More praise for
RASCAL MONEY

"An entertaining account of how the good guys prevent the villain from foreclosing on the farm . . . This one is recommended."

Library Journal

"Illuminating and timely . . . A suspenseful and compelling thriller."

Booklist

"Garber has a good time with his first novel, and readers will too . . . [An] outrageous yet pointed commentary on contemporary business . . . A significant message about the manner in which we do business today is hidden in all the hilarity."

Publishers Weekly

"A very funny first novel."

The Kirkus Reviews

RASCAL MONEY

Joseph Garber

FAWCETT GOLD MEDAL • NEW YORK

A Fawcett Gold Medal Book
Published by Ballantine Books
Copyright © 1989 by Joseph R. Garber

Library of Congress Catalog Card Number: 89-35495

ISBN 0-449-14692-8

This edition published by arrangement with Contemporary Books, Inc.

Manufactured in the United States of America

First Ballantine Books Edition: October 1990

"*I stand merely upon the defensive. I have no positive inferences to make, nor any novelties to bring forward, and I have only to defend a common sense feeling against the refinement of a false philosophy.*"

—William Hazlitt

"*It was without a compeer among swindles. It was perfect, it was rounded, symmetrical, complete, colossal.*"

—Mark Twain

To: J.

Book One:

T.F.T.B.W.

"Ban, Ban, Ca-Caliban.
Has a new master—Get a new man."

The Tempest
William Shakespeare

THATCHER WAVED HIS ARM. A CAB, one of the new Checker models that had just begun to show up on the sweltering streets of New York, darted out of the traffic and jolted up to the curb. Thatcher rattled the coins in his pocket, parsimoniously comparing the expense of a taxi ride downtown to the cost of a subway fare: $1.50 for a cab versus twenty cents for the subway—a not inconsequential difference for the president of a company that was going to have trouble making its August payroll. Still, it was important for him to arrive in style at this, the most important meeting in his young company's short history. If the meeting was a success, then his newly formed corporation, PegaSys, would be a success. If the meeting was a failure, then, in a matter of weeks, PegaSys would be bankrupt. Three years of backbreaking work would be wasted, and with his life's savings staked on the fledgling company, Thatcher himself would face the distasteful prospect of applying for unemployment benefits.

He winced at the thought. No member of the Thatcher tribe had ever gone on the dole. Besides, the bureaucrats who administered Lyndon Johnson's Great Society were considerably more interested in extending help to those who had never had a chance—not people like Thatcher, people who had a chance and blew it.

"Where to, Mac?" asked the cabbie, flipping down the flag on the meter. Fifteen cents rang up.

"Corner of Twelfth Avenue and Fourth Street."

The cabbie's face fell. It was a destination to which no taxi driver relished going. When he had spotted this well-dressed executive, the driver had assumed he was on his way to Wall Street. In the Wall Street area it was always easy to find another fare heading back uptown. Easy money and good tips. Instead he was being directed to a run-down neighborhood near the waterfront. The odds of finding another fare there were slim. Longshoremen did not indulge in the luxury of commuting by taxi. And if they did, they rarely tipped more than a nickel.

The cabbie tromped on the accelerator in disgust. "Whaddaya goin' down there for?"

"Craftsmen's union hall."

"Oh yeah, the craftsmen. Jeez, they say those cookies are tough cookies. We think we got us a tough union, but we're sissies compared to those guys. Them guys are pure mean. And that guy who runs the place—jeez, the stories you hear about him just give me the creeps. They say he's an animal, a real animal. So what's it wit you? You a lawyer or sumpin? One of them arbitrator guys the mayor is always cryin' about?"

"No. I'm in computers."

"Huh? Oh, them things. The big deal electronic brains that everyone is talkin' about. Gonna take over the world someday, they say. Sounds like a bunch of baloney to me, ya know. Is there anything to 'em? I mean are they really any good, or is it all just a bunch of crap?"

Always ready to spread the gospel of technology, Thatcher leaned back on the vinyl seat and began to explain. The cabbie was profane, skeptical, close minded, ill educated, and hostile to technology. Thatcher guessed that in these regards he had as good an opportunity to rehearse for his afternoon's audience as he was likely to find.

2

THREE YEARS EARLIER A $1.50 CAB ride would not have been a debatable issue for Scott C. Thatcher. Nor would the subway have been an option. Back then, his sole method for moving about the island of Manhattan was a chauffeured company limousine. IBM vice presidents traveled in style. As one of the youngest and brightest stars in an organization of young bright stars, Thatcher had adapted quickly to the comfort perquisites of rank—and to the gratifying rewards of success. Success looked easy in those days. The recipe was clear. It was the recipe Tom Watson, Jr., wrote at IBM.

Tom, Jr., had taken his father's pokey old company (best known for its punch-card equipment, time clocks, and meat slicers) and turned it into a technology powerhouse. Good products, better service, and absolutely the best salesmanship had transformed IBM into a force to be reckoned with. During the late 1950s and early '60s IBM began to catch up with Burroughs, Univac, and the other leaders in the arcane, little-known, but rapidly growing market for computer equipment. Little more than a decade earlier, Tom Watson, Sr., had forecast that the twenty largest companies in America might buy a mainframe computer. By the time John Kennedy took office, Tom Watson, Jr., with messianic enthusiasm, was making the outrageous prediction that every company on the Fortune 500 would own *more than one* computer some day. Everyone laughed at this prophecy except, of course, the employees of IBM.

The careers of the men who had joined Tom early, who shared his vision and who worked like demons to prove it, progressed very, very quickly indeed. Scott C. Thatcher was one of those men. Scott C. Thatcher was on his way to the top.

A week before Thatcher resigned, Jack Loeman called him into his office for a personal chat. Loeman was a brusque old-timer, a few years away from retirement, and one of Tom Watson, Jr.'s, inner circle. He was also Thatcher's immediate boss.

"Scott," Loeman said, "I think there is something you should know. It's confidential and off the record. And, I don't want it to go to your head. OK?"

"Sure, Jack," replied Thatcher in his slow New England drawl.

"You are in line now. As of this morning, Tom put you there."

"In line, Jack?"

"In line to walk through a very narrow door. The one with the star on it."

Thatcher leaned forward. "Tell me more."

"You know how old Tom is and you know how old I am. In about ten or twelve years, maybe less, it will be time for him to retire. Me, I'm going to be put out to pasture in two years. So

Tom's got that long to train a successor for me, and whoever it is who holds my job may—I say may—be the man who will lead IBM after Tom retires. Tom figures a decade is about how long it will take to teach someone what he needs to learn to run this ship. He's getting ready to start the process now. He is looking at the men who are maybe twenty years or so younger than he is, the guys he thinks can do the job. As of this morning, you're one of them.''

Thatcher arched his shaggy blond eyebrows in a way that could have meant surprise, or that could have meant he had just filled an inside straight. He folded his hands in an almost prayerful gesture. Resting his chin on his fingertips, he looked upward at Loeman's ceiling, as if soliciting the advice of angelic counsel.

After a moment's thought he said, ''Well . . . of course, I am honored at this. It, ahh . . . hmm . . . is not something I expected. Or had even thought of. I mean, after all, it is hard to think of Tom retiring. He is still a young man. And, the '70s are a long way off.''

''Not at IBM. Not in Tom Watson's office. We plan in decades. Sometimes I think we even plan in centuries. It's the prudent thing for a chief executive officer to think about his successor long in advance. Hell, he could get run over by a truck tomorrow, or, God forbid, have a coronary. You've got to ensure the continuity of top management. Can you think of anything more important than that?''

''Sure. I mean, no, I can't. Makes sense.''

''OK, then, got any questions?''

''Well. . . .'' Thatcher paused, reluctant to broach the obvious.

''Yeah, sure you do. You want to know what it means right now? Salary, title, office, reporting relationships, perks, all that kind of stuff.''

''The topic did cross my mind.''

''The answer is: nothing. Doesn't mean squat. All it means is that you keep doing what you're doing, only doing it better. And, that the folks who watch you closely will watch you even closer—myself being chief among them.''

In a curious way, the honor of being recognized as a potential heir to the IBM throne made Thatcher turn in his resignation sooner than he otherwise would have. He had been toying with the idea of starting up his own company for more than a year. Now he had it on the authority of no less a figure than Tom

Watson, Jr., maybe the greatest executive America had ever produced, that he, Scott Claymore Thatcher III, just might be good enough to run IBM someday. Someday. Well, if he was good enough to run someone else's company, he reasoned, then clearly he was good enough to run his own. And if you are that good (which is very good indeed), why should you wait ten years or more to move into the number-one slot? Why not do it now?

For the next week he spent his evenings agonizing over the business plan he had put together earlier in the year and from time to time reread wistfully. The plan outlined the structure and operations of a new computer company—one that would make a better computer than IBM, sell it at a lower price, and support it with all the care and commitment to customers that were IBM's hallmark. A company that would out-IBM IBM. Ho wanted to call it "PegaSys" and he already had a logo design in mind: a winged horse soaring into the sky, flying high, high above the competition.

The risks involved in leaving IBM to start his own company were not inconsequential. He would be abandoning a satisfying and successful career, and with it the $5,000-a-month paycheck that guaranteed his wife and children a comfortable life and considerable security. Now frugality would supplant comfort, and the wolf, heretofore distant, would camp by the doorstep. Further, his personal status would drop to zero. No longer would he be introduced at cocktail parties as "Scott Thatcher, a rising young exec at IBM," an introduction sure to garner instant respect and attention. Now people would say, "Meet Scott Thatcher, he runs his own business," words that in the early '60s evoked images of aluminum-siding salesmen and used-car dealers—words that snickeringly described a man who had been unable to succeed in corporate America.

Most terrifying of all, building his own company would consume all of his inheritance and all of his savings—$200,000, a sum equal to what the average American worker starting his career in the 1960s could expect to earn during the *full course* of his working life. It was a sum Thatcher knew he could never accumulate again if he left IBM, started his own company, and then failed.

But the rewards . . . if he could make it work, and now he was sure he could. His *own* company, his *own* wealth, his *own* master of his *own* destiny. For the next ten years, no matter how hard he worked at IBM he would be working for someone else.

No matter how high he rose, he would be rising behind someone else. No matter what he accomplished, even if he became president of IBM, he would always be an inheritor, not a creator. IBM would always be Watson's company, not Scott Thatcher's. He would always be the tenant, not the architect.

For someone of Thatcher's intellect, drive, and talent, the idea of running *someone else's* company was insufficiently demanding. There are, Thatcher thought, two kinds of people: those who do what others know to be right, and those who do what they themselves know to be right. In the business world, 99.9 percent were of the former. He counted himself of the latter. He typed up his resignation.

"You can't be serious," said Loeman.

"I am, Jack."

"Have you really thought through the implications of resigning? Resigning now, after what I told you last week?"

"Yes, I have, Jack. Give me credit for that. I've been thinking about this for a long time. I know that I have got to do it. If I don't do it now, I never will. It's time, Jack. It's *the* time."

"Scott . . ."

"I don't want you to think me disloyal. It's not that. I love this company, and I'll hate leaving it. It's a privilege working here. It's just that . . . well, I can't fail here. I've gotten to the point that no matter what I do, I can't fail. At best—or at worst—all I can do is plateau out. Jack, try to understand, I can't do my best work if the only risk I'm haunted by is the risk of just plateauing out. I have got to have a bigger risk than that. For me to be at my best, I need the right to fail."

"Now that *is* an interesting observation, Scott. Dumb as hell, but interesting. Well then, if that is your orientation, so be it. It will break Tom's heart; he's really fond of you, you know."

"Yes. I'll talk to him myself, if you don't mind."

"I don't know as that's necessary or appropriate, Scott. I'll check on it for you."

"Fair enough. I guess that's that, then. I'll go start cleaning out my office."

"Sure. But check with the security people on any papers you want to take with you. Jerry what's-his-name is going to be security officer on the 360 project; I'll have him or someone else stop by this afternoon."

"OK, Jack. Let me just say that it has been good working for you. You are high on the list of folks whom I'll miss."

"Same here, Scott."

Thatcher stood and grasped Loeman's hand. They gave one another the obligatory virile shake, and Thatcher turned toward the door. Loeman spoke up, stopping him, "Oh yeah, Scott. Look, if this thing of yours doesn't work out . . . I mean, if you do it for a couple of years and it's a failure, you'll probably be back on the job market. It's not that I don't wish you well, Scott, but you know most new business enterprises fail. So if you find that running your own business is a disaster and you need a real job, and you decide you'd like to come back here to IBM to find employment, I want you to know just one thing. I want you to know that you are a Judas Iscariot and there is no way in hell we will ever take a traitor like you back."

Three years later, entrepreneurship had proved to be no fun, no fun at all. Scott C. Thatcher was wiser, poorer by $193,000, and in debt by another $200,000, and at the end of his rope. His pale blond hair had turned prematurely white, as white as a sheet in an Ivory Snow ad. He had grown an equally white moustache, in part to be trendy, in part to soften the harshness of his straight, narrow, New England puritan's nose, but mostly because IBM didn't like its employees to sport facial hair. Equally in opposition to the IBM dress code, he had taken to wearing blue shirts or, if he was feeling particularly racy, striped ones from Paul Stewart. But he rarely felt racy, not anymore.

He had hired his team during the two months immediately following his resignation. First, Joe Jonas and Doug Wheeler, both enormously talented members of IBM's vast middle management ranks, and both several years younger than he. Then two dozen top-flight engineers, electronics experts, programmers, salesmen, and technical writers. And finally, the others he needed: secretaries, bookkeepers, and the like.

Thatcher's team, the PegaSys team, had worked hard and had worked smart. In eighteen months, putting in seven days a week and sixteen hours a day, the team produced a working prototype of a computer superior to anything on the market. By the twenty-fourth month they had debugged it and turned the prototype into a production model. By the twenty-sixth month they had manufactured an inventory of fifteen machines. By the twenty-ninth month they had developed software applications for accounting, payroll, inventory, and order entry systems that did twice as much as IBM's computer programs in half the time and at a third of the cost.

By the thirty-sixth month they had not sold one computer. Not one.

Thatcher and his team made sales calls on about 300 companies. They wrote proposals without number. PegaSys salesmen and technicians and executives flew to San Francisco and London, to Dallas and Milan, to Seattle and Rio, and to most stops in between. No one would buy a PegaSys computer.

"Yeah, look, you guys have got a good machine here, but hell, you can't compete against IBM no matter how good your hardware is."

"I'd buy one if somebody else already had one installed. But look, guys, I don't want to be the pioneer for your computer. You know who a "pioneer" is, don't you? He's the guy who gets the arrows in his ass. Call on me after you've got a track record and maybe we can do business."

"There is only one thing wrong with your computer. It doesn't say 'IBM' on the front."

"It's an impressive technology and I like the price. Come back and see us in a couple of years if you're still around."

"Let me level with you. All us computer managers have a saying. Sort of a proverb, you know. It goes like this: 'No one ever got fired for buying IBM.' "

And so, on a particularly hot and humid July day, in the middle of the worst water shortage in New York's history, Scott C. Thatcher found himself in hock up to his proverbial eyeballs, weeks away from bankruptcy, and with one and only one potential shot at salvation: the International Brotherhood of Craftsmen Union and Fraternal Society. The union was thinking of buying a computer system, an exceedingly large computer system indeed.

3

"OK, MAC, HERE WE ARE. THAT'S a buck twenty-five on the meter." Thatcher reached for his wallet as the cabbie continued, "One other thing, pal. These computer things you been tellin' me about are kinda interestin'. Sounds like you might have something there. Maybe the wave of the future, as they say. Like TV was a few years ago. Now I got this kid, see. I just put him through NYU, the bum, and now he ain't doing nothing but slinging hash at some lunch joint on Maiden Lane. He gets straight A's in everything except foreign language, which he flunks twice if you can believe that. Smart as hell, anyway. But he can't figure out what kind of work he wants to do. Leaves me worrying and waiting for the draft to nail his butt. With this Vietnam thing, I get nervous. I worry about him a lot. He's a great kid, but he don't know what to do with his life. You think maybe I should tell him to get into computers?"

"Absolutely. It is the best place for a young man to be," replied Thatcher, giving the cabbie a dollar and a fifty-cent piece. In an impetuous fit of generosity he added, "Keep the change."

"Gee, thanks. Here, let me give you a hand with that junk you got there." Thatcher was wrestling with the paraphernalia he needed to make his pitch to the craftsmen: a portable slide projector, a briefcase full of slides, and a screen. The driver turned off his engine and helped him carry it into the seedy, cinderblock union hall.

"Thank you very much," said Thatcher.

"Hey, no problem, pal. But look, maybe you can do me a favor. If I send my kid by to see you, will you talk to him? I mean, he really is a good kid. Maybe you can find a job for him."

"Sure, why not. Here's my card. Have him give me a call in,

oh . . . four weeks," Thatcher answered, knowing full well that in four weeks he would either be hiring as many smart young people as he could find—or would have had the phones disconnected.

"Great! Hey, my name's Ash, Don Ash, like at the end of a stogie. And my kid's named Mike."

"Good. I look forward to hearing from him."

Thatcher entered the building to confront the union's receptionist, a Selma Diamond lookalike. She eyed him with the reptile-eyed suspicion that only a New York receptionist can muster. "Good afternoon. My name is Scott Thatcher. I am here to make a presentation to Mr. Varrazano and his colleagues. I believe that I am expected."

"Spell it," she muttered nasally.

"T-H-A-T-C-H-E-R."

"And the first part."

"S-C-O-T-T."

"Two T's?"

"Yes."

She picked up a phone, slowly dialed three digits and muttered, "Hi. It's Martha up front. Tell Joey the Bridge that there is some guy named Scott Thatcher, capital S, small c, small o, small t, small t, space, new word, capital T, small h, small a, small t, small c, small h, small e, small r, out here to see him and the boys. Yeah, honey, read it back to me. Yeah, OK, you got it right. Good job, honey."

She hung up and squinted at Thatcher, "That's Sylvie, Joey's gal. She don't spell too well. Siddown and take a load off. They'll be out to getcha in a couple minutes."

Giuseppe Varrazano, alias Joey the Bridge, was president of the International Brotherhood of Craftsmen Union and Fraternal Society. Both Joey and the brotherhood earned their share of popular notoriety via frequent appearances on the third page of the *New York Daily News*—that section of the tabloid commonly referred to as the "rape page."

Not that the *Daily News*'s third page *always* dealt with rape. Indeed, the editors' preferred page-three themes were more on the order of photogenic ax murders, lurid love-pact suicides among the artistic classes, or blood-spattered gangland slaughters, ideally those involving crowded restaurants awash with the remains of innocent victims. In the lamentable absence of these editorially appetizing events, a brutal rape (or better still, rape-murder) would fill the bill—optimally, one with a nurse, nun, or schoolteacher as the victim. New York being the kind of town it was (and is), if nothing else suitably entertaining could be found, there was always a good rape story on page three of the *New York Daily News*.

Or at least there had been until Joey the Bridge showed up on the scene. Joey preempted the rape page. He positively hogged it, more than satisfying the *Daily News*'s editorial appetite for calculated mayhem, random slaughter, indiscriminate bloodletting, and the efficient mass production of terminal violence. The floating bodies of Teamsters, longshoremen, and others foolish enough to compete for labor dominance had become so numerous that they were beginning to represent a hazard to navigation in the Port of New York.

Giuseppe Varrazano was not a hands-off manager. He did not, according to such nervously anonymous rumors as the *Daily News* could accumulate, merely order this carnage. He participated in it—gleefully, by most accounts.

According to one hushed and jittery informant, Joey's nickname stemmed not from his having almost the same name as the recently completed bridge linking Brooklyn to Staten Island. Rather, it had arisen from Joey's practice of entombing the bullet-riddled remains of former colleagues in the still-wet concrete used to construct that bridge. Eighteen of them, to be precise.

Another tale-teller whispered in the ever interested ear of a *Daily News* reporter that Joey's missing and presumed deceased predecessor had been flayed and filleted—and that his tanned hide now served as a toilet-seat cover in the union hall's executive washroom.

Thatcher, who was cool to the prospects of investigating the veracity of this rumor, had carefully avoided drinking any liquids for the entire hellishly hot day, and had with equal care emptied his bladder before traveling down to his meeting with Varrazano and his cronies.

The union's executive conference room was a peculiar affair, a windowless room deep in the bowels of the building. It's walls, inside and out, were lined with cork. Likewise its ceiling. Utterly soundproof, it had no telephone and was silent as the grave. Thatcher entered it with understandable nervousness.

The room was dimly lit and thick with the haze of cigar smoke. In its otherwise bare center stood a long, narrow conference table, an inexpensive metal model, topped with imitation wood veneer—the kind that is easily washable and never stains, no matter what substance is spilled on it. The table was flanked by modest, military-surplus chairs, six to a side, and at its head stood another, obviously more expensive chair. This piece of furniture seemed to Thatcher to have been customized. It was easily three inches, perhaps four, higher than the other chairs.

Through the smoky gloom he could make out a handful of bulky men clustered at the back of the room, standing far out of what little illumination there was. They all were wearing hats—the model favored by Mickey Spillane.

One of them lumbered away from the crowd. He was a distinctively batrachian type who, apart from an enormously tasteless raw-silk suit, looked as if he would be more at home on a lily pad catching flies with his tongue. "You Thatcher?" he asked.

"Yes, I am. And you are Mr. . . . ?"

"Liscone. Marty Liscone. Call me Marty. I'm treasurer. Here, lemme introduce you to the boys."

Liscone drew Thatcher back into the gloom at the end of the room, rattling off eight or nine names that ended with sounded vowels. Thatcher shook an equal number of clammy, corpselike hands, hearing a hoarsely muttered, basso profundo "Please-tameecha," with each icy shake.

The top management of the International Brotherhood of Craftsmen Union and Fraternal Society resembled the sort of people—well, not quite people—who belonged in trees, peeling bananas with their toes. Thatcher calculated that there was not six inches of forehead among them. But what they lacked in cranial height, they more than made up in prognathous jaw. He tried to make idle conversation with them, but found their vocabulary limited to indifferent grunts and a quite small number of obscenities. All that could be said in their favor was that each pressed a few cigars into his hands: Upmanns and Monte Cristos, the likes of which he hadn't been able to obtain since Eisenhower cut off trade with Cuba and which, in any event, he hadn't been able to afford since resigning from IBM. Win, lose, or draw in his sales pitch to the union, he had a week of aromatic ecstasy ahead of him.

Thatcher was in the process of trying to frame a cogent response to a question about his moustache ("Why'd a guy like you grow one of them sissy pussy ticklers?") when the conference room door flew open. Two hulking giants who might have qualified as tackles for the Detroit Lions, had they not been a bit oversized, lurched in. With their hands beneath their jackets they eyed the room slowly, ultimately focusing on Thatcher and the men around him with what, in Thatcher's opinion, seemed to be lethal menace. Thatcher heard a rustle as each union executive grasped the lapels of his suit coat, spreading them wide.

Liscone gave him a nudge. "Open yer jacket, ya jerk, so they can see you ain't heeled."

"Heeled?"

"Carryin' heat. A gun, asshole."

"Oh." Thatcher imitated the gesture of the others as closely as he could and reflected that, if nothing else, he would have an interesting tale to tell at the next gathering of the Harvard Business School Alumni Association.

The two gorillas nodded their simian heads and let their hands fall from beneath their jackets. One gave a guttural bark. A moment later Giuseppe Varrazano walked through the door.

Joey was as thin as a whippet and stood almost as high. He wore a black silk suit, a black silk shirt, a yellow silk tie, black patent-leather elevator shoes and the obligatory porkpie hat, also black. His watch was solid gold, and appeared to contain enough precious metal to retire the Mexican national debt. The number of carats in his diamond pinkie ring was exceeded only by that in the ring he wore on his thumb.

Without saying a word, he strode to the head of the conference table and sat down. Equally soundlessly, the union executives to whom Thatcher had been speaking moved to the table and took their places. Joey the Bridge took off his hat. They all took off their hats. Joey set his hat on the conference table. They all set their hats on the conference table. Joey unwrapped a fresh cigar. They all unwrapped fresh cigars. Joey licked the cigar and put it in his mouth. They all lunged forward with lighters.

Joey inhaled deeply, and let the smoke sigh out of his mouth. He waved his hand in a bored gesture reminiscent of a Roman emperor. *Let the games begin.*

Liscone began the meeting with one of the most monumental misuses of an English word Thatcher had ever heard. "Gentlemen," he said.

"Gentlemen, we're here today because our great union needs computers. Things here have just gotten too complex. We've gotten too big, too fast. Through the dedicated efforts of our esteemed president, Mr. Joey the Bridge, our beloved union has come from nowheres to lead the pack. We got more members than we can keep track of, more dues than we can count, and more company contracts than we even know anymore. And, need I add, we got lots of problems keepin' track of those to whom we lend money and makin' sure they honor their debts or face the consequences which we find as unpleasant as they do, if you know what I mean.

"So what with one thing and another, Joey he tells me to go get a computer to keep control of all this shit. Now I don't know from computers and nobody here knows from computers. So we look in the phone book under 'computers' and there are these eight guys listed, of whom no one has never heard nothin'. So we call 'em all up and they come down to see us, and most of 'em go back and we never hear from them again. Which they may regret, but that is business for another day.

"So three of them come back and ask all of these questions, many of which no one in his right skull would answer even if you hadn't taken the oath of silence. Then they write in these big thick books with lots of charts in 'em and words which are Greek to a simple craftsman—unless he is Greek, in which case they are Chinese. And, there is one thing I can understand in each of these books, and that is we are lookin' at very serious money here with this computer thing. Like, we are talkin' about more than a million dollars, which is not hay.

"So I say to Joey, I say, 'Joey, I don't know. Joey, are you sure we need one of these computer things?' And Joey puts it all in perspective by tellin' me what he will do to me if I don't get a computer in here so fast that works, which then causes me to go to the library and learn a lot about computers before doin' anything else. But I still don't know much, to tell you the truth.

"Now we got Mr. Scott C. Thatcher here this afternoon. His company is called PegaSys. This mornin' we saw the guys from the other two companies that want to sell us their computers. We're gonna pick one. And I do mean we. I ain't makin' this decision myself. Everybody understand that? We're gonna vote, and I'm gonna list down who voted for what so that Joey can remember in case he don't like what happens and I don't wanna get no blame in case he doesn't.

"So lemme begin by tellin' you guys this. Them guys we saw this mornin' have sold hundreds of computers. Thatcher here ain't sold none. That right, Thatcher?"

Thatcher stepped forward from the back of the room. "Absolutely true, Mr. Liscone. However, I can assure you, Mr. Varrazano, and your colleagues, that our computer, the PegaSys computer, is superior in all regards to any other product on the market today. And, it will remain superior for many years to come. It was designed and built by the best brains in the business and we are proud of it."

"So how come you ain't sold none?"

"Because we are small, and no one likes dealing with the little guy," replied Thatcher, coyly glancing at the diminutive Joey the Bridge. "The little guy always has to work harder when he is competing with the big guy. I'm sure you know that. And, like your union, we, too, are trying to come from nowhere. But, Mr. Liscone, while we were slow away from the gate, we are riding the best horse on the track."

"Level with us, Thatcher. If you don't sell us a computer, what happens to your company?"

"I level with everyone, Mr. Liscone. If I can't persuade you this afternoon that PegaSys is the best solution to your needs, then I will be forced to close down my company."

Liscone leaned back and whistled. "Well, I guess that's as level as you can get. If things are so rocky, tell us why we should buy your stuff."

"First and foremost, the PegaSys computer is technologically superior. It is, if you will, a 'smarter brain' than anyone else makes. It is faster, larger, and more reliable. Second, and equally important, if—no, when—when you buy our computer you will be getting considerably more than any of our competitors can offer you."

"Whaddaya mean?"

"When you buy from us, you will be getting our full attention. Our *entire* company and all our resources will be devoted to serving you. You will be our first customer. Everyone on my payroll will be working for you and you *alone*. Until you are happy, they will work on nothing else. Mr. Liscone, you will not simply be buying a computer when you buy from PegaSys. You will be buying the full-time services of an entire company! How many other companies can make a promise like that?"

"Interestin' thought. You guys prepared to deal?"

"When you say 'deal,' I presume you mean negotiate our price."

"Nah. Shit, raise your price for all I care. It all gets paid outta union dues anyhow. When I say 'deal,' I mean *deal*. You know, we write you a check, you write us a check. Not much, you know, but a little somethin' to show your appreciation. Nobody sells nothin' to the craftsmen if he don't *deal*."

"I don't *deal* and my company doesn't *deal*. At least not in that sense."

"Sense? Thatcher, the only sense involved is that it sounds like you ain't got none. You're between a rock and a hard place, ain't cha? Sounds to me like you got a choice between gettin' our business or gettin' out of business."

"Then I will choose the latter."

"Look, Thatcher, if you asked all those people who work for you if they'd rather pony up a little grease or go see the bankruptcy judge, whaddaya think they'd say?"

"They would all elect to shutter the doors. If they didn't think like that, I never would have hired them."

"Hmpf. OK, make your life tough. I just hope your presentation is good. It better be real good, after what you just said. Go ahead, pal, make your sales pitch."

Thatcher flicked on the slide projector. The room was so dark that there was no need to dim the lights. PegaSys's logo illuminated the screen, a winged horse outlined in bold blue strokes against a white background. He began to speak.

"Thank you, Mr. Liscone. And, on behalf of my colleagues and fellow workers at PegaSys, I would like to thank all of you for your time this afternoon. During the next hour or so I will describe the system we propose to install in your union. I will cover five topics." He pushed a button and a new slide, labeled "Agenda," appeared on the screen.

"First, 'Background.' I will describe briefly what our company, PegaSys, is and what it stands for. Second, 'Needs Analyses'; during this section I will tell you what we believe your union's computer system must do. As you know, we had a team of five business systems analysts spend three weeks down here examining your current operations, interviewing people, and identifying the specific processes and workflows that a new computer system might improve. Third, 'Hardware,' in which I will discuss not only the features of our computer, but those of the peripheral equipment such as tape drives, printers, and so forth. Fourth, 'Software.' This section contains a description of what we call *programs*, the instructions that dictate the actions the hardware performs. Fifth and finally, 'Costs/Benefits'—what your true expenses for hardware, software, training, documentation, personnel, and other categories will be and the ultimate savings and operational improvements that the investment will produce.

"Now, I know that none of you are technologists. Yet computers are a highly technical topic. During my presentation I may use words or concepts that are new to you. So, if you do not understand, or if you have any questions whatsoever, please do not hesitate to interrupt me at any point with any question you wish. First, let me begin telling you a bit about PegaSys. . . ."

The first section of Thatcher's presentation was easy sailing. He breezed through the credentials of his staff quickly. The second section seemed equally smooth. He told them how he thought the union worked, and which of its manual processes he believed could be automated.

He paused before beginning the next part of his talk. "Now, are there any questions, any questions at all, on the material I've covered so far? Gentlemen? Have I and my team captured a good understanding of your operations? Do we understand what your new computer system must do? Ahhh . . . no questions then. OK, I will move on. The next section is highly technical, so please interrupt me if I go too fast or if I am unclear on any point."

For the next fifteen minutes Thatcher talked about bits, bytes, bauds, and characters per second. CPUs and I/O, main memory and DASD memory, streaming and spooling. Buffers, front ends, controllers, line printers, autocoders, terminals, modems, multiplexors. His slides portrayed flowcharts awash with strange symbols and linked by arrows. Often the slides were annotated with numbers prefaced or followed by such symbols such as Σ, B, Δ, μ, $\sim$, and ζ.

Every few minutes he stopped, looked up, and asked for questions or points of clarification. He received silence in return. The silence was profound. He began to worry about it.

Next he talked about software. Operating systems, applications systems, monitors, debuggers, COBOL, FORTRAN, machine language, hexadecimal notation, rem's, maintenance, coding, compilers, ANSI standards. "Now, does everyone understand this? I know it is quite technically complex. Questions? Anyone? Questions? No. Well, then on this slide . . ."

In the thick silence that surrounded him, Thatcher began to sweat. Something was wrong. No one could listen to this kind of material without asking at least one question.

The longer he spoke, the more he sweated. And he wasn't hot. Not at all. Indeed, he felt quite chilly. His audience wasn't hearing a word he said. Or if they heard, they were ignoring him. As soon as he had refused to even broach a discussion on kickbacks, he worried, they had decided to tune him out. Or maybe find a nice, wet patch of concrete . . .

It was all over, he thought. PegaSys's last possible customer was going to buy from someone else. He didn't have a chance. Three years gone. Savings gone. Everything he could mortgage or borrow against gone. And all the loyal people who had put their lifeblood (and, for most of them, their life savings) into PegaSys—why, they were gone too.

He sweated some more. It was soaking through his shirt and dampening his suit by the time he finished.

". . . and ultimately, not only cost savings totaling in the millions of dollars, but smoother, better functioning operations as well. Not only can we do the job, we can and will do the best job. Are there any questions? . . . No, I thought not. Then let me thank you again for your time. Mr. Liscone, have you any reaction?"

Thatcher looked at Liscone. Liscone looked at Thatcher. Seconds passed, each seeming an eternity. Finally Liscone broke his stare and turned to Joey the Bridge. Joey looked back, his eyes hooded and uncommunicative.

More moments passed, then Joey the Bridge nodded his head at Liscone, tossing his hand up with a sharp, brutal chop. Liscone nodded back. Joey seized his hat and stood up. The two gorillas rushed to the door and threw it open. Joey stepped briskly toward it, his elevator shoes clacking on the linoleum. As he reached the door, he paused, looked over his shoulder, and spoke for the first time since entering the conference room. "Thatcher, I got one t'ing to say, and dat t'ing is dis. T.F.T.B.W. Dat's all, Thatcher, T.F.T.B.W."

Then he left.

"Congratulations, Thatcher," said Liscone. "You guys got the job."

"We do?" asked a stunned Scott C. Thatcher.

"Yeah, ya got lucky an' ya got smart," said another hood. "Dincha hear Joey? He said ya got da job. An' Liscone, he got lucky too, he don' have ta make no decision himself. An' all of us got lucky 'cause we don' have t' vote on dis fruity t'ing. Ya done good, Thatcher. 'Specially tellin' Liscone here ya won' pay no grease. Dat was real smart. Ain't nobody here wants to do business with no fuckin' crook. Us guys is all businessmen here."

"Ahhh . . . well, yes. Yes! I am honored. We are honored. All of us at PegaSys. I promise you will get your money's worth.

Really. But, look, one thing I don't understand. Those letters—or I thought they were letters . . . what Mr. Varrazano said when he left the room. I'm not sure I quite understood what he said.''

The hood smiled. Thatcher thought it was a particularly unpleasant smile, but doubtless the fellow meant it to be in good cheer. '' 'T.F.T.B.W.' is what he said. You know, 'T.F.T.B.W.' Short for 'Da Fuckin' T'ing Betta Woik.' ''

4

I⊤ DID.

Book Two:
Attila Rides

"I know who I was when I got up this morning, but I think I must have changed several times since then."
Alice's Adventures in Wonderland
Lewis Carroll

1

It was another hot, sticky New York morning, more appropriate to July than to mid-October, when Mike Ash began his daily walk to work. It was a short walk, extending a mere ten blocks from his $2,800-per-month East 58th Street apartment (5 rms, lux bldg, hi flr, r/vue, frplc, 24 hr drmn, mod kit) to the PegaSys skyscraper at the corner of Madison and 54th. As walks in New York go, Ash's route was comparatively pleasant. Not that he ever noticed.

Like all New Yorkers, he walked briskly, his eyes aimed slightly downward and focused on the middle distance. New Yorkers do not amble, do not meander, and do not hesitate. Nor do they pay much attention to the world around them.

New Yorkers are that way of necessity. To preserve a modicum of sanity in a city of borderline lunacy, they learn to screen out Manhattan's nerve-racking sights and sounds. They become impervious to the scream of sirens, the rumble of traffic, and the shattering din of heavy construction. By the same token, they wholly ignore the usual denizens of New York's crowded streets. Anyone whose neighbors were beggars, bag ladies, junkies, pimps, pushers, three-card-monte operators, and lawyers would do the same.

Ash, however, was not merely impervious during his morning walk to work. Ash was very nearly in a trance.

He was never at his best first thing in the morning. Best did not become a consideration until sometime after 11:00 A.M. Fair did not even enter the picture until about 9:30, after he had downed three cups of coffee, read the *New York Times*, and smoked the first of his self-allotted ten daily cigarettes. If anyone in the office made the mistake—and few did—of greeting his entrance with a hearty, "How are you this morning, Mike?"

25

Ash glowered and responded by growling, "It's too early to tell."

At the ungodly—in Ash's definition—hour of 8:40 A.M., he was mostly asleep. Although his body moved, his mind was on autopilot. His limbic system, the most primitive part of the brain, was all that was functioning; the low-order cranial cells and structures that mankind shares with alligators and iguanas directed his steps, animating him like a very dull robot with mechanical, preprogrammed precision from his home to his office. Until some honest caffeine hit his stomach, his early morning condition was generally indistinguishable from brain death.

That is why he made it halfway across Third Avenue before he noticed that something was amiss.

Ash likely would never even have looked up had not the woman in front of him dropped her purse, letting it lie in the middle of the street as she bolted for the sidewalk. Such an uncommon event was sufficient to stir even Ash from his morning stupor. Ash's brain was slow to respond. Very slow. It stirred grudgingly, reluctant to process incoming sensory signals.

Groping for something upon which to focus, Ash first contemplated the fleeing woman's shoes. He did so with the remote interest of a distant and disinterested observer. Most Manhattan women wear jogging shoes for their morning's walk to work. While ungainly and ugly, jogging shoes are comfortable, cheap, and sturdily resistant to the offal that lines the city streets. Consequently, otherwise fashion-conscious females galumph their way to and from their offices in joggers, keeping their less sturdy, more fashionable footwear safe, dry, and unscuffed in a shopping bag or briefcase.

What caught Ash's attention was that the woman who had dropped her purse was wearing beige leather pumps. They forced her to run with an awkward and obviously uncomfortable stride. *Ahh,* thought Ash, *another reason for women to wear jogging shoes in Manhattan. They let you run faster. A fine subject for an ad campaign: "You'll never get away from that mugger in a pair of Guccis. Be sure to put on your Nikes when you come to New York!"*

Cynicism always raised Ash's spirits. The fog of sleep was lifting and he was becoming more aware. As his protesting cerebral cortex awoke, he saw the woman glance over her shoulder. She was watching something—or someone—on the uptown side of Third Avenue. The look on her face was fear: genuine, unmistakable fear.

He followed her eyes, staring for a moment at the spectacle in the middle of the street without any understanding of it at all. A battered Checker taxi was stopped, straddling two lanes. It was one of the old models, the sort that Ash's father had driven up until the day he died. Ash studied it fondly. It was a rarity, a relic of his younger years that was no longer manufactured.

A few yards in front of the cab, a police car was stopped. It had been brought to a halt at right angles, blocking the cab's way. Behind and to the left another police car had also stopped. Uptown, behind the three vehicles for 100 yards, Third Avenue was empty—as empty as Dodge City at high noon.

A nice metaphor, and an appropriate one, thought Ash dreamily, as he sorted out the rest of the picture. There were four police officers surrounding the taxi. They were hunched in the combat firing position: legs were bowed, backs arched forward, and arms locked straight before them. They clenched their pistols with both hands, tilting their heads slightly to the right, the better to draw a bead on the taxi. The expressions on their faces communicated no reluctance to fire. If anything, they looked eager. Ash, still rather remote from events, thought to himself that they looked almost posed, like models in a still photograph from a made-for-TV movie, *New York Vice*.

A man in a grey suit holding a dark-brown attaché case came strolling down 56th Street, turned the corner onto Third, saw what was going on, blinked, gasped, and scurried back the way he had come.

All the while, Ash stood dumbly in the field of fire, the seriousness of his position slowly registering on a stuporous brain.

Finally wide awake, he put it all together. The man in the taxi had done something terribly wrong. Whatever it was, it was bad enough to stir New York's finest to action. The police had brought the cabbie to ground after a high-speed chase down Third Avenue in the middle of rush hour. Now they had him, and if the poor hapless bastard so much as twitched an eyebrow, bullets would fly. Some of those bullets would fly . . . exactly . . . toward . . . the . . . spot . . . Ash . . . was . . . standing . . . on.

Ash woke up and ran like hell.

But, as he ran he noticed something disquietingly familiar about the cab driver. Something that almost, but not quite, made him pause. It was the expression on the driver's face—a look of disgust, of resignation, and of desperation. And above all, a glimmer of mad hope in his eyes. It was this glimmer that scared

Ash. Ash could tell that the man was thinking that maybe, just maybe, he could outdraw or outrun those four cops. Despite apparently hopeless odds, maybe it wasn't all over. Maybe he still had a chance.

Ash found this expression utterly terrifying. The reason he found it so terrifying was that he had seen the same expression in the mirror that morning when he had shaved.

2

THE FIFTY-THREE-STORY TOWER ON Madison Avenue between 53rd and 54th had once been the headquarters of Universal Tin Can Inc., the world's largest maker of food packaging. But, in the early '70s, "the Can," as its employees fondly called it, moved to Dallas, sold all its factories to a Japanese conglomerate, changed its name to Techno-Dynamics Corporation, and got into cable television and satellites in a big way. It left behind fourteen floors of unoccupied and—in those days of economic recession—unrentable office space.

With the city of New York on the verge of bankruptcy and property values plummeting, the building's owner was positively ecstatic when a young, upstart data processing company offered to sign a twenty-year lease for five floors as its new headquarters. On certain conditions, of course.

First, the name of the building was to be changed. No longer was it to be the Universal Tin Can Building. It was to be known as PegaSys Center. Next, Universal Tin Can's memorable, if time-worn, logo was to be removed from the building's entrance and replaced with PegaSys's highly stylized, electric-blue flying stallion. Further, rental costs were to be guaranteed not to increase at a rate greater than that of the consumer price index—and PegaSys was to be given an ironclad five-year right to rent up to twelve additional floors under the same terms. Finally, PegaSys was to be offered an option to buy the entire building and the land it sat on at a price equal to ten times the cash flow generated by the property. "Said option being uncancellable for a period not to exceed ten (10) years from the date of exclusion of this document, and being exercisable solely, exclusively, by the discretion, of the lessor, PegaSys Inc., or its successor company, without recourse, negotiation, litigation, or arbitration on the part of the lessor Ezra J. Epstein and Associates, Inc."

The president of PegaSys, a soft-spoken and taciturn Yankee named Scott C. Thatcher, paid $500,000 for the option. Given the moribund nature of the New York real estate market, Ezra J. Epstein almost felt bad about taking his money. Almost.

Three years later, boom times returned and Epstein filed his first lawsuit to break the deal. He lost. He lost the second, third, and fourth ones too. And in 1983 when PegaSys exercised its option to buy the building, Epstein lost that case as well. After his heart attack he moved to Georgia, where he subsequently made a killing by developing a sixty-acre industrial park in Norcross.

Now, as the 1980s spiraled to their conclusion, the building's sole tenant was PegaSys Inc. And PegaSys Inc. was no longer a young, upstart data processing company. It was a twelve-billion-dollar enterprise whose name usually appeared near the top of those lists of the most admired companies in America— the ones that *Forbes*, *Fortune*, and *Business Week* put together every year. It was, in fact, the second largest computer company in the world.

At One PegaSys Center, the ground floor and two above it were devoted to showrooms. Next there was a floor consisting solely of conference and training rooms. Above that was the employees' cafeteria. The remaining forty-six floors housed PegaSys's employees, among them Michael John Ash. And, of course, Scott Claymore Thatcher III.

Thatcher was nothing if not a traditionalist. "I am," he once said during an appearance on *The MacNeil/Lehrer NewsHour* "a capitalist, a churchgoer, and a Connecticut Yankee. Not necessarily in that order." Consistent with his older, sterner values, Thatcher sometimes thought of himself as the last practicing proponent of the "carrot and stick" school of management. It is the job of management, Thatcher contended, to make employees eager for success and fearful of failure. It is the job of

judicious management to wield both the carrot and the stick—
to reward good employees and to penalize bad ones.

PegaSys Center was a reflection of Thatcher's carrot-and-stick
philosophy. It, or rather the space and furnishings it contained,
was part of the reward system. The lower floors were sticks; the
upper floors were carrots.

The forty-six stories given over to PegaSys offices began with
a warren of linoleum-floored cubicles, each cubicle barely containing enough room for a chair and a desk. Those who worked
there were at the bottom of the corporate pecking order. As one
moved higher in status, seniority, and salary, one moved up the
tower. On higher floors the linoleum gave way to wall-to-wall
carpeting, and the cubicles metamorphosed into small but well-
appointed offices. Higher still, the offices grew in size. One
hundred and twenty-five square feet. One fifty. One seventy-
five. Along about the two-hundred-square-foot mark, painted
plaster walls disappeared and a variety of wallpapers materialized. Up around two hundred and fifty square feet, parquet floors
and scatter rugs began making themselves noticed. And in the
uppermost suites, the scatter rugs became Oriental carpetry.

Ash's office was at the low end of Persian rug territory, two
stories down from the top floor and hence from Scott C.
Thatcher. Ash was PegaSys's vice president for corporate development, a position sometimes described as "VP of 'all
other' " or as "the highest paid gofer in the company." But
mostly he was known as "Mad Mike," the creative dervish.

Ash looked rumpled that morning. He looked rumpled every
morning. And every evening as well.

It was not that he was sloppy. On the contrary, all his buttons
were buttoned, his shirttail always tucked in, his tie impeccably
knotted, his shoes brightly shined, his cheeks smoothly shaved,
and his light-brown hair tidily trimmed. Nor was it that he was
overweight. His metabolism kept him on an enviably even keel
at 178 pounds and a perfect size 40—just right for his broad-
shouldered, five-foot, eleven-inch frame. His features were bal-
anced and symmetrical. He didn't have dandruff. His posture
was erect. His gestures were incisive. His gaze was clear and
his voice direct. But . . . he looked rumpled.

There was something about him that seemed indefinably
askew. Wearing a Brooks Brothers suit, new from the store, he
would remind you (just a little) of Walter Matthau in *The Odd
Couple*. His custom-tailored shirts, freshly returned from a Chi-

nese laundry, looked as if they were on their second wearing. And, when he put on the reading glasses that he had begun to need once he passed the age of forty, visitors to his office would get the uncomfortable feeling that one of the earpieces was loose. It wasn't.

In sum, Michael Ash was the sort of guy at whom people would take one look and ask, "Long flight?" even though he hadn't been on an airplane.

Few women were impervious to his rumpled charm and faint self-deprecating grin. Women found him a little endearing, rather like a slightly disreputable teddy bear. They sensed in him a vulnerability and a need for help that he really didn't have. He made them want to straighten his tie and smooth down his cowlick, though the truth of the matter was that his tie was already straight and he had no cowlick. From the lowliest file clerk to the most case-hardened Harvard MBA, women eyed Ash and decided that they wanted . . . wanted to . . . to help.

Ash neither realized nor exploited this peculiar fascination. Instead, he simply remarked that he seemed to work extremely well with women, and chalked it up to being a bit more enlightened an executive than most of his generation.

"Morning, Phyllis," said Ash.

"Good morning, Mike," his secretary replied, eyeing him to see if he needed some sort of assistance—say, a wet umbrella that needed to be hung somewhere, or a loose thread that needed snipping. Unconsciously disappointed to find nothing that needed fixing, she continued, "The *Times* is on your desk and you got a telex from Germany. I'll be right in with your coffee."

Ash was an open-door, bright-office man. Consequently, from her station outside his door Phyllis could keep a watchful eye on him as he went through his morning rituals.

First, Ash hung his suit jacket in the small closet that was one of the perquisites of his rank. Next he poured a cup of coffee from the carafe that Phyllis had brought in. Then he picked up the German telex from where it lay on top of his *New York Times* and, taking care not to look at its contents, set it aside.

During the next twenty minutes he downed two cups of coffee, glumly reviewed the dismal news of the day, and studied the stock market's results with mixed emotions. With his third cup of coffee in hand, he lit a cigarette, inhaled deeply, and began to look more purposeful. Phyllis, like all good secretaries, could read the signals. She picked up Ash's appointment diary and came into his office.

"Let's see. You have a ten o'clock meeting with Louise and Frank to review the Engineered Systems marketing plan. Then you have a twelve o'clock lunch at the Harvard Club with Mr. Lechner from Salomon Brothers. You've got to be back by one-thirty for a conference call with the San Francisco office. Those consultants Mr. T. hired want to interview you for an hour at two. Oh, and don't forget tomorrow is the EMC meeting. Louise says to tell you that Mr. T. will probably ask about the Engineered Systems plan. It begins at four o'clock sharp. While you were reading the paper, you got a call from a Mr. Clarence."

"Get him back on the line, would you?"

"Sure. And do you have any response to that telex?"

"Telex? Oh! Telex. Aw, hell, I haven't even looked at it yet," Ash said, confirming a fact of which Phyllis was well aware.

Down forty-some floors from Ash's office, Marty Feinman was punching keys on a computer console. Marty was PegaSys's chief of computer operations, responsible for running all of the complex hardware PegaSys used for its own internal needs. Fifty million dollars' worth of sophisticated computing power was under his personal control. Every day at this hour he had to run the company's accounts payable system.

">LOGON. EXEC SUMMARYAP/PEGAS s1 5 RT" typed Marty, the characters appearing on the computer screen in front of him.

">PEGASYS OLYMPIA MAINFRAME. ENTER PASSWORD," responded the computer.

">TY18687 IOHY," answered Marty.

">OLYMPIA AUTHORIZED USER VERIFIED. ENTER TERMINAL."

">PEGAS CENTRAL."

">OLYMPIA AUTHORIZED TERMINAL VERIFIED. ENTER I/O."

">DASD/ALL. LOCALREMOTE/ALL. SBUS/ALL. GOTO PEGAS CENTRAL H/S."

">OLYMPIA PROCESSING," replied the computer. Marty heard the whine of the high-speed printer as it began outputting PegaSys's accounts payable report. He strolled over to glance at the printout.

"ONE TRILLION BOTTLES OF BEER ON THE WALL, ONE TRILLION BOTTLES OF BEER. TAKE ONE DOWN, PASS IT AROUND, NINE HUNDRED AND NINETY-NINE BILLION, NINE HUNDRED AND NINETY-NINE MILLION, NINE HUNDRED AND NINETY-NINE

THOUSAND, NINE HUNDRED AND NINETY-NINE BOTTLES OF BEER
ON THE WALL . . ."

Marty looked at the printout in horror. "Oh, shit!" he bellowed, diving for the phone. He punched in Roy Knight's number.

After one ring, a voice answered. "Security, Knight."

"Roy, this is Marty Feinman in Computer Ops. Wintergreen's back and he's fucking up Olympia!"

"Oh, shit!"

Five minutes later Knight lurched into the computer room. He glared myopically around the room, the light flashing off his thick, wire-frame spectacles. Feinman was madly ripping paper out of the high-speed printer and stuffing it into fifty-gallon trash containers. Unfortunately, the printer was faster than Feinman, and the floor was now ankle deep in printouts. Knight kicked his way over to the printer and looked at what it was spewing out.

". . . NINE HUNDRED AND FIFTY-SEVEN THOUSAND, THREE
HUNDRED AND SIX BOTTLES OF BEER ON THE WALL. TAKE ONE
DOWN, PASS IT AROUND, NINE HUNDRED AND NINETY-SEVEN
BILLION, NINE HUNDRED AND TWENTY-THREE MILLION . . ."

Knight was the only corporate security officer in America with a Ph.D. An infant prodigy from the remote outback of Mississippi, at the age of twenty he had taken his doctorate degree in computer science at the Massachusetts Institute of Technology. His professors were happy to see him go; he intimidated them and, besides, his personal habits were appalling.

Knight was a hacker. He lived and breathed computers. They were all that interested him. Food, sleep, sex, friends, personal hygiene all fell by the wayside when Knight had his hands on a computer. In a trance of ecstatic concentration, he would spend days, weeks, crouched in front of his computer terminal performing spectacular feats of electronic brilliance. And as he performed his mechanized acrobatics, mounds of rancid debris—pizza crusts, Colonel Sanders' chicken bones, half-eaten eggrolls—would rise around him to stupendous heights. In the mystic trance of an obsessive hacker, he worked miracles and conjured magic. Oblivious to this sordid, mortal sphere, Knight, an anchorite of automation, would let his body go unwashed, his teeth unbrushed, his face unshaved and his linen unchanged. Within the closely knit computer aficionado community, the very word "Knight" became a synonym for, indeed a measure of, untidiness. "Ugh," one hacker might remark to another, "this kitchen is a bit Knightish, I'd rate it at three mega-Knights."

Knight's particular specialty was breaking into other people's computers, defeating their security systems, and examining their programs and files. His intentions were neither malicious nor felonious. He was merely curious. He simply wanted to know how things worked. Consequently, after graduating from MIT he was recruited, naturally enough, by the National Security Agency. There he was employed as something called the "deputy director of computer analysis," a disarmingly polite title for someone who was a career computer burglar.

At the NSA, Knight had electronically crept into every kind of computer ever made, picked its microchip locks, pilfered its coded secrets, and digitally looted its innermost treasures. The antiaircraft guidance system for the missiles that protect Muammar Khaddafi? A piece of cake. The triply impenetrable, cryptographically secured computers used by Swiss banks and their paranoid Arabian customers? Kid stuff. The KGB's closely guarded mainframe at Dzerzhinsky Square? A bit tricky, that one, but no more than an honest day's work. Ultimately he went too far (President Reagan was obliged to write a personal letter of apology to the British prime minister) and was fired. Scott personally hired him. "Set a thief to catch a thief," Thatcher had remarked as he appointed the twenty-seven-year-old Knight to be PegaSys's vice president of security.

Knight was good. Knight was the best. Or so they said until Wintergreen showed up.

"NINE HUNDRED AND NINETY-SIX BILLION, NINE HUNDRED AND NINETY-NINE MILLION . . ."

"When did it start?" asked Knight.

Marty, moving slightly upwind, glanced at the glowing green computer terminal. "I started exec'ing at 9:46 and eight seconds."

Knight, whose ability to perform complex mathematical calculations in his head was legendary, said, "Unless we do something, it will take until 2:20 in the morning before it ends."

"Yeah, about that."

"No, precisely that. Sixteen hours, thirty-four minutes, and fifty and one-tenth seconds."

"Yeah." Marty scooped up more printouts. The paper was piling up to his knees now and he was not about to challenge Knight's computations. Behind his back PegaSys's employees had nicknamed the rail-thin Knight "the cerebellum on a stick."

"How do you know Wintergreen is responsible for this?"

"Who else could it be?"

"You're right. Who else could it be? OK. Let me see if I can abort Wintergreen's latest merry little prank."

"I tried."

"I'm sure you did," Knight said with the disdain of superiority addressing mere competence. He shoved the growing flood of paper away from the console, sat down, and began to type. His fingers flew over the keyboard. Electronically he poked and prodded at PegaSys's central computer system—a system that he knew to be the most secure in the world, because he himself had designed its security features. With the perfect concentration and sure stroke of a master brain surgeon, Knight started to operate, using computer programming instructions to slice his way down to where the disease was.

". . . PASS IT AROUND, NINE HUNDRED AND NINETY-FIVE BILLION . . ."

As he typed, the rapture overtook him, the rapture of computing. Knight loved them, the beasts. Magnificent, intricate, and enormous, computers were abstract mathematics made material. The beauty of theorems made concrete. The poetry of equations turned physical. Formulae became corporeal in a body of silicon and metal more alluring than any biological creature could hope to be. The only machine there is that is controlled not by muscle but by mind. The only truly logical beings in the world. The only truly reliable beings in the world. Computers were the only thing Knight loved and, with one exception, the only consummation he desired.

What else did he desire? He desired Wintergreen. More specifically, he desired revenge on Wintergreen, the otherwise anonymous, grubby little hack who had the temerity to violate his beloved security system and bewitch this sleek and sexy machine, Olympia, his mechanical lover.

The console screen flashed an apparently incomprehensible display of hexadecimal characters. *Ahh*, he thought, *there it is. Elegant, Wintergreen, truly elegant. As crafty a piece of computer hacking as I have ever seen, and I have seen a lot. You almost outfoxed me, pal. But, to quote Edward G. Robinson, you are good, kid, real good; but as long as I'm around, you are only second best.* With a flourish, Knight typed a line of code into the console. There was a pause, the screen went blank, and then slowly, painfully slowly, a message appeared.

">NOT BAD, KNIGHT, BUT YOU HAVEN'T CAUGHT ME YET. BETTER LUCK WITH YOUR NEXT TRY. XXX WINTERGREEN."

Knight hissed with fury and glanced over at the high-speed printer. ". . . EIGHTY-TWO THOUSAND ONE HUNDRED AND TEN BOTTLES OF BEER ON THE WALL, NINE HUNDRED AND SEVENTY-SEVEN BILLION, FOUR HUNDRED . . ."

Knight hunched forward and started to type anew.

3

ASH WAS IN TROUBLE.

Oh Jesus, he thought, *here I am mooning like a sex-struck teenager again. When we broke up, we should have stayed broken up.* He tried to steer his attention back to Louise's analysis of Engineered Systems. Instead, he found his eyes tracing the handsome slope of Louise's long and lovely calves. He followed them up to her hemline, just below the knees, then traced the path of her thighs, *Oh God, her thighs,* upward and . . .

Ash was in trouble. Especially where Louise Bowman was concerned.

Like Mike Ash, Louise Bowman was a vice president of PegaSys—its youngest vice president. She was a full ten years younger than Ash, as trim as he, and in considerably better physical condition. At best, Ash's exercise regimen consisted of his daily twelve-block walk to and from the office, spiced by an occasional frantic dash through the interminable corridors of LaGuardia Airport to catch a plane. Louise, on the other hand, exercised religiously for an hour each and every evening. Sit-ups, push-ups, leg lifts, aerobic jumps, side bends, toe touches, knee squats, running in place, and a little light weight lifting. On the weekends she was unable to get out of New York, she made a point of walking ten miles through Central Park. When she could escape the city, she rode horseback all summer and skied cross-country all winter.

Or at least she had, until she became involved with Ash. In Ash's company she exercised just as hard, albeit in different ways . . . and sometimes longer.

The result of this physical discipline was a woman whose shape could (and in towns smaller than New York, did) stop traffic. She was tall, five-nine, and, because she refused to be seen on the streets wearing jogging shoes, her footwear added another two inches to her height. She strode shoulder to shoulder with Ash when they walked together, her long legs matching his stride to the very inch. Her hair was black. Not brunette. Black. Black as a raven's wing, and tightly wound in a chignon that she unloosed only in bed. It drove Ash mad when she undid her hair.

She was born and raised in Minnesota, won a scholarship to Stanford, and moved on to finish third in her class at Wharton. After graduating from business school she joined McKinley-Allan, the bluest of the blue-chip management consulting firms, and three years later was hired by Joe Jonas, then PegaSys's executive vice president and chief operating officer. Every eighteen months since, like clockwork, she had been promoted.

For most of her years in New York, she shopped with reluctant pickiness at B. Altman's, Saks, Bloomingdale's, and a host of discreetly stylish boutiques. Trying to find just the right wardrobe was difficult and time-consuming. She hated it. Then Alcott and Andrews opened its doors. The store's low-key, subtly stated office wear suited her to a tee. She spent thousands of dollars a year there, year in, year out.

Suits of dark natural fabric or a tasteful combo assembled out of a light (but not bright) skirt and dark jacket became her stock-in-trade, worn with a starched white blouse and set off by a parti-colored Hermés scarf or single strand of pearls. Louise's style quickly became the standard role model for PegaSys's young, aspiring women. Both secretaries and professionals watched her closely, imitating what they envied. Further, despite their conservatism (or perhaps because of it), her dress habits fostered rich and lurid daydreams among more than a few of her male subordinates.

Had Ash spoken of such things, he could have stated authoritatively that the most extravagant dream was but a pale reflection of reality. But Ash did not speak about sex. He was uncommonly reticent on such matters, and tried as best he could to keep away from such basic male rituals as sexual boasting. Not that he had much to boast of until Louise entered his life.

Ash's sex life was not a failure. It was merely unnoteworthy. In college he had a few hurried, clumsy encounters before marrying the woman who had done best at resisting his inept advances. Together they grew in mutual sexual competence, and declined in mutual sexual enthusiasm. At some point a few years after joining PegaSys, he stumbled into a brief and mechanical affair with a striking young computer programmer in the Government Systems Division. He stumbled out of the affair just as quickly when an observant colleague warned him that Scott C. Thatcher adamantly disapproved of office romances.

After twelve years of childless marriage and claustrophobic New York apartment dwelling, Ash and his wife divided up their property and went their separate ways. Each had a career and each had concluded that their careers were vastly more important—and interesting—than their life together. With neither acrimony nor affection, they divorced.

After the divorce Ash felt obliged to date new women. But he didn't know how. He tried going to a singles bar once, an upper East Side meet market called the Incontinent Behemoth. After fifteen minutes, he decided that he was out of his league. Joe Jonas, Ash's immediate boss in those days, introduced him to various unattached ladies of a libertine bent. Few of these ladies made it to the second date, fewer still to the third—and there was never a fourth. He perused the personal ads in the back of the *New York Review of Books* with some interest. However, he couldn't work up enough nerve to respond to those few advertisements that appeared to have been written by someone whose company, alone and in an empty room, wouldn't make him feel nervous.

Months passed. And years. Every now and then he would wake up in the morning with a woman in bed next to him. It was, however, a rare event. It became rarer still with the herpes scare, and then the AIDS epidemic, and finally the ever-growing time demands of his executive responsibilities at PegaSys. Ultimately, Mike Ash became celibate without even thinking about it.

Then, some ten months earlier, he had found himself spending countless weeks in Chicago, trying to clean up one of the messes created by Joe Jonas's resignation. Louise Bowman joined him, assigned to work with Ash in solving a particularly complicated set of marketing and financial problems.

Neither had known much about the other before this assignment. During the course of their entire careers they had spent only one day in each other's company—and that a notoriously bad day involving an aborted attempt to acquire a small company in Missouri. They occupied different floors of the PegaSys tower, and had spent their working days in different organization units. Both had, at best, secondhand information about one another: Mike's reputation as an erratically brilliant and unpredictably moody executive, Louise's reputation as "a sixteen-hour-a-day lady" with a razor-sharp mind and a full-time, no-nonsense commitment to her career.

At PegaSys, like most other corporations, executives were frequently dubbed with less than complimentary, but often accurate, nicknames. For example, Scott Thatcher was widely referred to as "El Exigente," the demanding one—a reference to an otherwise long forgotten advertisement for Colombian coffee. Reflecting on Ash's manic energy and unpredictable flights of soaring creativity, the junior staff secretly called him "Mad Mike." No-nonsense Louise was known as either "the Iron Nun" or, when she was driving her subordinates to work late into the evening hours, "Midnight Mary."

Ash looked with some trepidation upon his prospects for working successfully with the Iron Nun. Bowman, in turn, was far from certain that she could accomplish anything saddled with Mad Mike. Both were pleasantly surprised.

Soon enough, they discovered that they worked well together, and, once their long and hard hours in the office were through, still enjoyed one another's company. Over an afterwork drink. Over dinner. Over an after-dinner drink.

Soon enough, each found that the other's corporate and private personalities were strikingly different. Mad Mike, the sharp-tongued creative whiz kid, was modest, self-deprecating, introspective, and boyishly amusing. The Iron Nun was shy, a little lacking in self-confidence, homesick for her Minnesota farm life, and surprisingly prone to girlish giggles. *Mike,* thought Louise, *is actually a pretty analytical guy. Louise,* thought Mike, *really has gotten some unfair bad press on her creative skills.*

Soon enough, each found that, off the job, they shared a good deal in common.

Cats: Mike named his stately Russian Blue Ivan, short for Ivan the Purrable, a name he would *never* confess to anyone but blurted out one evening to Louise. She was charmed; her Burmese's secret name was Prince Pitterpat Paws, Prince for short. Opera: Louise's love of Rossini was so great that she actually left the office before 7:30 P.M. whenever *Barber* or *Italian Girl* was being performed. Mike was a sucker for Puccini and would tie his business schedule into knots to ensure that he made a performance of *La Bohème*. Books: Iris Murdoch and Stephen King, John Fowles and Ed McBain, Gore Vidal and Bernard Cornwall. Laughter: Increasingly it boomed from the conference room they shared in Chicago, giggles, titters, guffaws, and deep, long, happy laughs. Ambition: . . .

They complemented one another. The problems arising in the aftermath of Joe Jonas's resignation were getting solved, and the solutions were better than either had expected. "We make," said one or the other (neither could remember which), "one hell of a good team." "Yeah, we're a pair."

So much a pair that once when they were checking into the Ritz-Carlton, the preferred Chicago hotel of PegaSys executives, the receptionist summoned a bellman to "take care of Mr. and Mrs. Ash's bags." Mike blushed at that, but Louise giggled.

On one particular Monday in early March, Ash flew to Chicago by himself. Louise followed the next day, checking into the Ritz-Carlton before going to the office. That evening, as she and Ash were dining together, a surprise snowstorm swept into Chicago. They left the restaurant to discover two inches of snow on the ground—and, the streets empty of taxicabs. Cursing their luck, Chicago's wretched winters, and, especially, the icy wind off the lake, they trudged a cold and weary mile back to the Ritz-Carlton. They stopped in the hotel bar for a warming glass of the exquisite Fonseca '66 port the bartender kept secret from all but his most special customers. They chatted idly about their day's work, about what the next day would bring, and about the rumors and gossip that flew around the halls of PegaSys.

Then they rode the elevator up to their rooms, discovering that, for the first time during their stints in Chicago, they were housed on the same floor. Indeed, by a quirky coincidence their rooms were side by side, two parts of a suite that shared a common foyer.

Louise reminded Mike that she had brought a report he needed with her from New York. Mike followed her into her room as she went to fetch it. She pulled the report out of her briefcase and handed it to him. As he stood flipping through it, Louise stepped back, arching her back in a long, languorous stretch. She pulled her shoulder blades together as she stretched, and, human anatomy being what it is, her breasts pushed forward, straining at the soft fabric of her blouse. Her blouse was a loose, creamy-white silk affair, with six rows of double pleats down the front. Around her neck she wore a subdued sea-green scarf tied in a half rosette. Her suit was a very dark navy blue, and, as she stretched, her jacket fell back to surround and highlight her breasts. Deep down in her throat, she sighed, making a sound like a contented tabby cat.

The blue jacket, the green scarf, the loose cream blouse now tightly outlining every curve and swell of her bosom . . . It was the most sensuous thing Ash had ever seen. He kept flipping through the report.

"Ummm," Louise said, "that felt good. I don't know where they got all that furniture in our Chicago office. It feels like it was custom-designed by Torquemada. After a day sitting in those chairs, I'm stiff all over."

Ash grunted and turned another page.

"Here," she continued, plucking a nearly invisible piece of lint off his lapel, "let me get that off of you."

"Ahh, thanks." He squinted down at a table of numbers, and turned another page.

"No problem"

"Ahh, look, Louise, there's no reason for me to keep you up while I look at this thing. I'll just go back to my room and—"

"Don't be silly. Sit down." Her voice seemed almost harsh. Ash noticed that her "sit down" very nearly ended in an exclamation mark. He also noticed that her very fair skin had turned a little, just a little, redder than could be accounted for by a long cold walk, a glass of port, and a warm hotel room.

He folded the report closed and looked at her. Absentmindedly he twisted it in his hands, tightly rolling the document into a baton and idly tapping it against his leg.

"Ahhh, Louise?"

"Yes."

"I may be way out of line here but would you mind if I gave you a kiss?"

"No. That would be nice."

"Would you mind if I gave you a serious kiss?"

"No. That would be even nicer."

Ash was in trouble.

He was supposed to be concentrating on the vitally important report about PegaSys's Engineered Systems Division. Instead, he had an erection and was concentrating on what Louise might do about it if only they were alone.

Louise kissed differently from any woman he had ever known. She started with a series of quick pecks, a handful of seemingly dispassionate, cocktail party-style busses. Then, without warning, she thrust her tongue into his mouth with an insatiable hunger, producing a high-voltage shock of sensuality. Holding her in his arms, there in the Ritz-Carlton Hotel, he felt an effect not unlike that of a strong drink hitting an empty stomach.

He pulled her closer, eager to feel her softness firmly against him but still trying to be gentle. Hugging her with his left arm, he slowly stroked the palm of his hand up and down her back. She in turn caressed his shoulders softly with her fingers. As they kissed and clutched, she made a soft, satisfied sound. "Mmmmm."

It was all very good to Ash. It all felt quite wonderful. However, as the heat of an obviously mutual passion rose, he wondered and worried about exactly what he should do next. Long celibate and quite inexperienced in the rituals of contemporary seduction (he was the seducer, after all, wasn't he?), he fretted about how to proceed. He didn't want to appear too eager, for fear that aggressiveness would scare Louise off. Nor did he want to appear too hesitant for fear that her appetite was for something . . . well, more macho.

Another worry. It had been a very long time since he had made love. Too long. Suppose he was overly anxious and couldn't perform? Or, worse, suppose he was overly impatient and his performance was a short one. Like most men, he had experienced both problems before. With this lovely, warm (and most interestingly wiggling) woman in his arms, he most sincerely did not want to have either problem now. Least of all now.

Or suppose that Louise was only interested in a little kissing and cuddling. Would she be satisfied with just that? Would she break their clutch, step back, smile, and send him on his lonely way to bed? He'd had that experience with women, too.

He knew now that he wanted to go to bed with Louise. He wanted it maybe more than he had ever wanted anything. Over the course of a few brief moments, that want had become the most important thing in the world to him. The want had been there, hidden in his unconscious, for weeks—for longer. Louise's kisses unlocked it, leaving Ash with the shaken recognition that he very likely was, *God help me*, in love. *No, Ash*, he thought. *It's just sex. No, it's love. I'm in love. I have been all this time and just haven't known it. Nah, it's sex. No it's not . . .*

Louise pulled her head back, loosened her hold on him, and rested her cheek on his chest. Without his noticing it, she had slipped out of her shoes and now stood a few inches lower than he.

Anxious to keep the moment, Ash said, "I think you like to hug,"

"Mmmmm," she replied, "and to be stroked, too. I've got a high stroke requirement. Isn't that a silly thing to say? A high stroke requirement. I sound like a computer engineer talking about electrical requirements."

"No, hugs are good for you. There was an article in the science section of the *Times*. . . ."

"I saw it. I've got a high hug requirement, and a high stroke requirement, too." She giggled with embarrassment.

"It's OK," said Ash, "I can handle that kind of requirement."

He squeezed her harder, and began lengthening the sweep of his strokes up and down her back. She sighed another contented, "Mmmmmm. You give good hug, Ash."

After a few more hugs and back rubs, Louise lifted her mouth back to his. Another handful of quick pecks, and then an even more potent kiss. Ash, frantically trying to calculate his odds of success, decided that the time had come to take a risk or two. Tentatively, ready to withdraw quickly if Louise froze up at the action, he let his hand drift down over her rump. A quick, light stroke and he pulled it away. Louise just snuggled closer. He did it again, slower this time.

Encouraged by success, he let his hand roam further and wider. Still cautious and prepared to retreat, he sidled over her breasts. She didn't flinch, so he touched them again, a bit more authoritatively. She squirmed, but it was an encouraging sort of squirm. He enfolded one breast in his hand and began to squeeze it. The softness of it all amazed him, and the way it moved. His fingers tingled and the palm of his hand, cupped around her, seemed radiant. *Is this what a woman's breast feels like?* Had it been so long that he had forgotten? Or was it that Louise was different and special? Or, special to him.

Daring even more, he fumbled at her blouse. *Where the hell are the damned buttons on this doubly damned thing?* He couldn't find them and so merely reached beneath it, its looseness leaving ample room for his explorations. *What the hell is this? Oh, bra. Right, I'd forgotten about those things. There's a clasp in the back you've got to undo. I was never any good at unhooking the bloody clasp. Damn!*

But the gods were smiling on Michael Ash, because on his first try and with the merest flip of his fingertips, he managed to unfasten Louise's bra. He gently took what he found beneath it in his hand. What he found in his hand gently took his breath away. It was the warmth that staggered him, the silky smooth, unknowable warmth. Firm, but not too firm. Large, but not too large. Eminently caressable, more than he could have imagined. Alive and eager for his touch. He kneaded her breast softly, his fingers alternately squeezing the entirety and tenderly teasing the nipple. It was magic.

Louise's kisses rose a degree or two in intensity.

Ash concluded that the time had come to move from stand-up kissing to something else. What else, he wasn't quite sure of. He opened his eyes. Louise's were still closed. With his lips still firmly pressed against hers, his glance darted around the room. Surely there was a place to sit or lie. *The bed? No, too early and too risky at this point. The floor? Don't be silly. Ah-ha! A sofa! At the far end of the room. Now the question is how to manipulate her down there without seeming too obvious.*

Louise solved the problem for him. Again she pulled away from his kiss. Opening her eyes, she looked up, saw his wide open, and said, "Hey, handsome, no peeking." Then she rested her head back on his chest.

Ash felt her hold around his back slackening. He could tell she was trying to wind down. She was working up to a nice way to say good night.

Clever Ash. Crafty Ash. Cunning Ash. "Louise, let's sit down for a minute and talk."

"Mmmmm, OK."

With his arm around her waist (she fit against him just perfectly), he led her to the sofa. Still holding her carefully against his side, he eased her down. "But first, let me handle your high hug, high stroke requirement again." Without waiting for an answer, he wrapped his arms around her. She hesitated for just a moment, then rose to the invitation on his lips. Pecks—countdown, 5-4-3-2-1-0. Tongue—ignition. All systems go. And, as for lift-off. . . .

Mike worked his hand up under her skirt, caressing her thighs with a long circular motion, then stroking between them. In barely audible tones Louise breathed, "Don't. I get nervous, Mike. Mmmmm. Don't. I get nervous. I get . . . mmmmm . . . very . . . mmmmm . . . nervous about this."

Ash answered by reaching beneath her panty hose, his hand pressed closely against her by the tug of the elastic. "Nervous. Very nervous. Mmmmm." And that was all she said for ten minutes.

Mike watched her carefully, almost studiously, as she moved in response to his fingers. Her eyes were closed, her long lashes lying nearly against her cheek. Her face looked like that of a Botticelli angel in innocent sleep. Thus her face, but for the rest, little innocence was in evidence. She opened to accept him. The ball of his middle finger slid up and down against her clitoris, and with each each slide she clenched her thighs and lifted her hips. Quite soon she was ready for him to go deeper, and he inched his finger into her. She was more than moist, he found; she was wet, and slick. As he pushed back as far as he could, she groaned with pleasure, the sound coming from deep in her chest, and she shivered from her shoulders to her toes. Unless Ash was profoundly mistaken, it was an orgasm, a very fast one that had come mere moments after he had first touched her sex.

More shivers and more groans followed, each more intense than the one before it. Louise's back arched higher and higher, and she writhed from side to side, forcing her body to take the fullest advantage of Mike's probing touch.

At the end, she gasped five or six times, lifted her hips high above the sofa, and fell back. Then she rolled away from Ash's hand and said, "Mmmmm. Nice. That was really nice. I'm going to sleep well tonight."

In what was, to say the very least, the heat of the moment, Ash hardly noticed her comment, although in later months, he would remember it and think about it much. Instead, he was thinking (not clearly, but thinking nonetheless) that in his admittedly limited experience he had never seen a woman whose climax was so . . . so . . . downright sincere. He was also thinking that he wanted to share the next one with her. Urgently. Right now.

"Uff," she said, sitting up and tugging down her skirt in one fluid gesture, "and it is past my bedtime."

There was a message here that Ash did not want to hear. "Louise? Ahhh, look, Louise. Speaking of bed, ahhh . . . What

I would like to do, what I *very* much want to do is take you over to that bed and, ahhh . . .''

"Mike, I'm not using any method."

"Huh? What?"

"Method. You know, birth-control method. You know, no pills or diaphragm or anything."

It took Ash several seconds to work out the implications. Lamely he offered, "Well, ahhh. I *could* be careful, you know. I mean, Louise, we are talking desperate straits here."

She reached out her hand and touched his cheek tenderly. "Poor baby, I know. But there is no way I'm going to risk it without protection."

Ash thought his voice was going to break. "Louise, look, I mean, ahh, *desperate* straits."

"Well, I suppose . . . I suppose you could run out and buy some condoms. Or we could wait until tomorrow. That would be better, wouldn't it? I'll still be here tomorrow, Mike." She examined the look on his face for a moment and then added, "No, I suppose it wouldn't, poor baby. Well, then, go ahead."

Mike lunged forward hungrily but was stopped short by her outstretched hand, "No, I mean go ahead out and get some protection. And hurry back."

With a maddening blend of reluctance and eagerness Ash rose and, hampered by an all too obvious erection, hobbled to the door. He grabbed the topcoat he had draped on Louise's table at some point—he wasn't quite sure when—and wrapped himself in it to hide his aroused condition from anyone he might encounter in the hallway. "Back in a flash," he said. "I'll be waiting," she answered.

His tumescence did not subside as he scurried to the elevator. Nor did it leave him while he waited impatiently for its arrival. It was still there as he rode the elevator down to the ground floor. It stood proudly beneath his coat as he trotted through the lobby. Indeed, it survived a full three minutes of the subzero winds and blinding blizzard that completely shut down the city of Chicago, every store in the city of Chicago, and, coincidentally, the sexual expectations of Michael J. Ash.

A frustrated Mike Ash called Louise Bowman to tell her of his defeat. From the sound of her voice he could tell that he had woken her from a sound and relaxing sleep. That disappointed him even more.

The next night Louise made up for his disappointment. More

than made up for it. She kept making up for it nearly every night thereafter.

Senior executives drawing six-figure salaries are supposed to spend their office hours thinking about their work. Not their sex lives. Least of all are they paid to indulge in romantic fantasies about other senior executives who also draw six-figure salaries. Ash knew that. He also knew that the quality of his thought and the caliber of his management style had gone clean to hell since his affair with Louise had begun.

With each passing day, his work got a little worse. *Especially*, he thought, *since Louise started getting a bit kinky. Don't even think about it. Get back to work! Back to the Engineered Systems Division.*

"I'm sorry, Louise, I didn't quite understand that last point. Could you and Frank back up a page or two and go over it again for me?"

"Sure, Mike."

Ash was in trouble.

4

. . . Eight hundred forty-eight billion, seven million, four hundred and forty-six thousand, eighty-nine bottles of beer on the wall, eight hundred forty-eight billion . . ."

Knight brushed a lock of salt-and-pepper hair out of his eyes and looked around. They were watching him, all the women from the data entry department that Feinman had brought in to help keep the mounting piles of computer printout under control. There were some members of the programming department there, too. And people from EDP audit. Technical services. Telecommunications. The room was crowded with people silently watching Knight in the battle of the century. *Knight versus Wintergreen! The heavyweight bout for the world computer-hacker championship. Live from Madison Square Garden in New York. "It's an excited crowd here tonight, Dave." "Yeah, I know. Just look at those fans. They know that this is the big one. Winner take all. They're expecting blood at this match, Frank." "Yup. And Wintergreen, the youthful contender, is in great shape. He's had Knight, the champ, on the ropes most of the evening." "Well, I wouldn't count the champ out yet, Frank. He may be older and slower than Wintergreen, but he's an experienced fighter. I bet he has some surprise moves left in him still." "Well, time will tell, Dave, and now, as the bell sounds to start the fifth round of this historic prizefight, Knight moves into the center of the ring. He's looking mad, Dave, real mad."*

Knight stared at the computer terminal. The computer terminal stared back.

". . . BEER, EIGHT HUNDRED AND FORTY-EIGHT BILLION, SEVEN MILLION . . ."

Whatever the notorious hacker prince, Wintergreen, had done, it was exceedingly clever. More clever than Knight would ever have imagined.

It was not uncommon for young technology enthusiasts to hook their personal computers up to a telephone line and try to pirate their way into a major corporate computer installation. It was a rite of passage in the hackers' strange, subterranean culture. For the most part, the pirates simply dialed in, browsed around for a bit, and then moved on. Sometimes they perpetrated minor tomfoolery or left silly messages: "CONAN THE COMPILER WAS HERE." "IBM SUCKS SILICON." "STOP ME BEFORE I SYSGEN AGAIN." A few indulged in mischief of a more malicious sort; where especially unpopular corporations were involved, serious damage was sometimes done.

It was Knight's job to protect PegaSys's computers from the prankish depredations of hackers. He did his job very well. No hacker had made it through even the first level of PegaSys's computer protection. Except, of course, Wintergreen. Wintergreen made it all the way. He wasn't even breathing hard when he got there. Smiling, he rode the wires, cruised the circuits, surfed the software, cavorting clownishly in plain view . . . but always just out of reach.

Nor was PegaSys the only target of Wintergreen's pranks. From some secret location, the pseudonymous Wintergreen blithely browsed through the computers of every corporation in

America, and when the mood was upon him, it was Halloween; trick or treat, Wintergreen calling. His specialty was elaborate practical jokes. Like, for example, seizing control of the PegaSys Olympia computer and forcing all of that machine's $50 million of computing power to devote its single-minded efforts to printing out the lyrics to "One Hundred Bottles of Beer on the Wall," upping the denomination from one hundred to one trillion.

Very funny, Wintergreen, Roy Knight thought. *I am really laughing my butt off. You little twerp. Well, pal, you've met your match. I know what you're doing, and I am going to shut you down. Right now.*

Knight smiled. The watching crowd leaned forward. Liston turned to face Clay, Manolete turned to face the bull, Casey turned to face the pitcher, Knight turned to face Wintergreen. Knight's fingers danced gracefully over the keyboard. Green rows and columns of numbers flickered over the console screen. Knight depressed the "enter" key and leaned back with a self-satisfied smirk.

" > YOU CAN RUN AND RUN AS FAST AS YOU CAN, BUT YOU CAN'T CATCH ME, I'M THE GINGERBREAD MAN. XXX WINTER-GREEN."

Knight slumped.

"What the . . . ," said Scott C. Thatcher, pausing for a moment to let the crowd in the computer room fill in the obscenity, profanity, or expletive that he himself never articulated, "is going on here?"

Knight jerked his head up and swiveled his chair around. Thatcher stood at the entrance to the crowded computer room, glaring at its occupants with wrath. A wrathful Scott Thatcher was a sight to behold, and an event to avoid. When he frowned, storm clouds gathered on his brow, his voice deepened, and those nearby waited fearfully for the flash of lightning, the rumble of thunder, and the tangy aroma of fresh roasted sinner.

"I repeat. What the . . . (*pause*) is going on here?"

Knight stood to answer. *Bless me father, for I have sinned.* "Hacker, Scott. Chap named Wintergreen. He's busted into Olympia again."

"Again? Again." Frost formed on the "A," snow on the "g-a-i" and glacially thick glare ice on the "n."

"Uhh, yeah. This is his second trip in. No, third. Third, isn't it, Marty?"

Feinman, wrapped in reams of computer paper, appeared to

be trying to audition for the lead role in a remake of *The Mummy*, or better still, given the look on Thatcher's face, *The Invisible Man*. He mumbled something of a vaguely affirmative nature.

"And," Thatcher thundered with finally honed sarcasm, "is this event of such nigh on universal, indeed, apocalyptic interest as to demand the reverent study of an audience numbering, as near as I can tell, in the hundreds if not the thousands? Is this the second coming of Christ, ladies and gentlemen, that it demands your rapt and unstinting attention? For if Christ has returned, and chosen the computer operations department of this corporation in which to first manifest his epiphany, then my responsibilities as chairman and chief executive demand that, at a minimum, I notify our public relations department so that they may issue a press release. Doubtless such a release would have a far more salubrious effect on the performance of our stock than one that described the antics of our employees standing around idly watching the pranks of some . . . (*pause*) computer hacker."

On the very period of Thatcher's last sentence the room emptied.

Thatcher was a handler. Some years earlier Joe Jonas, since resigned from PegaSys, had told Mike Ash, "Old Rock Jaw is a handler. He's a manipulator, a puppeteer, and most of all a handler. He knows how to handle people. Back when I worked for him at IBM I had a bad case about my salary. The headhunters were telling me I could make twice as much money if I left IBM and went into industry. So I kept harping on Thatcher about how little money I was making. Now Thatcher had sold this 1401 system to a big Wall Street brokerage house, and he told me to manage the installation. One day he took me down to meet the customer. Well, the guy the customer put in charge of the project was a retired pro football player. The brokerages like to hire jocks because their customers like to rub up against 'em. This guy . . . this guy doesn't have a neck. If you hit him upside the head you'd hear an echo. Between his ears it's the Carlsbad Caverns. He can't count higher than twenty-one with his pants down. And he's making fifty grand a year more than I am. So in the limo coming back uptown I say to Scott that I am fed up with starvation wages, and I don't think this guy can write, and I know he can't read, and he is making a lot more money than I am. Scott looks at me and smiles and says, 'Yup.

He does. But, Joe, that's all *he'll* ever make.' Right then and there, I knew I'd been handled.''

Thatcher sighed deeply and shook his head. Then he grinned elfishly. ''OK. Knight, you'd better fill me in. And, you, Marty, get out there, circulate among the troops, and make sure they're all back at productive work. And make sure I didn't scare them more than I intended. One other thing. Call the janitorial department and have them clean up this mess. OK, pal?''

Feinman nodded, ''OK, Mr. Thatcher.''

Thatcher pulled an armless computer operator's chair over next to Knight, spun it around, straddled it, and sat down. He crossed his arms on the back of the chair and propped his chin on them. He knew that Knight was under pressure and tensed up; the best way to calm the man down was to appear utterly casual and relaxed himself.

''All right, Roy, tell me all about it. Take your time.''

The man who sat with self-imposed casualness facing a distraught Roy Knight was no longer a hustling, upstart entrepreneur. More than a quarter of a century had passed since Thatcher left IBM to create PegaSys. The passing years had changed his appearance little, and what alterations they had worked were of a kindly sort. He still was lean, trim, and wiry. His hair still billowed in unruly curls, powder white. His nose remained a bit too narrow and sharp, and so, to soften it, he kept his moustache, letting it flow out in a style that had not been fashionable since somewhere around the year 1907. His sight was almost as clear as ever; he would never need eyeglasses, although from time to time he felt the need to squint. Such few wrinkles as appeared on his face were clearly laugh lines. All in all, on first glance, Scott Thatcher might appear to the uninitiated as a modest, kindly old gentleman, the sort of amiable codger one might expect to find rocking slowly in a porch swing in the house next to grandmother's somewhere in Kansas or Nebraska.

However, on second glance, the observer would be driven to form a different impression. The old man's carriage was a bit too erect, his forehead a bit too high (a long-disused phrase might come to mind: ''leonine brow''), his chin jutted with too much authority, and the look in his eyes was imperial. He commanded attention, respect, and obedience. On second glance, Thatcher seemed less like a charming old coot and rather more like someone whose bust belonged in the senate of ancient

Rome—a patrician, a philosopher, or a warrior-priest. Someone experienced and gifted in wielding absolute power. Wielding it well, and enjoying every minute of it.

The power involved in running a multibillion-dollar corporation is not inconsequential. PegaSys employed 70,000 people, and each of them ultimately looked to Thatcher for his or her paycheck. PegaSys disbursed billions of dollars each year to the thousands of smaller companies that supplied PegaSys with parts, components, services, and support. Ultimately, they looked to Thatcher for their earnings and *their* ability to pay *their* employees. Another 100,000 people and organizations owned PegaSys stock; the value of that stock and the dividends it paid hinged on Thatcher's actions. PegaSys's customers, who were legion, relied on the company's computer hardware, software, and services as integral to the conduct of their business. Thatcher's decisions profoundly influenced them as well.

Perhaps Thatcher did, after all, look like a Roman emperor—one of the better ones, say, Marcus Aurelius. But whatever the extent of the resemblance, the power Thatcher held would have been the envy of any Roman emperor, good or bad. "Of course I have a lot of power," he once snapped at a pushy writer for *Fortune* magazine. "And I use it. That's what it's there for."

The most striking element in Thatcher's administration of his enormous power was using it to proper effect. Nothing he did could seem arbitrary and nothing could seem thoughtless. He had to add to his power an element of drama, an element of acting. Indeed, Nelson Tongue, Thatcher's closest friend since his falling-out with Joe Jonas, insisted on calling Thatcher "Actor Man," or sometimes "Many Masks." Thatcher found Tongue's nicknames offensive. But then Nelson was a witch doctor, and could call anyone anything he wanted.

Thatcher donned a mask, taking on the role of Roy Knight's smiling old uncle. "Speak to me, Roy. Tell me all about it."

Knight spoke haltingly, "Guy calls himself Wintergreen. No one knows who he is or where he came from. He started hacking into every computer in the Fortune 500 a couple of months ago. Signs all his messages 'XXX Wintergreen,' like he's an artist and proud of his work."

"If he signs his name, why haven't the Feds been able to catch him? Computer burglary is a federal offense," said Thatcher.

"There are thousands of people named Wintergreen. Thousands of them. The FBI hit them all, and none of them had the horsepower to pull the stunts that this guy does."

"So Wintergreen is a pseudonym?"

"Yeah."

"What is Wintergreen's specialty?"

"He's got two. First, he gets in. He gets into anything and he gets in everywhere. Hell, Scott, our computer security system here beats the CIA's—you know that—and he cakewalks through it. From what I hear, he's cakewalked through everybody else's, too. So, his first specialty is that he gets in; no matter what you throw in front of him, he just sails down the phone lines and into your computer. His second specialty is that he plays outrageous practical jokes."

Thatcher gestured at the mountains of printouts. "Clearly. Can you give me another example?"

"You know Globalcare Insurance?"

"How could I not? They're one of our competitor's biggest customers. I positively yearn for Globalcare's business. I crave it. I desire it. I dream of it, and in my dreams I smile."

"Sure. Well, they've got all these video terminals all over the country to process insurance claims. And most of the claims clerks are little old ladies. These ladies sort of have the reputation of being like your maiden aunt, you know, the proverbial maiden aunt from Peoria. So one morning they come in to work and their computer screens are all doing the same thing. Everywhere. All over the country. Every screen is printing out these limericks. And every limerick begins with the line 'There was a young man from Nantucket.' "

Thatcher's eyes open wide. "Every limerick?"

"Every limerick. For about an hour. After that there were a bunch beginning, 'A pretty young maid named Hunt.' "

"Oh, dear. I get the picture," Thatcher chortled. "How long did it go on?"

"Four hours, and he never repeated himself once."

"Do I detect a hint of admiration in your voice, Roy?"

"Well, you can't help but admire . . ."

"Emm, well, yes. But, I would admire it more if Wintergreen weren't a criminal. You know it was in large part due to our lobbying efforts that computer penetration was made a federal offense. And, while I might find brother Wintergreen's antics amusing, I am not amused by the fact that he is mucking around with our systems."

Knight nodded. The dullness was leaving his eyes, and the

sparkle of the hunter stalking his prey returned. "He's going to regret that, the twerp. I've had trouble figuring out exactly how he has programmed himself to seize control of Olympia, but I'm on his trail. I can get him, Scott. Wintergreen, oh Wintergreen," he snarled, facing the computer terminal, "you are mine, punk."

The rise in Knight's spirits made Thatcher smile. The first step in getting an employee back on the tracks was to improve his attitude. "Ok, Roy, look, I've got a couple of spare minutes. What say I try to give you a hand? After all, I used to be pretty good at this stuff myself."

Knight looked up with pleasure. "Yeah, sure, Scott. Maybe I need a hand."

"Have you tried handles?"

"No, Wintergreen is too subtle for that."

"Let's try a few anyway."

Handles are highly personalized code words and phrases that hackers hide in their programs. If you type in the right code (say the magic word and the duck will fly down), you automatically unlock their secrets and cause the program to abort. The hacker culture is not generally a malicious one, and most hackers view it as merely sporting when the target of one of their pranks discovers the handle that ends the joke.

Hackers' handles are drawn from the art forms hackers admire most: old movies (the kind that appear on the late, late show, during the hours when only hackers are awake), comic books (every lounge in every university computer department in America is knee deep in them), science fiction novels, and similar sources.

Knight gazed upward for a moment, searching his memory for what was most popular among the hacker community. Then he began to type, muttering as he pounded the keys: "Badge? Badge? I don't got to show you no stinking badge. Those aren't pygmies, they're dwarves! More wine, you waddling toad. For a man who has not yet lived a lifetime, you know far too much. Gort Klaatu Varata Nitku. Beam me up, Scotty, there's no intelligent life on this planet. Cerebus doesn't love you; Cerebus just wants all of your gold. I am Judge Dredd and I AM the law. Snakes, it would be snakes. . . . ''

As Knight typed, Thatcher's eyes suddenly hardened. He snapped his fingers, "Wintergreen, is it? Wintergreen? Roy, what was the first prank that Wintergreen pulled?"

Knight thought for a moment. "I'm not sure I remember. It

was a while ago and—no, wait, he did something strange. Just printed out a dozen pages of gibberish. Actually, what he did was send the same gibberish to every computer in every major company around. Or so I heard.''

"When you say gibberish, what do you mean? Do you remember any of it?'

"Not really. Some of it dealt with a church or a funeral or a graveyard or something, and then it talked about a Greek or an Egyptian or—''

"Aha! Was it a Phoenician? By any chance did it talk about Phlebas the Phoenician?''

"Maybe. Yeah. How did you know that?''

"Roy, you don't read anything but math books, do you?''

"No, I read physics texts too. Some science fiction. Why?''

Thatcher sighed with resignation. "Nobody reads anymore. Well, no matter, I think I know who he is. Or rather, what he is,'' said Thatcher spinning to the computer console. "Ex-PFC Wintergreen was a character in *Catch-22*. That's a novel, Roy, a very popular one. Anyway, in the book Wintergreen was, well to put it into terms you might understand, sort of a first-generation hacker. His favorite prank was sending the words "T. S. Eliot' to army officers expecting battle commands. It drove them crazy.''

"Who was T. S. Eliot?''

Thatcher resisted with difficulty the urge to say something unpleasant.

"T. S. Eliot,'' he said patiently, "was a very well-known poet. His most famous poem is called *The Wasteland*. The first message Wintergreen sent to us, and I guess everybody else, was the text of *The Wasteland*—what you call a dozen pages of gibberish. I am willing to bet I know Wintergreen's handle!''

As he spoke, he reached out to the keyboard and pecked, "> T. S. ELIOT.''

There was a pause while distant circuits connected, and then a message came back, "> YO. THAT YOU, YOSSARIAN?''

"> NO, WINTERGREEN, THIS IS SCOTT C. THATCHER.''

"> YOU'RE SPOOFING ME.''

"> IF YOU ARE AS GOOD AS PEOPLE SAY YOU ARE, YOU CAN RUN A VALIDATION, CAN'T YOU, WINTERGREEN?''

"> NO NEED. ANYONE WITH THE GUTS TO ISSUE ME THAT CHALLENGE IS EITHER GOING TO BE REAL SORRY FOR SPOOFING ME OR TELLING THE TRUTH.''

"> JUST SO.''

">HEY, I MEAN REALLY. LIKE I AM JUST BLOWN AWAY. IT'S REALLY YOU."

">YES, IT'S REALLY ME."

">YOU ARE ONE OF MY ALL-TIME HEROES, MR. THATCHER. I MEAN REALLY, THE WAY YOU STAND UP TO THOSE WEENIES AT IBM. AND YOUR COMPANY. WOW! GREAT COMPUTERS, MAN, YOU JUST MAKE GREAT COMPUTERS."

">IF YOU LIKE US SO MUCH, WHY ARE YOU CRIPPLING OUR INTERNAL COMPUTER SYSTEM, OLYMPIA?"

">OH, DON'T TAKE IT SERIOUSLY. I WAS JUST FUNNING AROUND. HERE I'LL SHUT IT OFF NOW."

There was a sudden silence as the printer clicked off. It ended with 785,736,315,438 bottles of beer left undrunk on the wall. After a moment, Knight spoke. His voice was soft and his tone wistful. "I could have gotten him, Scott. It would have taken me only a little more time. I could have gotten him."

"Of course you could have, Roy. I know that. Of course you could." Thatcher turned again to the keyboard.

">THANKS."

">HEY, IT'S MY PLEASURE TO HELP YOU, MR. THATCHER."

">WELL, YOU CAN HELP US BEST BY LEAVING OLYMPIA ALONE."

">AW, IT WAS ONLY THAT YOUR GUY KNIGHT IS SUPPOSED TO BE HOT STUFF AND I WANTED TO SEE HOW GOOD HE IS."

">HE'S TOP GUN, WINTERGREEN. HE'S THE BEST."

">MAYBE SO, MAYBE NOT."

"I could have gotten him, Scott. Really, I wasn't that far away."

"I know, Roy, I know."

">WELL, WINTERGREEN, IT'S BEEN INTERESTING, BUT NOW WE ALL HAVE TO GET BACK TO WORK. SO I WILL BID YOU GOOD-BYE."

">SURE. YEAH. GREAT. TALK TO YOU SOON, MR. THATCHER. XXX WINTERGREEN."

"Now there's an unappetizing thought," Thatcher reflected. "What did he mean, 'talk to you soon'?"

"He'll be back, Scott. I know he'll be back. And he'll find me waiting for him when he comes. I'll get him. I'll clean his clock."

Thatcher shook his head. "I think he will leave us alone, Roy. PegaSys has his respect."

"No. He'll be back. And I'll be ready for him."

Knight turned thoughtfully to his computer console. *Ahab*

sharpens his harpoon. Pat Garrett loads his guns. Zorro unlimbers his whip. Come on, Wintergreen, make my day.

5

TWELVE HUNDRED MILES AND ONE time zone to the west, an unremarkable and unremarked-upon corporation known as American Interdyne Worldwide—AIW for short—was preparing to meddle in the affairs of PegaSys, and in so doing make the lives of Scott Thatcher, Louise Bowman, Mike Ash, and, for that matter, all of PegaSys's employees and executives, a living hell.

The traveler compelled (usually against his or her will) to visit this corporation quickly discovers that no major airline serves AIW's hometown, Desuetude, Missouri. Desuetude can be reached only via a connecting flight through Chicago's O'Hare Airport. This connecting flight requires travel on an airline named Auk Airways.

Auk's only boarding gate (and only plane) is located at the end of a *very* long cinderblock corridor in an otherwise unused terminal building. There being no jetway, passengers must walk out onto the tarmac to board the plane. At this point travelers unsettlingly observe that: (1) the plane is a quite small prop job, and consists of an airframe built in Czechoslovakia, powered by an engine built in Mexico; (2) the pilot generally is outside the plane, doing something noisy with a wrench; (3) other passengers who fly the route frequently hold rosary beads, glance at the sky, and kiss their crucifixes; and, (4) when one enters the plane the only sanitary facilities to be found are airsickness bags—more than one for each passenger.

What happens after the Auk flight to Desuetude, and hence to AIW, is airborne is best left unspoken.

AIW's corporate headquarters are located approximately

twenty miles south of the Desuetude airport in a reclaimed land-fill. This office complex occupies sixty or seventy acres of man-icured, rolling greensward. Visitors cannot help but be impressed at how well kept the grounds are. The spacious lawns in particular are richly green and closely cropped; visitors to AIW frequently speculate that the reason the lawns are so neat and tidy is that this is where its employees graze.

The main corporate office building is among the more outré examples of architectural excess in America. Stylistically, it looks like a collaboration between the Hyatt Corporation and Albert Speer. Dripping with swirled concrete grillwork, it would not be out of place gracing the Las Vegas strip. One of the hallmarks of corporations such as AIW is the predisposition of their leaders to squander corporate resources on matters wholly unrelated to the health of the corporation or the best interests of its shareholders. And, when it comes to squandering resources, hardly anything is more effective than a gargantuan, grotesque new corporate headquarters.

Outside of this extravagant architectural folly, and immedi-ately abutting AIW's chrome and glass entrance, is the executive parking lot. Each space is clearly labeled with its occupant's name. The number-two space, right next to the chief executive officer's, bears a woman's name. Does this mean that AIW is an enlightened corporation with women in the top executive ranks? No, sadly it does not. This parking spot belongs to the CEO's voluptuous secretary. It is occupied by a sporty, all white Mer-cedes 580 convertible, doubtless a gift from a close friend.

Upon entering AIW's corporate headquarters building, the first thing a visitor will notice is that the receptionist is located in a protective glass booth—doubtless to protect her from the onslaughts of outraged customers. This receptionist wears a uni-form and doubles as a security guard. She is armed. She will insist that all arriving guests immediately sign their names to a logbook so that if silverware disappears from the executive din-ing room during their visit, AIW will know who to track down. Moreover, she will oblige guests to wear visitors' badges so that they may be readily identified as alien entities unworthy of walk-ing freely through the corporation's corridors.

Because the announcement of visitors is not among the re-ceptionist's top priorities, guests will have ample opportunity to study AIW's reception area while they wait, interminably, for their host to come greet them.

The receptionist area is carpeted with indoor/outdoor rugs,

the kind that used-car dealers put in their showrooms. AIW's janitorial staff cleans them with a hose. The lobby walls are hung with paintings of a rather blotchy, awkward, and primitive style—still lifes, landscapes, portraits of vapid little children, and the like. They all illustrate a common technique; indeed, they all bear a common signature: that of AIW's president's wife. These paintings were not contributed to AIW gratis. Picasso would have charged less.

In addition to these paintings, the walls are decorated with aerial photos of AIW's factories and advertisements for its products. These are "image ads," which talk about AIW's commitment to growth, to "excellence," and to the quality of its management. They contain precious few words about how growth will be achieved or what the company's actual lines of business are, a topic AIW's executive management prefers not to discuss too openly.

There are a few other ads hung on the walls here in AIW's lobby. They portray AIW's chief executive brandishing a bottle of Old Shipwreck, a low-priced rye whiskey. Old Shipwreck is not distilled by AIW; indeed, AIW has nothing to do with the liquor trade. What has happened is that Old Shipwreck's advertising agency has come up with a crafty new ad campaign. The agency has dubbed Old Shipwreck "the drink of overachievers," and pays $25,000 in cash to any company president willing to prostitute himself by appearing in one of their ads. AIW's president appears in three separate advertisements for Old Shipwreck. He likes the spare cash and he *really* likes being called an "overachiever."

Tired of strolling around the lobby waiting for their eternally tardy hosts, visitors finally decide to sit down and read such publications as are lying on the inevitable glass end tables and coffee tables (the latter being useless, since the receptionist does not have the courtesy to offer guests a cup of coffee). This literature consists of outdated copies of unintelligible, technical trade publications: *Foundry and Forge*, *Toxic Waste Engineering*, *Modern Antenna Design*, *Bargeman's Quarterly*, *Byte*, and others. The janitors have been instructed to retrieve these magazines from employees' trash baskets and bring them to the lobby. Waste not, want not.

Buried somewhere in the depths of these publications one usually can discover a copy of an AIW annual report. This is a document that should be read with awe. An immense amount of talent and ingenuity went into producing it. It is a masterpiece of lavish graphic design. It is beautifully prepared, gorgeously laid out, and elegantly executed. It is a thick document, printed on the highest grade chrome glossy paper. Full color, of course. The cover is illustrated with a dramatic photo of a lightning bolt flashing down through the night from stormy clouds over a major city. Emblazoned across the photo are some particularly stirring words: "AMERICA INTERDYNE WORLDWIDE—Electrifying the Competitive Landscape! Our Annual Report on Excellence, Achievement, and Growth." The contents of this volume are as fictitious as its cover.

Beyond the reception area, guarded by a locked and alarmed door, lie a seemingly endless series of corridors and vast, football field–sized bullpens, furnished with ghastly grey, chest-high fabric and metal dividers, all acquired from the SteelCase Corporation. The workers in these bullpens are uniformly white, uniformly male, and uniformly unoccupied.

At the nethermost reaches of this maze is AIW's executive wing. It is easy to identify this area as housing senior management. The carpets are thicker and there is not a SteelCase product to be seen. Here is to be found the spacious office of Brian W. Shawby, chairman and chief executive officer of American Interdyne Worldwide, a muddleheaded incompetent whose maladroit mismanagement has brought AIW to the brink of bankruptcy.

On the day in question, Brian W. Shawby should have been at the end of his tether. The more than twenty-year period during which he led AIW, having inherited the once prosperous enterprise from his robber-baron father, had been an unmitigated disaster. Nothing he did ever seemed to work right. No strategy he set ever succeeded. No business he entered ever prospered. No new product he launched ever sold. The amount of money AIW had borrowed bordered on the total worth of the company. The banks' demands for payment were becoming strident, and Shawby did not have the funds needed to satisfy them.

But Brian Shawby was not depressed. Brian Shawby was not discouraged. Brian Shawby smiled. Brian Shawby looked eagerly and hopefully to the dawn of a bright new day of abundant wealth and triumphant corporate success. Brian Shawby was planning to mount a hostile takeover raid against PegaSys.

In Tokyo, nine time zones to the west of Missouri, or, if you will, fifteen to the east, it was shortly after midnight. Most Japanese workers had long since gone home, the women between 5:30 and 7:00 P.M., the men between 6:30 and 8:00 P.M.

Okinakao Hidetake frowned when he reflected upon the growing decadence of his nation's labor force. Leave at 8:00 P.M.! And there was still work to be done! Bah! At that rate, everyone in Japan would be driving Korean-made Hyundai cars before the decade was over. Or worse, Chryslers. "Where is the spirit of our workers?" he asked in one of his morning harangues to his employees. "Have we become a nation of fat and lazy decadents, like the squalid Americans? Have we no loyalty to our nation, our Emperor, and our company, that we talk in terms of ten-hour workdays? That we think of Sunday as a day of rest? That we leave the job before the job is done?"

Harangue or no harangue, at Seppuku Ltd., no one would even think about leaving before the job was done. Least of all, when the job that was being done had been ordered personally by its fearsome chairman, Okinakao Hidetake.

Hidetake stood facing the enormous floor-to-ceiling window behind his desk, his squat frame outlined by the lights of Tokyo and the night above them. He ran his palms backwards along his temple, smoothing down his glistening grey hair. "And what of this man's ancestors? What of them?" he asked the exhausted team of Seppuku executives cringing before his desk.

"Ancestors, sir?"

"It is said that if you would know a man, know first his ancestors."

"Hai! Wisdom from the ancients."

"No, wisdom from Okinakao Hidetake, you simpleton. Now tell me of this Thatcher's ancestors. Tell me all."

"Hai! His progenitors are historic figures by American standards. He traces his line back to the third boat of puritans to arrive in America—"

"Merely the third?"

"Hai! Merely the third. Newcomers, then, but historic newcomers. His forefathers fought in the American Revolution, and then—"

"Which side?"

"The American side, sir."

Hidetake hissed through his teeth. "His ancestors took up arms against their emperor. His is a disgraceful bloodline."

"Hai! Disgraceful, sir. Just after the turn of the century, the family sold their farm and moved west to a town on the great Mississippi River—"

"It is shameful for a farmer to leave his land."

"Hai! Shameful. There Thatcher's great-grandfather was a judge. His grandfather moved further west, becoming a banker and earning his great wealth as the trustee for the estate of a young American pornographer."

"You mean a newspaper publisher?"

"Hai! And magazines, too. When the pornographer came of age, Old Thatcher retired to Connecticut. There Thatcher's father was born, and became a doctor, a most successful surgeon. He served with General MacArthur during—"

"I know precisely what Thatcher's father did in the war. And after. Precisely. As for his other ancestors, you will give me the details in writing."

"Details, sir?"

"Do you mean that is all you know? All? All! You dare to sully my ears with trivial gossip, the scribblings of journalists for the American press, the nonsense that our employees in America have copied out of books! You dare to do this and think that you have satisfied my demand for information about Scott C. Thatcher! A painted geisha girl could do a better job, and at least she would sing me her story in soothing tones, serving hot sake to ease my spirits. Get back to work, you men, and do not leave the job until the job is done!"

With hurried bows and hoarse "hai's," Hidetake's minions scurried out of his office. Their clogs clacked noisily on the cherry and teak parquet floor. Hidetake watched them with a knowing smile; by the time he returned to his office at 7:30 A.M., there would be a full report on Scott C. Thatcher and PegaSys on his desk.

He stood up, rolled his shoulders to loosen them, and moved closer to the window. With his hands folded behind his back, he stared out into the night. Thirty-five stories below him, traffic swirled and flowed, looking, from this great height, like tiny luminescent insects. One out of every seven of those insects was a Seppuku car. Five out of every eleven people driving those cars owned a Seppuku television or VCR—and usually both. Three out of every seventeen banked at a branch of the Seppuku Global Marine Trust. Three out of every four owned a Seppuku watch.

Like all major Japanese corporations, Seppuku was a conglomerate. Its interests spanned mining, shipping, electronics, transportation vehicles, appliances, financial services, and almost anything else that Okinakao Hidetake thought he might be able to make (or if not make, at least sell) cheaper than his competition.

Like all Japanese executives, Hidetake admired General Electric more than any other company in the world. Its vast size, enormous reach, and sprawling diversification were his role model. He admired its ability to secure the number-one or number-two position in any arena in which it chose to compete. Its hungry preference for acquisition—its ability, for example, to buy an operation the size of RCA, strip it to the bone, digest it whole, and swiftly move on to another meal—struck him as being more than merely admirable. It struck him as worthy of imitation.

At the age of sixty-nine, he knew he had no more than one last opportunity to secure his position in the annals of Japanese enterprise, one last chance at leaving his mark on history, *Hai*, he thought, *so much to do and so little time to do it in.*

He turned away from the window and walked to the large, glass-enclosed display case on the distant wall of his office. There, staring at the contents, he performed his respect to his ancestors (and hence to himself).

The case contained weapons, two swords of great antiquity dating from the days of the Fujiwara hegemony. They were the swords of his ancestor, a noble retainer to the Heike clan. They had been salvaged from the tragic carnage at the battle of Danno-ura 800 years earlier.

Within the case, lying on a red silk pillow, was another, more contemporary weapon. It was an automatic pistol, a Nambu model 94. Its eight-millimeter clip lay next to it.

The swords and the pistol were weapons of defeat. The swords had been carried by Kagetsune until the very day that the despised Minamoto destroyed him and all but a handful of the Heike. The Nambu had been carried by Hidetake until the very day the British-American occupation army marched into Shanghai.

At first, Hidetake had been reluctant to display the gun in his office. It was, after all, the standard weapon of the Kempeitai, an organization that combined in one single corps all of the responsibilities held in Nazi Germany by both the SS and the Gestapo. The Kempeitai boasted of the fact that not only were their duties broader and more onerous than those of their German analogs, but that they, the Kempeitai, executed those duties with considerably more efficiency. And enthusiasm. Thirty-four million dead Chinese were the evidence of this *esprit de corps*.

It was an elite body in which one could take considerable pride
. . . at least until August of 1945.

Then things changed. For a few years one did not acknowledge having been an officer of the Kempeitai. One usually did
not even acknowledge that one knew such an organization existed. *Kempeitai? Ahh, Yankee-san, I do not know the meaning
of this word. How does it translate in my language?*

But Western memories are short and Asia is far away. Soon
all was forgotten, and, by the 1970s old war medals were donned
for the Emperor's birthday. By the 1980s all references to World
War II had been expunged from Japanese grammar and high
school textbooks—and the most popular movie of the year was
Zero, the thrilling saga of a hotshot fighter ace who blasted
legions of inept Western pilots (of unidentified nationality) out
of the blue Pacific skies (during an unidentified period of war).

Hidetake reached into his pocket, searched out a small key
and unlocked the display case. He reached in and took the pistol
in his hand. He withdrew it, slapped the clip home, and drew a
bead on an invisible target standing somewhere before him.
"Bang," he said, "you're dead."

Four thousand, six hundred and fifty miles west, in Moscow,
it was about 6:00 P.M. Andrei Bezukhov shot a rat. The rat had
been gnawing at the cables powering the KGB's mainframe
computer. At least once a week, and sometimes more frequently, the hungry rats would chew through an electrical line,
thereby consigning themselves and the computer to a smoky
demise.

It had not been that way a few years before, when the computer was located in the warm, well-lit, vermin-free environ of
KGB headquarters at Felix Dzerzhinsky Square. Those were the
good old days, the happy days, the days before some perfidious
(and doubtless American) hacker had electronically invaded the
Dzerzhinsky installation and wreaked unspeakable havoc. Bezukhov glowered as only Russians (and, coincidentally, Finns)
can glower. *Damned fools,* he thought. *Damn the KGB and
damn Yuri Andropov's bones and damn that American. Doesn't
anyone realize that the only way to protect a computer is electronically? You can't guard it with walls, you have to guard it
with software. But no, not the KGB. If there is a security violation, you pull out the guns and unleash the guard dogs and
put bigger locks on the door.*

Or, case in point, relocate the entire computer center to a

more physically (but not necessarily electronically) secure location. Say, Lefortovo Prison. Say, the deepest dungeon in Lefortovo Prison. The deepest, dampest, dirtiest, dingiest, *rattiest* dungeon. *Damn them.* Bezukhov heard a squeak and the scrabbling of tiny claws coming from behind a disk drive. He thumbed back the hammer on his revolver and waited as patiently as he could.

In Great Britain, in the City of London—as the English call their financial district—at the Queen Street offices of Quint and Claggart the business day was drawing to an end. Given the nature of their business, 3:00 P.M. was rarely too early to close. As was the practice at this firm, the workday ended with a stiff drink. Quint clicked his glass against Claggart's, and they each tossed back three fingers of not particularly expensive scotch whiskey.

"In honor of the day," said Quint.

"In honor of the day," agreed Claggart.

"I propose that we have another."

"In honor of the day, I second the motion."

"We are on our way."

"Back again."

"Beyond back, dear boy. Beyond back."

"Indeed. Not merely back. No! To the top, we are on our way to the top!"

"Just so. A third libation might be in order, might it not?"

"Indeed, it might."

The scotch bottle gurgled.

In certain Eastern religions it is held that life is but a great cycle of everlasting birth, death, and rebirth. There is no end and no beginning. The wheel of eternity rolls remorselessly across endless infinity. Through the countless aeons, the cosmological wheel turns, and with each turn, the puny souls of mankind, and indeed all creatures, are reincarnated. Throughout millennia beyond reckoning, the cycle of reincarnation spirals downward, ever downward. Through the timeless void, each creature is reborn more diminished in status than it was before. As the great cycle passes, those who lived once live again, reincarnated as lower life forms. What was, for example, once a man might be reborn as a cockroach. Lower, ever lower, what was once a cockroach might come back as a New York landlord. Lower, ever lower, that same soul, reborn again, would then return as a commodities trader.

For Quint and Claggart, it was the end of the line. They were lawyers.

6

WHAT ASH DIDN'T REALIZE, AT least not until much later, was that Louise herself had been as single-mindedly celibate as he—and for about as long.

After the collapse of the fifth of what she liked to think of as her four-and-a-half rotten affairs, she found that, yet again, she could not bear the idea of sex. Even the thought of the prolonged but platonic company of a man, much less intimacy, repelled her. Her muscles clenched at the very concept. To reduce the likelihood of meeting a potentially datable man, she added extra hours to her already long workday; she arrived at the office early and went home late. She applied an additional layer of ice to her already frosty style of dealing with such men as might approach her. She avoided invitations that were likely to put her in the way of an introduction. Her friends, long familiar with her post-romance behavior, recognized the symptoms and didn't even bother. At those few parties she attended, she arrived solo and solo departed. She had been sleeping alone for the three years prior to taking Ash as her lover.

Louise Bowman was, of course, an intensely moral woman. People who were less than intensely moral did not rise very far in PegaSys's hierarchy. Thatcher had an almost supernatural instinct for catching out those whose professional and personal standards of conduct (which are more or less the same thing) fell short of the mark. Louise was not disposed to casual or recreational sex. She took such things too seriously. Moreover, despite—or more likely because of—her stunning looks, most men left her alone. Calculating their odds in advance, as all men do, they concluded that she was either out of their league, or was sure to already have a lover. Probably of the Greek god sort. Big. Muscular. Athletic. Possessive. Jealous. Violent.

Thus, for the most part, those offers that Louise got were not worth getting. They came from the predators, the lotharios, the office Don Juans, and professional cocksmen. She squelched even the most persistent with little more than a word.

On the rare occasions that something better appeared to offer itself, Louise was cautious, slow, and introspective. She could spend a week or more pondering something as trivial as an invitation to have a drink after work. She would worry and fret anxiously, looking into every nook and cranny for flaws in the character of the invitation's author. By the time she worked herself up to accept, the opportunity was gone, and the man who'd had the temerity to approach her likely was making the kind of grousing remarks that only added to the frigid reputation of PegaSys's "Iron Nun."

Louise's wariness was the result of her belief that she was a lousy judge of men, and a consequence of the lousy judgments she had made.

Consider, for example, her first lover. He was named Robert—not, he insisted, "Bob." He was a director at the small advertising agency that had hired her right after she had graduated magna cum laude and cautiously virginal, from college. He was twelve years her senior. He was soulful. He was romantic. He was married, with a house and two young sons in Scarsdale.

Their lovemaking was limited to Monday through Thursday evenings, because Robert liked to get home early on Friday in order to have a full weekend with his boys. During the week, such time as he and Louse spent together was bracketed at one end by the hour at which they left the office and at the other by the 8:45 P.M. express to White Plains. These limits, further constrained by the amount of time it took Robert to get up to Louise's tiny studio apartment on West 81st Street and then to dash back to Grand Central Station, left them together for, at best, a span of two-and-a-half hours. Usually it was a bit less.

They would couple twice, three times if Robert was feeling particularly randy, and then Louise would fix a light meal. There was never quite enough time for them to go out to dinner. They might talk for a few minutes somewhere along the line. Then Robert would give her a kiss, check his calendar in case he had a late meeting scheduled for the next day, and run for his train.

Robert was in love with her. She knew he was because he

said it all the time. He planned to divorce his wife and marry her. He was eager. He wanted to do it immediately. It was, however, going to be difficult. Difficult. After all, his sons were at particularly impressionable ages. He was up for promotion to vice president. The economic considerations were very serious. His wife was not a stable person. His parents had to be softened up. He needed Louise's support more than ever. He had to catch that damned train, but they would talk more about it on Wednesday night.

Louise was twenty-one and extraordinarily intelligent. And naive. She was the product of an honest Lutheran upbringing, raised in the kind of community where lies dealt only with the size of fish that had escaped or the virility of bulls that were for sale. She simply did not know any better.

Besides, she was in love. She was ready to postpone her dreams of a career. She and Robert would wed. They would move to Darien, so much more fashionable than Scarsdale these days. *She* would have two sons. Only after they were in school would she go on to business school and start *her* career. *She* would be a success. A success—unlike that woman, that unstable, grasping woman, that woman whose name she never even learned.

New York is a smaller town than most people think. On a Friday night two years into her affair with Robert, Louise went to the Music Box Theatre with her old college roommate and best friend, Marilyn Lefkowitz. Marilyn's husband was away at a business conference. As the house lights went up after the first act, she spotted Robert rising from his seat some ten rows in front of her. He was laughing and talking to a very attractive, very well-dressed woman. He had his arm around her waist, helping her into the aisle. The woman needed help, being, rather obviously, seven or eight months pregnant.

She and Marilyn missed the second act. That is what best friends are for.

A year later, partway through Wharton, convinced that she was now over Robert, she went out on a date with one of her classmates. At the end of the evening he leaned forward to kiss her. She responded with a kiss that convinced him that kissing was merely the beginning of what she was prepared for. After a heated half hour of exploration he parted her legs, stretched himself between them, and pushed to enter her. She screamed in pain, thrust him away violently, and, after he left, cried herself to a humiliated sleep.

Her gynecologist diagnosed the condition as nervous vaginismus. "It's a fairly common response," he counseled, "to emotional upset or sexual rejection. The muscles clench up and squeeze some very tender nerve endings. Hurts like hell, as I suppose you know. But you shouldn't worry about it. Time, they say, heals all wounds. Physical and psychic. Once the psychic hurt cures itself, the condition usually disappears. In the meantime, try Valium."

On the next date, which was understandably harder to get, Louise gulped her Valium on the way out of the restaurant, climbed into the young man's car, and promptly fell asleep. Wharton inculcates a fine sense of cost/benefits analysis in its students. Listening to Louise's soft snores, the young man in question calculated that investing in a third date with Louise would be an imprudent business decision. He would spend his money elsewhere.

Upon awaking more humiliated than ever, Louise resigned herself to a year or two more of chastity. It turned out to be a cure she had to take after parting with three of her subsequent four lovers. Each of the three had brought on the vaginismus condition again. Both the condition and the cure were something that caused her to be very thoughtful and very cautious and very slow in picking her subsequent lovers, including the sixth, Michael Ash.

But what about the fifth lover?

He was another story. He didn't cause her pain. He did not reject her. He did not even break up with her. Not once in their ten-year, on-again, off-again relationship. Technically speaking, he was lover number two. Also number four, number six, and, if she had wanted, number eight. He always came between the others. She always went back to him. He was her best friend's ex-husband, David Lefkowitz.

"So ask Dave," said Marilyn not three weeks after the divorce.

"Oh, Marilyn, come on, this is a serious problem. I need some real advice."

"No, really. Dave's a nice guy. He's always liked you. You get along with him just fine. He's good company and very presentable, and we both know he's available."

"Marilyn. Marilyn, he's your husband."

"Not anymore. The courts of the state of New York have made it official. You know, divorce. It's legal now, they don't make you wear a big red 'A' on your blouse."

"I couldn't. I mean, I've known him as long as I've known you. Besides, I just couldn't be seen . . ."

"Of course you could. Who's to know? Look, lady, you just joined this fancy consulting company, which pays fancy Wharton B-school graduates fancy salaries so they can live in fancy East Side apartments, and now you have to go to their fancy annual dinner dance. You want to look dumb, don't go. You want to look dumber, go alone. So you've got to go. So you need a date. So Dave's available. He's there. Just ask him, he'll do it. I know he will."

"I just can't. I know him and I know you and . . ."

"The fact that you know him is the principal qualification, babe. After that rat Robert—oh, God, I can't even say the bastard's name without getting mad—you haven't exactly been in circulation. How many other single men are you on friendly terms with?"

"Ahh. Well. Not a lot. But you and he . . ."

"Were married for a couple of years. We lived together. We slept together. Right here. Right over there on that bed in the back room. It wasn't bad. It wasn't. We were high school sweeties in Boston and we got married on the day I graduated. And we came to New York and lived in this crummy little apartment—"

"It's a nice apartment."

"—in Brooklyn Heights because my father bought it for a wedding present. Then we grew up and split up. That doesn't mean that he's a creep or a space cadet or a lousy lover. Nor, my friend, does it mean that I own him or he owns me. I still like him, in fact. He'll make somebody a nice husband."

"Marilyn!"

"Well, he will. Not that I am offering you his hand in the wedded bonds of holy matrimony. Although given your taste in men, you could do worse. All I'm saying is that you need a date for your debutante ball in the business world, and you have only one option."

"No way, Marilyn. Forget it. Help me find another man. Not Dave. I won't do it."

But she did.

And she did it again eighteen months after splitting up with Frank, for whom she (and by actual count six simultaneous others) did not prove woman enough. And two years after her disastrous interlude with Barry, who left her to live with Lionel. And yet again following the one who had been worst of all, Martin, another ("Oh, Louise baby, how could you be so dumb? Come here and cry on Marilyn's shoulder.") married man. Which is why she counted David Lefkowitz as her fourth, sixth, and nearly eighth—had not Ash materialized—lover. He had been there, quiet, undemanding, patient, and good company. She knew that if she and Mike Ash couldn't make it work, Dave would be there patiently waiting for her to get over it. The knowledge made her comfortable.

Mike Ash knew it too. The knowledge made him queasy.

7

IT WAS THATCHER'S PRACTICE TO have a dinner party at his Sutton Place pied-à-terre every Wednesday evening. His guests were always an eclectic crowd: outspoken foreign diplomats, opera stars, rising (or risen) politicians, popular writers, Wall Street power brokers, critically acclaimed painters, lionized academic theorists, SRO nightclub comedians, or anyone else who seemed interesting and entertaining, and who could hold his or her own in confronting Thatcher's nimble mind.

Thatcher's hard and fast rule for these affairs was that, no matter what the rest of the guest list looked like, one of PegaSys's young vice presidents ("together with spouse, lover, friend, or what the Californians insist on calling 'significant other' ") must be invited. Thatcher knew that a significant component of anyone's success in the business world depended on that person's network of acquaintances. Accordingly, he went out of his way to help his young executives meet as many movers and shakers as possible. His dinner parties were his principal tool in achieving this goal, and once or twice a year each PegaSys officer could expect an invitation; it was always a most welcome invitation. Tonight was Louise's turn.

Protocol demanded that she be accompanied by a guest, so she brought David Lefkowitz. Thatcher's vocal disapproval of office romances made Louise and Mike cover their affair with a KGB-like cloak of secrecy. Whenever Louise had to attend a PegaSys social affair, she went with Dave. Mike, in turn, went with Marilyn. When Mike was with Marilyn, Louise stayed home and caught up on her paperwork. When Louise was with David, Mike stayed home and sulked.

The taxi turned off 57th Street and stopped just outside the Sutton Place cul-de-sac. A bored security guard standing in front of the United Nations Secretary General's residence just down the street jotted in his notebook, "7:33 P.M Taxi NT 803 M. Cauc Fem, tall brunet. Cauc male brown. Well drest. Enter SP. Thatcher Wednesday?"

Louise and David strolled to the end of the cul-de-sac, and stood silently for a moment watching an oceangoing steamer sail south beneath the Queensborough Bridge and on down the East River. The sun sinking behind them sprinkled the thick humid air with flecks of gold. Across the black flowing water, the trees of Roosevelt Island had darkened to a deep, rich green. The steamer burst into the last rays of the setting sun and glowed redly for a moment. Louise sighed and wondered about its destination. Some exotic port of call? The tropics? The China coast? The antipodes? Was there any romance, in the classic sense of the word, left in the world? If so, where?

The ship sailed on. Louise and Dave turned to the red-brick, white-doored pied-à-terre that was Thatcher's city home. Louise reached out and pushed the doorbell. A soft chime sounded within. A moment later Olivia Thatcher opened the door.

"Hi, Livy, it's me."

"Louise, dear, and who's that behind you? Oh, Dave. You two certainly seem to be seeing a lot of one another. Well, come in out of the beastly heat, children, come in."

Livy Thatcher, Louise thought, as she did every time she encountered Olivia. *My God, may I look as good as you thirty years from now. May I look half as good, I'll still be satisfied. So will all the men. If there are any then.*

Olivia spoke in a quick, soft whisper. "OK, Louise, Dave, very quickly here's tonight's starting lineup. I think you know only one of them, Evér Dhrajkovic, Yugoslavian minister of trade, call him 'Ernie' unless you're feeling formal. Don't call his wife anything; she can't speak English for beans and her name sounds like something with bronchitis anyway. Don Banks and Stacy, he's number three or four or something at Morgan, Teech & Kidd. She's a CCB, a Charitable Cause Bore, but better than you would expect. Luke Stern from Stanford University . . ."

"The Nobel Prize in . . ."

"Economics, you got it, and his wife is going to get one in medicine, unless I miss my bet. And last, but not least, your friend and mine, the inimitable, the unforgettable, the unsinkable, the unspeakably overdressed Red Queen and her hubby of the week, whose first name is Harry. His last eludes me but is not worth remembering because there will be a new one the next time you see her."

Dave, who was studying the quirky Paul Flora pen-and-ink drawings that lined the foyer walls, looked up. "Red Queen?" he asked. "Am I missing something? Who is—"

Dave's question was interrupted by the abrupt appearance of a petite, raucous, shockingly crimson tornado. It rushed into the foyer, ricocheted against Olivia, spun up to Louise, and then turned on Dave, saying breathlessly, "Lies, all lies. Ignore these people, prevarication comes as naturally to them as truth does to me. It is the essence of my profession. Justine Gold at your service."

"Dave Lefkowitz," he said reaching his hand down toward Justine. She, from her diminutive height of five feet two inches, grabbed it and gave him a judo-like tug. As he head jerked down, she planted a noisy kiss on his cheek, leaving a livid smear of lipstick behind. As Louise moistened her handkerchief and began rubbing it off, Dave asked, "Ms. Gold? Ms. Gold, are you the—"

"Justine, please. And yes, I am. Founder and president of Gold Associates, *Ad Age's* 'Ad Man of the Year'—they wanted to make it 'woman' but I told them to stuff it. Cover of *Venture*, cover of *Inc.*, cover of *People*, cover of *Savvy*, cover of *New York*, hell, I'm cover girl of the year."

"She also," interrupted Thatcher, stepping into the foyer, "is, as of this afternoon, the proud recipient of PegaSys's business. I have dropped Leslie Smart as our public relations agency and awarded Justine the account. Lavish her with your congratulations later. Meanwhile, can we move this gathering out of the foyer and into more spacious and appropriate quarters?"

* * *

In 1978 PegaSys's advertising agency had been one of Madison Avenue's oldest, most respectable, and most pretentiously stodgy firms. The agency was developing a new print campaign for PegaSys and the time had come for Thatcher to review its proposals. In deference to the fact that PegaSys had become a billion-dollar company, the agency set aside its largest conference room for the meeting. As the review meeting progressed, Thatcher singled out some copy for particular praise. His account executive responded, "Why, thank you, Scott. It's the work of the newest member of our team. I don't think you've met her, Justine Gold, she just joined the firm two months ago." With this he pointed down, down to the nethermost reaches of the conference room, where the team's minor members, munchkins, and worker bees were seated. A tiny figure rose, a brunette with an unrepentantly unbobbed nose, who was wearing a fire-engine red blazer, a wine-dark skirt, and a pink blouse of a shade defying adjectival description.

Because junior staff are allowed only seconds in the spotlight, and are rarely to be seen, much less heard, the account exec turned to Thatcher to continue his presentation. He did not get very far. Justine, flouting all the laws and protocols of the firm, did not drop a curtsy and return to her seat. Rather, she began to speak. At length. She even walked to the head of the conference table, chattering every step of the way. The essence of her remarks was that, while the copy Thatcher had seen was good, the original copy she had written was even better. Had the agency's editors not emasculated her draft, she argued, Thatcher would be even more impressed. She then dropped a typescript of her original version of the ad in front of Thatcher.

A hush filled the room. The account exec glared at Justine as Julia Child might glare at a cockroach in the aspic.

Thatcher read the copy, smiled, and said, "She's right. It is better. Use it instead."

Three days later, he received a note from Justine announcing that after being fired she had found a job as copywriter at another agency.

Thatcher reflected over the note for a moment or two. The way *he* handled employees who had the guts to challenge his decisions was simple. If they were obviously wrong he fired them; if they were obviously right he promoted them. If it was unclear who was right and who was wrong, he stuck with his original decision and gave the challenger credit for being creative. He expected every executive in PegaSys to do the same. If they didn't, he fired them too. He did not want anyone who could not recognize and respect the intelligence of his or her subordinates on PegaSys's payroll.

Accordingly, he called his account executive and three other large agencies to order a "bake-off," the ritual combat between competing advertising agencies for the affections of a large account.

A few years later, Justine decided to change careers by starting her own public relations firm. By then she had joined the ranks of Scott's and Livy's intimate friends. Her crimson presence graced their dinner parties and enlivened already lively weekends at Thatcher's Connecticut estate. She was part of the Thatcher inner circle.

Scott and Livy stood by Justine during her frequent marriages and equally frequent divorces. Supporting Justine in these matters came naturally to Thatcher; he was a Marine Corps veteran and had a strong stomach. Justine's divorces were not peaceable affairs. Harmonious partings were not her strong suit. Violent ruptures were her stock-in-trade. Her divorces commonly commenced with the soon-to-be-ex-husband in a hospital bed. In traction. In a cast. Breathing through a tube. They concluded with the husband's lawyers extracting a large settlement from Justine. Justine's diminutive size belied her strength. Her amicable, red-lipped smile belied her temper. Her parting shot at a discharged spouse was typically a right hook of formidable potency. On more than one occasion, Justine had terminated a relationship with such devastating effect that she was convinced she had murdered her partner. Once she had fled the country to avoid prosecution.

For the next forty-five minutes or so, Louise, sometimes with Dave in tow and sometimes without, circled around the oversized red and brown Kazakh carpet lining the Thatchers' living room, speaking to her fellow guests. From Dhrajkovic she learned that the Yugoslavian economy had gone to hell in a hand basket and that the government was prepared to make a deal under almost any terms if PegaSys would locate a plant within its border. She asked Don Banks what he recommended in the market and he, grimacing, replied, "A good bomb shelter, canned food, and plenty of hollow-nosed bullets for your thirty-ought-six."

Dragging Dave away from where he stood in rapt devotion

before two Botticelli studies for the *Primavera*, prizes in Thatcher's much-prized art collection, she headed for Luke and Leslie Stern. Justine intercepted her, seized Dave by the elbow, aimed him at a Paul Delvaux oil painting, and herded Louise off into a corner.

"So what do you think, Louise?"

"About what?"

"Harry. What do you think about Harry? You know, Harry. My new husband. *Harry*."

"Oh," replied Louise. "Oh, I don't think I got his name over there. Harry, huh? Well, he is, ahhh, tall, isn't he? Kind of cute, too, I guess. Ahh, what does he do, anyway?"

"Keep this to yourself, for God's sake. He's a lawyer."

"Lawyer!"

"Ssshhh. In whispers, please. You know how Scotty is about lawyers. The other thing is, he's a Catholic. Can you believe that? Me, I'm humping a Catholic. If my mother only knew. Every time we have a fight, I worry he's going to yell 'You killed Christ!' "

"But you love him, don't you? Justine? Justine? *Justine!* Well, at least you like him?"

"Oh, yeah. He's the best so far."

"Justine, you can't think like that. 'The best *so far*.' Marriage is a long-term proposition."

"Look who's talking, thirty plus who knows how much and still unwed. Anyway, I . . . don't look at me like that. It's true. Look at you, I mean just look at you. You've got so much more to work with than me, and you can't even bag one lousy little husband."

"I guess like they say, I'm just waiting for Mr. Right."

"Well, baby, let me tell you, I found Mr. Right. Five times already."

"Six."

"So who's counting? Is it really six? Jesus, how could I forget."

"Could we all move into the dining room now," said Livy, slowly rounding up her party and discreetly steering them in the right direction. She was always the perfect hostess.

And so, unknown to one and all, Thatcher's guests sat down to dinner with the authoress of *The Poisoner's Passion*.

Mike Ash was the only person other than Thatcher who knew Olivia Thatcher's naughty secret.

Wife of one of America's most respected businessmen, professor of English literature at Hunter College, mother of three gorgeous daughters, fund-raiser for a dozen worthy causes, member of the board of directors of the Metropolitan Opera, and clandestinely . . .

It had happened on a lazy Sunday afternoon in the spring two years before. Thatcher and Ash had been working for weeks on a new production program that was due to be announced at the annual shareholders' meeting the next day. Thatcher spent his weekends relaxing—or, if need be, working—at his multi-acre estate on Long Island Sound. On the morning of that particular Sunday he discovered that some last-minute changes in the program were needed. He called Ash, and Ash offered to rent a car and drive up to help work out the details.

Ash arrived at about two. Livy led him out to the backyard where, very much to his surprise, he found Scott with a bow and arrow in his hands. Not merely a bow, but a seventy-five-pound draw weight, thirty-one-inch draw length, gunmetal grey, Bear composite bow. *The damned thing*, he thought, *is nearly as big as Thatcher himself.*

Fifty yards away, a not inconsequential distance, a target perched on a tripod. Thatcher stood at a fourty-five-degree angle to the target, his legs planted wide. He took a deep breath, drew back slowly, and then released. The arrow, a hollow aluminum Easton Game Getter tipped with a field point, soared high, seemingly destined for a spot some two feet above the target. But as it slashed through the final twenty yards of its flight, it dropped steeply and thwacked with a satisfying slap into the bull's-eye. From where Ash stood, it appeared to bury twenty inches of its length in the target. Thatcher grinned and muttered, "Take that, John Wayne."

He turned toward Mike. "Hi. Glad you could come up. Didn't know about my latest crackpot hobby, did you? I recommend it. There is something eminently satisfying about archery. Something that soothes the mind and refreshes the spirit. It almost makes me think that there is something in all that hogwash about Zen Buddhism."

"Zen Buddhism?" Ash asked, trying to keep a neutral tone of voice.

"You needn't worry. Senility has not set in yet. All I mean is that the Zen types use archery as an aid to meditation, and . . . no, Ash, I am not into New Age zaniness. What I mean to say is that the technique for meditation is as good for relaxing as . . . aw, nuts. Look, I do this because it's fun."

"Can I give it a try?"

"Nope. No one draws Odysseus's bow but Odysseus. Now go into my study, find yourself a drink, and give me ten minutes to finish what I'm doing here. OK?"

"OK."

With drink in hand, Ash prowled through Thatcher's study, a room that was less an at-home office than a library. The walls were covered with floor-to-ceiling bookshelves, and the shelves were overflowing with volumes of every size, every shape, and every topic. History, biography, science, philosophy, archeology, novels, and short stories. Among the novels, Ash spotted what appeared to be, curiously enough, a complete set of the works of Leonora Argive, bestselling creator of countless bodice-rippers notorious for the frequency and variety of their heavy-breathing sex scenes. Ash couldn't imagine what they were doing here. They were not the sort of thing that Thatcher would read. Nor Livy. Indeed, Livy, in her capacity as a noted academician, had been called upon to write a review of Madame Argive's latest triple-decker for the *New York Times Book Review*. In it she had called the authoress "a butcher of syntax, a slayer of grammar, and a slaughterer of style. Ms. Argive's prose, when coupled with a plot more turgid than that of *The Decline and Fall of the Roman Empire*, characterizations less deep than those to be found in a Daffy Duck cartoon, and an overdose of overcooked sex scenes, suggests that the author has set her sights at high parody, but (alas for literate readers) has fallen short of the mark by a distance to be measured not in inches but in miles."

Ash pulled down the first of the Argives from its shelf: *Duke Montoni's Wench*, eighteen weeks on the *Times* bestseller list, $600,000 cash advance for the paperback rights, made into a movie by Dino de Laurentiis that reputedly lost $20 million. He flipped it open. On the title page there was a handwritten inscription, "To 'S'. From the author of the book to the author of the joy. 'O'."

Whoops.

He grabbed the second book, *The Inquisitor's Daughter*. "To my husband, who inspired me to make this one even worse than the one before. 'O'."

And the third, on which was simply written, "To Scott, whom I have always loved, and who deserves far better than this. Livy."

As he reached for the fourth, he heard Olivia speak behind him. "Young Michael Ash, to die at an age such as yours would be tragic, don't you think? All those promising years ahead of you."

"Livy. You didn't? You aren't really?"

"As one of my heroines might say, 'Honor and truth, you churl, mean more to me than my poor paltry life.' Actually, they all say that. Usually by chapter ten. Yes, I did write that. And all the rest of them, too. Now, young Michael Ash, are you going to swear a mighty and solemn oath of secrecy, or are we going to spend the next few minutes discussing the disposition of what little of your mortal remains I intend to leave unchopped, diced, and sliced?"

"You *really* are Leonora Argive?"

"Indeed I am. The name is a barely disguised plagiarism, you know. And, if you look on the shelf above, you will see that I am also Ceoilia Mountbatten. You know, *Shadows Over Moongate Moor, The Secret Passions of Eagle's Brood Keep, The Dark Lord's Dark Desire*."

"The high priestess of the 'Gentle reader, had I but known!' school of gothics."

"Actually, I've used that line twice in Mountbattens. Both times just before the heroine discovered the Thing in the Attic. But don't try to distract me, Mike: we were discussing your fate and your future, if any. No one, no one in the world except Scotty, knows that I am the perpetrator of these things. And I want it kept that way. I'm serious."

"Aw, hell, Livy, you've known me for twenty years. Sure I'll keep my mouth shut."

"Be sure that you do. Scott wouldn't be humiliated if the world found out that I wrote this trash, but, I can assure you, I would be. Now be a good boy and put those books back where you found them."

Over coffee, the strong, rich "Major Dickenson's Blend" that Thatcher had air freighted in from Peets in San Francisco, Dhrajkovic said the wrong thing. "We have, in my country, been more capitalist than socialist ever since Tito broke with Stalin. But still, I think, we are not capitalist enough. We need to learn more from America. I have read a book and believe that we can learn much from it. It is called *In Search of Excellence*."

Louise, sitting next to Justine, whispered, "Ooga, ooga, dive, dive." Justine grinned. *In Search of Excellence*, a bestselling self-help book for business people, was one of Thatcher's personal bugbears. The very mention of the book stirred him to a fine froth of sarcastic indignation.

Thatcher leaned forward, thrusting out his jaw. His unruly eyebrows bristled. "You mean the gospel according to Mr. Thomas J. Peters? I consider that tome to be a sort of *Dr. Ruth's Book of Good Sex* for inept managers. The issue for most companies is not achieving excellence. The issue for most companies is overcoming shabbiness. The question is not *In Search of Excellence*. The question is *In Search of Shabbiness*. I shall write a book on the topic some day."

"Shabbiness," asked Dhrajkovic, "is a word not in my vocabulary. What is shabbiness, please?"

"Ernie, you know what the word 'best' means and what the word 'worst' means, don't you? Well, Ernie, between the 'best' and the 'worst' lies the merely average, a vast realm that is ignored, overlooked and, of course, overpopulated. Within this realm there are many gradients, and as one approaches the boundaries of the 'worst,' one comes upon the second-rate, the mediocre, and the *shabby* things of life. Here are found people, places, products, organizations and, indeed, whole countries, which, all things considered, would be better off swept beneath the carpet. It is to this too-often neglected multitude that the word *shabbiness* applies. What then is shabbiness? It is the word that describes the essence of those people, places, things, and acts that lie *at the low end of mediocrity*. The shabby never reach the peak of excellence, nor do they plummet to the nadir of failure. The very hallmark and vital essence of shabby corporations is their ability to survive, to muddle along, to cause those who hear their name to arch an eyebrow and ask, 'Oh, are those guys still in business?' Shabby managers lack the flair, the special panache needed to create a resounding success; by the same token they are devoid of the hell-for-leather, kamikaze spirit needed to create a truly spectacular failure. They simply don't have the spunk required. They don't have 'the right stuff,' they don't have what it takes—in fact, they don't even have what it takes to be average. The domain of the shabby is that rather grey-green mildewish area lying well below average, but just above bad."

Dhrajkovic shook his head slowly back and forth. "Surely," he said, "you describe the way factories work in my country. I am not insulted. It is true, but we become less so every day. And surely this shabbiness is not found here, not here in America."

"Ahhh. On the contrary. *Surely* here in America. Let me tell you a story. Let me tell you something that happened to me out in Missouri last year. Louise was there, she will vouch for the truth of every word."

Louise spoke. "Oh no, not AIW. You're not going to tell that story again?"

"Yes. It is a salutary and moral tale, and one from which our foreign friends might learn a profitable lesson," said Thatcher. "Brian Shawby is the president of American Interdyne Worldwide, the worst company in America."

Banks asked, "AIW? Are those guys still in business?"

Thatcher barked triumphantly, "See what I mean!"

8

IT WAS THREE O'CLOCK IN THE morning, Thatcher's dinner party had long since ended. The streets of New York were quieter now, and empty. Traffic lights cycled through their measured progression of changes for no one in particular. An occasional night-owl taxi slowly cruised up and down the avenues looking for fares that were not there. Such pedestrians as were about stayed near the curb, stepping hurriedly from streetlight to streetlight, avoiding dark doorways.

On Sutton Place, Scott and Olivia Thatcher were fast asleep. They lay side by side, as they had for nearly forty years, with their hands intertwined.

Thatcher was dreaming. He dreamed he was nine and it was the bright morning of a nearly perfect summer's day. The sky was cornflower blue, with no clouds at all. You could tell that the day would turn hot, but it was not hot yet. His father had taken his black doctor's satchel and gone off to his office. His mother was doing her household chores. It was the best time of the day for an adventuresome boy in knee pants who, filled with much energy but no mischief, had happily forgotten that school would be starting again in a few weeks. The house was clapboard, white with blue trim, and had three gabled stories and a high, red-brick chimney. It stood far back from the road, well away from rare passing automobiles and more frequently passing horse-drawn carts. Stretching a long, long way down to the mailbox was a dry, hard-packed dirt driveway, made for running. The green front yard, speckled with dandelions and fringed with flowers, ended a short pleasant distance from a shady, screened-in front porch. On the porch were a shiny walnut glider and two wickerwork easy chairs for evening sitting, iced-tea drinking, and conversation. Between the grass and the road lay a tangle of high, tall weeks and grasses, Queen Anne's lace, towering sunflowers, a tangled blackberry ramble, and an old, old pear tree. A good-natured, sloppy dog of dubious ancestry named ''Mick'' was out in the weeds, busily matting his brownish coat with burrs while pursuing those pursuits that appeal to good-natured dogs on a summer day. Mick's archenemy, an irascible marmalade tomcat of infinite cunning, slept beneath the porch digesting his mornings catch of field mice. The young boy steered clear of both of them. They made him sneeze. Back around the house his mother was hanging snowy sheets up on a clothesline to dry. A light breeze made the linen swirl and billow like the sails of a Spanish treasure galleon drawn by N. C. Wyeth. She wore a pale blue apron, fringed with white piping, over a yellow flowered dress. The apron lifted in the breeze. Her mouth was full of clothespins, and she smiled at him as he dashed around the house. He grinned back, running onward. Behind the backyard was a ramshackle shed that housed his father's tools. He wasn't allowed in there. Behind the shed was the vegetable patch, also off limits. And behind that, deep dark woods began. The forest stretched who knows how far, and hid who knows what kind of lurking, probably hungry, but maybe cowardly, creatures. A small, shallow, clear, astonishingly cold creek marked the outermost boundary of his adventures to date. Someday he and his pal from next door, Gary, would suitably arm themselves and mount an expedition to explore the terra incognita beyond the creek. The boy felt that their odds of finding buried Indian treasure were pretty good, if they survived the unquestionably perilous trek through the forest. Maybe a larger party than just he and Gary was required if anyone was to make it back alive and unscalped. Around the corner from the backyard was where the well and the springhouse were, and a very big maple tree with slats nailed up its trunk for climbing, and a good stiff rope tied from a thick branch for swinging and screaming like Johnny Weissmuller going to rescue Jane from the cannibal dwarves. "Pygmies?" "No! They're dwarves!" That was the best part of the movie, and he didn't understand why his dad laughed at it. Underneath the maple tree there was a horseshoe pitch. His father's skill at horseshoes was amazing, a phenomenon of nature. The boy himself could barely toss a horseshoe the length of the pitch, but his father threw a ringer every time. Or, almost every time. There might be something interesting to do inside the house. He had a cap pistol he could get, or a bow and arrow, or a ball and bat. But going indoors didn't feel right. The morning might disappear if he left it. Besides, Gary, who had a really good scab on his knee from a spectacular scooter accident, would be coming over any minute. Gary was going to bring the latest version of the lost Indian treasure map that they planned to find buried in a soup can. The map, now on its fifth draft, was becoming an impressive piece of work. However, it needed to look a bit more aged before it would be acceptable. The boy made a mental note to ask his dad how to make papyrus or maybe parchment. If the ancient Egyptians could do it, it couldn't be that hard. On the other hand, making smoke signals, another ancient skill, and one that looked easy in the movies, had proved to be a tough art to master. His mother's reaction to what happened to the blanket had been surprisingly strong. His father had been much more understanding. It was an old blanket, anyway. The boy wandered partway down the dry, dusty driveway, picking up pebbles, examining them carefully, and selecting those of the right size, shape, and smoothness to serve as slingshot ammunition. He and Gary would practice their marksmanship on rusty tin cans later in the day. His eye turned to the blackberry ramble. The berries were glistening now, rich and tart and ready to be picked for a pie. Mom would want him to fill a bucket with them today or tomorrow. He decided that while he was waiting for Gary, while it was still not cool, but at least not hot, he would pick those berries. So the boy turned back to the house, and, shuffling his feet to raise as much dust as possible, rattling a dozen good pebbles in his pocket, went to get a deep galvanized steel bucket to fill with ripe blackberries on a warm, buzzing summer morning.

Thatcher turned in his sleep and the dream was gone.

* * *

A few blocks to the north and to the west, Mike Ash was turning fitfully on his sofa. Unable to sleep, he had decided to read for a while. Unable to concentrate, he dozed off, dreaming of disturbing conversations with Louise that he had never had. Ivan, whose secret name was Ivan the Purrable, lay beside him, watching his troubled rest with the tolerant skepticism of a very wise cat.

Still farther north, Louise Bowman slept fetally curled into her accustomed spot on the far right corner of her bed. She never visited Ash at his apartment; it was situated far too close to Thatcher's. She did not want to run the risk of being seen leaving it at some odd hour in the night. Or, worse, in the morning.

Five blocks west, the Laocoön was being reenacted in Justine Gold's bedroom, with Justine, softly snoring, cast in the role of the serpents. Her legs twined about Harry like twin boa constrictors, pinning him hungrily where he lay. Her sleeping arms, with surprising strength, clutched him in a fierce hug. Her hands rested firmly against the tenderest portions of his anatomy—sharp, crimson nails outstretched, mere millimeters from his flesh. Harry was not asleep. Harry was awake. Harry needed to get up and pee. Given the weaponry aimed at his sensitive parts, Harry was understandably hesitant to move. However, his need was becoming urgent. He would have to get up soon.

To the south in PegaSys's headquarters building, Roy Knight's haggard face broke into a grin. He leaned back from his computer terminal and folded his arms with smug satisfaction. He had finally puzzled out the software techniques that Wintergreen had used to break into PegaSys's main computer system. The piracy program that Wintergreen had written was no mean feat. Rather, it was an enormously complex and quite thoroughly brilliant piece of software, one that must have taken its hacker creator months to design. It was also very nearly unbeatable. Unlike the buccaneering efforts of other hackers, Wintergreen's masterpiece did not actually load itself into the mainframe computer it was seeking to subvert. Rather, guerrillalike, it lurked outside the central computer, hiding in the jungle of printers, disk drives, telecommunications devices, and other peripherals that surrounded the mainframe. From these hiding spots, it struck quickly, then withdrew again, camouflaged, blending into the background. Knight smiled with grudging admiration; Wintergreen had invented a brand-new technique for computer penetration, one that doubtless would raise holy hell with computer managers worldwide for months to come. It was slick. It was elegant. It was a good hack. He envied the talent of its creator. But, on the other hand, it had taken Knight mere hours to unravel a piece of work that it had taken Wintergreen months to put together. Maybe Wintergreen wasn't so good after all.

About twelve hundred miles and one time zone farther west, Brian Shawby, chairman and chief executive of American Interdyne Worldwide, was unable to sleep. Tomorrow—no! today!—was his big day. A major press conference. Television news. The cover of *Business Week*. Maybe even a feature in *People*. He had to be at his best. He had to demonstrate the calm command of a captain of industry. He got up and took another pill.

Eighteen hundred miles west of Brian Shawby and his dreams, at the Palm Restaurant on Santa Monica Boulevard, it was midnight. Joe Jonas's host called for the check. The waiter looked at the empty place and uneaten meal that Jonas had left behind when he stormed out of the restaurant. "The other party," he said. "Is he coming back to finish that steak?"

"No. I think not," replied the diminutive Japanese as he peered at the bill through his wire-rimmed glasses. *So expensive*, he thought.

"Do you want a doggie bag?"

The Japanese looked perplexed. Was this a Chinese restaurant? Had the peculiar Mr. Jonas ordered dog?

In Tokyo the business day was nearly over. The women workers would be leaving soon, and in an hour or two the men would pack their briefcases, roll down their sleeves, and, in clumps of three or four, head for the door. Except, of course, at Seppuku Ltd.

At Seppuku, the pace of work had yet to slacken. Indeed, in one particular department, the pace actually seemed to be picking up. That department was the message center. It found itself having to type and transmit an enormous number of telex messages, all of which seemed to have been generated by Seppuku's corporate vice president of finance. All of which seemed to be in code. All of which were directed to European banks and brokerage companies. Later, similar messages would be sent to similar companies in America. The clerks would work all night typing them. They would not leave the office until the job was done.

In Moscow, in the basement of the Lefortovo Prison, it was late morning, nearly lunchtime. A bored KGB computer operator was buffing her fingernails. She hated Lefortovo. She hated the basement. She hated the unknown Yankee pirate, whoever he was, who had subverted the old computer center at Dzerzhinsky Square, causing the paranoid panic that resulted in the KGB relocating all its facilities to this rat-ridden dungeon.

A bell clattered on a teleprinter, signaling an incoming message. She glanced over at it. It was a relay to the KGB Economics Division from Tokyo. She watched the noisy printout clatter through its first line, through its second line, through its third line . . . and then, with an off-key boing, the bell rang again. Something was wrong. Trouble on the communications line from Tokyo? No. It was something else. Something far worse. She looked on in horror as the teleprinter began printing out . . . A picture. A picture of an animal. With ears. Big ears. A rabbit. Not just any rabbit. It was the Yankee cartoon character Bugs Bunny. He was leering hideously and extending his hand in a cheery wave. Boing, boing, boing. The printer printed, " >EH, WHAT'S UP DOC? IF KNIGHT CAN DO IT, SO CAN I! XXX WINTERGREEN." Boing, boing, boing. Every printer and terminal in the KGB suddenly turned on: " >ONE TRILLION BOTTLES OF BEER ON THE WALL, ONE TRILLION BOTTLES OF BEER. TAKE ONE DOWN, PASS IT AROUND, NINE HUNDRED AND NINETY-NINE BILLION, NINE HUNDRED AND NINETY-NINE MILLION, NINE HUNDRED AND NINETY-NINE THOUSAND, NINE HUNDRED AND NINETY-NINE BOTTLES OF BEER ON THE WALL . . ."

Oh God, not again, she thought. *This time they'll move the computer center to the Kamchatka Peninsula!*

On Queen Street in London, at the offices of Quint and Claggart, Solicitors, the business day had just begun. As was traditional, it began with the clinking of glasses.

"In honor of the day," said Quint.

"In honor of the day," responded Claggart.

Quint glanced at his watch, a stainless-steel, digital Seppuku Globemaster, whose electronic intricacies were well beyond his ability to master. "Any moment now."

Claggert tugged on his watch chain, retrieving from his

checkered waistcoat an antique Whitfield Greenwell nautical repeater, the last unpawned heirloom in his family legacy. "Any moment indeed."

In the outer office a bell rang, signaling an incoming telex message.

"List! But I do believe I hear opportunity knocking," cried Quint.

"Quite clear, quite clear. Let us send to know for whom the bell tolls," replied Claggart.

"It tolls for thee."

"And thee."

9

THATCHER'S ALARM CLATTERED AT 6:30 A.M. He loosened his hand from Olivia's and shut off the buzzer. Donning an old pair of jeans and a sweatshirt, he left the house for his morning walk. A mile north to 78th Street and a mile south back home. During the night the unusual October hot spell had broken, and a cold front had moved in from the north. Thatcher threw his head back, inhaled deeply, and thought for a moment that he could smell the distant New England autumns of his boyhood.

Mike Ash's dreams had worsened. Now he was dreaming of conversations that he and Louise had really had. Shortly Ivan, merciful for a cat, would awaken him by nuzzling his very cold, very wet cat nose into Ash's very warm, very dry human armpit. Ash would neither understand nor appreciate the nobility of this gesture, and, as a result, Ivan would sulk for the remainder of the day.

* * *

Louise, too, dreamed. She dreamed of the Barbie doll her mother had refused her. Mother, a living example of the stern, Minnesota sort of liberalism, saw in Barbie the crassest exemplification of calculated Madison Avenue consumer exploitation. Louise saw in Barbie the prettiest, most desirable doll there ever was, a doll whom she could love and who in turn would love her.

Harry groaned. The pain had not subsided. "It couldn't," said Justine testily, "have been *that* bad. I mean, you didn't have to scream like that, did you?" Harry replied, "Like hell," in a voice that still squeaked high up among the soprano registers.

Knight wiped his hands against his jeans. After solving Wintergreen's conundrum, he had treated himself to a scrumptious hacker's feast: spicy Szechwan chicken and sweet-and-sour pork from Pei's All Night Chinese, a fifteen-incher from Famous Ray's Pizza (with pepperoni, sausage, onion, anchovy, green pepper, chilies, mushrooms, et alia), an oversized bag of Wise's barbecue-flavored potato chips, a dozen Oreo cookies, and two cans of Orange Crush. PegaSys's nighttime security forces were familiar with Knight's eating habits. At Thatcher's personal direction, they kept sufficient petty cash on hand to pay the endless string of delivery boys who showed up during the odd hours when Knight got hungry.

Fed, relaxed, and refreshed (*Did I sleep? No. Gotta do that sometime.*), Knight returned to his computer terminal, cracked his knuckles, and punched in a string of programming code followed by the words " > T.S. ELIOT."

There was a lengthy pause while distant circuits clicked. Then a message returned, " > YO. THAT YOU, YOSSARIAN?"

" > NO, WINTERGREEN, IT'S ME. ROY KNIGHT."

" > HEY, NOT TOO SHABBY, MR. KNIGHT. HOW'D YOU FIND ME?"

" > IT WAS EASY, WINTERGREEN."

" > EASY! LIKE HECK! COME ON, MR. KNIGHT, DON'T GIVE ME THAT."

" > IT WAS EASY, WINTERGREEN, I'VE GOT YOUR PROGRAM."

" > BALONEY, MR. KNIGHT. PURE UNADULTERATED BALONEY. I SHUT THAT PROGRAM DOWN AND PULLED IT OUT WHEN THATCHER ASKED ME TO. NO WAY DO YOU HAVE THAT PROGRAM."

" > DO YOU RECOGNIZE THIS, WINTERGREEN?''

Knight tapped a series of keystrokes and the screen filled with programming notations. Seconds passed.

'' > WOW! MR. KNIGHT, I AM IMPRESSED. HOW'D YOU DO THAT? HOW'D YOU GET MY PROGRAM?''

'' > FIRST THING I DID WHEN YOU BROKE IN HERE WAS WROTE A BLOODHOUND AND STUCK HIM ON THE END OF EVERY WIRE IN AND OUT OF THE BUILDING. WHEN YOU ISSUED YOUR ABORT, HE FOLLOWED WHERE IT WENT, HELD IT UP FOR A NANOSEC-OND, TOOK A PICTURE OF WHAT WAS THERE, AND THEN LET IT GO. AND WHILE YOU WERE TALKING TO THATCHER, HE SNIFFED DOWN YOUR TRAIL, TOO.''

'' > THAT'S MAYBE A GOOD HACK, MR. KNIGHT. MAYBE. SO IF YOU KNOW WHERE I AM, WHERE AM I?''

'' > EAST COAST, WINTERGREEN. PENNSYLVANIA, 412 AREA CODE. CARNEGIE-MELLON PREFIX, I THINK. SOMEWHERE IN THE ROBOTICS INSTITUTE LABS, I BET.''

'' > WRONG. WRONG, WRONG, WRONG. THAT'S JUST A RELAY STATION. ONE OF THE MANY. YOU CAN RUN AND RUN AS FAST AS YOU CAN, BUT YOU CAN'T CATCH ME, I'M THE GINGERBREAD MAN.''

'' > RELAY? OH YEAH, I SEE IT NOW. WELL, NOT TO WORRY, WINTERGREEN, I'LL GET YOU.''

'' > NO YOU WON'T, MR. KNIGHT.''

'' > YES, I WILL.''

'' > NOPE. I'M TOO GOOD. I'M BETTER THAN YOU ARE, MR. KNIGHT.''

'' > OH?''

'' > YEAH. I'M FASTER, I'M SMARTER, AND I'M YOUNGER THAN YOU, MR. KNIGHT.''

'' > I'M ONLY 32, WINTERGREEN.''

'' > THAT'S OLD, MR. KNIGHT, OLD AND SLOW AND OUT OF TOUCH AND OLD.''

'' > SO YOU THINK YOU CAN TAKE ME, SON?''

'' > I KNOW I CAN TAKE YOU, MR. KNIGHT. I'M GOOD. I'M WINTERGREEN. I'M THE BEST.''

'' > SO YOU HOPE, BOY.''

'' > SO I KNOW, MR. KNIGHT.''

'' > I'D WORRY SOME ABOUT THAT, IF I WERE YOU, SON.''

'' > I GOT NO WORRIES, MR. KNIGHT, NO WORRIES AT ALL.''

'' > SEEMS TO ME YOU'RE A BIT SCARED OF ME, BOY.''

'' > SCARED? SCARED! I'M NOT SCARED OF YOU, MR. KNIGHT. NO, SIR. YOU DON'T SCARE ME AT ALL, MR. KNIGHT.''

"'>OH? WELL, IF YOU AREN'T SCARED OF ME, BOY, HOW COME YOU KEEP CALLING ME 'MISTER'?''

The computer screen went blank. Knight looked at it, smiling the faint, self-deprecating smile of victory. *It was an old star and battered, this tin star he wore. But it stood for the law, and the young punk (played by Skip Homier) respected it for that. The punk rode on. Gary Cooper looked up the street. The womenfolk were coming back out now. Dodge City was safe again. The camera pulled up and back slowly, as the sheriff ambled down the dusty street to his office. A Dimitri Tiomkin soundtrack rose in the background. The closing credits rolled.*

10

THE EMC, THE EXECUTIVE MANagement committee, of PegaSys Inc. convened promptly at 4:00 P.M. on the second Thursday of each month. Promptly. Thatcher liked promptness.

The committee was composed of all the officers—that is, vice presidents and above—of PegaSys. There were thirty-eight of them. However, eleven were based overseas or in California (another foreign country as far as Thatcher was concerned) and were expected to attend EMC meetings only once each quarter.

Of the remaining twenty-seven, eight were women and nineteen were men. All were between thirty-three and forty-four years old—with two exceptions.

The first exception was Doug Wheeler, PegaSys's executive vice president, chief operating officer, and heir apparent to Scott Thatcher. Wheeler was fifty-three and had been the third employee of PegaSys when Thatcher founded it more than two decades earlier.

The other exception was Scott C. Thatcher himself.

There had been a third exception to the general youthfulness of PegaSys's executive cadre, Joe Jonas. Joe had been the second person Thatcher hired. He also had been very visibly earmarked as Thatcher's successor-to-be and good right hand. But almost a year ago, at the age of forty-nine, Joe Jonas had resigned. Doug Wheeler moved up in rank to fill his shoes.

Had a visitor from another corporation been invited to sit in on a PegaSys EMC meeting, he or she would have been, at a minimum, taken aback. In most companies a gathering of executives is a solemn affair. Management meetings are occasions upon which the owners of exceedingly expensive suits don the richest and darkest of their wardrobes. Quiet and decorum reign. Poker-faced participants sit in somber, calculating silence. If called upon to speak they do so carefully, weighing their words for maximum political impact upon those who are in favor—and to contradict those who are not. They watch their neighbors warily, guarding their own backs and waiting eagerly for a political foe to fall into error. In most companies, an executive meeting is like a dinner at the Borgias'.

The traditional rituals, ceremonies, and blood sacrifices of boardroom America were not celebrated at PegaSys. Its executives were a different breed. They were younger than most, and mostly had been hired during the company's early years. In a very real sense, they had grown up together, were classmates, and members of the same fraternity. Further, it was Thatcher's particular genius to manage his people so that, unlike so many corporations' managements, they performed not as a balkanized agglomeration of warring fiefdoms, but rather as one, single winning team. Indeed, PegaSys's executives *were* the winning team. They worked together and played together. They did both equally hard. They made little distinction between the two.

Accordingly, the atmosphere in the monthly EMC meeting sometimes was rather more reminiscent of a locker room than a boardroom.

At four o'clock (promptly), Thatcher rapped his Caran D'Ache pen sharply against a water glass to call the meeting to order. Speaking slowly and with a pronounced New England twang, he said, "Shall we begin? Is everyone here? Let us see, I note that brother Darcy is missing. Does anyone know where he is and whether he has found the time in his busy schedule to grace us with his presence this afternoon?"

Someone remarked that he had been summoned over to AT&T's remote headquarters in New Jersey by one of PegaSys's most important customers.

"Then we will grant him a dispensation. Revenue generation takes precedence over bureaucracy. All right, let's begin. Our agenda starts with Doug's review of the usual matters. Later in the evening I will call on Frank Mason to give us an evaluation of what those villains at IBM are likely to do next. And I want Doug Wheeler to bring us up to date on how the consultant's study is progressing. Then, we will have Louise Bowman and Mike Ash fill us in on the Engineered Systems plan. Perhaps brother Michael might also shed some light on how we can turn that troubled organization into a profitable enterprise. Or whether we should bother. Now, Doug, how do operating results look?"

Wheeler stood up and switched on a slide projector. A bar chart appeared on the screen behind him. "Let me give you the bottom line first. We will be finishing this quarter with year-to-date sales up by about 8 percent, that's within two-tenths of a percent of plan. Gross margin is right where we expected it at 47 percent. Net is off by 11 percent because we took a big hit on the deal we lowballed to General Motors. We knew it was coming but we don't like it anyway. It's something we're going to need to make up next quarter or we're going to louse up our annual results. On the next slide you can see the balance sheet. Everything's OK except receivables. We've got some slow pays out there, ladies and gentlemen, and I'd like those of you who have customer responsibilities to get on the case. The collection department can't handle some of those situations all by themselves."

Thatcher grunted. "I want it recognized that we are not in the business of providing credit services to the Fortune 500. With the economy in the shape that it's in, a lot of companies out there are slowing down their payables. They may call themselves prudent financial managers but I call 'em deadbeats. Now I know you all think that I am an ogre on this issue—you all think that I am an ogre on most issues . . ."

Thatcher took a carefully calculated pause to sip some water and ignite a cigar, thereby allowing everyone to reflect that, while he occasionally spoke like an ogre and occasionally looked like an ogre, Scott C. Thatcher most assuredly was *not* an ogre. Rather, he was a tough-as-nails executive who had built nearly single-handedly one of the most prestigious businesses in the world. He cared about that business and the people it represented more than anyone could know.

". . . But I refuse to let a bunch of lackluster companies, whether they're our best customers or our worst ones, use our financial strength to cover up their financial weakness. I want the bills paid, and the customer relations department will just have to manage its way around any problems my irrational insistence on timely payment causes. Let me note in passing that if I personally have to intervene in this issue, those problems may be materially greater than they would be if the people in this room resolve the issue. OK? OK. Sorry for the interruption, Doug. Please continue.''

Wheeler put up the next slide and began to review the details of PegaSys's financial performance. Ash's attention slipped away as he began to worry how to cover up the deficiencies in the Engineered Systems plan. He was supposed to be a whiz kid, a superbright, supercreative, super solver of unsolvable problems. The quick-fix artist, the brain surgeon, Mad Mike who could come out of left field with the craziest idea anyone had ever heard. Just crazy enough that it might work. Well, this time everyone was in for a disappointment. Mad Mike had gone dry. Not only did he not have a *good* idea, he didn't have *any* idea about how to remedy Engineered Systems's problems. Thatcher was going to ask for a solution, and Mike Ash was going to disappoint him.

It was Louise, of course. He spent all his time thinking about Louise. *Damnit, damnit, damnit all*, he wanted to scream, *I love you! Can't you see that? Can't you understand what I have been trying to tell you? Can't we . . .*

Gladys, Thatcher's secretary, walked into the room holding a large courier envelope. She whispered something in Thatcher's ear. Wheeler paused in his presentation while Thatcher examined the contents of the already opened envelope.

In a quiet, serious voice, Thatcher said, ''Better turn the lights up, Doug, and shut off the projector. It appears that we have a slight change in agenda and I don't think we will be getting to the matters I originally asked to cover. Ladies and gentlemen, we have a letter here. It comes from someone known to me, one Brian Shawby, chief exec of AIW, American Interdyne Worldwide.'' There was a murmur of whispered question and answer from around the table. More than one person asked his or her neighbor, ''AIW? Are those guys still in business?''

Thatcher said softly, ''The letter is brief. I will read it to you in its entirety. It is addressed to me.''

≡ ≡ ≡
American Interdyne
Worldwide

Brian W. Shawby
Chairman and Chief Executive

Mr. Scott C. Thatcher
Chairman and Chief Executive Officer
PegaSys Inc.
One PegaSys Center
New York, New York, 10017

Dear Mr. Thatcher,

PegaSys is a company for which I have long had the highest respect and regard. Its record of achievement is one which many companies in America might envy. We at AIW (American Interdyne Worldwide) in particular have followed PegaSys's progress with great interest. Indeed, we have been so impressed by your company's results that, from time to time, we have taken substantial investment positions in PegaSys's stock. These investments have always rewarded us with handsome dividends and with strong capital appreciation.

Given our considerable investment position in your company and on-going interest in its progress, we have now concluded that our mutual interests might be best served by an even more substantial investment in PegaSys. Consequently, on the advice of our legal and financial advisors, and with the approval of our Board of Directors, we are now planning on accumulating a significant portion of PegaSys's stock. We anticipate that this accumulation will result in our securing a controlling interest in the company.

The mechanism we plan to use in acquiring the stock we desire will be a tender offer for eighty percent of the shares outstanding as of this date. This letter represents our formal notification to you and to the Board and management of PegaSys of our intent. Within fewer than ten calendar days we will file a formal detailed description of our proposal with the Securities and Exchange Commission, the Department of Justice, the Department of Commerce, the Chancery Court of The State of Delaware, The Governors of The New York Stock Exchange, and other appropriate parties. A copy of this proposal will be forwarded to you and each member of your Board of Directors. Our offer will be at $85 per share cash and/or cash and equivalents, a sum which you, your board, and the public shareholders of the company will recognize as generous.

We look forward to PegaSys's joining the AIW family of companies.

Very truly yours,

Brian T. Shawby,
Chairman of the Board, President,
Chief Executive Officer, and
Chief Operating Officer

Thatcher handed the letter back to Gladys. "Ladies and gentlemen, it seems that we are the target of a takeover raid. There is a press release accompanying this abomination. And a photograph. Gladys, make Xerox copies of this package for everyone. We will now adjourn this meeting for thirty minutes. This man Shawby is known to me, and I have a few phone calls to make."

11

It HAD BEEN ABOUT A YEAR EARlier that Thatcher, to his subsequent regret, had first stumbled across American Interdyne Worldwide. At the time PegaSys had been losing share in its once lucrative video display division. The problem was that PegaSys needed new video technology, and by unfortunate coincidence, the technology it needed was patented by a small, marginally profitable electronics subsidiary of AIW.

Thatcher reviewed the problem with his board of directors, ultimately deciding to try to buy AIW's operation. After several months of telephone negotiation, AIW's president and chief executive officer, Brian Shawby, agreed to sell. He invited Thatcher and his acquisition team to visit his corporate headquarters to sign the final papers. Thatcher, always courteous to a fellow executive, agreed. Louise, Mike Ash, and Thatcher then booked their reservations . . . via Auk Airways.

The trio, understandably shaken by their in-flight experiences, arrived in AIW's lobby to be greeted by a tiny, primly dressed, smiling grey-haired woman in her late fifties. "Mr. Thatcher?" she asked with a winning smile. "I'm Martha, Mr. Shawby's junior secretary. Would you and your party come along with me?" Martha bustled out. Thatcher, Mike, and Louise followed behind her. After a seemingly interminable walk through AIW's enormous mazelike office complex (Louise whispered to Mike, "There's a lever here somewhere and if you push it you get a food pellet."), they finally arrived at Shawby's palatial suite.

The anteroom to Shawby's office contained floor-to-ceiling mahogany wall shelves on which was displayed a cornucopia of AIW's products. Few visitors ever noticed these items because even more on display was Mr. Shawby's senior secretary, a sultry, pneumatic redhead of prominent, far from understated charms.

She was one of those women who tan well; during her recent vacation in Acapulco she had developed that tawny, warm brown color that so nicely complements gold. This was indeed a felicitous coincidence, since about a year's worth of Cartier's inventory was decorously strewn about her neck, waist, wrists, fingers, and ankles. Like every third woman born between 1955 and 1965, she was named Jennifer.

Jennifer was, of course, on the phone. To her sister. The one on vacation in Greece. She had been on the phone since she arrived that morning at 9:30. It was now 11:30 and she hadn't even had time to take the cover off her typewriter. Not that she would have even if she hadn't had all those calls to make. When she wasn't on the phone, she spent her time reading Danielle Steele's latest novel. Slowly. Moving her lips.

To Mike Ash's disappointment, Jennifer appeared utterly unaware of his presence—or, indeed, of anything other than the telephone. Martha ushered the PegaSys trio into Brian Shawby's office.

Louise's jaw dropped at what she saw. Money had been spent on this office—not tastefully, not well, but nonetheless money had been spent. The chairs and sofas were covered in lime and purple pastel-dyed leather. Shawby's desk had been hewn out of one solid, massive hunk of granite. Likewise the matching credenza and coffee table. The floor, Louise thought, must have been reinforced to support these pieces. There was a bathtub-sized model of the corporate jet, Shawby's prize possession, sitting in a corner. Shawby's walls were hung with enormous stone ornaments retrieved from the rubble of demolished art deco buildings. There were a red sandstone gargoyle, a series of three-foot concrete medallions bearing weatherworn images of Roman emperors, something that looked like a Reichstag Eagle, six pseudo-Corinthian plinths, and an enormous, rusty cast-iron grill. And on prominent display was a poster-sized photo of Shawby shaking hands with the president of the United States—not the current incumbent, but rather Shawby's role model of managerial acumen, Jimmy Carter.

Shawby rose from his chair to greet the three visitors, extending his hand over the barren expanse of his desk. He was a handsome man in his late fifties and was deeply tanned from his recent vacation in Acapulco. The scars from the chin tuck and hair implants he had obtained during this trip hardly showed at all. He was wearing a tailor-made grey wool suit and an off-white shirt. His tie and pocket handkerchief were of matching color. He said, "Scott, delighted to see you."

"Glad to be here, Brian."

"Good. And who are these charming people with you?"

"Let me introduce Mike Ash, my vice president for corporate development."

"A pleasure to meet you, Mike."

"And Louise Bowman, currently vice president for video terminal operations, but due to move up to the corporate offices in a month or two."

"Always delighted to meet a pretty gal, Scott. Please, please do sit down. Welcome to American Interdyne Worldwide. After all those phone calls, at last we finally get together, huh? Tell me, how was your trip?"

"Fine, up until we climbed on board Auk Airways. That's an unusual airplane they fly, Brian."

"Oh, Auk Airways. Ha! Well, it's one of those little inconveniences we all have to put up with for living in this part of the world. I don't like flying it myself. But, I think if you asked any of my employees whether they'd like to live here or someplace where they could fly TWA, they'd tell you that they'd rather stay here. But of course, I'm prejudiced; you know, I was born in these parts. That's one of the reasons why I had our new corporate headquarters built here. But look, enough of this chitterchatter. Let's get down to business. What brings you folks out this way?"

"We're here to close the deal, Brian."

(A pause.) "Deal?"

"The contract, Brian."

(A longer pause.) "Contract?"

"The one we've been talking about for the past three months. It was in the package we sent you."

(A long, long pause.) "Package?"

"Yes. My letter, our attorneys' comments, the investment banker's analysis, the proposition binder, and the contract itself. We had it couriered to your attention two weeks ago."

"Oh that! Oh yes! Right! Of course. Yes, I saw it. Yes. And I've had my people go over it with a fine-tooth comb and give me a detailed analysis. Very thorough. Very complete. Every facet. Ahh. . . . And, I gave it a pretty good going-over myself."

"What is your reaction?"

"My reaction? Well. Ahh. Ehh. Hmm. Well, interest. Yes, interest. I have some questions, of course. One or two points. They're in the folder with your letter and my staff's report. The folder is right here . . . no, it isn't. Let's see. Maybe I put it . . . no. Now what did I do with that thing? Is it in this drawer? Down here? Pardon me while I . . ."

After further search proved fruitless, Shawby finally yielded to the inevitable and buzzed his senior secretary, Jennifer. She was still on the phone and refused to respond. So he buzzed Martha.

Martha immediately located the file, and bustled in with it. She paused for a moment to ask if anyone would like coffee or something else to drink. Thatcher, who had not had a cup of coffee since leaving New York, was so moved by her offer that he was speechless and could only nod prayerfully in the affirmative. Martha bustled out and Shawby, flipping vigorously through the file to refresh his memory, began to speak again.

"Well, Scott. Yes. I must say, yes. Certainly, yes. Yes, we have indeed reviewed your package. And reviewed it closely. Really given it a good looking-over. Nothing cursory. A really thorough review. Comprehensive. We take this kind of thing seriously here at AIW. If it's worth doing, it's worth doing right. We like detail here at AIW, and detail is what you've given us. We appreciate that, Scott. I appreciate it."

"Then we're agreed on the transaction, aren't we, Brian?"

Shawby looked up like a hunted animal. His brow furrowed with perplexity. He thumbed through the file folder, desperate to discover what the meeting was about. He had no recollection of Thatcher's letter, no memory of the material enclosed with it, and not a clue as to what his staff had recommended. In fact, he had clean forgotten that he had scheduled a meeting with the PegaSys executives. Finally, he stumbled across the memo containing his staff's recommendation. His eyes lit up, he sat more erect, and his voice became perceptibly deeper. He prepared to make a genuine executive decision—an opportunity that he rarely confronted.

"Let me respond to that question directly, Scott. Candidly. You know, we see several propositions every year. (*Buzz, buzz.*) Some good, some not so good. You know, we haven't done anything quite like this yet. But that doesn't mean we won't. (*Buzz, buzz.*) Or at least it doesn't mean we won't consider it seriously. Very seriously. Now this package, Scott, is well done. (*Buzz, buzz.*) The best offer we've ever received on this particular topic. We've gone over it. I've gone over it. And speaking for AIW, I think I can say that our reaction is one hundred percent . . . (*Buzz, buzz.*) Damn phone. Just a second, let me take this. Yes, Martha. Yes. Oh, he is, is he? Yes. Well, I'd better talk to him. Excuse me, Scott, this is urgent. Could you and your people step outside for a moment while I take this call? I won't be but one minute."

As Thatcher, Mike, and Louise slipped out of Shawby's office, Martha bustled in with a coffee tray. The coffee was on the inside and Thatcher was on the outside. He considered asking Martha to fetch the coffee out, but decided to wait because Shawby said he would be on the phone only a minute or so.

But the one minute turned into thirty. The coffee stayed in Shawby's office, growing colder with each passing moment. Thatcher, in contrast, was growing hotter.

Shawby finally emerged from his lair. He looked different somehow. Shorter. About three inches shorter. AIW's chief executive officer had carefully concealed a platform behind his desk to add a badly needed quarter of a foot to his height. He rushed toward the exit, saying, "Sorry about that, Scott. Really sorry. Look, let's all get back together right after lunch. Right after lunch. Say about 3:00 P.M." Then he was gone.

Jennifer looked up, dog-eared a page in his Danielle Steele novel, removed her chewing gum and began to sashay toward the door. "Out to lunch, Martha," she said over her shoulder. Then she was gone. AIW's employees frequently remarked that Jennifer and Shawby always seemed to leave for lunch at about the same time.

Thatcher, Mike, and Louise stood in stunned dismay outside Shawby's office. Martha smiled up at them, telling them that Shawby had a previous luncheon engagement and was sorry that he could not join them. However, he had arranged for two other AIW executives to take the three visitors out for lunch. She also assured Thatcher that Shawby's calendar was open for the entire afternoon, and that he would be able to reconvene the meeting at 3:00 P.M.

At this point Louise performed a hurried consultation of her pocket flight guide. "Arrgh," she said. "The only flight out of here is at 3:00 P.M. If we stay to finish our meeting with Shawby, we'll either be stuck in Desuetude or have to drive a hundred and some odd miles to the nearest major airport."

"We'll drive."

"These things wouldn't happen to us," Louise grumbled, "if we owned a corporate jet."

"A frivolous waste of money," Thatcher shot back. "The alleged savings in time and convenience are not worth the cost."

"But are they worth avoiding a night in Desuetude?"

Thatcher glared at her.

As Louise stuffed her flight guide back in her briefcase, a rather porky-looking chap wearing a plaid jacket, grey slacks, and no tie ambled in. He was Joe Casey, AIW's vice president of engineering, one of the PegaSys trio's luncheon hosts.

Thatcher introduced himself, as did Mike and Louise. Casey responded, "Delighted to meet you, Scott. And I'm always delighted to meet a pretty gal."

Casey remarked that their other lunch partner, Carl Bitzer, the VP in charge of AIW's computer systems, would meet them at the restaurant. He then herded the three out of the executive suite, through the endless maze of corridors (Louise noted that at lunchtime every desk in AIW was unoccupied and the sole sound to be heard was the ring of unanswered telephones), and out into the parking lot to his car.

Only it was not a car. Not really. It was a truck or a van of some sort, nearly two stories tall, with four wheels in the back, two in the front, and a row of multicolored spotlights across the roof. Its wheels looked as if they belonged on a 747. It was just the sort of brute you would want on a two-month trek across the Kalahari desert. A bumper sticker was affixed to the rear of the vehicle: "Is there life after death? Fuck with my truck and find out."

The three PegaSys executives clambered in, taking care to avoid bumping their heads on the gun rack. On the dashboard was a little plastic statuette of St. Jude, the patron saint of lost causes.

Joe fired up the engine and, over the deafening roar, yelled, "We're running a bit late, so hang on." He then laid rubber the length of the parking lot. For real heart-stopping thrills, the trip to the restaurant compared favorably to a flight on Auk Airways. It was the sort of ride the folks at Disneyland charge an 'E' coupon for.

After what seemed an eternity (or at least a close confrontation with it) the truck arrived at its destination; Joe shut down the afterburners, activated the air brakes, and taxied into a parking lot. Thatcher seemed to stumble as he climbed out of the truck. Mike hypothesized that he was kissing the ground.

The restaurant at hand was named Madame Sylvia's Parlour. For Desuetude's environs it was considered to be a very classy spot, because it was the only restaurant in town at which one did not pay the cashier on the way out the door.

Upon entering Madame Sylvia's Parlour, the PegaSys executives discovered that Desuetude's finest eatery was decorated with red velvet hangings, beaded curtains, gilded, berhinestoned lamps, and paintings of undraped ladies of the sort admired by Peter Paul Rubens. The restaurant was, Louise observed, also terribly, terribly dark inside.

Thatcher, Louise, and Mike, guided by Joe, made their way through the gloom to their table, there meeting Carl Bitzer. Bitzer was wearing a brown blazer, dark brown slacks, brown shirt, and matching tie. He looked as if he had fallen into a vat of chocolate. Joe Casey introduced them.

"Carl, this is Scotty Thatcher, from back East."

"Pleased to meet you, Scotty."

"And his development guy, what was your name again?"

"Mike Ash."

"Welcome to our little company, Mike."

"And Louise."

"Always delighted to meet a pretty gal, Scotty."

After they had all seated themselves, a waitress ambled over. Louise did a double take. The waitress appeared to be wearing a semitransparent negligee—red velvet garters—black mesh stockings—and five-inch stiletto heels. *My God*, Louise thought. *This isn't a restaurant, it's a bordello.*

The waitress asked for drink orders. Both Casey and Bitzer ordered Bloody Marys, stating, for what was probably the ten thousandth time, that they wanted them "heavy on the bloody and weak on the Mary." For what was probably the ten thousandth time, the waitress giggled appreciatively. She turned to Louise and Mike, who both ordered glasses of white wine. Thatcher asked for a Campari and soda.

The waitress responded, "A what?"

"Campari and soda."

"Could you spell that?"

"Ahh. C - A - M . . . Never mind. On second thought, I'll just have a glass of white wine too."

The waitress disappeared off into the darkness to fill the drink orders. Awaiting her return, Bitzer told Thatcher that opportunities for dining out in Desuetude were limited. However, he assured him, Madame Sylvia's Parlour was absolutely the best. "You all will," he said, "find it every bit as good as any place back East. Besides, even if you don't like the food, there's always the after-lunch show."

Show? thought Thatcher.

The scantily attired waitress returned with the drink orders. Casey's and Bitzer's Bloody Marys were in enormous vessels, less glasses than buckets. Casey eagerly hefted his glass, no mean feat given its size, and said, "Well, here's to our guests." He downed about half the contents in one swallow. Thatcher tasted his wine. It was not, Thatcher concluded, a vintage year. It was not even a vintage month. Likely the beverage came from upstate New York, and was sold in fifty-gallon drums.

Everyone ordered lunch. The food returned with startling speed. The only way it could be served so fast was if the orders were precooked and sitting on a warming tray. One bite persuaded Thatcher that the meal was indeed precooked, probably the night before. As she served the meals, the waitress said, "Now y'all enjoy your meals. And enjoy the show, too."

Show? thought Louise.

For the next hour or so the PegaSys team suffered through a less than gratifying conversation with Messrs. Casey and Bitzer. Their interest and conversational repertoire seemed to be limited to football, fishing, and off-color jokes. As for the latter, they preceded each tasteless tale with an obviously insincere apology: "Well now, Scotty, I sure do hope that Louise here isn't offended by ris-kay stories."

As the ordeal finally seemed to be drawing to a close, both Casey and Bitzer ordered monumental desserts and massive after-dinner drinks. When these were consumed, Thatcher glanced at his watch and suggested that they ask for the check and head back. Casey, looking like a disappointed three-year-old, said, "What? Leave now and miss the show?"

Show? thought Mike Ash.

Just as Thatcher was going to ask what this "show" business was all about, the lights in the restaurant came up. There was some sort of platform running the length of the restaurant; Thatcher hadn't noticed it in the dark. The maitre d' stood on it with a microphone. He began to speak, "Howdy, gentlemen. Oh, and I see we've got a lady here, too. Always nice to see a pretty gal in the audience. Welcome, y'all, to Madame Sylvia's Parlour. Hope y'all enjoyed our fine food, our fine drinks, and now, our renowned after-lunch fashion show. Today our lovely models will be showing intimate apparel and fetching swimwear from the famous Fredericks of Hollywood collection. If any of y'all see something you want to buy (and I just mean the clothes, boys), anything at all for your wives or girlfriends, our lovely waitress will be happy to take your orders. That goes for you too, ma'am, if you've got a hubby or just a good friend, I'll bet he'd just love to see you in one of these outfits. Perk his old attention right straight up."

Louise winced.

Then a rather busty young woman strolled out onto the platform . . . or, more accurately, slinked out onto the runway to model what might best be called a minimalist bikini. She was followed by other ladies wearing either less fabric or more; but where it was more, it was not in the right places.

Throughout this spectacle, Casey and Bitzer leaned toward Louise and joshingly asked whether or not she would like to add the piece on display to her wardrobe. Their comments represented progress of a sort, because this was the first time during the entire day that any employee of AIW had addressed her directly. The "fashion" show proceeded. Louise found it not wholly lacking in interest. For example, this was the first time she'd ever seen a V-front, thigh-length nun's frock. Done entirely in leather, too.

During the course of the show, the check arrived at the table. Thatcher waited for Casey or Bitzer to pick it up. And waited. And waited. Casey eyed it like a dead frog. Bitzer affected not to have noticed it. It just lay there.

The day's events had left Thatcher more than a little irked. He reflected on the matter, and decided that he had no intention of adding to the already lengthy list of insults he had endured the injury of paying for so appalling a lunch. After an interval of sufficient length to ensure that he was making his point, he gave Louise a signal. She slapped her American Express card on the bill. Both Casey and Bitzer promptly lunged for the check rather than endure the humiliation of having their lunch paid for by a woman. Thatcher gave Louise another signal and she smilingly withdrew her credit card. Casey, to his chagrin, was left holding the bill. He grimaced at it for a moment or two, then started to check the math with the aid of a pocket calculator. As he did so, Thatcher thought to himself how truly sweet was even the small and petty revenge of sticking these two with the tab. Having validated the math, Casey looked up, and said, "OK. That's $22.50 for me, $19.00 even for Carl, and $67.80 for your party, Louise."

By 2:45 P.M., the trio, even gloomier than they had been before they left, were back in Shawby's office. It was almost 3:30 when Shawby breezed through the door, looking rather ruddy-cheeked and content. A few minutes later Jennifer sashayed in. Everyone at AIW commented that Jennifer and Shawby always seemed to come back from lunch at about the same time.

Shawby announced that he was delighted to see them and was well launched into introducing himself before he remembered that he'd already met the three earlier in the day and was merely reconvening that meeting. Once this fact dawned on him, he proceeded to steer them into the executive conference room, saying, "Now you folks just make yourself comfortable here for a minute or two. I want a few other people in on this discussion."

At about 4:00 P.M. three other executives drifted into the conference room and introduced themselves. There were AIW's corporate chief counsel, the division vice president responsible for the subsidiary PegaSys wished to acquire, and AIW's chief financial officer. The latter was a thirty-five-year-old Wharton MBA of considerable intelligence, talent, skills, and ambition; he also was Shawby's son-in-law and heir apparent. There was something about him that reminded Thatcher of Shakespeare's *Julius Caesar*, something about a character with a lean and hungry look.

At 4:30 P.M. Shawby drifted in. After six unproductive, time-wasting hours in Desuetude, the PegaSys team was at long last about to sit down and do some business. Or so they thought.

The meeting began with Shawby asking Thatcher to restate the purpose of his team's visit. During the preceding three months there had been countless face-to-face meetings, innumerable phone calls, and vast reams of correspondence on the matter. Thatcher personally had discussed the situation via telephone with Shawby some eight or nine times. Everyone in the room should have already known what was going on. Accordingly, Thatcher kept his comments brief.

"In a nutshell, your video display operation would be a good fit with our company. The reason is simple. Video terminals are an important portion of our business, and are not a meaningful part of yours. In fact, I believe it the only computer-related business that AIW has. It is a business that is not a major contributor to your bottom line but is to ours. More important, your people have patented manufacturing processes that could be of considerable use to my company. For us to replicate it would cost a good sum of money and consume a good deal of time. We have the money, but we do not have the time. The only other corporation in the world that has these processes is Bakayaro of Japan; Bakayaro is poised for near-term entry into the U.S. and will not license its technologies to our company. We need the processes to remain competitive in the face of this Japanese threat. Consequently, your video display facility is important to us. It is worth more to us than it is to you. Therefore, we are prepared to pay $35 million, a sum slightly more than five times the annual cash flow you receive from the operation. We believe that this price is more than fair. You have agreed. Two weeks ago we sent you our formal offer and all the relevant paperwork. We are here today to conclude the deal."

The corporate chief counsel looked perplexed. He began to scribble on a yellow legal pad.

Meanwhile Shawby turned to the divisional vice president into whose bailiwick the video display plant fell, asking him to review that plant's operations and results. The divisional VP pulled out a set of vu-graphs, clicked on an overhead projector, dimmed the lights, and began to talk. The material he used dealt with 1987 results; the vu-graphs were dusty, scratched, and marked over with a felt-tip pen. This was not the first time that they had been used.

The chief counsel slid his pad beneath Shawby's nose. Shawby looked perplexed. He began to scribble a response.

The divisional vice president responsible for video displays rambled on. Not only was the ground he covered ancient history, but it was also ground that Thatcher's team had covered before. More than once. They knew it better than he did.

The yellow legal pad whizzed back to the chief counsel. He scrawled one word on it and flipped it back to Shawby. Shawby silently mouthed something that seemed to be an obscenity. His son-in-law snatched the pad, scrutinized it, and mouthed the same word. He glared at the chief counsel, who responded by pulling a typewritten piece of paper out of a portfolio and handing it to him. After reading this page, the son-in-law scribbled in very large letters (Thatcher could read them from his end of the table), ''WRAP IT UP AND SIT DOWN!'' on the yellow pad. He flashed this message at the speaker, who obeyed.

The overhead projector was turned off and the lights came on. There was a silence. It was a silence of the more enduring sort.

Thatcher sensed that something had gone awry, but could not imagine what it might be at this late date in the negotiations. It fell to Shawby's son-in-law to enlighten him and his colleagues. ''Scott, we all owe you an apology. You know, even in a tightly knit management team like ours there sometimes is a little breakdown in communications. One thing or another falls between the cracks. Maybe we don't handle something as well as we should. And, when that happens, all we can do is say we're sorry. And, Scott, we are sorry. We seem to have made a bit of a mistake, in fact an outright blunder.''

He glared accusingly at Shawby, who responded by squirming in his seat. He sighed and continued, ''As I'm sure you know, our board of directors has been interested in selling off the video operation for quite some time now. Well, while Brian was aware of your offer and preparing to move on it, I was unaware of it. Indeed, I approved the sale of the facility to another corporation and told our chief counsel to conclude the deal. The fault for this mistake is entirely mine.''

He glared again at Shawby, who was now intensely studying his shoes, and proceeded to explain that the sale had been executed and that a press announcement on the transaction had been released early that morning. This press release was the sheet of paper the chief counsel had pulled out of his portfolio. It was passed to Thatcher, who read:

FOR IMMEDIATE RELEASE: Today AIW, a leading multinational diversified manufacturer, announced that it had concluded the sale of its video display manufacturing division in Squirrel City, Missouri.

In disclosing the sale, Brian Shawby, AIW's CEO, said, ''The termination of our video business should be viewed as a healthy sign. Computer-related products are not, and never have been, part of our mainstream business. While video displays were a profit-maker for AIW, it represented a diversion of management attention from the other higher growth segments upon which we are strategically focusing. Moreover, the sale of this facility will yield cash resources which we plan to prudently invest in future growth opportunities in our core business sectors.''

The Squirrel City plant was acquired by Bakayaro Ltd. of Japan for a price of $28 million.

Thatcher returned to New York hoping never to hear of AIW again.

12

FOR IMMEDIATE RELEASE: St. Louis, Missouri. At a press conference held late this afternoon at St. Louis's Lambert Field, Brian Shawby, President and Chief Executive Officer of American Interdyne Worldwide (AIW), announced his company's plans to acquire the assets of PegaSys Inc., a large manufacturer of computers and computer-related equipment. AIW is a leading multinational diversified manufacturer headquartered in Desuetude, Missouri.

Standing in front of the AIW corporate jet (***PHOTO***), Mr. Shawby remarked, "Our interest in PegaSys is not to be taken as hostile. On the contrary, our offer to acquire the company should be recognized as not only friendly, but as being in the best interests of both parties. Pegasys clearly needs the kind of technological resourcefulness and vision that a more diversified company such as AIW can muster. Within the past twelve months, for example, PegaSys tried to acquire one of our leading edge technology divisions. It was this attempted acquisition that called to my attention the unarguable fact that PegaSys could profit from the kind of creativity and excellence in innovativeness in which we at AIW specialize.

"Further, let me say that computers and information technology are the wave of the future. These businesses are going to be very big and very important some day. As we look forward at AIW, we intend to be major players in the arena. Acquiring PegaSys will give us an important start in developing a meaningful position in the market. Of course, PegaSys will only be a small first step and we will need to build upon it."

AIW's Vice President of Finance, Mark Cass, who is also Mr. Shawby's son-in-law, added, "I agree wholeheartedly with Brian."

When asked about financing the acquisition, Mr. Shawby replied, "I and my Board of Directors have been counseled throughout our deliberations on this important matter by Nicholas Lee from Lee, Bach and Wachutt Investment Bankers. As you know this firm is a premier specialist among investment banking firms in arranging the financing of major acquisition transactions. Nicholas Lee, as President of Wachutt, has issued us a feasibility letter, and, accordingly, I am completely confident of our ability to raise the sum necessary through the creative use of international debt instruments. Shareholders of PegaSys need have no concern about our having the funds in hand two months hence to pay fully and fairly for the shares they tender."

Vice President of Finance Mark Cass, added, "I agree unreservedly with Brian."

After concluding the press conference, Messrs. Shawby and Cass continued on their flight to New York, where they are expected to conduct a round of intense meetings with members of the New York financial community.

PegaSys's executive management committee had varying reactions to the press release. However, the male members shared a common enthusiasm for the photograph that accompanied the document.

"Who's the woman in the picture?" someone asked.

"Whoever she is, she is some good-looking lady. How come we don't have one like her with our corporate jet?"

"Because we don't have a corporate jet. Scott thinks they're a waste of money."

"Maybe we should get one anyway—if the stewardess is standard equipment, I mean."

"That's not a stewardess. It's probably Shawby's daughter, the wife of this Cass guy."

"Yeah, well, if that's Shawby's daughter, young Mark did not merely marry for money. Does anyone here know if that is her?"

Louise sighed, "No one is going to believe this, but her name is Jennifer and . . ."

For the next hour, while they all awaited Thatcher's return, Louise told her fellow executives what she knew of AIW and Brian Shawby. The executive ranks of PegaSys were aghast—but nonetheless relieved. It was, after all, highly improbable that such a collection of featherweights could seriously hope to acquire a company of PegaSys's stature, talent, and wealth.

"The worst company in America," someone snickered. "How could those turkeys have the unmitigated gall to tender an offer for us? Shawby must be on drugs."

"We will eat their lunch," another concluded. "It will be like Bambi versus Godzilla."

"Yeah," added a third, "and the role of the big lizard is being played by a cigar-smoking old dude with a moustache."

Clink, clink. The Caran d'Ache tapped against the water glass. Thatcher had returned to the head of the table and was calling the meeting back to order.

"All right, ladies and gentlemen, recess is over. Let's get back to school. Leave some room for our guests at the head of the table. No, Larry, Roy, leave those two other seats empty too, at least for the moment. I believe many of you on the EMC know these people, but I will introduce them to you once again. They have changed their busy schedules to join us here, and I appreciate it. On my immediate left, Justine Gold. I think most of you know that Justine is one of my closest personal friends, and runs our corporation's public relations agency, Gold Associates. Next to her, Denniston Howe. Denny is a lawyer, but better than most . . . excuse me, I mean *and* better than most. He is a managing partner with Howe & Hummel, our law firm. And finally, Don Banks from our investment banker, Morgan, Teech & Kidd. They will be leading their firms' efforts as we stop this foolish takeover bid in its tracks.

"I have asked them to dash over here this afternoon so that they and you can hear the same message at the same time. The message is this, business as usual. Do I make myself clear?

Business as usual. I do not want the unwelcome attentions of the lamentable Mr. Shawby and his shabby conglomerate distracting any of you. You will continue to make the smooth functioning of PegaSys's daily operations your top priority. You will keep your hands on the wheel and your eyes on the road. It is imperative that you do. I do not wish to have one customer lose confidence in us because we have been singled out for attack by some hapless simpleton from Missouri. Our competitors will be prepared to encourage such a loss of confidence. You are to be prepared to counter them. By the same token, I do not want one creditor thinking that this cornbelt yahoo's imprudent assault on PegaSys means that our attention is elsewhere. No one who owes us money, goods, or services is to think that they can forget about us because our minds are elsewhere. So then, business as usual. We shall be dispatching Mr. Shawby and his minions to their justly deserved rewards rather quickly, I think, and when we are through, I do not wish to learn of one glitch, one blip, or one hiccup in the orderly operations of this enterprise that we all have built.

''I trust I make myself entirely clear. Now, I count twenty-six executives in this room. All but two of you are either currently heading line operations or managing major headquarters departments. Only two seem to be floating loose with staff functions. Ms. Bowman, Mr. Ash, congratulations, you draw the short straws. Please come to the head of the table, you are both now assigned to the defense team. Tell your subordinates that they are now in charge of whatever you were in charge of. You two are going to be otherwise engaged for the next few weeks. That's right, take those seats there.

''In case anyone is wondering, I myself will head the effort to fend off the wretched Mr. Shawby. As you all know, I have a keen appetite for vengeance, and will relish the opportunity of not merely defeating the sniveling little worm, but positively humiliating him. Therefore, and until further notice, Doug Wheeler will act as chief executive officer for all day-to-day matters not directly related to this takeover offer.

''With that out of the way, let me address the obvious questions. I would be surprised to learn that any of you were intimate with AIW—except Louise and Mike who, to their everlasting sorrow, have actually visited the dismal place and met the equally dismal Shawby. I have here a copy of AIW's annual report. You will all find copies on your desks when you return to your offices. It is an unedifying document, but not without its lighter moments. Let me make a few observations about the financial status of this blot on the landscape of free enterprise. Please restrain your laughter as I do so. AIW is a $2.8 billion company. We are a $12 billion company. AIW netted $80 million in profits on its sales, that's a 3.7 percent profit margin. We netted a bit more than $1 billion, an 8 percent margin. AIW has fifty million shares outstanding and about a billion dollars in equity. Its stock is trading at nineteen bucks a share—less than equity, in other words. We have nine billion dollars in equity, and 210 million shares outstanding. Our stock closed this afternoon at seventy-six and five-eighths. We are trading at three times equity. To acquire 80 percent of our common stock at $85 per share would take $14 billion in cold hard cash, and that ain't hay. On the balance sheet, AIW shows exactly $200 million in cash and marketable securities. That means it can buy right now a pitiful two million of the 170 million shares it needs—cash on the barrel head. Good luck, folks, and God's mercy on you. The rest will have to be debt. AIW already has a debt-to-equity ratio of 0.96 to one. It carries an S&P rating of triple 'B' minus. They are fiscal lepers. No one will touch them. How much more debt can they draw down to finance this deal? Would you lend this organization $14 billion and change? Would a bank lend this organization $14 billion and change? Would Guido the loan shark down on Flatbush Avenue lend this organization $14 billion and change? I think not! What we have here is a company one-fifth our size with no money to speak of trying to buy us. What we have here is a mouse trying to eat an elephant. And the mouse has no teeth. Well, what will be eaten here is mouse soufflé. I trust that no one in this room believes otherwise."

Banks spoke. "Overconfidence could be a mistake, Scott."

"Don, I am confident. Indeed I am overconfident. I am positively exalted with confidence, and rise heavenward in its rapture. How can these shabby fools succeed? Do they need $14 billion or do they not? Which they have not, and which they can get not. Or am I missing something?"

"Scott, maybe we should have this discussion off-line."

"No, go ahead, Don. I make it a practice—"

"To share everything with your management. I know, I know. Look, Scott, everyone, the thing is this. The man has made the offer. He has gone public with it. He is on the hook for it. He has got to deliver something. And, he has the most murderous group of thugs on Wall Street, Lee, Bach and Wachutt, promising to raise money for him. They're killers. They're piranhas. They wouldn't be backing this thing just because it's a slow day in the market and so what the hell. They are up to something. There is something behind this that we don't know yet. You should be worried, not arrogant.''

"Don, I pride myself on the openness of my mind. Go ahead, make me worried.''

"In the car coming over here I had a chance to take a look at *your* balance sheet, Scott.''

"Yup?''

"Cash and marketable securities to the tune of $1.1 billion.''

"Hmpf. It's too much, I know. But we've been accumulating it against some major plans. The new European research center—and we've got the folks over at Broadview trying to find a good software company for us to buy. Some other things, too. So maybe we've socked away a little too much cash.''

"Pensions overfunded by at least another billion.''

"A bit more than that, really. By design. People who spend their careers with PegaSys should not worry about the future.''

"An exceedingly valuable hunk of Manhattan real estate carried at cost, not current value. Plus God knows how many acres out in the hinterlands, including some highly desirable areas around San Francisco, Phoenix, and San Diego.''

"The accountants don't let you do it any other way.''

"I know, but say it's another four or five billion in undervalued assets, if you count in the value of the PegaSys patents and a few other goodies.''

"So?''

"And no debt.''

"We work for PegaSys's profits, not for the banks.''

"What I'm saying here, Scott, is maybe about half the money Shawby needs is represented by PegaSys's cash hoard and by some other pretty nearly liquid assets. All he has to do is round up a buyer and pledge those assets to line up a peepot full of money.''

"In other words, he raises some of the money he needs to buy us by promising to sell off our land, buildings, patents, and other assets as soon as the deal goes through?''

"Effectively, yes. And, if he does, he won't have to worry much about the rest. It won't be easy, but it won't be hard either. He can borrow it.''

"What! How? The man is in hock up to his eyeballs. AIW doesn't have an inch of credit left. It is already carrying a debt load equal to 96 percent of the company's net worth. It is leveraged to the hilt. Shawby doesn't have any assets he can borrow against."

"He doesn't need them. He can borrow against yours."

"Don, are you telling me that AIW, that Shawby, that . . ." Thatcher paused for an unspoken profanity. "That someone can buy my company *with my own money*?"

"Yes, I am telling you that maybe it can be done. Weirder things have happened."

"I don't believe it's possible."

"Hey, Scott, welcome to America, the land of opportunity."

Thatcher shook his head and softly murmured, "Capitalism sows the seeds of its own destruction."

"Excuse me, Scott, I didn't quite hear that. What did you say?"

"Oh, nothing, just a quote from Marx."

"Marx? Karl Marx? Scott, are you feeling OK? I know these things can be kind of a shock. Maybe you ought to go lie down for a bit."

Thatcher, accompanied by Mike, Louise, and the three advisers, had adjourned to his private conference room. The room, which abutted his office, was small and intimate, with seats for no more than ten people. Its dark walnut walls were hung with paintings from Thatcher's prized collection of Chadds Ford artists—Pyle, the Wyeths, and their followers.

Don Banks stood looking out the window warily. It faced east toward the United Nations building, the East River, and Queens. He lowered the venetian blinds and drew the curtains.

Thatcher complained, "Don please leave those open. I like natural light."

"There's a problem with that, Scott. Any eavesdropper with a hundred bucks worth of mail order equipment can hunker down on any roof within ten blocks of this building, point an acoustical reflector at this window, and hear what's being said. You draw the drapes to muffle the sound, to keep our voices from reverberating against the window. After today, any meetings on this acquisition situation should be held in an interior room with no windows. You'll want that room swept for bugs twice a day at a minimum."

Thatcher's eyes flashed. "I will not play childish James Bond games."

"It is going to get worse."

"Not if I can help it."

"You can't help it."

"Oh." Thatcher leaned back in his chair and cupped his arms behind his head. He looked up at the ceiling. "I am a wholly honest man," he said. "It is a failing, I know. Not even the most diligent application of my best-intentioned efforts have sufficed to break me of the regrettable habit of truth telling. Nor have the tireless exertions of lawyers, consultants, competitors, and my own sales force prevailed against my unhealthy appetite for veracity. It is a problem. Sadly having no choice in the matter, I shall be honest, and honestly say that I consider this situation to be a shabby joke in poor taste. At worst it is an unsavory affront to this corporation's dignity. At best it is an annoying gnat to be summarily swatted. However, Don Banks, upon whose advice I rely, tells me that the affair should not be shrugged off so lightly. Quite frankly, I will confess, I don't know beans about this takeover game. I don't know beans about how the Wall Street game is played. I don't know beans about how you investment bankers—"

"With all due respect to my profession and to my colleagues," said Banks, "an investment banker is just a three-card-monte operator in a three-piece suit."

"Well, I knew *that* all along. Anyway, what I am saying is that I, that we, that PegaSys, might need some help from you, Don."

"That is how we all collect our fees, Scott."

"In that case, let us begin to extract some value from them. From yours, Don, and Denny, and Justine."

"OK, what we need to do first—"

Justine, flourishing a scarlet Dior sleeve, interrupted, "What we need to do first is brief you for the press conference."

All eyes widened and turned toward her. Thatcher's eyebrows arched upward, looking like a shaggy McDonald's sign. His moustache twitched. His voice dripped sarcasm. "Press conference. Press conference. You mean you expect me to discuss this matter with some silly twit from the Action News Team?"

"Yeah," answered Justine, "at precisely 5:30 this afternoon, right outside the front entrance of the building. I've already called the *Times*, the *Journal*, the wire services, the networks, and . . ."

"Justine," Thatcher extended the word into far more syllables than it contained. "Justine. I have nothing against the media. Freedom of the press is superior to the alternative. But don't you think we have more important things to do than worry about show business?''

"In Justine's defense," Don Banks said, "at the moment, no. At the moment, having a press conference is about the most important thing you can do. This is a very big story. It is front-page news. It will make the networks.''

"I already checked," added Justine. "This story gets a minute and forty-five seconds from NBC and a minute-fifteen from the other two nets. Don't give me that look, Scott Thatcher, that's a lot of time, an amazing amount of time, for a business feature on prime-time TV.''

"God help us all," sighed Louise. "The second largest computer company in the world. Twelve billion dollars in revenue. Seventy thousand jobs at stake. And it's worth 105 seconds or less.''

Ash, who to his pleased surprise finally found himself confronting a situation more absorbing than Louise's legs, spoke up. "Forget about the seconds. The point, I think, is this. Shawby and AIW have gone public with this thing. Shawby already held a press conference to make the announcement. If he has any sense—''

"Which he does not," interjected Louise.

"He took the opportunity to make himself look good and sound smart and establish himself a lot of credibility with the public and the investment community. Half the fight here is sounding believable, sounding like a winner. Correct me if I'm wrong, Don.''

"No, you're right, Mike. For most people, Shawby is an unknown quantity. He is coming out of nowhere, from a very small company, with a very big offer. Put yourself in his shoes. He needs to make people take his tender offer seriously. He needs them to think he can pull it off. His formal tender offer will probably have all sorts of contingencies in it. If investors don't believe in him, then they will worry about those contingencies. People won't tender their stock if they don't believe that he can succeed.''

Thatcher leaned back. The humble look was gone from his face. "Lesson number one, huh? One of our jobs is to make sure that investors don't believe the twerp can win.''

Justine, bobbing with excitement, answered, "Not *our* job, Scotty, *your* job. You are the big cheese, pal. Numero Uno. You are chief exec of PegaSys. The spotlight will be on you. You have got to make this a personal contest. Thatcher versus

Shawby. The press will love it. The public will love it. It's classic. You built this company with your bare hands. You are the last American entrepreneur. Now it—no, you—are under attack from this obnoxious little predator. This is a fight to the death. *Morituri te salutamus*. Into the arena, gladiators.''

13

BRIAN SHAWBY WAS IN HIS SUITE at the Hotel Pierre on Fifth Avenue. The Pierre had been his preferred hotel since the '60s, when Shawby's attorney, Dick Nixon, kept his apartment on the floors above.

Shawby lay in bed watching the evening news. He sipped cautiously at his drink: three parts water, one part Smirnov, and two Alka-Seltzer tablets. Flying always upset his stomach. Jennifer, as usual, was in the bathroom. She had taken occupancy when they had arrived forty-five minutes earlier.

On the television screen the announcer said, ''Next, a major corporate takeover battle erupted today, pitting two giant companies against one another in what promises to be one of the most fiercely contested battles for control in recent history. Details after these messages.''

Not bad, not bad at all, thought Shawby. *"Giant companies." I like the tone of that. Could do without the fierce battles though. Nick Lee says Thatcher's too much of a sissy gentlemen to get into a fight.*

''Hey, Jennie, come on out of there. The story is going to be on in a minute.'' Jennifer sashayed through the bathroom door. She was wearing a scanty little leather costume. It looked a bit like a nun's frock. She swirled girlishly to show it (and certain other matters) off. Shawby whistled in appreciation.

''Today in St. Louis, the president of American Interdyne Worldwide made a surprise announcement. We will hear from

Sherri McMillian of affiliate KLOT at St. Louis's Lambert International Airport. Sherri?''

"Thank you, Jack. Arriving in his corporate jet on the way to New York, Brian Shawby, president of American Interdyne Worldwide, headquartered here in Missouri, told a surprised group of reporters that his company planned to take over computer giant PegaSys Inc., a corporation five times the size of American Interdyne. Reading a prepared statement, Shawby said . . .''

"Aww, Brian, look at your face there. The green from when you upchucked shows up on television. I told you to let me put some of my makeup on your cheeks.''

"Ssssh, let me hear this.''

". . . the kind of technological resourcefulness and vision that a more diversified company such as AIW can muster. Within the past twelve months, for example, PegaSys tried to acquire one of our leading edge technology divisions. It was this attempted acquisition that called to my attention the unarguable fact that PegaSys could profit from the kind of creativity and excellence in innovativeness in which we at AIW specialize.''

"And you slurred your words. Brian, I told you not to take those Dramamine. They always make you such a sleepyhead.''

"Ssshhh, I said, damnit, hush.''

". . . who will give us PegaSys's reaction from New York. Cindy?''

"Thank you, Jack. It was a grimly smiling Scott Thatcher who met with reporters here in New York today. Referring to AIW and its investment bankers, Lee, Bach and Wachutt, as (and I quote), 'Termites gnawing at the foundations of American technological and industrial leadership,' Mr. Thatcher went on to say . . .''

"See, *he* doesn't look green.''

"Shut up, goddmamn it!''

"Well, you just be that way. I'm going back to the bathroom.''

". . . Hard words, I think you'll agree, Jack.''

"Absolutely, but it's refreshing to hear a man who says what he thinks, Cindy.''

"Yes, and Thatcher has the reputation of a man who does not pull any punches. He lived up to that reputation in response to one of my questions.''

"Mr. Thatcher, you sound like a man ready for a fight.''

"Indeed I am. I didn't seek it, but I will not flinch from it.

If a fight is what AIW wants, then a fight is what AIW will get. Brian Shawby has flung a gauntlet in my face. I intend to see to it that he now dines on a meal of gauntlet burger.''

"You sound like you see this as war."

"I do, and my battle command to all of PegaSys's employees and my warning to AIW is this: let no grass grow where my warriors' horses have trod!"

Jennifer stuck her head out of the bathroom. "And another thing . . . oh . . . oh, Brian, honey, your face is all green again. Poor baby, is your tummy still upset?"

Book Three:
The Instrument
of the Devil

"And now I've told you, and you don't know. That's how it is between us. You talk to me—I talk to you—and we don't know."
                                                                    The Rescue
                                                                    Joseph Conrad

1

LATE IN THE SUMMER OF 1902 A Yankee peddler, a traveler in ladies' unmentionables, passed through the town of Desuetudo, Missouri. During his brief visit he sold six foundation garments, four sets of bloomers, and a particularly effective line of smooth talk to Elsie May Shawby, the more buxom than bright fifteen-year-old daughter of a tenant farming couple. At the time Elsie May was not quite sure what it was that the traveling drummer persuaded her to do. When, some nine months later, the act—and its consequences—were explained to her, she belatedly vowed to be more careful next time.

The Yankee salesman's visit had been so short and his departure so hasty that no one could remember his name. Elsie May, who certainly had the closest contact with him, thought that it was Robert . . . or Robin, or Roger . . . or, in any event, something that began with "Ro." Therefore, after a necessarily abbreviated discussion with her distraught parents, the squalling infant was christened Roger Shawby.

Young Roger Shawby's boyhood was far from happy. Born, as it were, on both the wrong side of the tracks and the wrong side of the blanket, he was the butt of coarse humor and snickering innuendo. Nor were his prospects improved by the fact that he was a black-haired, coarse-skinned child in a town otherwise populated by ruddy-cheeked, fair-haired German immigrants.

Roger Shawby matured into a singularly malignant and devious young man. Always a loner, he skulked through adolescence beholden to none, trusting no one, and viewing the world around him with an unwholesome combination of suspicion and avarice. Along the way he managed to develop certain profitable

121

skills relating to the nimble manipulation of three walnut shells and a pea, the dexterous dealing of marked cards, and the adroit rolling of weighted dice. Like W. C. Fields, Roger never played games of chance.

At the age of seventeen, having graduated with high marks (but universally low esteem) from Desuetude's high school, he managed to secure a position as salesman for the town's principal manufacturing company, the South-Central Missouri Button Foundry, Inc. During the next four years he traveled the Midwest selling buttons, and by the age of twenty-one had become the most successful route salesman in the company. He achieved these results by enticing his customers with irresistible payment terms: double or nothing, high card wins.

Ostensibly as a reward for his accomplishments, but more motivated by the familial concerns of Klaus Fylfot, the founder and owner of the South-Central Missouri Button Foundry, Roger found himself assigned to new responsibilities. Following fast upon the day on which he had expressed his ardor and almost honorable intentions to Miss Desdemona Fylfot, daughter of Klaus, Roger Shawby was dispatched eastward to New York, the Babylon in which the South-Central Missouri Button Foundry, Inc., had never realized a scintilla of success. Klaus Fylfot breathed a sigh of relief when Roger climbed aboard the train, and as it puffed out of the station whispered a prayer that he would never return. That evening, as they went to bed, Roger's mother and grandparents addressed similar requests to the Deity.

Thus it was that, in the verdant spring of 1923, Roger Shawby arrived at Pennsylvania Station, New York, New York. All his wealth and earthly possessions he wore on his back or carried in a twine-wrapped cardboard suitcase clutched tightly to his side. No one contemplating this diminutive, reptile-eyed bumpkin would have predicted that, within the brief span of six years, Roger's wealth would be stored not in a Montgomery Ward suitcase, but rather in the vaults of the Chase National Bank, and that Roger himself would be well on the way to becoming the president of a Fortune 500 company.

Roger launched upon his business endeavors in New York slowly and with care. First he scrutinized the telephone book to discover the location of the city's principal clothing manufacturers. He discovered that they all clustered within an area a few blocks south and west of Times Square. Next, dressed casually, he roamed idly about the streets of the garment district, jotting down observations about each company and noting the names of their owners as they appeared on building directories.

In so doing, he made several perplexing discoveries. First, the streets of the garment district were aswarm with people who looked nothing at all like the tall, Teutonic citizens of Desuetude; on the contrary, the neighborhood was populated by bustling legions of short, willowy, dark-haired folk. Second, their names, unlike any to be found in his hometown, were multisyllabic, full of consonants, and commonly ended with "-stein," "-man," or "-berg." Third, the denizens of the garment district spoke a language that seemed to Roger's midwestern ears to be a curious admixture of English and something only faintly Germanic. And, finally, they all dressed in peculiar clothing of black, wearing tiny, sometimes colorful, swatches of cloth pinned to the back of their heads.

These anomalies baffled Roger. Like any good salesman, he recognized the necessity of looking, speaking, and acting like his customers. But who, he mused, were his customers? What was the cause of their unusual physiognomy, speech, and clothing? It was not until he revisited the area on a Saturday and discovered that every sweatshop in the garment district was closed that he realized the horrible truth. *It was the Sabbath. These people were all Jews!*

Roger had never seen a Jew before. None lived in Desuetude, nor in any other place he had ever visited. Nonetheless, despite his lack of firsthand experience with this accursed tribe, Roger Shawby reckoned himself something of an expert on their perfidious behavior. During his childhood in Missouri he had heard many a Sunday School sermon on the devious behavior, unending cupidity, and cunning scheming of the Jews. Indeed, Roger had been awarded a blue ribbon by his pastor for a theme paper he wrote on the degenerate laws and blasphemous practices of the Jews as embodied in their principal textbook, *The Protocols of the Elders of Zion*.

Three weeks later, his yellow-checked suit freshly dyed black, his gold-plated watch fob hidden away, and his face darkly bearded, Roger Shawby picked up his sample case and went on his first sales call. His target was Emmanuel Belenberg, owner of Belfashions, Inc., and brother-in-law of the nearby Temple Sinai's influential, ultra-orthodox rabbi.

"Whaddaya got ta show me?" asked Belenberg.

"I got but'ns," Shawby (whose business card now read "Schwartz") replied.

"You got but'ns, I got but'ns. Everybody got but'ns. Only I got more but'ns than I need. Who needs but'ns?"

"I got better but'ns and I got a better price."

"So show me."

"Here they are. You ever seen such good but'ns? A bargain at twelve cents the hundred."

"Dese you call good but'ns? Dese? Dese are schlock but'ns, dat's vat dese are. And I pay ten cents the hundred, too."

"So show me."

"Look. Right here in dese bins. Metal but'ns, cloth-covered but'ns, bone but'ns. Ten cents the hundred and better than your but'ns, which are schlock but'ns."

"So vat can I say, you wanna buy pig-bone but'ns from some goyisher momser, you get 'em cheaper than I can sell my cow-bone but'ns. Vat can I say, kosher costs more."

"Vat? *Pig* bone! You say dese but'ns are *pig* bone . . ."

Young Roger soon opened his account with the Chase National Bank, and a large account it was. Into his coffers money poured from three sources: a very small weekly sum generated by his modest salary; a somewhat larger monthly sum representing his sales commission; and a truly enormous daily deposit accumulated from the two cents' difference between the South-Central Missouri Button Foundry's price per hundred buttons (ten cents) and the price Roger charged his customers for "kosher" buttons (twelve cents).

Six months later, the South-Central Missouri Button Foundry had to break ground for a new factory to meet the demand generated by Roger's flow of orders. This factory was, of course, located on land abutting the foundry's principal supplier of raw material, the Desuetude Hog Rendering Works. Six months after that, Klaus Fylfot employed his excess profits to buy the hog works outright.

Roger, with his country boy's distrust of New York's financial community, did not lose a nickel when, in November 1929, the stock market crashed. Roger did not play the stock market. Roger did not play games of chance. Roger believed in the almighty power of cash or, in its absence, the equally almighty power of a stacked deck. However, as the shares of the South-Central Missouri Button Foundry plummeted from eight dollars to forty-five cents per share, Roger calculated that some heavenly power had been kind enough to arrange the cards for him. He was perfectly positioned to do what he had always planned on doing: buying the whole company, lock, stock, and barrel. In January 1930, he returned to Desuetude triumphant, the new owner of the button foundry. The very first of his cringing employees he confronted was Klaus Fylfot.

Klaus listened in despair to Roger's simply stated, forthright proposition: either Klaus gave Roger his daughter's hand in matrimony or Roger would see to it that Klaus starved in the snow. Klaus thought long and hard about which was the lesser of the two evils, and then, in the wee hours of a January morning, having thought his situation through to its logical conclusion, blew his brains out. Roger was keenly disappointed; insurance companies refuse to pay life insurance policies on suicides.

The wedding was in March.

While America sank deeper and deeper into the Great Depression, a bright, new, vigorous, visionary force was stirring abroad. Imbued with the ardor of confident youth, new voices were speaking and new songs were being sung. Specifically, they were singing the *Horst Wessel*. Roger joined the chorus enthusiastically. He enrolled in the Bund and displayed prominently in his office the symbols of the new regime: the fasces and twisted cross.

In February 1935, he and Desdemona were vacationing at Locarno. By coincidence, less than a day's drive south, at Stresa, Roger's two idols had scheduled a conference. Roger, donning his badge and arm band, drove down for the day in the hope of catching a glimpse of them. The drizzling winter rain of northern Italy made the roads slick and treacherous. Roger throttled down to a crawl of twenty miles an hour. Rounding a hairpin mountain curve, he came across a large, black Mercedes limousine tipped over on its side, looking for all the world like a gigantic dead cockroach. Its passengers, a group of uniformed, high-ranking Germans and Japanese, huddled damply beneath an umbrella. Roger pulled over to offer them a lift. They were most appreciative and, during the remainder of the drive to Stresa, Roger held a lively and rewarding conversation with his passengers. There were, he learned, certain supplies that the Reich needed. Oh, not today, perhaps, but soon. And those same supplies might be needed even sooner by the Japanese, who were, after all, desperately short of natural resources. Buttons, yes: particularly brass buttons, since the Germans, Italians, and Japanese were allocating their brass supplies to the fabrication of bullet casings. Meat, too; especially ham canned in small ration containers. Leather as well; pigskin makes fine belts.

By the time he arrived at Stresa, Roger had the two things he most desired in life: an invitation to dine with both the *Führer* and *Il Duce*, and a very large order.

Roger returned to Locarno busting with the virile vigor that a major business coup inspires. That very evening he sired on Desdemona his eldest son, Brain Shawby.

As the volumes of foreign orders mounted, Roger Shawby renamed his company "American Dynamic Industries International." It grew swiftly in size and profitability, and, as it grew, events that made peaceful men shiver made Roger smile: Austria, Guernica, Nanking, the Sudetenland. To his chagrin, the outbreak of hostilities between Germany and Britain halted Roger's exports to the Reich, but his trade with Japan continued unimpeded until 1940, when Roosevelt severed trade relations with that country. By then Roger didn't care. Roosevelt had signed the Conscription Act, the ranks of the U.S. armed forces were filled with young draftees, and every soldier needed buttons, rations, and belts. All Roger needed to do was change the design of the eagle stamped on them.

World War II and, shortly thereafter, the Korean War were good to Roger Shawby. American Dynamic Industries prospered. In particular, its canned-ham product developed a worldwide reputation—as the one and only military ration that soldiers complained of more than Spam. Indeed in chronicling the Korean War, some military historians ascribed the abrupt halt of the Chinese Army at the 36th parallel to the side effects of the tons of defective American Dynamic Industries International rations left behind by retreating Americans.

Roger invested his company's war earnings wisely. Once peace broke out, he rapaciously executed dozens of acquisitions, turning American Dynamic Industries International into the thirtieth company on the Fortune 500 list of the largest industrial companies in America. Coupling an almost supernatural canniness with the blood lust of a true predator, he scooped up plastics companies, uranium processors, construction concerns, appliance manufacturers, television stations, motel chains, and a host of other organizations perfectly positioned to profit from the greatest boom years in economic history. On Wall Street they called him "Jolly Roger"; he was the most feared pirate to sail the seas. In later years, business historians would compare the acquisition antics of latter-day acquisition artists to Roger Shawby's buccaneering legacy, and conclude that their depredations were but pale imitations of the now-deceased master of the game.

In the early 1960s, God (or more likely His adversary) called Roger Shawby to his reward. The legacy he left to his son was an empire. Young Brian Shawby returned from Monte Carlo to don his crown and follow in his father's footsteps. But the crown was the wrong size, and he could not match his progenitor's stride. By the late 1980s two decades of Brian Shawby's peculiar management style had transformed the company, now renamed American Interdyne Worldwide, into the 140th-something entry in the Fortune 500.

Once upon a time, in the distant past, asinine and ill-informed people had criticized Brian Shawby's performance as an executive. Business reporters, investment analysts, stockbrokers, litigious shareholders—riffraff like that. Some used harsh words; more fools they. One had even written that Brian was an incompetent blunderer and had gone so far as to recommend that AIW's board of directors replace him as chairman. Shawby sued him. He lost, but it was the principle of the thing that really mattered.

Of course, now things were different. Now, the carping faultfinders had shut up, and shut up for good. Now they were singing a different tune, now that AIW was back up in the top tiers of the Fortune 500. Now that Brian had successfully taken over PegaSys.

Things began to change the very day he took occupancy of the PegaSys building, booting the weeping loser's bony butt out onto the street. Idly, Shawby wondered what Scott Thatcher was doing with himself these days. Probably drooling in his tea at some home for senile old folk. Well, no hard feelings for the useless old fart. After all, he had turned out be the sort of creampuff pushover that Nick Lee had predicted. No, Thatcher had not put up much of a fight after all. Ever generous in victory, Shawby made a mental note to send him a card come Christmastime.

The rewards of success were estimable. Shawby accepted them with humble pride and a boyish grin. The honors, the respect, the dignity, the stature, the lavish praise, the power, the money, the perquisites, the fast cars, the palatial homes, the nubile young women. He adopted a lifestyle modeled on that of every red-blooded American businessman's hero: J. R. Ewing. Only, unlike the television character, Shawby was never the victim of bad reviews. Indeed, Brian found the unending stream of favorable personal publicity as gratifying as the enthusiastic admiration of world-famous celebrities. The appearances on the Carson show, the dinners at the White House, the hobnobbing with bejeweled socialites, the features in *People* magazine, the features in the *National Enquirer*, the warm attentions of various soap opera starlets, game show hostesses, and a full complement of Warren Beatty's former girlfriends.

Speaking of whom . . . He was in bed with one right now, the blond one with the big boobs, now what was her name? He rolled over and stretched out his hand to grab her tight little butt. Whoops, not there. She must have gotten up to take a leak.

Brian.

Huh?

Briannnnn!

Whose voice was that?

Briannnn, come on and get up, honey.

A sort of nasal whine.

Briannnn, come on, you promised to take me shopping. We've been here in New York for five whole days and I haven't even gotten to one little old store yet. You promised, Brian. Now quit your dreaming and get up, you sleepyhead.

Dreaming?

'Sides, you got that meeting with Mr. Lee at lunch, and you're going to leave your poor little Jennifer all alone for the whole afternoon. And you want to see your ad, don't you? It's in all the papers this morning.

2

This announcement is not an offer to purchase nor a solicitation of an offer to sell Shares. The Offer is made solely by the Offer to Purchase dated October 17 and the related Letter of Transmittal and is not being made to, nor will tenders be accepted from or on behalf of, holders of Shares in any jurisdiction in which the making of the Offer or acceptance thereof would not be in compliance with the laws of such jurisdiction.

Notice of Offer to Purchase for Cash
170,000,000 Shares of Common Stock of

PegaSys Inc.
at
$85.00 Net Per Share
by
AIW Acquisition Enterprises, Inc.,
a wholly owned subsidiary of

American Interdyne Worldwide, Inc.

AIW Acquisition Enterprises, Inc., a Delaware corporation (the "Purchaser") and an indirect wholly owned subsidiary of American Interdyne Worldwide, Inc., also a Delaware corporation, is offering to purchase 170,000,000 outstanding shares of Common Stock, $10.00 par value (the "Shares"), of PegaSys, Inc., a Delaware corporation (the "Company"), at $85.00 per Share, net to the seller in cash, upon the terms and subject to the conditions set forth in the Offer to Purchase dated October 17 (the "Offer to Purchase") and in the related Letter of Transmittal (which together constitute the "Offer").

The Offer and Withdrawal Rights Expire at 12:00 Midnight New York City time on Friday, December 24, of this year unless the Offer is extended.

129

The Offer is conditioned on, among other things, there being validly tendered and not withdrawn by the Expiration Date at least 170,000,000 of the outstanding Shares on a fully diluted basis.

The purpose of the Offer is to acquire control of, and of a majority portion of the equity interest in, the Company.

The Offer is subject to certain other conditions set forth in the Offer to Purchase, which should be read before any decision is made with respect to the Offer.

The information required to be disclosed by paragraph (e)(1)(vii) of Rule 14d-6 of the General Rules and Regulations under the Securities Exchange Act of 1934, as amended, is contained in the Offer to Purchase and is incorporated herein by reference.

The information Agent for the Offer is:

LW Queen & Co., Inc.

384 Adder Avenue
Butte, Montana 59799
(406) 911-9119 (call collect after 5:00 P.M., Pacific Standard Time)
The Dealer Manager for the Offer is:

Lee, Bach and Wachutt Investment Bankers

One Ophedian Street
New York, New York 10011
(212) 555-1111 (collect calls will not be accepted)

3

THATCHER FUMED. EVEN THOUGH he had known for a week that it was coming, the sight of AIW's announcement in Friday's *Wall Street Journal* infuriated him beyond measure. "Cash?" he growled. "I still do not understand how in the . . . [pause], the no-good . . . [pause] can offer cash? Don, you promised me that we would be facing some *flaky* offer of warrants, junk bonds, and watered-down equity. Not much cash at all. Not an all-cash deal. Now where the [pause] are they getting it?''

Don Banks looked glum. He shared this expression in common with everyone in the room except Thatcher, who looked purple. "Scott, I am damned if I know. These bastards are putting $14 billion on the table. I will be dipped if I know where it is coming from."

"Take a guess. Even a guess is better than what we've got."

"I can't make a guess. Anyone who raises real money, and God knows $14 billion is as real as it gets, does it with bank borrowings, lines of credit, debt offerings, asset sales, equity issues, any of that stuff. And when they do, they disclose things to the public, to the Securities and Exchange Commission, to somebody. But not AIW. Hell, AIW isn't even saying they found some spare change in a sock under the mattress. The problem is Lee, Bach and Wachutt. The problem is Nick Lee. He is a clever devil and, I swear to God, the son of a bitch is behind this thing. He's set up some scheme, some plot, and it will be a doozy. If we can figure out what he's up to, then we will know where Shawby is getting the bucks from. Jesus, I would like to know what Lee has concocted this time."

Thatcher's voice sizzled and crackled. "Well now, hadn't you better find out? It would be a rather useful little insight, don't you think? Or do I ask too much of my investment banking firm, which will, I hasten to point out, draw down a minimum of $35 million even if we lose?"

"Scott, with all respect, I have half the talent in my firm tying themselves in knots trying to do just that."

"Then put the other half to work. It'll do 'em good."

"We are doing our best, Scott, and I don't think—"

"Neither do I, Don. My tone is uncalled for. I apologize. I know you and your people are doing your best, and that is all I can ask for. It is . . . I say this to all of you in this room . . . it is that I am a bit shaken by this whole thing. Such ill temper as I might show under these circumstances may be understandable, but it is not productive. If I start to fly off the handle again, will someone please tell me to shut up and take my medication. Look, it's nearly lunchtime, and we've been at this since seven. Let's take a break. I need the time to cool off, and the rest of you need it to clear your heads. We are all getting a bit fuzzy on the issues. I'll have Gladys take your order for sand-wiches. Let's reconvene in . . ." Thatcher consulted his wrist-watch, "a half hour, 12:15. Whoops, wait a second there. I want the sleeves rolled down, the ties tightened up, and the heads held high when you leave this conference room. None of you are to slink about the hallways looking liked whipped puppies. I want you people to look calm, controlled, and cool. Would somebody please help young Michael straighten out his tie there."

Ash's tie was already straight.

Thatcher, accompanied by Don Banks, returned to his office. "I hate," he said, "windowless conference rooms."

"Get used to it. This game has become—"

Gladys stuck her head through the door. "Excuse me, Mr. T.," she said, "but you have a call. I told him you were in conference but he insisted. It's a Mr. Nicholas Lee from Lee, Bach and Wachutt."

Thatcher glanced at Banks, raising his eyebrows in question, and picked up the phone.

"Don't take it," said Banks, too late.

Thatcher spoke into the mouthpiece. "This is Scott Thatcher."

"Good day to you, Scott. I am Nick Lee."

"Yup."

"I thought it good that we talk, you and I."

"I have nothing to say to you. You already know my position. PegaSys is not for sale. Not to Shawby, not to you, not to any-one. I hold AIW's tender offer in nothing but contempt. We have nothing to discuss."

"I think not. We've much of which we should speak. I should much like to meet you face to face. We've never met, you know, and I'd like to."

"You want a meeting, now why would that be?" replied Thatcher. Banks shook his head broadly, silently mouthing, "No."

"That each of us might know the other better. That you might see that my hoof's not cloven; that I wear no forked tail behind."

"Ahh, but perhaps a forked tongue."

"Touché. A man of wit, as I have heard. What say you, then? Brian and I, late today?"

"Brian Shawby will never set foot in this building."

"But he will. And your office too, I think. The day's not far off when he will be there."

"I wouldn't bet on that."

"I have, dear Scott, I have. And steeply too."

"Of course you have, and it will prove to be a losing gamble. You are playing the wrong game at the wrong table this time. PegaSys is not for sale. I will not see this company stripped and plundered. That's your specialty, isn't it?"

"Only one act in a broader repertoire. My own talents are multifaceted, but I excel at high-stakes gambling. Do not hope to play against me and win. No one ever has and no one ever will."

"Then perhaps you would be willing to risk a side bet. Shall we say a bird?"

"A bird? Oh, a bird. Do you mean a crow?"

"Of course."

"To be eaten?"

"Clearly."

"At a certain place?"

"The front steps of the New York Stock Exchange would be the appropriate spot, don't you think?"

"At a certain time?"

"High noon, the day after the tender offer expires."

"Cooked or raw?"

"It will be your lunch, Nick, and I leave the choice to you."

"Done! The wager's set. I'll pluck the bird for you."

"Nick, I hope you choke on the feathers, sitting there eating crow for your Christmas dinner instead of turkey. And speaking of turkeys, you are welcome to share a bit with Brian Shawby."

"He will share little of any bet I win. But we digress; Scott, if you'll not meet with the both of us, surely you'll meet with me."

"A meeting here alone with me . . ." said Thatcher, looking at Banks. Banks grimaced and turned his thumbs down. "Well . . ." Banks threw his hands up, making the football referee's time-out sign. "Well." Banks drew his hand across his throat in a chopping motion, then stood up and began to mimic the contortions of a man strangling himself. "That might not be a bad idea." Banks squeezed his throat harder, his tongue lolling out. "Shall we say first thing Monday morning?" Banks collapsed back in his seat, whistling the *Dies Irae* from the Catholic mass for the dead.

"Saturday I fly to Tokyo. Might I come up late this very afternoon?"

"Nope. I am, as you might expect, rather busy these days. But, if you really think it important that we get together, I can meet you if you come up right now."

"I'd a luncheon planned with Brian Shawby, but doubtless we will lunch again on other days. I'll leave now. You may expect me shortly."

"Good. I'll see you soon." Thatcher hung up the phone and looked quizzically at Banks. "Don, setting aside for the moment the dubious caliber of your acting skills, precisely why didn't you want me to meet with the man? What harm can it bring?"

"Plenty," said Banks grimly. "Everyone on Wall Street will know that you've met face to face with that son of a bitch. They'll know it about five minutes after it's happened, because Lee will put the word out. It will be perceived as a sign of weakness on your part, on PegaSys's part. Everyone will think that you are willing to talk, to discuss, to negotiate. By meeting with Nicholas Lee you are calling into doubt the sincerity of your opposition to this acquisition."

"Piffle. But if it worries you, I'll call Justine and have her put the word out *before* the meeting. You know, 'An irate Scott C. Thatcher summoned the notorious takeover raider, Nicholas Lee, to his office today and administered a stern rebuke. Restating his adamant opposition to the acquisition of PegaSys and the role Mr. Lee's firm, Lee, Bach and Wachutt, is playing in it, Thatcher, ever-righteous in the face of the Lord, scourged the moneylender out of his temple' And so on and so forth."

"Yeah. Well, yeah. Do it now."

"So I shall. Meanwhile, do me a favor, and rustle up the file on Lee and his outfit."

When Gladys announced that Nicholas Lee had arrived and was waiting in the visitor's lobby, Thatcher decided not to send her to fetch him, but rather to go greet him himself. He found Lee sitting immersed in a copy of PegaSys's annual report. Extending his hand, he greeted Lee, "Hi. Welcome to PegaSys. I'm Scott Thatcher."

Nick Lee stood up. He was tall and lean, and bore the grace of a tango dancer. His gaunt, angular face was as sharp as a new-honed ax, and his features were almost Oriental. He looked to Thatcher like a prince from the Arabian Nights. Thatcher could not decide if Lee was extraordinarily handsome, or extraordinarily ugly. Regardless, his presence was powerfully striking.

Lee took Thatcher's hand, shaking it firmly with a warm, dry grip. Smiling, speaking in a soft clear voice, with just a hint of a southern accent, he said, "Let me introduce myself. I am—"

"Nicodemus Liebowitz," said Thatcher.

"Ahh, a small show of strength. Gloves off, is it?"

Nicodemus Liebowitz was born in Newark, New Jersey. When he was ten his father, who was a functionary with the telephone company, was transferred to Lynchburg, Virginia. Neither Nick's father, Conrad, nor Nick's mother, Rosemary (née Thorn), was Jewish. Indeed, search the family tree as they might, neither could ever quite find out why the family bore a name so obviously inappropriate to members of the Anglican High Church.

The young family found life in Lynchburg different from life in Newark. In Newark, no one burned crosses in their front yard.

Nicodemus Liebowitz's school years were an unremitting hell of misaimed anti-Semitic prejudice, insult, and torture. He vowed that he would devote his life to wreaking a subtle and vindictive vengeance—not merely on the citizens of Lynchburg, but on all mankind. After graduating from Yale (where he was denied membership in all fraternities) and before entering the Johns Hopkins School of Medicine, young Nicodemus took a one-year sabbatical. He went to Los Angeles and studied acting. When he returned, his name now legally changed to Nicholas Lee, he adopted a faint, soft southern accent.

"Nicholas Lee, ma'am, of Virginia. I am pleased to meet you."

"Oh, a pleasure, Mr. Lee. Lee? Now, you aren't by any chance related to . . ."

"Distantly, ma'am, distantly," Lee would reply, thinking of Adam and Eve.

It worked wonders. Nick Lee left his past behind him (he didn't even attend his father's funeral). And when, after practicing abroad for a few years, he quit the medical profession to become a financier, no one denied him anything.

"Why this is a charming office, Scott, though smaller than I'd have expected. But handsome, for its size. And these paintings on your walls—is that a Murillo? And there a Tintoretto? And this chalk, surely Palma Vecchio? Infinite riches in a tiny room. Hidden assets, I'll warrant, with values not shown upon your balance sheet. I must redo our valuation, don't you think?''

"Private property, Nick, not corporate. They are part of my personal collection. Like Pegasys, they are not for sale.''

"Ahh, now, that is too bad. I do so love to buy and then to sell things of beauty. That is the difference between us two. You the collector, I the auctioneer. You accumulate, I gleefully dispose.''

"Nick, with such courtesy as I can muster, let me suggest that there are many demands on my time. I am quite busy these days. Undoubtedly you have some topic in mind, some new wrinkle in this takeover offer that you are funding for Shawby. . . . ''

"Funding? I? For Shawby? Perish the thought!''

"No? Well, orchestrating then.''

"Less a conductor than a puppeteer.''

"Shall we continue to trade bons mots for the remainder of the afternoon, or do you have something specific that you want to say to me?''

"So abrupt. To business, then. We made a tender last week to buy your company. The price we pose is not our highest offer; we can pay more, and will if need be. You may seek such defenses as you can find, others who will offer greater sums, and greater still, or perhaps through leveraged buyout try to up the stakes so high as to elude our grasp. You can only fail. Our wealth is limitless for this endeavor. No matter how dear you may sell yourself, you can sell only to us. The die is cast, *jacta alea est*, said Caesar. Thus I say to you, resign yourself. Concede. Abandon a hopeless resistance. Bow to the inevitable. Things will go easier for all—you, your colleagues, all—if you do.''

Thatcher clenched his fists and started to speak. Lee cut him off.

"No, let me say what I would be saying, then you may speak your piece. Circumstances beyond your control—indeed, beyond your understanding, confront you now and are arrayed against you. Do not doubt that sixty days hence when our tender offer falls due, PegaSys shall be ours. Whatsoever you contemplate to prevent it, we have contemplated before you and have with foresight prepared a countermeasure. No action of yours, nor of any man, shall suffice to stop or slow our strategy's remorseless success. At most you can but erect such difficulties which I and mine can with ease of effort surmount. Still, despite my certainty that we shall prevail, I would avoid a trying and tedious confrontation, if I could. We seek victory, not a bloody battlefield, and confident in our victory, we are prepared to be merciful now. Resist me, and in later days forfeit mercy. Surrender today, this week, and I'll show not only mercy but generosity, too. Now here's my generosity made concrete. For you, you'll keep your chairman's role, for who would trust poor Shawby in a job as big as that. Beyond this, I'll give you three seats upon the AIW board of directors. I myself will hold three as well, and between us we will wield a majority, and bend the destiny of the combined organizations to our own liking. And money? Well, of course. Not that it matters to you. But what of your people? What of them? Cash for their loyalty, $100 million to be divided among your senior managers as you wish. Such a sum is only fair, only generous, only merciful if you will only concede.''

Lee reached beneath his suit coat and drew forth a folded piece of paper. Holding it between his long, slender fingers, he offered it to Thatcher. Thatcher sat in unmoving silence. Lee placed the document on Thatcher's desk, took a filigreed gold pen from his shirt pocket, and set it down on the paper. ''Here's a contract,'' he said. ''Sign and you will lose little, and gain all that can be gained. What do you say, my friend, what do you say?''

Thatcher said, ''I say, get out of my office.''

''Come now, let us be friends; yes, be my friend. Sign and I'll be your friend, I'll be your ally. Even more, I'll be your unwearied slave.''

''Get out of my office. Do it now.''

''You'd rather have me as a friend than a foe. I can be a most deadly opponent. I am the spirit of opposition.''

''Get out of my building. Get out of my company. If you are not off these premises in five minutes, I will have the security guards carry you bodily to the street. And take your deal and your pen with you.''

''Keep the pen as a remembrance of the opportunity once had and then missed. Good-bye, Thatcher, I think we'll not speak again.''

''Good-bye, Lee, and if I don't see you again, good.''

4

A GOOD DAY'S WORK," JUSTINE Gold said, looking up with a smirk.

Her husband Harry, lost in the depths of one of the giant bean-bags that Justine used as a proxy for chairs in their very contemporary apartment, grunted neutrally. He was trying to concentrate on a Friday night basketball game that was being imported to his Mitsubishi forty-inch television set with the compliments of Ted Turner and Manhattan Cable Television, Inc.

Justine, fishing for a more interested response to her career and her day's labor, continued, "Yeah, this little baby is going to give Nick Lee and his minions conniptions."

Harry aimed his remote control at the screen, depressed the "mute sound" button, and asked, "What do you mean?"

"Here," replied Justine, "take a look at this." She brandished a half dozen pink pages of double-spaced dark red typescript at Harry who, through a series of yogalike contortions, managed to free himself from his seat and stand to take them. "Written," said Justine, flourishing a set of sharp, blood-red nails, "with my own little hands. Typed by these dainty little fingers."

"What is this?"

"A story I wrote and gave to one of the wire-service reporters. She got an exclusive and all she had to do was insert her own byline right there on the top. It's what we in the trade call a 'plant,' my love."

Harry read:

PEGASYS STRIKES BACK
Chairman Thatcher Blasts Investment Banker
by XXXXXXX

EXCLUSIVE

New York. October 29. An irate Scott C. Thatcher, Chairman of computer giant PegaSys Inc., lashed out today in response to a hostile takeover attempt being mounted against his company by Missouri-based American Interdyne Worldwide (AIW) and sponsored by leading Wall Street investment bankers, Lee, Bach and Wachutt.

Summoning Lee, Bach and Wachutt president Nicholas Lee to his offices for what Thatcher later called a "stern lecture" . . .

Harry read on, pausing only to ask if the part about the side bet to eat crow was true. When he was finished he handed the draft back to her and said, "This is a nasty piece of work, babe."

"That's what I get paid for, hon. Lee will just shit when he sees this tomorrow morning. It's out on the wires now and every paper in the country will run it."

"How come you didn't give it to the *Times* or the *Journal*?"

"They're harder to plant. Of course," Justine sighed, "they will be miffed that I didn't give them a chance at the story. But I'll make it up to them. I'll give them an exclusive when Scotty decides to run for president."

"Huh? Since when?"

"Oh, since about two days after this takeover raid is done with. Thatcher's star material. I'll put him in the White House, just you see if I don't."

"Does he have a say in any of this?"

Justine raised her hand and drew a blood-red nail down the line of her husband's cheek. "What man ever has a say where I'm concerned? You know that by now, don't you, lover?"

Harry nodded his head slowly. Then, asking Justine to remind him that he had to make a phone call during halftime, he went back to watching the game.

Scott Thatcher lay supine on the sofa, reading, his head resting in Olivia's lap. Olivia held her own book in her left hand and with her right gently stroked his forehead. This was how they spent their quiet evenings together, both of them reading, one occasionally stroking the other.

Thatcher was an omnivorous reader. This evening he had returned to one of his best-loved topics, the Icelandic Sagas.

The sagas, true-life histories of Iceland's earliest families from the years A.D. 900 to 1200, thrilled and moved him, touching him deeply in ways that contemporary literature could not. There was a cold and pure power to these tales of distant days, when Viking settlers created a society unlike any known before—a parliamentary democracy rich with freedoms still unknown in most of the present-day world. Its equal and uncompromising citizens (who numbered among their ranks the most fiercely independent women in all of history), confronted their harsh northern island with an austere joy, celebrating triumph, defeat, and even the commonplace things of life with song, poetry, and sharply pointed wit. The Icelanders were Viking merchants, warriors, and farmers (usually all three at the same time) who clung to a fatalistic philosophy of predetermination. None, however, passively accepted the chill inevitability of fate with gloom and resignation; rather, the Icelanders laughed in the face of destiny, defying gods, devils, and men to do their worst. The Norns spin their threads, weaving the fabric of life and death, and each man's and woman's doom is written as they are squeezed from their mothers' wombs; we are all held fast in Wotan's grip and cannot escape; laugh, then, and bite the deity's hand, and bravely fling your challenge at him: *do your worst, oh one-eyed god, for an even greater hand holds you, and your doom is as surely writ as mine.*

The sagas were first translated into English during the late 1800s, deeply influencing Victorian thought, politics, art, and literature. Those held in thrall by the sagas and the haughty, unyielding philosophy they embodied were said to be "in the Northern Thing." Scott Thatcher, in whose veins a strain of fatalistic Calvinist blood still ran, was this evening "in the Northern Thing."

He was reading the greatest of the sagas, *Njal's Saga*. As the tale unfolded, Gunnar, a farmer of great humanity and equally great pride, had fallen victim to the conniving plots of his political opponents. A conspiracy was set against him and Gunnar was unjustly condemned to outlawry. He had either to exile himself from Iceland for a time or risk living outside the law at home. As an outlaw, he would forfeit the protection of Icelandic law, and could be preyed upon, even killed, by whomever wished to attack him. Choosing the safety of exile over the perils of staying with his family and farm, Gunnar rose up one morning and packed his things in preparation to depart. "When he was ready to leave he embraced them one by one. The whole household came to see him off. With a thrust of his halbard he vaulted into the saddle and rode away. He rode down toward Marker River. Just then Gunnar's horse stumbled and he had to leap from the saddle. He happened to glance up toward his home and the slopes of Hidarend. 'How lovely the slopes are,' he said, 'more lovely than they have ever seemed to me before, golden cornfields and new-mown hay. I am going back home, and I will not go away.' '' So Gunnar returned home to face a doom woven upon the very moment that he was born.

The phone rang.

There were four phone lines into the Thatchers' Connecticut estate, all unlisted. One number was for PegaSys business and was known only by key PegaSys employees. One number was for Olivia's work, and was given to her fellow faculty members at Hunter College. One was for friends and was rather widely distributed. And one was for family use exclusively. The line that rang was Olivia's.

She lifted her receiver and said, ''Hello. Yes, this is Livy. Oh. Oh! Joe! Joe Jonas! Joe, how are you? It's so good to hear your voice again. Oh, Joe, let me get Scott on the line. No, no, Joe, he's right here. . . . Joe, can't you get over this silliness? You're grown adults, you've got to . . . What? This is the stupidest thing I have even seen. You are acting like a three year old. So is Scott. You are both babies . . . All right, have it your way . . . Yes, I'm listening. . . . Yes, I've got it. Look, Joe, don't go. Don't . . . Well, at least call *me* again, won't you? . . . Yes, love you, too. Bye now, Joe. Bye.''

Livy hung up the phone. ''That was Joe Jonas.''

Thatcher said nothing, did not even set his book down.

''I told him that I think you and he are acting like absolute infants, refusing to talk to one another.''

''I heard.''

''You won't talk to him, will you?''

''Nope.''

''Not even on the telephone.''

''The telephone is the instrument of the devil.''

''You are an impossible, stubborn man sometimes.''

''The legacy of a moral New England upbringing.''

''You simply are not going to budge, are you?''

''Nope. It's too comfortable on your lap.''

''That's not what I mean and you know it.''

''Yup.''

''Well, Joe gave me a message for you.''

"Emmm?"

"Do you want to hear it?"

"Emmm?"

"He said, and I quote, 'Watch your back, pal. Zeros at twelve o'clock high. Remember Pearl Harbor. Beware of the Nips.' That's all he would say."

Thatcher shot erect, dropping his book to the floor. "Excuse me, Livy, I have to make some phone calls. I'll do it in the study. Don't want to disturb you. I might be awhile."

Thatcher entered his study and sat, lost in thought, by the telephone. Hanging on the wall above him—and not in a particularly prominent place—was a framed, yellowing photograph. The photo showed a very young marine corps lieutenant lying in an anonymous military hospital bed. The young lieutenant's left arm was in a cast, as was his right leg. General Douglas MacArthur, bareheaded and without his trademark aviator's glasses, stood next to the supine lieutenant, shaking his hand and pinning a medal on his chest. A small brass plate was mounted on the photograph's wooden frame: "Second Lieutenant Scott C. Thatcher III. Inchon, Korea. Silver Star."

MacArthur looked older than his photographs. His face was deeply lined, especially around the eyes, and his belly sagged with the droop of the genuinely aged. The young lieutenant had never realized how truly old "the Old Man" was.

The general, who was dressed in battle fatigues, stood next to the bed. He turned to face the PIO photographer. "This OK?" he asked.

"A little to your left, sir. Press your left leg up against the bed. Good, that's it. Half turn. OK, we got it. Go ahead."

MacArthur reached out his hand, taking a typewritten citation and a small velvet box from one of his aides. He looked down at the citation and read, " 'For uncommon valor in the face of hostile fire and at the risk of his own life, Second Lieutenant Scott C. Thatcher III . . .' Thatcher. I know that name. I knew your father, son. Hope you're easier to get along with. Let me look at this thing, here. Lord of mercy! Says you single-handedly charged a tank. Ran headfirst into oncoming machine-gun fire from a enemy tank. Says you jumped on top and fed a grenade down the hatch. Says you saved your whole platoon. Did you really do that, son?"

"Yes, sir, I guess I did."

"We've got a minute or two before these damned feather

merchants make me go somewhere so they can take more pictures. Tell me about it. Tell me what happened.''

"There's not much to tell, sir. It was a couple of weeks after the Inchon landing. My company was assigned to do some mopping up to the north. The captain told me to take my platoon up the road a bit, recon, then come back. Well, you know how those roads are, sir. In places they're worn down, really worn down. So many people walking back and forth on them over the centuries have made them like gullies. They're deep. The one we were on was really deep, maybe eight feet top to bottom. It was raining off and on, so the clay was slick as oil. There was no way anyone could climb up one of those gullies. It was like walking through a canyon. The men and I were marching along in the drizzle. It was a cold, wet day. We had our ponchos on, and we had our M 1s slung muzzle down under the ponchos to keep the water out. We got about two miles up the road, up that gully, and came around a corner. There was a beat-up old Soviet T-34 sitting there, maybe twenty-five meters up the road. A Korean lieutenant was perched in the hatch. I saw him and he saw me. He yelled something and dropped down into the tank. I heard the hatch slam down. Then the tank started rolling toward us. There just wasn't anything to do. We couldn't turn around and run, because he'd be right behind us. We couldn't climb up out of the gully because the walls were too steep and too slick. And we sure couldn't stay where we were. So I just went for the tank. They opened up with machine-gun fire, but they couldn't seem to hit me. Or so I thought. I guess they got me pretty good in the left arm. I remember feeling like I'd bumped into a door or something, but it didn't hurt, and it didn't stop me. All of this happened pretty fast, I guess, because I was running as hard as I knew how. Then I was at the tank, and I dived up on it. I suppose that's how I broke my leg, but I didn't notice that either. I pulled myself up on top to the turret. It was just blind luck that the tank commander forgot to secure the hatch. I lifted the hatch, pulled the pin on a grenade, and dropped it in. There was a thump, and the tank stopped. That's all that happened, sir. Then the men carried me back to sick bay."

MacArthur ran his hand gently across the young lieutenant's forehead, and softly asked, "And what were you thinking about, son? What was going through your mind when you charged that tank?"

"Nothing, sir. I didn't think of anything. I didn't think about it. I saw that tank coming, and, well, it seemed to me to be the only thing to do.''

MacArthur turned to his aides and murmured, ''They all say the same thing. All these boys, the brave ones, all say the same thing. 'It was the only thing to do.' Where would this country be if God didn't send us boys like this?'' Then he looked back at Thatcher and said, ''Well, son, this Silver Star is for you. It probably should have been the Medal of Honor. I'd say you deserve it, and I'd pin either on you with equal honor. I knew your dad, you know. I said that, didn't I? He served with me in the islands, and then in Japan. Colonel Scott C. Thatcher, Jr. Doctor Scott C. Thatcher. Well, he was an iron-willed old cuss with a wild hair up his butt, and he was dead wrong, and he wouldn't shut up, so the lawyers and I had to get rid of him. Sent him home. I didn't care for him at all. But, I will say his boy has done him proud. You are the sort of son anyone would be proud of, even a hard-nosed old puritan like your father. OK, you with the camera. Let's get this over with.''

The photographer waited until MacArthur grasped the lieutenant's hand, then fired his flash gun. He popped another flashbulb into the camera, shoved the Speed Graflex's film advance lever forward, and took a second shot of the same scene. ''OK. I've got it, sir. Lieutenant, we'll have your picture to you in about a week. One copy to your hometown newspaper, two to each of the wire services, and one to the *Stars and Stripes*. Unless you have any problems.''

''No problems,'' the young lieutenant said.

MacArthur shook Lieutenant Thatcher's hand again, smiled affectionately at him, and turned to leave. As he walked away the wounded young man called out, halting him, ''General, I just want to say one thing. My dad was right, and you were wrong.''

MacArthur did not turn to look at him. Instead he raised his jutting chin upward and, addressing whatever deity resided in the skies, sighed, ''Wasn't one enough? Did you have to curse this planet with two of them?''

Thatcher didn't even notice the old photograph. He stared at the telephone, deciding whom he would call first.

Mike Ash tickled his fingers beneath Ivan's chin. Ivan purred, tilting his head back so that Ash could get him . . . ahh, just there. That's the spot. Ivan squinted. His ears folded back, and the tip of his tail twitched with pleasure. Excellent, just excellent. It had taken him a while, but Ivan, ever patient, finally had trained and housebroken this large, ungainly, and quite slow-witted creature.

Mike Ash, whose taste in furniture ran toward the delicate, simple lines of the so-called Williamsburg style, was sitting on a plump blue and white easy chair, his bare feet resting on a low mahogany coffee table. Ivan, of course, was firmly ensconced in his lap. Ash glanced over at the engraved Tiffany ship's clock on his mantle; the clock was a gift given by Thatcher to all his vice presidents in commemoration of PegaSys's twentieth anniversary. Time was passing slowly for Ash. He still had another forty-five minutes before Louise got home from work. It was too early to go to her apartment. *Maybe,* he thought, *I should call her at the office. No, maybe I shouldn't. Maybe I ought to think about this. Think about the problem. No, the problems. Plural.*

There was the sex part. That was a problem. Unexpectedly, Ash had discovered in himself an untapped wellspring of sexuality. His now nearly forgotten years of marriage, the days of occasional, mechanical bachelor sex that followed it, and then the long period of chastity following that had left him persuaded that his sexual appetites were at best tepid. He had (with only a little smugness) considered himself virtually impervious to ardor, and well beyond the age of risk. The sight of a pretty woman aroused in him, at most, aesthetic appreciation. Peacefully at one with himself, approaching in the not-far future the gentle autumn of his life, he felt he could view the mating rituals of others with the dispassionate amusement of an uninterested observer. He did not miss sex, and, perhaps, even felt good about his imperviousness to feminine charms. No midlife crises for Mike Ash. *(Midlife crisis! Joe Jonas once roared, Yeah! Yeah! Know all about it. Brought on by a fundamental, profound existential angst about one's own tenuous mortality, and by an equally fundamental, profound male itch for blonds with big tits!)*

Louise changed things. Ash's monastic self-image crumbled into dust. Saint Michael the Lukewarm metamorphosed into a particularly goatish satyr. To his surprise, possibly to his chagrin, Mike found that he had not only an unquenchable appetite for sex with Louise (and Louise only), but also a dishonorably ingenious aptitude for the act. In all its infinite variations. His enthusiastic craving was boundless, insatiable, and limited only by the durability of human flesh. His talent and creativity seemed endless.

It was Louise, of course, who inspired in him these feats of superhuman innovativeness. Her mere presence in the room, a whiff of her perfume, the very sound of her voice on the phone, made blood rush to his head. There was something in him that tumbled out of control when he approached her. She was like a drug, a potent aphrodisiac, racing through his veins. Addicted, he could not get enough.

Ash treasured self-discipline, and found the loss of it jolting. It put the lie to what truths he knew—or thought he knew—about himself. His passions defied his ability to govern them. In Louise's company he lost self-control, and with it, self-identity. In those increasingly rare moments when he was able to reflect upon the matter, he worried about his stability, and wondered if, after all, he had really managed to avoid the disturbances of midlife crisis.

He had (*that goddamned trip to Greece, goddamn it*) broken off his affair with her. The rift hadn't lasted three weeks. His biochemistry whipped him back to her in a starved frenzy. *I despise myself. No control. No control at all.*

And there was another problem. It is at the age of forty, or thereabouts, that Death first notices you. Stopping on his rounds, he looks you over carefully, sizing you up the way a used-car dealer does a new customer. Then he jots a note in his little black book to stop by your house more frequently. You become part of his regular schedule of appointed checkups.

Ash had passed forty, and been chilled by the Reaper's calculated stare. He felt *time* now, the wind made by calendar pages turning, the tiny tremor of a ticking clock, the winding down of things. He was not old, not by any measure, and surely was fit enough to reckon his future in decades. But neither was he young enough to ignore the implications of his age or forget the mathematics of his future. For example, marriage (another problem, that) and children (add that to the debit ledger as well). Were he and Louise to marry (as he desired) and she to conceive (equally desirable) then he would be . . . how old, when the child reached adulthood. In his sixties. Two children, spaced two years apart . . . still in his sixties. Three, you're pushing your luck, Ash. And what kind of an age is that for a father? Can such a downright elderly—we're talking senior citizen here, pension fund and all—old duffer be a good father? Can he play football with the boys? Can he be anything other than a liver-spotted embarrassment to the girls? Or, suppose he went senile? His grandmother had. She was barely sixty when it happened. Imagine subjecting teenagers to that. "Oh God, look at your dad. He's slobbering. Oh, grossout to the max!"

There are other problems as well, Ash thought, *but let's just begin with those. Louise and I have to talk, my God, we've got to talk.*

Talking was another problem, the biggest one of all. The time had come to confront it. Ash set Ivan down and went to the phone to call Louise.

Louise Bowman stalked like a prowling tiger through the stacks of the PegaSys corporate library, sending legions of dithering clerks scampering in fear. Rounding the shelves containing "Foreign Periodicals—UK to USSR," she copied her prey and descended upon him. Dan Johnson, assistant librarian, flinched.

"Damnit, Dan, this is not enough. I need more, lots more. I want numbers. In numbers there is truth. Do not feed me this qualitative, squishy, touchy-feely crap. Give me numbers."

"Ahh, Louise . . . Ms. Bowman—"

"Look, let me be as clear as I know how. Monday morning, first thing Monday morning, I am on the hook to give Scott Thatcher every piece of information he needs to know about AIW. Everything. All of it. So he never has to ask another question about AIW again. Now, I want to know the size of every market in which AIW participates. I want to know the price of every product AIW sells. I want to know the prices their competitors charge. I want to know shares. I want to know margins. I want to know distributors' markups. I want to know shipping costs. I want to know manufacturing costs. I want to know component costs. I want SG&A. I want to know raw-materials costs. I want to know it all. All, goddamn it!"

"Louise, Ms. Bowman, look. It's not that easy. AIW has seventy different divisions doing seventy different things. It's a can of worms. It's—"

"So what? What do you think we hire smart people for? What do you think we've built this library for, second in New York City only to Citicorp's? You people are supposed to be researchers, so let's see some research."

"It's coming, it's coming. All it takes is time. If you'll just get off our backs . . ."

"OK. OK, I can respect that. OK, you want time, you got time. You want me off your back, you got me off your back. It is now, let's see, 8:15. You have until 9:00 tomorrow night, twenty-four hours—no, you'll need more time than that, make it until early evening Sunday, say around 5:30 or 6:00, for you and your people to produce the material I want.''

"Gee. Thanks, Louise. Thanks a lot."

"Yeah, well, and don't let your people make any plans for going home Sunday night, 'cause I'm going to have plenty more questions once I see the stuff I asked for. Good night.''

"Night, Louise. Always a pleasure working with you."

Louise returned to her office, closed the door, locked the door, drew the drapes, unlocked the file cabinet, removed the strongbox in the file cabinet, went back and double-checked the door lock, unlocked the strongbox and pulled out a pack of cigarettes and a Bic butane lighter. She lit it up and inhaled deeply. *Damn, damn, damn, and damn again,* the forlorn cry of an ex-smoker, fallen from grace when a crisis materialized. *Ugggh, tastes like an old army sock.* She took another drag and, waving her hand through the smoke to dissipate it, sat down at her desk to unenjoyably enjoy the hateful nicotine.

Maybe Mike has the right idea, she thought. *Maybe the trick is not to quit, but just to discipline myself to a certain number. Say, five a day. Well, maybe ten. No, no, no! It's a filthy, disgusting habit and I don't need it and I wish I had never started it and it was just to show off anyway. I'll quit, I know I will, but, oh God, I never smoked a cigarette I didn't enjoy. I wish Mike wouldn't do it when I'm around. Mike . . .*

Mike, now there was a subject worth thinking about as one gratified a secret craving—two secret cravings for the price of one. Michael Ash: first the good news and then the bad. The good news was the sex. The sex was good, amazingly good, and, equally amazing, showed no signs of slackening even after all these months. Louise, like Mike, was taken aback, indeed overwhelmed, by the overpowering urgency of their sexual attraction. She found herself dampening with arousal when in his company. She responded to his merest touch with eager yearning. He satisfied her beyond the bounds of satisfaction, taking her places she had never known existed.

That was good, real good. No arguments from Louise, nor any complaints, on that point. But, in all honesty, that seemed to be all there was to their relationship. It was just sex, sex, and more sex. There was never much time for anything else *(snicker/ giggle)*. But, she wondered, was sex enough? As many times as she had asked herself that question, so many times had she answered, no, it was not enough. Sex for the sake of sex was a sour satisfaction.

The relationship was becoming empty and sterile. The personal warmth at its center was disappearing. With each passing day they seemed to have less and less in common. Now that she thought about it *(let's be cold, objective, and analytical here)*, Mike never spoke to her anymore. Before that first *(wonderful)* encounter in Chicago, she and Mike had had lovely, lively times together. They strolled through the streets chatting endlessly, and broken each other up with wisecracks, quips, and jokes in the office. They had discussed books, movies, cats, cars, parents, apartments, plays, operas, friends, enemies, dreams, disappointments. . . . They had, well, they had *meaningful* conversations.

Now, they only . . . well, no need to go into *that* again.

What was wrong? Was it Mike, was it Louise, or was it the whole relationship? Louise asked herself that question a lot, too. The answer varied depending on her mood, but, most commonly, it was item number two *(this is a multiple choice test, select one item only)*. Self-confident in every business endeavor, Louise lacked certainty in herself. Her personal history provided damning evidence, she believed, that she was not a woman who could attract or sustain real love. She had an unerring instinct for men who would abandon her or whom she herself, to preserve her sanity, would have to abandon. Her predictable preferences were for louses, rats, scums, and crumbs. Not that Mike Ash manifested any of the warning signs of those breeds. *Not yet, he hasn't.*

Of course, the early signs were there. There was something wrong. She wasn't talking to him, not really talking, nor he to her. *Yes, as you might have known, it is going wrong.* If it wasn't, wouldn't they be able to talk? Didn't they have something, anything, important to say to one another? And why had Mike quit saying that he loved her? At the beginning, silly thing, he would say it all the time. She couldn't get him to shut up. Now, he said nothing about love. Early warning signs. It would only get worse. And, sooner or later, she would get hurt again. Hurt badly. Then she would cry—but cry alone, certainly not in front of some god-damned man.

Meanwhile, since a bad end was inevitable, she decided to enjoy the good part. She stubbed out the cigarette and wrapped its remains in a handkerchief. She would carry the evidence of her weakness out of the office and throw it in a litter basket. She picked up the phone to call Ash. His line was busy, but what the hell, he was sure to be waiting for her in her apartment when she got home. Then . . . then . . . *why, that was a nice thought*.

Besides, the disturbing surprise and subsequent tension of AIW's tender offer had made her period late, and she was getting cranky. *Better to think of nice things*.

Louise locked up her cigarettes, opened and shut the door a few times to circulate the air, sprayed her mouth with Binaca, popped two Certs between her teeth, and left for the day.

Standing on the street in front of the PegaSys tower, Louise looked vainly for a cab. It was Friday night in the city. The theatre crowd was in town for supper and a show. No cabs were to be seen.

An enormous two-toned, grey-and-blue Rolls Royce glided silently up to the curb. It was trimmed in garish gold, and had smoked windows. *Gold hubcaps? Dear God! Donald Trump?* she thought. *It's extravagantly tasteless enough.*

A smoked grey window rolled down, and a thin dark face looked out. "Good evening, Ms. Bowman, I should like to talk to you. Step into my car. It will be my pleasure to give you a ride home. My name is Nicholas Lee."

Louise fumbled in her purse as she said, "OK, buddy, this is New York. Smart women don't take lifts from strangers in this town. Not even dumb women." She pulled a small tube out of her purse and pointed it at Lee. "And this is chemical Mace."

"No need, no need for such weapons, my dear. I merely desire to give you a ride—"

"I'm sure."

". . . And speak of career opportunities with my firm to our mutual profit and advantage. I have a rich employment contract already drafted for you to sign."

With one hand Lee held a sheet of paper out of the window, and with the other he extended a pen toward Louise.

"I'm going to count to five," Louise replied, "and if you aren't out of here, pal, you get Mace in the face."

"Silly girl, riches and wealth can be yours, and power too. Buying and selling deals. Why act as factotum to an aging master when you your own master can be? Lee, Bach and Wachutt need such souls as you. Come, join us. Sign here. Serve us and be served. We will guarantee—"

"One, two . . ."

"Occasions of easily won wealth are rare."

"Three, four . . ."
"Good night, poor foolish woman, and farewell!"
"Five!"
The window was up, and the Rolls purred luxuriously away.

5

THE HOUSE STOOD, AS IT ALWAYS had, staring somberly toward New York Harbor, its grim granite back turned on the financial district, its iron-grilled windows hung with heavy burgundy drapes, and its sober facade illuminated only by the flicker of what were surely the last functioning gas lamps on the island of Manhattan. The house was *The* House—The House of Morgan, Teech & Kidd, New York's oldest and most elite investment bankers.

Some said The House was built a century and a half ago. Others claimed it was far older. No one knew; or if any did, they would not tell. Its origins, like those of the firm within, were lost in antiquity. Abe Lincoln was known to have used Morgan, Teech & Kidd to underwrite bonds during the Civil War; there was some ambiguous evidence that the Continental Congress had done the same during the Revolution; indeed, in the archives of the New York Historical Society there was a water-stained and barely legible memorandum from Peter Stuyvesant that might, just might have been a plea that Morgan, Teech & Kidd syndicate shares in his New Amsterdam Company. It is, however, an absolute certainty that, high on the wall and deeply engraved in ageless stone, there are inscribed in the deepest chamber of the Great Pyramid of Cheops, hieroglyphics that translate as follows: "Project Financing Underwritten By Morgan, Teech & Kidd, Investment Bankers." Of course, most people think this inscription to be a waggish prank. Most people.

On the southern tip of Manhattan, where the value of a foot of land is enumerated in tens if not hundreds of thousands of dollars and construction engineers contrive to pile as many concrete highrise stories as is physically possible on every one of those feet, The House of Morgan, Teech & Kidd stands a mere five floors high. The House itself is fronted by a great sweeping lawn—a green island of grass and trees, bounded by a high stone wall, alone in a sea of concrete. Traversing this lawn is a narrow driveway, not of asphalt nor even macadam, but rather of good, honest, hand-laid cobblestone. At the head of the driveway stands the bronze-doored portico of The House, and before that door wait, day and night, a groom and a doorman. The groom stands ready with a bucket of fresh water, the doorman with a crystal decanter of fine Portuguese sherry. They and their predecessors have stood there with water and sherry since November 14, 1893. It was late in the evening on that date that Ukiah Kidd, the last surviving founder of the firm, hobbled out to his waiting barouche, remarking to his assistant, "I plan to be away for some time. When I return, I shall require water for my horses and a glass of sherry for myself." He was never seen again, but Morgan, Teech & Kidd being the kind of firm it is (and Kidd himself having the kind of reputation he had), the partners of the firm thought, and still think, it the course of wisdom to be forever prepared for his return.

Within The House are the high-ceilinged, wood-paneled offices in which Morgan, Teech & Kidd's three hundred employees and its forty-nine partners work—or rather, fifty partners, the fiftieth being Ukiah Kidd, currently on sabbatical. The partners and the staff do two things and two things only: underwriting, the principal business of the firm, and corporate financial counseling, a secondary service tolerated only to the extent that it ultimately leads to underwriting. As the rest of the Wall Street financial community decadently plumbed the fetid depths of such repugnantly ungentlemanly activities as trading, arbitrage, lending, or (most loathsome of all) commodities brokerage, Morgan, Teech & Kidd remained aloof—profitably dedicated to the purest expression of the underwriter's art.

Suppose that the chairman of a major corporation wished to raise $50 million by issuing one million new shares of stock—an admirable wish, but difficult in execution. For to whom would he sell the stock, and how? Would he call his friends, neighbors, and relatives? Would he take an ad? Might he stand in Maiden Lane wearing sandwich boards, with a sheaf of shares in his hand? No, selling such things is the role of the underwriter. He (and at Morgan, Teech & Kidd, the function is most assuredly male) buys the stock from its corporate clients and then resells it at a modest markup to its customers, buyers who typically are other large corporations, banks and pension funds. From such markups, usually less than a dollar or two a share, the investment banker profits handsomely—unless, of course, the stock in question has the regrettable attribute of not being salable at the price contemplated.

As relates to this latter distasteful possibility, Morgan, Teech & Kidd's philosophy was best evidenced by an enlarged reprint of a cartoon that hung on Don Banks's wall. The cartoon portrayed an elderly executive seated at his desk, lecturing a young man who obviously had just recently been hired. "Smathers," read the caption, "should you fail we will have you shot. We do this as a service to our clients."

On that Friday evening, Don Banks was pondering the likelihood of his partners shooting him as a service to Scott C. Thatcher. Denniston Howe, PegaSys's lawyer, sat across the desk from him, studying the cartoon and contemplating a similar fate. After six or seven consecutive hours of frustrating, fruitless work on the AIW takeover raid, they had reached the point where they were not so much talking to one another as talking to themselves.

"Writers get writer's block," Banks muttered. "Do investment bankers get underwriter's block?"

"Or lawyers, litigator's block?" Howe groaned.

Banks leaned back in his chair and gazed up at the ceiling. Like a child reciting its catechism, he again repeated the litany of improbabilities surrounding the takeover raid. AIW, a company with neither cash nor credit nor credibility, claimed that it was going to be able to raise $14 billion to pay for PegaSys. AIW's investment banker, Nick Lee, had held a press conference that very morning to announce that AIW would secure the funds without having to borrow, float junk bonds, or sell equity—all mathematical impossibilities, given AIW's balance sheet. Further, Lee had stated that "the funds are being secured at this very moment"—but had refused to explain how. Another anomaly: AIW's tender offer was open for sixty days rather than the traditional thirty. And, finally, $14 billion is a sum sufficient to cause more than a ripple in the world's financial markets, but the staff of Morgan, Teech & Kidd had not been able to find a scintilla of evidence that such an amount was being raised, moved, hoarded, or otherwise made available to anyone associated with the takeover. It was more than strange, more than bizarre, it was miraculous—possibly requiring, in Banks's opinion, an invocation to either the powers of light or the powers of darkness.

Summing up the sentiments of 349 of the most astute minds on Wall Street, Donald Banks sighed, "This whole thing is as queer as a plaid rabbit."

Denniston Howe, for his part, turned over the glum legal and political situations. The courts had long since become tired of the takeover game and impatient with the players. They would no longer call "time-out" whenever asked. The law offered little hope for PegaSys in fending off AIW.

On the political front, PegaSys's outlook was equally grim. Howe had been utterly unable to enlist the support of any political officeholder on PegaSys's behalf. For this, he had Scott C. Thatcher to thank.

Most businesspeople go to extremes to curry favor with the political community. They give money, they authorize their companies to create political action committees, they dispatch their juniors to attend countless boring rubber chicken dinner fund-raisers, they work silently behind the scenes for aspiring candidates (of the right persuasion), and they always find a kind word to say in public about incumbent officeholders (of any persuasion).

Scott Thatcher was not most businessmen. He held lawyers in low regard; most politicians being failed lawyers, his antipathy extended to them as well.

Thatcher had not had a charitable word to say of any president since Dwight D. Eisenhower. Eisenhower was not a lawyer, and Thatcher had remarked kindly on his golf game. The Kennedy clan never forgave him for terming their Cuban adventures the "Bay of Pigheads." During the Johnson regime he vocally opposed both the war in Vietnam and the war on poverty, viewing one as an ethical, and the other as an economic, blunder. Nixon gave Thatcher a prominent place on his White House enemies list; Thatcher responded by remarking to the *New York Times* that it was "an honor no less elevated than the Nobel Prize, but less arduous to obtain." As for Jerry Ford, Scott publicly speculated that Ford was walking evidence of the sensitivity of brain tissue to repeated sharp blows. Thatcher told Jimmy Carter to his face that he was uncertain that his elevator went to the top floor. Of Ronald Reagan he publicly concluded that his whole administration reminded him of something right out of a fairy tale—specifically, ''Ali Baba and the Forty Thieves.'' Most recently, President Bush had been termed by Thatcher as a typical Yale man, decorative and well bred, and good for nothing but decorating and breeding.

As with the President of the United States (and, naturally, all his appointees), so was Thatcher with senators, congressmen, governors, assemblymen, mayors, and even ward heelers. None took his wrath and criticism kindly, and none could be looked to for help in fending off AIW's raid.

Howe groaned, ''Ahh well, we can't expect much help from any government agency at all in stopping AIW—not Commerce, not Justice, not Defense, and not the SEC. Shit, the goddamned Russians could be behind this takeover, and the President would just smile, sign a waiver on the company's strategic technology, and let it happen. There's no politician in the country who wouldn't like to see Thatcher squirm. Christ! Why can't Thatcher keep his mouth shut about the folks in power?''

Banks sighed deeply. ''How long have you known Scott, Denny?''

''Oh, five or six years. And just professionally. It can't be said that we are personal friends . . .''

''Denny, don't feel bad about that. You've got to understand that Scott has got this thing—this phobia—about lawyers. Some people don't like snakes and some people don't like spiders and Scott Thatcher doesn't like lawyers. They make his skin creep.''

''Thanks a lot.''

''Sorry. I suppose I could have phrased that better. But look, lawyers are Thatcher's personal bugaboo. His definition of a lawyer, which I can quote from heart, is, 'A chameleonlike biped capable of instantaneously changing its colors to adapt to any background. Like other members of the reptile family, this animal is fast, slippery, cold-blooded, carnivorous, and has a poisonous bite.' ''

''You're telling me that I don't have my client's professional respect.''

''Denny, it's not just you. It's any lawyer. Learn to live with it. It's not personal. Anyway, if you don't know him well, the thing you have to understand about him is that he is a totally honorable man. He sees himself as—in fact, he really is—the last standard-bearer for all the old virtues. Integrity, honesty, fair dealing, objectivity, unflinching candor, truth—''

''Motherhood and the American way.''

"Uh-huh. All that stuff."

"What a pain in the ass."

"Ain't it the truth. All our lives would be easier if the old bastard just had a little larceny in his heart. Just a little, that's all I ask for."

Howe shook his head, stood up, and stretch. "Don, I don't know about you, but I'm worn out. We aren't accomplishing anything. I'm ready to go home, rest, and air my brain out. Maybe we'll come up with something fresh after we've let this thing sit for the weekend."

"Right. Let me just call Scott at home and give him a quick update." Banks reached back to the telephone on his credenza and punched in Thatcher's number.

In Connecticut, Thatcher sat in his study jotting down notes from the calls he had already made that evening. The study was dark, lit only by a single lamp on the antique rolltop desk at which he did his paperwork and by the cold blue light of a computer terminal that linked Thatcher to PegaSys's electronic mail service and its Olympia computer system. He was just preparing to call Banks when the phone rang.

"Thatcher here."

"Hi, Scott. This is Don. I've got Denny Howe here in my office with me. Hang on a second and I'll put you on the squawk box so we both can talk to you."

The phone went silent in Thatcher's ear as Banks pushed the buttons needed to activate his speakerphone. While waiting for the pair to come back on the line, Scott opened his desk drawer to find a fresh pad of paper.

"You there, Scott?"

"Yup."

"Good. You know, I can hardly ever get this damned squawk box to work. The telephone system has gone to hell since the government broke up AT&T."

As he spoke, Thatcher noticed a faint flickering out of the corner of his eye. A message was coming in on his computer terminal.

"Well, Scott, Denny and I have been here all afternoon, and we have come up with a few ideas. None of them are really profound; but . . ."

Thatcher leaned over and looked at the glowing screen. The message read, " > MR. THATCHER, HANG UP. THAT CALL IS BEING TAPPED. REPEAT, THE CALL IS TAPPED. THIS IS WINTERGREEN, AND I KNOW."

". . . we do have one that might slow down Lee. Scott, are you still there?"

"Yes, but, ahh . . . we, I mean, I can't talk right now. Let me call you at home tomorrow."

"Scott, time is short and if we are going to make any progress—"

"I said tomorrow. Good-bye now." Click. Click. Buzz.

In New York, Don Banks looked at Denniston Howe and said, "Now I wonder what the hell that was about."

In Connecticut, Scott Thatcher's fingers flew over the keyboard of his terminal as he tried to reestablish contact with Wintergreen. But Wintergreen was gone and would not answer.

"He's here!" yelled Roy Knight. "I've got you, you little . , , what? Aw hell, he's gone again."

Milo Skoropadiskyj, Knight's assistant and PegaSys's deputy manager for computer security, swung around in his chair looking querulous and asked, "What are you talking about, Roy?"

Knight glared from behind the screen of his computer terminal, his face white with frustration. "Wintergreen. It was Wintergreen. I've been waiting for him. I knew he would come back. I knew it wasn't over between us. Oh yes, I've been waiting. I've been watching. And then, suddenly, there he was, right in the middle of our electronic mail system. I was sure I'd track him down this time, but he just sent a short message somewhere and then disappeared. Goddamn it, I thought I'd be able to trace him to his lair, but he was too fast for me."

"Roy, calm down. Are you letting this guy get to you?"

"Get to me? Don't be silly! Get to me? Me! Roy Knight, let some pathetic little amateur hacker get to me?"

"Well, I mean you seem to be spending a lot of time trying to track him through the network, and—"

Knight shrieked, "I don't want to talk about Wintergreen! Got that? I don't want to talk about him!"

"OK, OK," Milo said soothingly, changing the subject to something less likely to rile Knight. "What say we send out for some Chinese?"

6

On what would prove to be a very bad Sunday, Mike Ash awoke in a very good mood. Somewhere along the route lying between his resolution to force a redefinition (or rather *any* definition) of his relationship with Louise, and the actual moment at which he planned to live up to that resolution, an opportunity for procrastination had raised its smiling face. If you were to ask Ash to portray the face it wore, he would have sketched out a lopsided version of the ubiquitous "Have a nice day" symbol.

He had been sitting, that Friday night, in Louise's apartment, waiting for her return from the office. As he waited he rehearsed, revised, and rerehearsed his speech. "Louise, sometimes I think you just use me like a service station. I can't . . ." *No. Wrong tone. Too confrontational.* "Louise, some months ago you told me to stop saying that I love you. Does that mean that . . ." *If you begin by putting the blame on her, you'll screw it up.* "Louise, will you marry me? I . . ." *Can't do that cold. You've got to build to it.* "Louise, when we are in bed together, what are we doing? Are we making love? Or are we just fucking?" *No good. She hates to talk about sex. Besides, sex isn't the issue.* "Louise, I don't think you know how badly I was hurt by that fling of yours in Greece. Although I didn't say anything at the time . . ." *Do you really think you can talk about that without screaming? No, you cannot talk about that without screaming. Choose something that won't make you sound like a jealous jerk.* "Louise, I know it's hard to concentrate on our personal affairs, on our relationship, with this takeover raid going on." *Not bad. Perfect, in fact. It positions both of us as neither the bad guy nor the good guy. Continue the theme.* "We both love PegaSys and we both love Scott, and neither of us wants to see

158

either of them hurt. We've been working our asses off and just haven't had the time to confront . . ." *Confront? Wrong.* ". . . think about ourselves." *Much better.* "And to think about where we are going . . . from here. . . ."

And with that, the happy face of procrastination beamed from ear to ear. For who could possibly be so smugly self-centered as to worry about their own trivial personal affairs when the fate of a great business enterprise was at stake? Certainly not Louise. She was woven into the very warp and woof of PegaSys's fabric. To ask her to distract herself with the issues that Ash wanted to raise was . . . downright unfair. Indeed, when he thought of it, was it not the case that by worrying too long and too hard about his relationship with Louise, Ash himself was doing a disservice to his company and to Scott Thatcher? Given the enormous intellectual burdens involved in fending off AIW's raid, how could anyone be expected to do his best unless he gave the raid and PegaSys's defense against it his full and undivided attention? Neither Mike nor Louise could be reasonably expected to sort out their personal lives while the takeover was looming. Both were the sort of people who put their lives and hearts into their work. Both found the idea of PegaSys being subjected to a hostile tender offer emotionally wrenching. *That's it, that's it. Emotions! We are spreading our emotions too thin. Between PegaSys and our relationship, we are trying to handle too much.* It just made good sense to wait until the fight between PegaSys and AIW was resolved. Once it was over, then they would be able to sit down and have the talk that Ash had been planning on having that night. Besides, he was feeling far too horny to put his heart into a conversation that might just result in his being kicked out and sent home to an empty bed.

By Sunday, having spent a fair amount of Saturday recovering from his Friday evening exertions with Louise, Ash felt like a new man. He had persuaded himself that his lackluster work and (at best) third-rate contributions to PegaSys's takeover defense was an unfortunate by-product of trying to handle one too many powerful situations. Now that he had diagnosed the situation, he was ready to fix it. Brimming with a newfound enthusiasm for his job, Ash decided to spend Sunday afternoon in the office catching up on his work.

A cold, grey November rain slicked the streets of Manhattan. Ash, a habitual loser of umbrellas, got soaked as he dashed from his cab and into the PegaSys lobby. Wiping the water from his face, he strolled over to the guard station and penned his name in the log that all employees were required to sign before entering and leaving the building outside of normal business hours. He quickly scanned the logbook to see who else was in the office. It was a large complement. Roy Knight, of course, but then as near as anyone could tell, Knight lived in the computer room, with his vacation home being the security office. Most of the shareholder relations department was in as well; they were readying a mailing blitzkrieg Thatcher had ordered for the coming week. Miscellaneous managers and munchkins from any number of operating departments were also at work. And, good news, virtually everyone from the library. Ash had hoped that some of the library staff would be around, because he needed some information about AIW and Lee, Bach and Wachutt.

He took the elevator up to the nineteenth floor and got off. The area around the elevator lobby was filled with cleaning equipment and wheeled trash bins. A small army of uniformed cleaning people bustled about, bearing brooms, brushes, and mops. Ash paid little attention to them. Mostly brown, mostly short, mostly dark-haired, and most assuredly not of Anglo-Saxon origin, they were members of New York's invisible class of service workers. Not everyone in the much-vaunted "service economy" is a banker, broker, or computer programmer. Indeed, most are janitors, waiters, and clerical menials.

Sunday is the day on which weekend janitorial crews clean New York offices. On Monday through Thursday, janitorial workers usually begin around 6:00 or 6:30 P.M.; they empty trash cans, cursorily dust desktops, and quickly damp-mop lavatories. The crews take Friday and Saturday off, returning on Sunday afternoons to clean up Friday's debris and to give the offices they maintain a thorough scrubbing.

Ash weaved his way through the maze of pails, buckets, and trolleys to the PegaSys library. He pushed open the glassed double doors and scanned the room. Things looked grim. The acrid odor of white-collar burnout hung in the air. Desks were piled high with styrofoam coffee cups; ashtrays, just cleaned by the janitorial crew, were overflowing again; and wadded balls of paper littered the floor around recently emptied trash cans. The library staff watched Ash's entrance with the dull, hostile eyes of hunted animals that have been pursued too long.

"Hi, guys," he said, looking around for the chief librarian. "Is Ann here?"

One of the junior staff replied, "No, she stepped out for a minute to get some fresh air."

"Been here long?"

"It's one of Midnight Mary's projects."

"Ah. My sympathies. Been at it long?"

"All weekend. Nonstop. Two all-nighters in a row. Louise said to be ready for her this evening. She's coming in to review what we've got."

"Well, Louise can get a bit obsessive, you know."

"I know. We all know. God knows that we know."

"Well, look, I'll try to keep out of your way. I just want . . . well, look, is Dan around? I'll talk to him."

"In the back. At the CompuStar terminal."

Dan Johnson was asleep. His head slumped on his arms, his arms slumped on the keyboard, he slept the dreamless sleep of an utterly depleted man. Ash looked at him, wondering whether or not to just let him rest. On the promise that it was better to awaken him than let Louise find him, as it were, asleep at the switch, Ash reached out his hand and gently shook Dan's shoulder.

Johnson shook his head and groaned. "Urrgh. No more, God, no more, they don't publish statistics on net imports to Albania, Louise, please . . . uh. Oh, it's you, Mike. What time is it?"

"About 3:00."

"Morning or afternoon."

"Afternoon."

"Day?"

"Sunday."

"Aw shit, she's going to be here in an hour or two."

"Yeah, that's why I woke you.'

"I'm ready for her. By God, this time I am fucking ready for her. I've got it all. There is no number in the known universe that we don't have. You want to know the atomic weight of the molecules in the plastic that AIW uses for coat buttons? Wait a second, I've got it right here. How about the model of the watch Shawby gave to his chief accountant when he retired in 1983? It's in the stack on Ann's desk. The number of doorknobs in AIW's executive suite . . ."

"Dan."

". . . is precisely . . . huh? What?"

"You're out of control, Dan."

Johnson's shoulders fell slack and he shook his head morosely. "You don't know what that woman can be like. She eats data like Godzilla eats Tokyo. And she's always hungry. I don't think I've ever worked harder in my . . ."

"You want some coffee, Dan?"

"Yes, black. Intravenously if you have the equipment."

A minute later Ash returned with an oversized styrofoam cup full of hot black coffee. Johnson had calmed down and was looking a bit abashed. He took a deep drink of coffee and said, "Sorry for the outburst, Mike. It's just that sometimes people don't appreciate what we do down here. What we go through. Nothing against you. You're one of the few guys from the top floors who even seem to give a shit."

"No, that's not so. I think everybody respects what you folks do—what all the corporate staff do. Even Louise. Especially Louise. Look, I'll drop a word in her ear. Try to get her to cut you guys some slack."

"May I be honest?"

"With me? Always."

"Then the only kind of rope that bitch is going to cut for anyone who works for her is the hanging kind."

"Ahh . . . Well, look, I'll see what I can do for you anyway."

"Thanks."

"Meantime, I need a favor. Nothing major, but, I need some qualitative stuff on AIW. Not any hard data or numbers. Feed that stuff to Louise, she understands it better than I ever will. What I'm looking for is the softer stuff, you know, kind of touchy-feely. Background articles on AIW—personalities, organization, culture, anything like—"

"Aw, hell! We had reams of that stuff piled up. We got it for Louise, but she refused to look at it. All she wanted was numbers. So we threw it out. I bet it's still in the trash cans out front. Let's go see."

But, of course, the trash cans were empty. "Hey," asked Johnson, addressing the staff at large, "anybody see what happened to all that junk on AIW we tossed out? Mike Ash here needs it."

After a general groan, one of the younger librarians spoke up. "Yes, one of the cleaning people got it. Just before Mr. Ash came in. He dumped it all into one of those big canvas bags they hang on those little pushcart things. He's probably still on this floor; when he left I saw him turn down the hall toward security. You might still catch him if you hurry. You can't miss the guy, he's some sort of Oriental—with a crew cut and wearing cowboy boots."

Ash trotted out of the library and hurried along the long L-shaped corridor that led to the security department. He turned the corner. Ten yards down the hall, a uniformed member of the janitorial crew was pushing a cleaning trolley toward him. The man was Oriental, and, yes, was wearing sharp-toed cowboy boots.

"Excuse me," Ash called out as he walked forward, "I want to look in that trash you've got there."

The janitor looked up, frowned, and began to move backward, tugging the trolley with him.

"Excuse me. Yeah, you, wait a minute."

The man picked up speed. Farther down the hall, behind the retreating janitor, Ash saw Knight come out of the security office. Knight was holding a can of Orange Crush in one hand and with the other was trying to manipulate a heavily overloaded wedge of Famous Ray's pizza toward his mouth. Idly, Ash wondered how Knight managed to eat so much food and still stay thin as a rail.

"Hey, look. Stop right there, fellow. I want that trash."

The Oriental looked furious. He reached beneath his grey work coat and began pulling out . . .

Knight was walking forward with his head back, a long string of mozzarella dripping towards his mouth.

. . . something shiny. It was metal . . .

"I am an officer of this corporation and you'd better stop. Who is your superior?"

. . . and long, like a gun barrel . . .

Knight's mouth was now tilted directly toward the ceiling. The pizza went in just as he collided with the janitor. The janitor spun toward the wall. The wall erupted. Ash heard the ringing in his ears before he realized that there had been a very loud explosion. A cloud of plaster blew outward into the janitor's face, the fragments blinding him. Knight threw out his gawky, uncoordinated arms in an awkward attempt to keep his balance. A half-dozen ceiling tiles, jarred loose by the force of the blast, rained down. The janitor reeled to the right, away from Knight's windmilling arms. His head bounced against the corridor's opposite wall and he collapsed in a limp heap.

Ash walked forward very cautiously, staring with amazement at the prostrate figure lying at Knight's feet. And staring with equal amazement at what he still held in his hand. It was the biggest handgun Ash had ever seen. Nickel-plated, ivory grips, a twelve-inch barrel, and a caliber suitable for Rambo.

"My hands are deadly weapons," said Knight. "It was the NSA, you know. They make you take all this spook training. I suppose I should have them registered. They teach you how to kill a man with a rolled-up newspaper."

Ash's ears rang. He couldn't concentrate.

Knight continued, "You know, we have a glitch here. I think maybe there is something wrong."

Ash muttered, "No shit."

"Yeah, really. This guy has a gun."

"I can see that. Why don't you take it away from him before he wakes up? He's going to wake up in a bad mood, you know."

"Good idea. Let me see, now. If I remember right, you can totally immobilize a man with his own belt. They teach you these things at the NSA. I think, you loop here . . . then down this way, then . . ."

"You're strangling him, Roy."

"No, no. See, you put it around his neck to keep . . ."

"He's turning purple, Roy."

"Oh wait, I forgot. Here, let me start over."

Three tries later, Knight actually did manage to get the job done right. In the meantime, Ash's head had cleared and the ringing in his ears had stopped. He had also managed to reach a conclusion or two.

"Roy. Roy, listen up. Do you know what I think this guy was up to?"

"Yeah, sure. He was raiding the office trash baskets. And probably everything else he could get his hands on. He's probably working for Shawby—or more likely Nick Lee—trying to get hard copy of our plans for countering the takeover. I'll put money on the fact that there are a dozen more just like this guy in the building right now."

"Ah . . ."

"I'll call the cops. Meanwhile, we've got to get this building sealed up tight as a drum. And someone should alert Thatcher. But you've already figured that out, haven't you?"

"Ah . . ."

"Look, you go downstairs to the guard desk. They have all the building monitors and control systems on that console there in the lobby. Tell 'em to shut down the elevators. They can do that from the fire alarm override panel. You know, whenever there's a fire alarm, all the elevators immediately go to the ground floor and then stop. Have them put a man outside the garage entrance, too. That's *outside*, Mike, I want him on the outside. Don't let anyone go down into the garage. Whoever is running this little operation probably has a getaway truck down there and may be armed. Just tell someone to wait outside and if any vehicles leave to get their license numbers. OK, Mike? We're just talking routine stuff here. Got it?''

Ash, who was seeing a side of Knight that he had not known existed, nodded in dumb affirmation. *Who,* he thought, *would have believed that this nerd actually is a competent security guy? Jesus, leave it to Thatcher to hire the ones who turn out to be surprises.*

"One other thing, Mike. Call me when you've got the building sealed, and leave the line open. And, for God's sake, if any of these people come down the stairs, stay out of their paths. I'll leave it to you to point the police in the right direction when they show up. Probably take 'em five or ten minutes. Meanwhile stay cool, you're doing fine so far.''

Am I hearing this right? Knight, nerd Knight, is all of a sudden John Wayne on the beach at Iwo Jima telling the troops to . . .

"On your way now, Mike.'' And Ash, shaking his head in wonderment, followed the orders of the man in charge.

Mike Ash had never seen so many police in one place at one time in his life. Twenty-nine stood in front of the elevator banks. Of these, twenty would be stationed in the PegaSys building's elevators; five others would ride up to the top floor and sweep down story by story; and the remainder would stand on guard by the elevator doors in the lobby. Two more were stationed by each fire exit—the exits emptying into the main lobby as well as those leading outside the building. Another dozen uniformed patrol officers, each of whom bore a riot gun, stood on the sidewalk outside looking menacingly efficient. Grey police barricades blocked the streets around the building.

Two plainclothes officers in charge of the silent, surprisingly efficient police cadres stood by the guard desk. One was on the phone, speaking to Knight. "Mr. Knight, this is Detective Ryerhurt in the lobby. All my people are in place and we are ready to begin the operation. Yes. Yes. Your Mr. Ash has called everyone who signed the entrance log and told them what's going on. Yes, he told them to stay in their offices and keep the doors locked. Yes, we have your people's locations and office numbers. No, we will be careful with them; there will be no trouble. OK, then, we are going to start. I am reactivating the elevators—now!''

Twenty elevators wooshed open. Twenty police officers

dropped to their knees, leveling pistols at the open elevators. They were empty. The policemen entered. The doors closed. Things were under way.

Ash turned to Ryerhurt, a tall, athletic man who looked precisely like the toughest cop on a made-for-television movie about very tough cops. "Mr. . . . ah, Detective Ryerhurt. Who's handling the garage?"

"My partner and I. I'm glad you asked. We'd like you to come along and help us identify any company vehicles that may be down there."

Ash had been feeling redundant and ineffectual. He was pleased to have something to do, to be someone other than the passive bystander who accidently uncovered the crime, to have some active role in this adventure that he could tell Louise about. Flanked by Ryerhurt and his partner, whose name Ash didn't catch, he marched resolutely toward a metal door leading out of the main PegaSys lobby.

Three flights of stairs lay between the lobby and the garage, which was the lowest level in the PegaSys building. The garage level was used to house four company limousines and a handful of utility vehicles. It was also the place where major deliveries were received. A freight elevator extended from the basement garage to PegaSys's highest floors and was also used for access and egress by the janitorial staff. The police had ordered that this elevator remain deactivated. They did not want an unknown number of armed men congregating in or near it.

As they stood at the top of the stairs, Ryerhurt reached out his hand to Ash's shoulder and whispered, "Metal stairs. Take off your shoes. If there is anyone down there, they won't hear us coming."

The three left their shoes by the door and began to descend. On the second level down, Ryerhurt waved Ash behind him, taking out his pistol. Ryerhurt's partner did the same. Now in the lead, the two plainclothesmen silently glided to the bottom level.

There was no door at the foot of the stairs, which opened directly onto the garage floor. Ryerhurt slipped out to the right. His partner moved to the left. Ash, the last on the floor, was between them. He watched the two officers edge forward slowly and, rather ill-advisedly as it turned out, decided to keep abreast of them.

Halfway across the garage floor, the trio noticed the man. The man had already noticed them. They could tell because he was pointing a rifle at them. Or rather, because the three were standing far apart, he was pointing the rifle toward the center of their small group. Which is to say, at Mike Ash's chest.

"Police officers. Drop the weapon." That was Ryerhurt's voice. Ash, who found himself suddenly numb and nearly petrified, glanced right. Ryerhurt was in a crouch, both arms locked in front, pointing a .38 police special at the man with the rifle.

The man with the rifle didn't move. It was dark in the garage, and the man stood in the shadows. He was not tall, but he was broad-shouldered and perhaps a little bowlegged. He held the rifle as though he knew how to use it. Ash peered at him, trying to make out his features. The man was Oriental.

"Come on, pal." Ryerhurt's partner was speaking. "Half the cops in New York are outside the building. Put your gun down."

Ash's eyes flicked right. Ryerhurt's partner had found a pillar and was hidden three-quarters behind it. Ash envied him.

"Nobody's been hurt and nobody's going to be hurt, so just set that weapon down and everything will be fine." Ryerhurt again. "The judge will probably let you off with a misdemeanor if you set that rifle down. That's the kind of city it is."

The man with the rifle had no place to go. Ash could see that. There was a wall behind him and another to his left. To his right, a big white delivery van blocked his way. Large red letters on the van spelled out "Eastern Superior Services," and smaller letters read, "A Division of Seppuku Ltd." The man with the rifle looked at the van for a second and concluded that it was too far to run. Ash concluded that there was no place for him to run either. Too bad.

The man spoke. He had a heavy Oriental accent. "I want the guy in the middle as a hostage."

Ash remembered a story about Hollywood—back in the old days, when tyrannical producers ruled the roost and aspiring actresses auditioned for roles lying on the "casting couch." It was said that one young starlet was cast in a very bad movie being shot under very bad working conditions with a very bad crew. The situation was so awful that, at long last, the frustrated starlet finally cried out to the director, "Who do I have to fuck to get out of this movie?" Ash considered the story to be a fine parable for his present situation.

Ryerhurt's partner spoke. "No hostages. You don't want to turn this into a hostage situation, pal. That means Feds and the tactical police and all sorts of crap. You don't want that. We don't want that. Let's just keep it simple. You put down the gun, we bring you in. We read you your rights, you call your lawyer. The lawyer comes, you go see the judge. The judge gives you bail, you go home. The lawyer cuts a deal with the D.A., and you cop a plea. Very clean, very simple, and no worse than getting a traffic ticket.''

The man with the rifle was silent. Nobody moved. Ash studied the man. He wore a thick belt with an intricate turquoise-and-silver buckle. Ash stared at in fascination. It took his mind off things.

Ryerhurt's partner again. "Look, no lie. Somebody spotted a guy stealing stuff upstairs and called the cops. We got what, how many do you think, Ryerhurt, officers upstairs?''

Ryerhurt replied, "An easy forty policemen are in or around this building. Maybe fifty.''

"Yeah, fifty or so. So look, there is absolutely no way you are going to get out of here. And like I said, why do you care? I mean all we can charge you with is stealing garbage. What court is going to put you in jail for stealing garbage? Come on, don't be a chump, don't make this into a big deal. Put down the gun.''

The man lifted the rifle. Ash felt a surge of adrenaline jolt his system. The man turned the butt of the rifle toward Ryerhurt, squatted down slowly, laid it on the floor, rose, and stepped back. Ryerhurt said to his partner, "Put the cuffs on him.''

Ash gasped, drinking in huge deep breaths of air. For who knew how long, he had forgotten to breathe.

"You OK, Mr. Ash?''

"Who do I have to fuck to get out of this movie?'' Ash whispered.

"What say?''

"Fine. I said I'm just fine.''

Ryerhurt's partner had handcuffed the man and was patting him down for other weapons. He yelled over to Ryerhurt that the prisoner was clean. Turning the now disarmed gunman to face the wall, he reached down to examine the rifle. He lifted it with both hands and cried out, "Holy Mother of God! Hey, Ryerhurt, Mr. Ash, come over here and look at this.''

Ash and Ryerhurt walked to the end of the garage. Ryerhurt took the rifle from his partner's hands and examined it with an almost reverential air. He held it up for Ash to look at. "Know what this is?''

"No. I haven't held a rifle in my hands since I was drafted into the Army. They got me just about a year after I joined

PegaSys, oh, more than twenty years ago. They gave us AR 14s back then. Let me look at this one. Christ, though, that thing has got a big bore, doesn't it?''

"Mr. Ash, big bore is an understatement." Ryerhurt broke the weapon open and extracted a gigantic bullet from it. "This round is a .470 Nitro Express. This gun is a Heym 88-B safari rifle with a Schmidt and Bender scope. This weapon costs more used than my car cost new. You can knock down a water buffalo with this gun. Or an elephant. Big game. Knock them down. Stop them dead in their tracks. Do you know what would have happened if our friend here had shot you with this thing? It wouldn't have put a hole in you. No, not at all. Instead, you simply wouldn't be here anymore. It would have blasted you into a fine red mist. There wouldn't be anything left except a bloody fog and some fragments of meat.''

Ryerhurt's partner added, "A bit like a phaser on *Star Trek*, only noisier and less sanitary."

Ash blinked. Ash screamed. Ash dived at the handcuffed prisoner. He slammed the man's head into the wall fast, fast, fast, one, two, three times. Before either of the two detectives could move, Ash had him down and was straddling him, his fists locked together, battering the Oriental's face with the pounding, furious frequency of a jackhammer. Ash was still screaming, and the blood from his fallen victim spattered muddy strings across his shirt. It took the strength of both policemen to pull him off.

The wrestled him over to a utility sink and held his head under the cold tap water until he stopped struggling. He was soaking wet again—the second time that day.

Ryerhurt asked, "You OK, Mr. Ash?"

Ash croaked, "Yeah. Yeah. OK. Cigarette. One of you guys got a cigarette? Mine are all wet." He giggled, then caught himself, and stood quietly while Ryerhurt's partner fished an unfiltered Pall Mall out of his pocket. He sparked a Bic lighter and Ash inhaled, filling his lungs with smoke.

"Jesus," said Ash, "Jesus. I . . . oh shit, I'm sorry. I haven't . . . Christ, I can't even remember the last time I hit someone. Oh, fuck! God, how could I do that? Look at the poor bastard. I can't believe I did that. Jesus, like some sort of crazy animal. Look at him."

Ryerhurt glanced over at his partner and nodded.

Ash continued, "How do you guys do it? How do you put up with some nut pointing a gun at you? How the hell do you keep control? How do you keep from killing them all? My God, if you hadn't pulled me off, I know I would have killed the son of a bitch. I would have drunk his goddamned blood. I was going to do it, I swear I was going to. Jesus God, but I am sorry. I . . . I didn't know I could do something like that. Aw, look at the poor bloody bastard.''

Ryerhurt's partner answered, "Here, take another cigarette. You went through the first one faster than I've ever seen. Now, let me tell you something. It happens. That's all, it happens. There's more violence in the world than nice people know, and it happens all the time. It's bad when it happens, but it happens. Sometimes it happens to nice people, and sometimes it's nice people who make it happen. I don't care if you're Mother Teresa, you can snap and go crazy and do bad things just the same as some wigged-out junkie in the South Bronx. I don't care if you're a nice guy or even a cop. It happens to cops too. Good cops, not a blemish in their records, real good cops with ten or twenty years of service. Then one night some punk draws down on one and we find this real good cop up to his elbows in blood and barking at the moon. And if we can keep it out of the newspaper, the department shrinks will put the guy on pills and a six-month leave and call it temporary insanity. And later that real good cop will go back on duty and have another ten years or whatever without a blemish on his record. It never happens again. So, what is it, Mr. Ash? No one knows. I think maybe it's that we all have an animal in us, say a dog, and we keep the dog on a leash. Whether we know it or not, we're watching that dog all the time and holding its leash real tight. But every now and then, some people get shocked or scared or something so badly that they forget about the leash, and let the dog go. That dog is a guard dog and a killer dog, Mr. Ash. When you let him go, he is going to destroy whatever is threatening his master. But what the hell, Mr. Ash, I'm not a shrink, I'm just a big dumb cop. What do I know?''

Ash, calmer now and far more rational, sighed, "Yeah, well. Look, thanks for getting me off him before I got into more trouble than I'm already in.''

In an innocent and honeyed tone of voice Ryerhurt said, "Trouble? Trouble, Mr. Ash? Why should you be in trouble? If anything, you should be commended for helping my partner and me subdue an armed and violent suspect resisting arrest.''

* * *

Ash had dried off. The recently arrived Thatcher, however, was dripping wet. And mad. He leaned into Ryerhurt's face and growled, "Yakuza? What in the name of all that is holy is a 'Yakuza'? I thought it was one of those whirlpool bath things. Or maybe a cowboy movie star of my youth, Yakuza Canutt."

"The Order of the Chrysanthemum," Ryerhurt replied. "Organized crime Japanese style, Mr. Thatcher. Kind of like the Mafia, only worse. You can tell them because they're all heavily tattooed—backs, shoulders, buttocks covered with exotic designs. Most of them are missing a finger or two. Whenever one of 'em screws up, he chops off a joint and gives it to his boss in penance. I used to think being a Catholic was tough. Anyway, they're the worst in the world, Mr. Thatcher. They make the Colombian drug crowd look like Girl Scouts. They started showing up in this country over a decade ago, mostly on the West Coast. They only started moving into New York this year."

"Sort of like Toyota's strategy back twenty years ago, huh?"

"I wouldn't know about that, sir. I'm a Chevy man myself."

"Hmpf! So, what are you telling me is . . . what?"

"In a nutshell, sir, it's this. There were eighteen of them in the building. They showed up at the same time as the regular cleaning crew. One of them went to the janitorial crew boss and said that unless he wanted his widow to have trouble feeding his orphans, he'd keep his mouth shut. The crew boss really had no choice. All of the Yakuza were armed. All of them bearing exotic weapons. Heavy firepower. Too heavy. Really stupid, expensive, overpowered stuff. Not the sort that experienced American thugs use."

"It is enormously comforting and extraordinarily refreshing to hear that the Japanese still have something they can learn from American expertise. And basic, individual craft skills too."

"Yes, sir. Well, the Japanese always have had a problem with handguns. Headquarters tells us it has something to do with their culture. Anyhow, all of the suspects had accumulated substantial collections of documents that your people assure us are not only very sensitive, but also never would have been thrown out. Moreover, we have found locked file cabinets and office safes forced open on several floors, and their contents fairly obviously rifled. I suspect we will get a substantial number of fingerprint matches."

"So we've—I mean you've—got them cold."

"Yes and no, sir. Usually our experience with the Yakuza is that they jump bail. We suspect that they hotfoot it back to

Japan, but, of course, we get no help from the Japanese police in tracking them down, much less extraditing them. We're told that the Yakuza is a pretty substantial organization over there, and that it is openly active in politics. So we get no cooperation at all on Yakuza matters. It's the same with every police department in the United States.''

"So deny them bail.''

"Not my department, sir. But off the record, the Yakuza keep the top criminal lawyers in the city on retainer. They always get bail.''

Thatcher's voice was rising, "There is something sadly awry with the political and legal system in this benighted city. It is that wretched, lazy, screw-loosened mayor! That slack-minded, slack-jawed monument to ineptitude. Koch was bad enough! This one makes Koch look like Lincoln! Ash, get his Honor on the phone!''

Ash made a conciliatory gesture. It had no effect. He made another. It didn't work either. He said, "Now, Scott, you know how you and the mayor get on. He really doesn't like you . . .''

"Nor I he. No matter, I will have words with him on this travesty. Even he, distracted as he is with foreign policy, nuclear regulation, the workings of the Federal Reserve Bank, and whatever other excuses he can muster for forgetting about the affairs of the city he was elected to serve, even he, even he cannot wholly overlook the fact that one of this city's premier corporations has been burgled, pillaged, and plundered, and that the perpetrators will likely escape free as a summer's breeze! Get. Him. On. The. Phone.''

"Scott, he won't answer. He has refused to talk to anyone from PegaSys since you accused him of bribery.''

"Oh, piffle. I never accused the man of taking a bribe.''

"No, worse. You accused him of paying bribes.''

"And what, pray tell, would you call it when he offers up hundreds of millions of dollars in debt and taxes extracted from the pockets of honest citizens to give to any corporation that threatens to move to Hackensack if they'll only stay in the city? Bribery, unadulterated, unabashed, and unrepentant bribery. That's what I called it and that's what it was. The phone, Michael. Reach out for it, pick it up, and get me that miserable man. Do it now.''

Ash did as he was instructed. Muttered a few words into the instrument. Winced and held it away from his ear. With a hand over the mouthpiece passed it to Thatcher, saying, "For heaven's sake, Scott, don't insult him."

"Of course not," said Thatcher. He smiled sweetly, took the phone and spoke into it. "Hi there, bunny brains . . ."

7

TOKYO: STREETS PERPETUALLY gridlocked with honking traffic; skies sweaty brown with pollutions; elevated trains packed to overflowing and clattering with a deafening din; pocket parks and playgrounds, once green but now greyly layered with industrial debris; stores and shops, perpetually holding going-out-of-business sales, their garishly packaged goods overflowing onto the pavement; sidewalks teeming with tensely scurrying hordes of tiny men and women, looking for all the world like laboratory animals on a treadmill; tawdry nightclubs, strip joints, and massage parlors with gimlet-eyed barkers in front and hard-edged women inside; neon lights and fast-food joints; neon lights and pornographic movie theatres; neon lights and corporate skyscrapers, neon lights and more neon lights. Tokyo: the Queens (borough) of the Orient.

The distance between Narita Airport and downtown Toyko (and specifically the Hotel Okura) is roughly the same as the distance between Chicago and Milwaukee. The price of a taxi ride at about $5 per mile, may be calculated accordingly. Brian Shawby blanched when Nick Lee stuck him with paying the fare.

Lee also made Shawby pick up the tab for dinner. Dinner for three cost nearly $500, even though Jennifer, having dashed to the ladies' room after her first encounter with sushi, had left well before the main course. (Shawby tracked her down some hours later, happily ensconced in a Kentucky Fried Chicken franchise, one of the flagship businesses of Jardine Matheson. Jardine's is thought by some to be the old-line Hong Kong trading house that served as the model for James Clavell's novel *Noble House*, a book that, curiously enough, discusses fried chicken not at all).

Setting aside Jennifer's runamok shopping spree, which added a measurable burden to his nation's already weighty trade deficit, Shawby's first four days in Tokyo cost him $3,000 cash out of pocket. It all added up alarmingly quickly: meals, taxis, tips, drinks, hotel rooms, admission fees, and his rather surprising first encounter with the traditional Japanese fortune-telling technique that Lee had insisted on introducing him to—an experience that involved the fortune-teller examining, manipulating, and reading the lines, texture, and patterns not of his hand, but of another appendage entirely.

Now, considerably poorer and by no means wiser, Shawby, led by Nick Lee, was on his way to meet Okinakao Hidetake, shogun of Seppuku Ltd. After crossing Seppuku's enormous white-on-white lobby, they entered one of the blinding chrome elevators. Lee touched the topmost button on the elevator's control panel and a computer-generated voice, repeating itself in six languages, spoke back to him confirming the number of the floor he selected. The elevator lurched upward, rose, and stopped on the third floor. The computer announced this fact in six languages. A handful of Japanese office workers trotted into the elevator, elbowing Shawby to the back. The elevator climbed another few stories and stopped. In Japanese, English, French, German, Spanish, and Mandarin Chinese, the elevator lectured the passengers on where they were. More Seppuku employees pushed into the elevator. Shawby caught a sharp elbow just below his sternum. The elevator paused and, in all six languages, recounted the floors upon which it was planning to stop. Then up it went, this time managing to make it to the twelfth floor. Shawby and Lee had forty-eight floors to go. The elevator, in flawless, impersonal digital tones, began speaking again. This time, in addition to litanizing the floor it was on and the floors it planned to visit, it rebuked its passengers for standing too far apart. "People riding elevators," it ordered (six times in six languages), "make room for other passengers. Important business must be conducted and our workers must travel from floor to floor. Please stand more closely together." Shawby collected two more bruises from jutting elbows.

By the thirtieth floor, the elevator's various pronouncements, requests, and commands were consuming a bit more time than Dan Rather's opening story on the CBS nightly news. Moreover,

Shawby was beginning to feel like a punching bag in a karate academy. Then one of the Japanese passengers made a serious mistake—he drove his elbow into Nick Lee's ribs. Lee growled a dozen words in Japanese, and a circle immediately cleared around the two Americans. On the very next floor, all the Japanese passengers evacuated the elevator, each punching in a code on the control panel that erased his or her request for a higher floor. In Japanese, English, French, German, Spanish, and Mandarin Chinese, the elevator announced, "This elevator is now in express service. Next stop will be top-floor executive suites."

Shawby, rubbing his bruises, looked at Lee and asked, "What did you say?"

"I merely observed that as a guest of Okinakoa Hidetake, I was disappointed at the impoliteness of his workers and would remark upon it to him during our call."

"Well that sure seemed to scare the hell out of them."

"Thus my intent. Were I a Seppuku employee, such a threat would frighten me."

"I'm going to be covered with bruises from where they bumped up against me."

"They will do that to any Westerner given the chance. 'Accidentally' elbowing *gaijin* is merely a peculiar artifact of the culture. It's not personal."

Okinakao Hidetake's office was not on the top floor, it *was* the top floor. Few foreigners, however, were permitted to learn this fact. The elevator exited on a reception area the size of a handball court. Decorated with burnished aluminum and rosewood, the reception room had only one occupant, a stunning, petite, young Japanese women, beautifully dressed in a flowered kimono. She immediately stood up and bowed gracefully to the two Americans. In lilting but perfectly accented English, she said, "You must be Mr. Lee and Mr. Shawby. Our company is very honored to receive you. My name is Mariko. If there is any way I may serve you, please tell me." Her smile displayed the most utterly exquisite set of dimples Shawby had ever seen. He began to picture any number of lurid ways in which she could serve him. "Now let me make you some fresh tea, and I will tell Mr. Hidetake of your arrival. He awaits you most anxiously." With tiny, swaying steps Mariko disappeared behind one of the four doors leading off the reception lobby.

One of these doors led to Hidetake's personal conference room. The other three led to the various and quite different offices he used for work and for entertaining (or intimidating, as the case might be) his guests. The first of these four offices was the one in which Hidetake spent most of his time, especially when meeting with his underlings. It was bare, indeed spartan. Its only furniture was Hidetake's desk, his chair, and a handful of hellishly uncomfortable hard-backed seats for those unfortunate enough to have to spend protracted periods of time with him; the sole decoration in this office was a tall glass case containing his ancestral swords and Hidetake's own officer's pistol from his days with the imperial army. The second office was more lavishly appointed; he used it for meetings with executives from other Japanese companies. This room was decorated in understated good taste; its walls were hung with drawings and watercolors by Tensho Shubun, Sessku, and Ike No Taiga, among other Japanese old masters; its chairs were well upholstered; its floors were deeply carpeted; and its bookcases displayed a sizable collection of popular, contemporary business texts—for example, such recent Japanese bestsellers as *The Key to Understanding World Competition Is the Zionist Conspiracy*, *How to Work with Women Now That Their Time Has Come* (the tone and substance of this latter volume being best communicated by its dust jacket, a photograph of a naked and plumply provocative female derrier) and, of course, a complete selection of the translated works of Tom Peters, *In Search of Excellence*, *A Passion for Excellence*, etc., etc., and etc. The third office was reserved for meetings with foreigners.

It was into this office that, moments later, Mariko summoned Lee and Shawby. As they entered, she dropped another incalculably graceful bow and said, "Honored sirs, I am available to act as translator for you if you wish." Lee replied that there was no need since he himself spoke Japanese fluently. Mariko set down an exquisite pastel Imari tea service, bowed, and began to leave. As she backed out of the office, Shawby watched her wistfully, thinking of gentle spring rains, blossoming flowers, fluttering butterflies and certain improbably athletic exotic acts.

Hidetake's third office was long, narrow, and dim. It was completely bare except for the woven reed mats that covered the floor, the two-foot raised dais at the far end of the room, upon which Okinakao Hidetake knelt, and a small teak table that stood before him. Hidetake wore a dark blue kimono decorated with an intricate yellow geometric pattern. His sheathed ancestral swords lay on the teak table in front of him. He watched silently with hooded eyes and an unreadable expression as the two Americans approached him.

Lee stopped a yard from the dais, bowed from the waist, and fluidly slipped into a kneeling position that exactly imitated Hidetake's. Shawby, operating under Lee's instructions to do exactly as Lee did, also bowed (an act that he found un-American) and knelt slowly. His tortured runner's knees popped explosively.

Lee spoke, rattling off rapid Japanese with what seemed to Shawby to be great eloquence. Hidetake spoke more slowly, his voice hoarse and guttural. When Hidetake concluded, Lee turned to Shawby and said, "Hidetake-san says he offers you his warmest personal greetings. He says that he is honored beyond measure to have an American executive of your stature illuminate his company with your presence. He says that he has long watched and admired your career from afar, and that, like all Japanese businessmen, he holds AIW in the profoundest respect and deepest admiration. He hopes that this first meeting between you and him is the beginning of a long, cordial, and profitable relationship between Seppuku and AIW, and that it will lead to a close relationship."

Shawby looked up at Hidetake and then said to Lee, "Yeah. Well, tell him I said the same sort of flowery crap. Then ask him about the money."

"In time, Brian, in time."

Hidetake and Lee again exchanged words, "Brian, he asks if your trip was good and if you have had a pleasant and enjoyable stay in Tokyo."

Shawby morosely swirled the dregs in one of the Imari tea-cups and muttered, "Tell him that if I have to drink another cup of green tea I'm going to puke."

Lee spoke at length, making a number of utterly uninterpretable gestures. Hidetake replied and Lee translated. "He has arranged a visit for our party tomorrow to Kyoto and he has assigned his personal bodyguard to guide us. On the day after, he himself will join us on a walk up Mount Fuji. This is a great honor, Brian, and I can assure you that these are unquestionably the most beautiful sights in Japan."

"The most beautiful sight in Japan is that little Nip piece out front. Two days with her is a better deal. Ask him if he wants to trade for Jennifer."

"Brian, you try my patience. I will thank Hidetake-san for the esteem he bestows on us and tell him that we will be ready at 6:00 in the morning. When I finish you will, I repeat, you *will* smile and bow forward politely."

Shawby did as he was told, and for the next half hour, Lee and Hidetake chattered unintelligibly back and forth. Occasionally Shawby, bored to distraction and squirming uncomfortably as his legs went to sleep, would look questioningly at Lee. Lee responded by answering tersely, "He says things are right on track." Or, "We've got no problems." Or, "I'll fill you in on the details later."

Finally, Lee and Hidetake finished speaking. Hidetake made a swift, nearly imperceptible bow forward, signaling that the meeting was over. Lee rose gracefully, and with equal grace, bowed in response. Shawby tried to get up, but found his joints in furious rebellion. Lee lifted him and, holding Shawby behind his neck rather as ventriloquist holds his dummy, forced his head forward into a bow. "Fuck, Nick," said Shawby, "how the hell do these Nips manage to sit like that all day? Are they built different from white men or what?"

Lee said nothing, but merely draped Shawby's arm around his shoulders and led the hapless, stumbling captain of American industry out of Hidetake's presence.

Hidetake, his poker face unmoving, watched them leave. Then, speaking softly to himself in the perfect English he had learned during his postwar education at Cornell University in Ithaca, New York, he muttered, "Asshole." Then he smiled and laughed. His laugh sounded like the rattling of scorpions in the dark. He was thinking of something he would like to do to Shawby; it was something he had learned as a lieutenant with the Kempeitai; it was something that involved hungry rats and a naked, staked-out prisoner.

Downstairs Lee and Shawby exited through the revolving doors and walked out on to the street. Lee stepped up to the curb and waved a taxi out of the congested, swirling traffic. Shawby stood back idly watching the passing crowd. He noticed a burly, broad-shouldered figure making his way toward the Seppuku building. The man was Japanese, muscular, and bowlegged; he had a bristling crew cut. His face was bruised, scraped, and heavily bandaged. Around his waist he wore a thick leather belt fastened with an elaborate silver and turquoise buckle. As he approached the Seppuku building's entrance, the man spotted Shawby and strode over to confront him. Brandishing a fist in Shawby's face (Shawby noted with dismay that the unfortunate man seemed to have recently had his pinkie finger amputated), he gruffly barked, *"Eigo o hanashimass Ka?"*

Shawby looked toward Lee for assistance. But Lee's back was turned, so he cautiously answered, "Ah, no, I am an American."

The man thrust his chin up into Shawby's face and, in heavily accented English, demanded, "You got anything to do with a company called PegaSys?"

Shawby, taken aback, was inadvertently honest, "Yes, I do. How did you—" The remainder of Shawby's statement were abruptly interrupted as the Japanese man drove a knee into Shawby's groin and a fist into Shawby's nose. Shawby was out cold well before he bounced off the sidewalk.

After a short wait, Mariko ushered another guest into office number three. This visitor was wholly impervious to her delicate charms, preferring far meatier women. He was the senior secretarial envoy for Far Eastern trade, technology, and exports, Union of Soviet Socialist Republics.

His Japanese was better then Nicholas Lee's, as was his command of the protocols and graces of visiting Japanese executives. He was a professional. Consequently, it took him a full quarter of an hour to get to the three sentences that summarized the reason for his visit: "Mr. Hidetake, my nation understands that you may be contemplating a certain investment in a certain company in a certain foreign country. I have been instructed to advise you that the very highest levels in my government wish to participate in this investment. In addition to assisting you with funding, Moscow will be pleased to grant to Seppuku Ltd. certain valuable trade preferences and import rights relating to certain technologies that you might access through your investment."

Hidetake smiled, nodded, and said, *"Hai!"*

The word *hai* translates as "yes"; but in Japanese, "yes" is ambiguous and can mean either "Yes, I agree," or "Yes, I understand." Upon the shoals of this ambiguity have countless Western businessmen foundered.

The Russian asked, "Will you make a portion of the transaction available to us?"

Hidetake smiled, nodded, and replied, *"Zensho shimasu."*

This phrase translates verbatim as "I will do my best." It can also mean "No way, José."

"How soon?"

"Kakyuteki sumiyaka." Meaning literally "with the greatest possible speed," or, alternately, "shortly after hell freezes over."

The senior secretarial envoy was seasoned in the ways of the East. He sought clarification and, after some effort, got it. With clarification came certain names and addresses—Brazilian names, Taiwanese names, Swiss names, Saudi names, Swedish names, Thai names, and, along with many others, the quite British names of Messrs. Quint and Claggart, solicitors of Queen Street, London, EC4R, 1AR.

Shawby groaned, slowly opened his eyes, and tenderly touched his nose. He was back in his hotel room, flat on his back in bed. Nick Lee stood over him with a damp washcloth. "What the hell was that all about?" asked Shawby. "Just another 'peculiar artifact of the culture'?"

Lee, candid for this one time in his life, replied, "Honestly, I do not know, Brian. And the fact that I do not know worries the hell out of me."

8

QUINT'S CLUB WAS NOT THE BEST. Unlike Claggart, whose pedigree traced back to a posthumously knighted naval hero of the Napoleonic wars, he could not command unquestioning entrance to Whites, The Reform, or any of the other prestigious, upper-crust clubs. On the other hand, neither was Quint's club the worst. His contacts and acquaintances were of sufficient stature to entitle him to membership in "acceptable" clubs.

Despite the dubiousness of his ancestry (common laborers as recently as the turn of the century) and the suspiciously snub angle of his nose (Irish, perhaps), Quint's father, a rising mem-

ber of the rising bourgeoisie, had ascended high enough to fi-
nagle his offspring into the right schools. There, despite a
marked lack of intellectual acumen, Quint's enthusiastic aptitude for buggery, flagellation, and bestial drunkenness ensured
his rapid academic and social progress. Blessed with low cunning, brutal appetites, and a native flair for falsehood, he selected the law as his chosen profession.

It was a profession in which he prospered, his specialty being
the extraction of kindred spirits from the untidy consequences
of such eccentric pleasures as he himself enjoyed, peccadillos
upon which unenlightened law enforcement officers, outraged
parents, shocked clerics, and dumbfounded livestock owners
more than frowned. British nobility being what it is, Quint's
special professional expertise brought him into contact with a
rather sizable cross section of the Empire's most august person-
ages. These grateful, but far from contrite, sinners were more
than happy to help their sympathetic solicitor and his recently
enlisted partner and soul mate, Claggart, dip their sticky, grasping fingers into such shady financial ventures as were known to
them. Thus did Quint and Claggart prosper. Thus did they grow.

Leaning against the bar, Quint eyed the amber of his malt
whiskey appreciatively. He held the glass up to the light, to study
it better. Warm and ruddy gold, it reminded him pleasantly of
the russet hair of a young Welsh working lad he'd corrupted just
two nights before. With a gesture that Oscar Wilde would have
thought excessive, he tossed the drink back and turned to his
companion, a mottle-faced retired brigadier and current director
of one of Britain's largest leather goods manufacturers. "Ahh,
Freddie," Quint remarked, "they say that the three distinc-
tive competencies of the Royal Navy are rum, sodomy, and the
lash. Let's give them credit for two wise choices, but with whiskey like this available to one and all, how can they tolerate rum,
eh, Freddie?"

Freddie peered over his parrotlike nose and answered,
"Weak-willed women, your navy boys. Can't do a man's work
and can't drink a man's drink. Never could and never will. The
navy went bad on the day they banned the cat and it will stay
bad until they bring her back."

Quint flapped his wrist at the bartender, summoned another
dram, and scrawled his signature on the chit. Then, quite casually, he said, "Oh, I say, Freddie, I do hope you listened to
my advice on that Yank company I told you about last month.
Made a bundle myself. PegaSys, eh, Freddie?"

"By God, I did, my boy! Been meaning to thank you about it. Damned fine recommendation. If I could pick horseflesh like you pick stocks, I'd be a rich man. Just wish I'd plunged a bit deeper. Honest soldier's retirement pay isn't much, you know."

"Quite so, and £4 a share in three weeks is not a bad return, eh Freddie? Oh, by the by, you have cashed out of it, haven't you, Freddie?"

"Can't say as I have. Eh, what? You subtle devil! Are you telling me I should?"

"Well, Freddie, old lad, I should say you should. Especially when there is something even better for you to put your gains in. Wealth beyond the dreams of avarice, Freddie. Wealth beyond all imagination. Speaking personally, I've pawned every asset I·own to put money into this one, Freddie. This one is a sure thing. That bank whose board you sit on might want to look into it too."

The brigadier lifted his glass to Quint. Quint lifted his own in response. Both tossed back their drinks. Brigadier Freddie smiled and said, "Next round's on me, I think."

A mile or two away at his (infinitely superior) club in Pall Mall, Claggart was having a less easy time of it.

The unwholesome outcome of fourteen generations of selective inbreeding, Claggart combined in one repugnant package the robust virility of Lassie, the sartorial sobriety of Liberace, and the sexual appetites of Humbert Humbert. His professional preferences bent toward the ever-lucrative necrophiliac side of the legal arts: wills, last testaments, inheritances, estates, and the profitable probating thereof. He reckoned among his clientele British black sheep of the sootiest hue—the sort whose profligacy blotted the noble escutcheons of the Empire's most ancient houses, who had Erred with a capital "E," and whose very existence were no longer discussed in polite circles, much less by their shamed relatives. Claggart's clients were exiled from the bosom of their families; their portraits were taken down from the walls, and their names stricken from their progenitors' wills. In this last matter, Claggart sought to serve. For when the paterfamilias had passed on to his just reward and the will was ready to be opened, Claggart, with the unerring instincts of a vulture, would begin hovering about the scene. On behalf of his disinherited clientele, Claggart left no bequest unchallenged, nor any legacy undisputed. More often than not, the legitimate heirs would sooner pay him off rather than subject themselves to the tedious litigation that he threatened.

Accordingly, the ripe aroma of carrion accompanied Claggart. His guest, a bearded, beturbaned and terribly butch Sikh, could smell it. And he flinched every time Claggart's clammy pale hands flapped his direction.

"See here, old boy," Claggart whined with growing frustration, "I've an O.B.E. after my name and hopes this year of having a Sir before it. If there was even the slightest possibility of this fiddle being not quite on the up and up, I shouldn't touch it with an Irishman's spoon."

"I do not question your integrity," replied the Sikh, "but I am not certain that this is legal in the United States."

"Bah! Whether it is or it isn't ain't the point, don't you know. I've been trying to tell you, my boy, that not one pence of your investment will ever see the dawn of a Yankee day. That's the beauty of it. It's all offshore, all away from the watchful eyes of their policemen—and, let me hasten to point out, away from the equally watchful eyes of the taxman, any taxman, be he Yank, Brit, or gentlemen of dusky hue, if you catch my meaning."

The Sikh did, and winced. "My son is in graduate school in America now, at UCLA in the business school. He has high hopes of finding employment in America and becoming a citizen. I should not want to do anything to sully our family's name or jeopardize . . ."

Claggart's supply of patience ran dry. This crafty little darkie was demanding too much information. Too clever by half, these Gunga Dins. It was boundingly apparent that the Indian had no intention of plowing his hard-earned rupees into what Claggart had in mind. Claggart stood up and snaked his hand out to the Sikh, who grasped it with visible reluctance. "Well then, my boy, I tell you what. You just think on it. Sleep on it. And if you decide you and that insurance company of yours want in, well, then you know where to find me. But if you do decide to take a flyer with us, you will have to move quickly. This little fiddle is hot, and I think we will have more buyers than we can accommodate. Now, let me summon over one of the porters, he'll find your coat and hat . . . well, I see you still have your, ahh, headwear . . . and show you the door. Ta-ta, now."

The Sikh departed. Claggart gazed around the reading room, seeking another victim. After a moment, his eyes lit on a horse-faced figure sitting in a dark green leather armchair, just below the bullet holes Mad George Gordon, Lord Byron, had placed in the club's walls as vengeance for being blackballed. The perfect candidate: minister—or was it secretary—of something to do with defense, or, perhaps, HM's prison, and a blood relation of—well, no matter who—but definitely on a first-name basis with the Royals, definitely on the ins with Maggie's government, definitely a financial advisor to certain wealthy peers of the realm, definitely rich as sin, and definitely a member in good standing, like Claggart, of another exclusive club, one ruled by a lady known only as Mistress Charlene. Claggart brushed a small storm of dandruff from his beetling brow and sidled over.

"Ahh, how good to see you, old boy, mind if I join you?" asked Claggart.

The horse face looked up, a dull fire burning somewhere deep in its hollow eye sockets, "Not if you are bringing that wog of yours with you."

Claggart looked innocently perplexed. "Wog? Of mine? Oh, good heavens, not mine, old boy, not my wog. Don't know who brought the bugger in, but it wasn't me."

"Don't like 'em. Never liked 'em. Shouldn't be allowed to rub shoulders with their betters. How did he get through the door? I thought we didn't let them in here."

"Oh, we have no choice. It was the last Labour government. They passed some bloody bugger-all law about discrimination."

"Well, damnation, I'll have words with Iron Maggie about that first thing next morning! Can't have the heathen Hindoo invading the privacy of our clubs, can we. Next thing it'll be your ruddy Kaffir, spear, shield, and all."

"Or worse yet, your snail-eating Frog."

The skeleton smiled. "Frenchmen least of all. They're all niggers, you know, all of them. If they ain't an Englishman, then they is a nig-nog, my nanny used to say. It's a well-known fact that niggers begin at Calais."

"Quite so, my lad, quite so. And speaking of the dark-skinned tribes, have you ever been to the Seychelles?"

"Arabs, ain't they? Bowing and chanting toward Mecca at the drop of a prayer rug. Yes, I'll warrant I have been. Stopped over with Mountbatten just before the end of the Raj. Lovely place, if it weren't for your burnoose boys. Why do you ask?"

Claggart leered and winked. "Well, I've just learned a bit about the place. About its banks, really. It seems that some of the more interesting turns in the world financial markets can be found in the back alleys down there in the capital, Victoria. Not the sort of thing for everyone, but the kind of fiddles that a man with the resources can profit from mightily. Yes, mightily. Especially if he is responsible for managing some small portion of the Royals' portfolio.''

"Hmpf! You wouldn't, I say, you wouldn't have come across anything that avoids the loathsome toils of Her Majesty's Inland Revenue Service, would you? I am looking at the devil's own tax bill this year.''

"Well," said Claggart, settling into his seat, "it turns out that I have. Now, I need your word that you won't breathe a word of this to a soul.''

"My lips are sealed. Tight as the tomb. Positively sealed.''

"Well, then . . .''

9

ANOTHER WEEK OF INTENSE, BUT fruitless, work had passed. PegaSys's legions found themselves thwarted at every pass. AIW, as guided by Lee, Bach and Wachutt, was mounting a startlingly effective campaign against its target. It sent brilliantly written letters to each of PegaSys's individual shareholders. Shawby and Lee made articulate (who would have believed it of Brian Shawby?) and compelling personal presentations to each of the fifteen largest money management firms in America. Since these organizations held rather more than $1 trillion in assets, their economic muscle was considerable. And all of them held substantial blocks of PegaSys shares.

AIW's unbelievable tender offer was becoming believable.

"Mr. Thatcher," Gladys's voice came out of the squawk box on Thatcher's desk, "you have a call on line one. It's Mr. Tongue. Do you want to take it?"

"Sure." Thatcher picked up the phone saying, "Thatcher here."

"Hi, masked man."

"Hello, Tonto."

"Hey! Come on, you don't call us Indians 'Tonto' anymore. Not ever. We don't like it."

"Well, I don't like being called 'masked man' either."

"But you are, Scott. You know you really are."

Nelson Strong Tongue was a Hopi medicine man. Thatcher had met him many years earlier while vacationing in northern Arizona. Although Thatcher never gave his time (money was another matter) to worthy causes, Nelson, whose tongue was both strong and silvered, had somehow persuaded him to work on behalf of the Hopis' endless fight against the land-grabbing encroachment of the Navajo. Much later Tongue would tell Thatcher that he had hoodooed him into working on behalf of the Hopi. Thatcher would respond by smiling condescendingly. Then Tongue would smile back at him, equally condescendingly.

Tongue said that Thatcher, like all men, was aligned with a kachina spirit—and in particular, the King Kong of the spirit world, an entity known among the Hopi as "Many Masks."

"Look," said Tongue. "What happens is all of us are close to the spirits of this world, kachinas, we call 'em. We're closer than we think. Now them kachinas give counsel, work magic, bring rain, lift curses, all that stuff. Me, I got the power to see who your kachina is. Which spirit, which kachina stands for you. You stand for him, too. Now kachina's not a ghost and kachina's not a god. He's what you might call an essence, sort of like the soul of something. Maybe the soul of river, or soul of corn, or even soul of practical jokes. Them dumb sociologists call 'em 'elementals.' Kachina stands behind me as the Protection Boy. He's the soul of protection. Pretty god-damned powerful kachina, that one. But kachina stands behind you, hell, he eats kachinas like mine for munchies. Kind of scared the hell out of me when I see who your kachina is, Scott Thatcher. Kachina that claims you for his own is old Many Masks. When a dancer dances the kachina dance, he puts on a kachina mask. Mask is the kachina you are, and you are what the mask stands for. The kachina mask you wear is you. Old Many Masks is all masks, all faces. Kachinas are the souls of stuff, right? Well, old Many Masks is the soul of the kachinas. He's got all the power and all the magic. He's the one who is all the rest, and so he's the one who can do it all. Meanest sonofabitch there ever was, too, leastways when he's mad. So old Many Masks comes up out the ground behind you, it means you are him and he is you. Welcome back, Many Masks. Guess I'm glad to see you again. And, do you know what?''

Thatcher replied, ''What?''

''Now that you're back, Many Masks, now that you're on our side, Scott Thatcher, I think them thieving Navajos are dog meat.''

''Yeah,'' Tongue continued, his voice fading in and out as it traveled across the wires of the Navajo Telephone Company, ''you're the one that's got all the masks. Nothing wrong with that, because you use 'em smart. One of these days, though, you'll take 'em all off and stand there with your naked face hanging out. And, know what, no one will recognize you. Heh, heh! Pretty funny, huh?''

''Nelson, why did you call? Is it time for the annual insult contest?''

''Nope. Called for two things. First thing is, we got your note down here about all that PegaSys stock we got in the tribal fund. Sure could use the extra money that selling it off to that fool of yours would bring . . .''

''He's not any fool, Nelson.''

''That's another funny thing, Scott. Seems he *is* your fool. You think about that some and you'll figure it out. Anyway, elders have talked it over, and we decided that there is no way we're going to sell that stock to your fool. Reason is you're a brother and we like you too much. Besides, nobody wants to piss off old Many Masks.''

''Thanks. Thank you very much. Please tell everyone that I genuinely appreciate the support. I wish I had it from more of our shareholders.''

''Second thing I wanted to tell you. We went down the kiva and woke up the Protection Boy and a couple of the others last night. Told 'em about how you're part of the tribe and how you been helping us with the thieving Navajos and all that stuff. Got 'em to agree to do some stuff for you. Or rather, to do some stuff to your fool. Can't say what, but I figure it's going to be pretty good.''

* * *

Shawby, back in New York after his week in Tokyo, glared darkly at the doctor, snarling, "What do you mean, you have to fill out a report for the health commissioner? Suppose word leaks out. Suppose some goddamned newspaper reporter gets ahold of it. Besides, I didn't even catch it in this city. Not even in this country. I mean, we're talking about a simple little body louse here, aren't we? It's not like it was AIDS or something."

"Yeah, pretty good. Every so often something real mean's going to happen to that fool. But the thing is, when our boys hoodoo him, they can only do so much. You're the one who can really get him, you and that damned kachina monster of yours, old you-know-who. So, what I want you to do is get on a plane and come on down here. We'll all go down the kiva with you and help you get your boy to put the biggest, ugliest curse on that fool that ever was. Nuke 'em, that's what we'll do."

"Nelson," Thatcher sighed, "with all due respect to you, your people, your culture, and your religion, I rank that suggestion as . . . let me be as polite as I know how . . . as, shall we say, lacking in credibility. Setting aside the unhappy consequences that would accrue should word leak out that the chairman and chief executive officer of a $12 billion company was practicing voodoo to stave off a takeover bid, I simply do not have the time even to try. Every minute of the day between now and Christmas is committed, scheduled and planned. Besides, Nelson, you'll forgive me for saying this, I do not have much faith in the power of the supernatural to extricate PegaSys from its problems."

"Figured you'd say that. No hard feelings at all. But, Scott, I tell you this, it'll work if you try. So if everything else fails, you just get your butt on down here. Then we'll fix 'em."

"Thanks, Nelson."

"Anything else we can do down here?"

"No, not really. Well, prayers, I suppose. And you might want to watch television tonight. I'm going to be interviewed on the Cable Business Network. They're taping interviews with Shawby and me this afternoon."

"Don't get cable down here. Hell, barely get telephone. But I'll see if we can do something with one of those satellite antennas some of the younger folks have out in the lands. Got to go now. Talk to you later. Good-bye."

"Good. OK. Thanks for calling. Good-bye."

10

NEW YORK'S SUMMER HAD BEEN
long, the hot days lasting well into October. Winter compensated for the long torrid summer by coming early and coming hard. The temperature was 27 degrees and falling when Thatcher stepped out of his limousine and onto the streets of lower Manhattan.

The Cable Business Network's television studios were located in a decrepit loft building in SoHo. As Thatcher, accompanied by Justine Gold, entered the building, they encountered Brian Shawby, who, his taping session just completed, was leaving. Shawby, looking uncommonly bright-eyed and alert, extended his hand. "Scott. I haven't seen you since you were out to visit us more than a year ago. Look, a thought just crossed my mind . . ."

"Short trip," growled Thatcher, walking on.

"Ahh, well, uh, look. I'm in town all the time, why don't you give me a call?"

Thatcher paused in midstride, then turned and glared at Shawby. After more than a moment's silence he said icily, "Sorry, I can't do that, Brian. We have one of those computerized telephone systems and it is programmed to block calls to Dial-a-Joke."

The producer was wearing maroon-rimmed power glasses; she absentmindedly tapped a gold Cross pen against her Rolex Lady Date just as she spoke to Scott and Justine. "OK. Here it is. *Newsmakers Tonight*. Thirty minutes air time, total. We got an eleven-minute interview with Brian Shawby already on tape. OK. We air that first. Commercial break. OK. We air eleven minutes with you. Commercial break. Two minutes of commentary from the anchors. Then on to the next segment. It goes out at 8:30 EST, ditto MST. 7:30 CST and PST. Prime time all the way. OK?''

"OK,'' said Justine, "one question. Are you taping the eleven straight up, or will it be longer and then edited down?''

"We'll go straight up if we can, OK? That's the way we worked it with Shawby, and that's the way we want it to work with you. He was real clean, real fast, real articulate. You be the same, OK?''

Thatcher spoke up. "Shawby was articulate? Brian Shawby? What did you do, put him on drugs?''

"Hey, no drugs in the television industry, OK! Now, I'm going to roll the Shawby tape for you now, OK?''

"OK.''

"I'll fast-forward the intro and lead in, OK? The interviewer is Walt Johnson, one of the regulars. Big-time management consultant. Actually Shawby's one of his clients, so he knows something about the guy and his company. We've got a different interviewer for you. OK, ready. Here we go.''

". . . of American Interdyne Worldwide. We're pleased to have you with us tonight, Brian.''

"I'm pleased to be here, Walt.''

"Tell me, Brian, why did you target PegaSys for takeover?''

"A number of reasons, Walt. First, it's a good company. Second, it's not as good as it could be. Third, and most important, it fits right in with our corporate strategy.''

"When you say that PegaSys is not as good as it could be, what do you mean?''

"The bottom line is that PegaSys could be more profitable than it is. Our analysis is that PegaSys has some lines of business, some divisions, that aren't as profitable as they should be; low-margin businesses that are holding down overall profits. I am certain that a fresher, tougher, smarter management can do something about those businesses.''

"How?''

"It's premature to say, but I imagine the things we will look at are downsizing the number of employees, moving some operations offshore, outsourcing some components and assemblies, and, if necessary, liquidating some operations.''

"Some people view PegaSys's chairman, Scott C. Thatcher, as one of the most able executives in America. Why do you think he hasn't taken those kinds of actions, Brian?''

"When it comes to his employees, Mr. Thatcher is old school, a bit of a paternalist, you might say. He has a fuddy-duddy mentality that went out of fashion in the 1950s. He is just not the kind of man to take tough action when tough times call for it. Another thing: we compete in global markets these days, and the only way to win is to strike alliances with those who have access to foreign markets. By that I mean setting up joint ventures with the Japanese and Europeans, licensing and transferring technologies, sharing the risks and sharing the rewards. Mr. Thatcher has consistently refused to let PegaSys give anything away to foreign partners. He insists on owning it all. And, he is out of touch with the economic benefits of moving jobs off shore. His attitudes toward the global business environment are a relic of a bygone day. He lacks the entrepreneurial business spirit that I pride myself on."

"Brian, you have been particularly secretive about how AIW plans to finance this takeover. I believe that there is some question as to whether you and your investment banker are in compliance with federal disclosure standards. Would you care to comment on that?"

"Certainly. First, let me note that our attorneys contend that we are in full compliance. These stories you may have seen in the newspapers are the result of a turf battle between the Securities and Exchange Commission and the Department of Justice. We are certain that the Department of Justice will prevail and that the SEC's various petitions to the courts will be found wholly lacking in merit. Does that answer your question, Walt?"

"Not entirely. It was a two-part question. I am sure all of our viewers are eager to know something about the details of how you go about raising more than $14 billion."

"Walt, I am certain they are, too. And if some of my competitors—and, for that matter, Scott Thatcher—weren't among the viewers, I would be happy to answer the question in detail. However, my point of view on the funding is that it represents a trade secret. We don't want PegaSys to know about it, or to use the same technique to buy money for its own defense."

"That is a fair answer, Brian. Let me ask you this, are you certain that AIW is doing the right thing by acquiring PegaSys?"

"Yes, I am. Of course you can never be completely sure that you're right. But at AIW we usually are. And if you are right 93 percent of the time, who cares about the other 8 percent."

"Brian, if you are successful in taking control of PegaSys,

how different will your strategy and management style be from the current team's?''

"We will be successful, Walt. You can count on that. As for the differences, they will be numerous. We place a premium on the creation of shareholder value at AIW. Our watchwords are steady increases in EPS, steady increases in P/E, and steady increases in ROE. Financial excellence is management excellence. Those who do not live by the numbers shall surely die by them. We don't believe in hoarding our cash, and we are very parsimonious about reinvesting it in current operations. It takes a lot of evidence to persuade my management team that capital investments for new equipment, upgrades or new facilities are really needed. Our operations management learns to make do, or do without. The same goes for R&D; we just don't like to waste a lot of money letting a bunch of research scientists amuse themselves. Further, we are committed to growth through acquisition. Today's business world is divided into the eaters and the eaten. We want to be like General Electric—at the topmost point in the food chain. If I were to sum up the difference between us and PegaSys in one word, it would be 'toughness.' Yes, toughness. I think that and 'excellence' capture the difference you'll see between us and PegaSys. We are tough with a dollar, tough with our customers, tough with our employees, and tough with ourselves.''

"Brian, that's as good a business strategy as I've ever heard. Now tell me, what is your vision of the future of computer technology? What do you see as the most important things for you to work on once you take over PegaSys?''

"Well, Walt, making forecasts is difficult, especially about the future. And of course I'm a businessman, not a narrow-gauged technocrat like Scott Thatcher. But I suppose that one of the key areas for us once we're in charge will be computer-generated animated graphics. I believe that advances in graphics will be so dramatic that, within our lifetimes, the motion picture *Casablanca Part II* will be released, starring the original cast. There just won't be any way to discriminate between the actors in computer-generated films and live ones. The realism will be perfect. Then, given the economics of moviemaking, Holly-wood will simply let live actors' contracts expire, I guess. Further, and for self-evident reasons, politicians will increasingly rely on computer-controlled clones for speech-making and television appearances. The TV networks, driven to distraction by the salary demands and erratic behavior of overpaid anchormen, will start relying on computer-generated newscasters. My vision of the future of computer technology is a press conference where a digital president is interviewed by software-driven reporters."

"Brian, we have time for one final question. Tonight I've heard you say two or three times that after PegaSys you see more acquisitions in the offing. Can you tell us the kinds of companies you see as complementary to your overall strategy once PegaSys is brought into the AIW fold?"

"Well, clearly, I can't name any specific names. But the kinds of businesses that might round out our portfolio once we own PegaSys are probably service businesses. We don't like manufacturing businesses at AIW. Indeed, as a nation we in the United States don't like manufacturing businesses. This is the age of the service economy. So, then, the kinds of service businesses I see fitting us over the long term might include leisure time—resorts, hotels, casinos, and that sort of thing. Probably some entertainment businesses such as TV and cable stations. Maybe hazardous waste management. All logical extensions of the strategy that led us to PegaSys."

"Thank you very much, Brian Shawby, chairman and chief executive of American Interdyne Worldwide. Next up, an interview with Scott C. Thatcher, defending PegaSys against AIW's tender offer. But first, this word from Nomura Securities, the largest brokerage in the world, with offices in New York, London, Tokyo . . ."

Thatcher, watching the tape of Shawby's interview in the Cable Business Network's green room, looked calm, extraordinarily calm, cool, and collected. That is what alarmed Justine so much. She had expected that he would be chewing the carpet into tatters, foaming at the mouth, and vowing bloody vengeance. Instead, he merely turned an icy stare toward the producer and said, "That was a very interesting performance."

The producer nervously tapped her Rolex and narrowed her eyes. "That's what I thought, too. The man was a disaster the first time I met him, OK? I would have sworn that he would never make it through the interview. Instead, he comes across like John Houseman playing the chief justice of the United States. Television is funny that way sometimes. I mean, look what happens during the election campaigns, OK? The camera can make the world's biggest bozo look statesmanlike."

Thatcher growled, "Well, it just has done precisely that. Television is the instrument of the devil."

* * *

The maitre d' was concerned. It was not good for business when a customer fell face down in the gazpacho. Twice. "Is the gentleman ill, madam?" he asked with as much solicitude as he could muster. "Would madam like some assistance? We would be pleased to take him someplace where he can lie down. Or, perhaps to another restaurant."

"Oh no," Jennifer replied, "it isn't anything to worry about. He'll wake up in a minute. He's been doing this all afternoon."

"Madam?"

"It's just a reaction to some medicine he took earlier. See, look, he's coming around again. Maybe you could get him another napkin."

"Indeed, madam. I shall bring several."

The maitre d' departed, looking over his shoulder with hostile despair. Shawby, his eyes glazed and rolling, lifted his dripping face out of the soup platter and muttered, "And so, therefore, in conclusion, in closing, let me say that, that, that . . . aw, what was I talking about?"

"The skin rash, honey. The skin rash you picked up in that Japanese sauna bath."

"Huh, oh, what? Yeah, well . . . ahh. Terrible, itchy thing. Have to coat it with this awful-smelling gunk. Huh, where are we, anyway?"

"Honey, I don't think you are in any condition to eat. Besides, you want to get back to the hotel to see yourself on television, don't you?"

"Ah, yeah. Television. Yeah. Got to see that. Whoo, I bet I'm going to be good. That stuff Nick gave me. Boy, was I on top of things. Cognetin. Halodol. And a few amphetamines to keep me going fast. Need some more of those, though. Anyway, I didn't forget a word of what Nick told me to say, did I? Oh, I was good. Oh, yes. Oh, my. Ohhhhh . . ."

Yawn. Thud. Splash.

Justine looked at the television monitor and shivered. The producer had told her that a different interviewer would be quizzing Thatcher, and Justine had forgotten to ask who. Now, far too late to protest, she knew. It couldn't be worse. It was Vidor Stark, affectionately referred to as "Viper" Stark by friends and opponents alike. Stark, a lawyer of more dubious practice than most, was the darling of the nethermost reaches of the "new" conservative movement. He owned, edited, and published *Right*

Reasoning, a magazine he had founded to combat the William F. Buckley school of bleeding-heart liberalism. Leader of the Jesse Helms for President campaign, zealous advocate of abortion clinic bombing, vocal proponent of the economic theories of Louis XIV, intimate friend of every dictator in Latin America excepting those in Cuba and Nicaragua, chairman of the Lycurgian Society, and dogged critic of the American Civil Liberties Union's hypocritical refusal to defend members of the Aryan Nation Movement, Vidor Stark rained down multisyllabic wrath on everything and everybody to the left of his sadly departed mentor and boon companion, Generalissimo Francisco Franco y Bahamonde. Scourge of the left and gadfly of the right, Stark possessed the uncommon talent of infuriating just about everyone. His arrogant sneer was a national landmark, and even when he was tying his shoe laces, he managed to look down his nose at anyone in his presence.

In the unctuous accents of New Orleans gentry, Stark began the interview. "Good evening. My guest is Mr. Scott Comstock Thatcher III, for the fleeting moment chairman of a computer company called PegaSys. How do you do, Mr. Thatcher?"

"Fine. And yourself?"

"Gratifyingly fit, thank you. Mr. Thatcher, whose company is being acquired by a prominent Fortune 500 firm, American Interdyne Worldwide, is here tonight to tell us a bit about himself and a bit about why he doesn't think that acquisition is such a good idea. Mr. Thatcher, you have a reputation for speaking your mind, do you not?"

"Having one, I am qualified to do so. Unlike the previous interviewee."

"Ah, yes. Mr. Shawby. I believe he accused you of paternalist predilections, did he not?"

"That was the word he used. I suppose he was referring to my policy of lifetime employment."

"To my nose, that phrase has the unfragrant aroma of the sort of socialistic attitudinizing that one might expect to emanate from our misguided brethren in the Soviet workers' paradise."

"Hardly. When I say 'lifetime employment,' I do not mean guaranteed jobs for incompetents. I mean that we do not lay off good people for bad reasons. We do not shutter factories, slash wages, or put our employees on welfare simply because those factories are producing profit margins a percentage point or two lower than what we might like. There is nothing wrong in sacrificing a minuscule amount of profit to help keep employment up.''

''Ah, but that flouts the iron laws of economics laid down so long ago by the sage Riccardo, does it not? Besides, is not this eleemosynary affectation a callous dereliction of your fiduciary obligation to maximize shareholder value? Are not profits the first, foremost, and overarching of your sacrosanct duties to your investors?''

''The duties of a corporation are not exclusively to its investors, despite such fiddle-faddle on the topic as is being currently promulgated by the business press. We are responsible to the nation, to our employees, to our suppliers, and to our customers as well.''

''Well, if you would drape yourself in the flag of patriotism, how is it that you steadfastly forbear selling your computers to the military?''

''Nonsense. That is not true. We decline to bid on military procurements only when we know that they're going to waste the taxpayers' money. These days too many corporations look upon the Pentagon as if it were the Lost Dutchman's Gold Mine. If a company's products don't work, if its technology is antediluvian, if its factories have been padlocked, if its customer service phones have been disconnected, if its bond rating is triple-C-minus, if its chief executive has been denied parole, and if its stock has been delisted, even then, *even then*, it can win a defense contract and make money faster than the U.S. Mint. The Pentagon is the last, best hope of shabby corporations. And I for one will not deal with it except on matters that I know make economic and technical good sense. If other corporations did the same, rather than encouraging federal folly and waste . . .''

''Have you the temerity to pose as the ultimate authority and arbiter of government policy?''

''I do, as may any citizen in our democracy.''

''This is a republic, not a democracy, a distinction to which you may be insensitive.''

''Rather, it is a constitutional, democratic, federal republic, and I pay equal respect to each of the four elements of that term.''

''Let me ignore for the moment your implication that I do not pay the same respect. Rather, let me return to what I believe is the fulcrum of your present predicament. The owners of your company, that is to say the shareholders, have been offered a pretty price for your stock. Do you not flagrantly deny them their inalienable right to an honest profit by resisting this take-over?''

"Short-term gains generated by predatory takeover special-ists and stock market speculators do not, to my way of thinking, represent anything that can fairly be called an *honest* profit. If you had invested a thousand dollars in PegaSys ten years ago, it would be worth $5,000 today. *That* is an honest profit. More-over, it would be the reasonable expectation of any rational per-son that, ten years from today, that same investment will increase another fivefold. That, too, will be an *honest* profit. I should add that, as chief executive, I cannot guarantee such an increase in value; however, it is toward such an end that our long-term strategy has been built.''

"Such a point of view summons up the somber specter of shareholder lawsuits against you and your board of directors. Or are you as disregardful of your board as you are of your inves-tors?''

"My board and I have been meeting face to face once a week since this affair began, and even more frequently by telephone. To a man and to a woman they agree an AIW takeover of PegaSys would be a disaster for the company, for the employees, for the customers, for the long-term interests of the investors, and for the competitiveness of the American computer industry. These concerns take precedence over short-term financial gains.''

"Beyond a doubt you will be sued.''

"Beyond a doubt, indeed. Courts of law are the only place where shabby companies like AIW can compete effectively. Having salespeople who cannot sell, management that cannot manage, and goods that are not so good, shabby companies would much rather confront their competitors in a courtroom than in the open market. The judicial system being what it is, they have considerably greater odds of making money through litigation than through free market competition. My board is more than willing to be sued. The litigation will be lengthy, and by the time it has begun—much less concluded—we are confi-dent that our corporate strategy will have produced sufficient stock price appreciation to moot the entire case.''

"That, sir, is pernicious disingenuousness, and you know it. I am beginning to conclude that further disputation on this point will be fruitless. Your intransigence awes me. Let us instead move on to other points. Mr. Shawby observes that you are loath to enter into partnerships with foreign firms. Would you care to comment?''

"At length . . ."

"I feared as much."

"Between the end of World War II and the present day, American manufacturing companies have granted by actual count considerably more than forty-five thousand technology licenses to Japanese firms. In turn, we have lost millions of manufacturing jobs to Japanese competitors. Objectively, one must conclude that cause and effect . . ."

"Objectivity, Mr. Thatcher, is in the eye of the beholder."

"May I continue without interruption, or . . ."

"Oh, by all means. But do let me prevail upon you to reflect on Mr. Shawby's tellingly accurate observation that ours is a service economy, not a manufacturing economy."

"Of course it is, now that all the manufacturing jobs are in the Tokyo-Osaka corridor! What's left except services? And, as relates to the so-called service economy, is it a good thing, and is it a situation that can continue? I think not. Setting aside the not wholly irrelevant question of precisely how many American busboys the Benihana restaurant chain can gainfully employ, you should recognize that the Japanese compete in the service sector as well. And they compete with the same set of predatory tactics in the service industries as they do in the manufacturing sector. If they are as successful in services as they have been in manufacturing, then all of those service industry jobs you and Brian Shawby are so enamored of will go the way of manufacturing jobs. Given current trends—the trade deficit, the enormous numbers of acquisitions that the Japanese are making in this country—I fear that in the not-too-distant future, we all may find ourselves taking the emperor's birthday off as a national holiday."

"Cassandra-like prophets of doom are to be found in every generation, Mr. Thatcher."

"Reread your Euripides, Mr. Stark. Cassandra was right."

"Doubtless our viewers can find other and better elucidations of the classics than either I or you can provide them with, Mr. Thatcher."

"On this one point we agree. Let me get back to the topic. PegaSys does not and will not make its patents, technologies, or licenses available to any foreign firm. We see no reason to give our fiercest opponents the weapons they need to defeat us. And, Mr. Shawby should be aware that PegaSys profits quite handsomely from international markets. Because we do not share our proprietary resources with foreign partners, our foreign customers face one simple choice: either buy from us or buy something that is not nearly as good.''

"I rather relish such jingoistic arrogance, Mr. Thatcher, ill advised and contrary to the fundamental economic imperatives of free trade as it may be. But what say you of the synergies Mr. Shawby finds between his company and yours? And what of his unstinting commitment to excellence?''

"Synergy is a meaningless neologism, coined by that fine old flim-flam artist Buckminster Fuller. Allegedly the word has something to do with the whole being greater than the sum of the parts. In actuality, it is an excuse used by inept executives for executing particularly imprudent transactions. As for 'excellence,' it is a generic and meaningless executive buzzword that increasingly is used by shabby managers to dissimulate in virtually every embarrassing situation. 'Excellence' has approximately the same vapid connotation as the phrase 'really awesome' when uttered by a Valley Girl.''

"Alas, I now perceive how out of touch you truly are with the pragmatic realities of contemporary business and social existence. However, since my researchers tell me that most of your stock is owned by institutional investors, pension funds for the most part, and since they have precious little tolerance of what you wistfully call 'long-term strategy,' I look upon you as someone to whom, rather soon I'll warrant, I'll have to extend my condolences.''

"Let me comment on the institutional investors. That really is the most important topic . . .''

"Sorry, but that flashing red light above the camera is telling me that our time is up. Thank you for your time. Next, this message from Dai-Ichi Kangyo Bank, the largest bank in the world.''

Her diminutive height notwithstanding, Justine towered with rage. She shook a red-tipped finger under the nose of the producer, hissing in fury, "You bitch! You let that jerk Shawby be interviewed by his own tame, trained pet dog, some jerk consultant on his payroll. And then you throw Thatcher to fucking Nero Caesar and all his fucking lions!''

"Don't you take that tone of voice with me, hon, OK? Besides, I'm just following orders. You know the bossman down in Dallas had to get some foreign sugar daddy to keep this network afloat, OK? So the word comes down that the sugar daddy wants tonight handled special, OK. Hey, hon, I only work here. I'm just hired help. I got to follow orders, OK.''

"Who the hell is the sugar daddy, the Odessa Pension Fund for Retired Nazi Storm Troopers?"

"No, honey, it's just some Jap, and I don't mean one like you.''

Justine arched her red-tipped claw, preparing to reply with deeds, not words.

In the studio, the mellifluous announcer intoned, "And now with a commentary on this evening's newsmakers interviews, here are our two guest hosts, Walter H. Johnson and Vidor Stark. Walt, what was your reaction?''

"Clearly, Brian Shawby represents the state of the art in American management thinking. He is attuned to the real issues: shareholder value, the pursuit of excellence, bottom-line performance, the value chain, ROE-driven immediate financial goals, global alliances, portfolio strategy, and disengagement from the manufacturing sector. I perceive in Mr. Shawby a refreshing, entrepreneurial creativity. He does not flinch from making the tough decisions and taking the bold departures. In my opinion, an AIW acquisition of PegaSys could be a good thing for PegaSys and a good thing for American enterprise.''

"Mr. Stark?"

"I wholeheartedly concur. Delicacy dictates that we do not comment on or reiterate Mr. Thatcher's politics of pinkish hue, his rampant xenophobia, his arrogant disdain for the rights of shareholders, his antediluvian paternalism, his . . . what is this? Who are those women and what are they . . . dear God!''

Walt Johnson replied, "The one in the torn slip with the broken eyeglasses is this show's producer.''

Stark, standing up to better view the carnage, asked, "And the other?''

"She's a public relations type.''

"Ah! How foolish of me not to have guessed.''

Justine, hearing Stark's sneering voice, let her whimpering prey drop to the floor. She rounded on Stark, narrowing her eyes, and crouching catlike, and snarled, "You!''

Stark, whose hobbies included big-game hunting, contemplated her posture and stance, concluding that they bore a striking resemblance to that of a hungry, ill-tempered leopard. Upon further thought, he decided that while subduing a 105-pound, five-foot-two woman was one thing, subduing a 105-pound, five-foot-two leopard was quite another. He started backing toward the exit.

He didn't make it.

As the sound of ambulance sirens faded into the distance, Detective Ryerhurt turned to his partner and said, "So what do you think?"

"I think about eight felonies, twelve misdemeanors, fifteen stitches, and $50,000 worth of property damage, that's what I think. That Gold woman is lucky her husband is a lawyer."

"No, I mean about these PegaSys guys. This is the second time in two weeks that this crowd has been involved in serious violence."

"Yeah?"

"Yeah."

"Well, you know what they say: one time is chance, two times is coincidence, and three times . . ." Ryerhurt's partner let his words hang in the cold night air.

"Due to technical difficulties, Cable Business Network's regularly scheduled program, *Newsmakers Tonight*, will not be seen. Instead, we are bringing you a special report on . . ."

11

Finnair flight 147 from Helsinki to New York had landed at John F. Kennedy International Airport. The passengers were clearing customs and immigration. Andrei Bezukhov, computer scientist and rat exterminator par excellence, breezed right through, compliments of his Swedish passport. *Name, Martin Waldvogel; profession, exporter; purpose of visit, business.* "Thank you very much. Exit through the green doors to your left."

Down the exit corridor two men waited leaning against the wall, two very large men. One looked tough enough to fight a rock crusher down a mine shaft. The other looked like the rock crusher. Both wore baggy-kneed, wide-lapeled, off-the-rack black suits from Moscow's GUM department store. Both wore wrinkled white shirts of Afghanistan cotton and lumpy polyester. Both wore Soviet army-issue brown dress shoes. Both wore disreputable-looking fedora hats. One of them had a copy of *Das Kapital* (in Russian, with a red cover and a picture of Marx on the spine) peeking out of his jacket pocket. The other one's gun was showing.

The two men were KGB agents in disguise. They were craftily disguised as KGB agents.

A third man, surely a blood relation of the other two, shambled down the corridor a pace or two ahead of Bezukhov. The two waiting thugs peeled away from the wall and greeted their compatriot. Nearby, a CIA man spoke into a walkie-talkie. Another snapped a picture. A third fell into step behind the lumbering trio. No one noticed Bezukhov. That was the idea. He walked, overlooked by all, out of the international terminal and up to the taxi stand.

New York is a cosmopolitan city. It is not an American capital, it is a world capital. It attracts the richest and most diverse ethnic mix imaginable. It affords infinite opportunities for cross-cultural encounters and exchanges. Where else, to choose but one example, could one witness a KGB computer scientist trying to communicate with a Rastafarian taxi driver?

"Take me to the Summit," said Bezukhov, whose English was really quite good.

"Da Summit, mon? Where dat she be?" answered the Rastafarian, whose English was not nearly as good as his passenger's, and whose lilting Jamaican accent perplexed Bezukhov immeasurably.

Bezukhov, whose knowledge of New York geography was considerably inferior to his knowledge of the city's native (but no longer principal) language, replied ineffectually, "Go across the river."

The Rastafarian groped for the greasy, tattered map he kept in his glove compartment, unfolding it and staring at it for several befuddled moments. Finally, his eyes lit up. "Da Summit. Da Summit. Here she be, 'cross dat Geor' Washin'on Bridge. Dat's a long way 'cross dat bridge, mon."

Bezukhov, ignorant of the implications and uncertain as to

the Jamaican's accent, grunted neutrally. The Rastafarian shrugged and started up his cab. Getting to Summit, New Jersey, was going to be a long drive and the traffic on Saturday, November 13, was as harrowing as that of any other day of the year. He decided to light up some of the sacred herb to mellow out his mood.

Mike Ash was walking home from D'Agostino's with a bag of groceries in his arms. A battered taxicab rattled up the street. Ash noticed that it was driven by a deadlocked Rastafarian, and that the passenger seemed to be screaming at the driver. The cab had jounced around a corner and was out of sight when the Rolls Royce silently slid up to the curb in front of him. The Rolls was huge, two-toned grey and blue, and trimmed with the most tastelessly elaborate gold fittings imaginable. Its rear windows were smoked, hiding the identity of its passenger from site.

The uniformed chauffeur rolled down his window and called out to Ash in a heavy British accent, "Beg pardon, sir, but would your name be Mr. Michael Ash?"

Mike warily answered, "Who wants to know?"

"Me guv'nor, sir. Mr. Lee he is. You are Mr. Ash, aren't you?"

The chauffeur stepped out of the car and opened the rear door. "He's in here, sir, Mr. Lee is. He'd like a word with you. Come on, sir, step in and we'll give you a nice ride home."

Ash took two steps back. "No way."

Lee leaned out of the open door. He was impeccably garbed in a dove-grey suit and held a gold-mounted walking stick in his gloved hand. He gestured with it, encouraging Mike to come closer. Ash didn't move.

In an amicable tone of voice Lee said, "Come, come, dear Michael. It's five long blocks home. I'll give you a lift. We'll chat on the way. I've followed your career with interest. Come, I am not trying to buy your soul but merely am offering you a short ride. We'll speak of what you'll do once PegaSys is owned by Brian and by yours truly, me. I think a sweet promotion may be yours when PegaSys is ours. Hear me on this subject and learn how you can ensure it."

Ash shifted the grocery bag from his right arm to his left, and answered in a thoroughly unpleasant tone of voice. "I think you don't know much about me, Lee. Neither you nor your fancy car is to my liking. I'm walking home. Why don't you buzz off?"

"Opportunity comes by but once. Don't let it escape ungrasped. It will not come again."

"Good-bye, Lee, and don't bother to bother me anymore." Mike walked off quickly. Lee's chauffeur shut the rear door, climbed back into the Rolls, and drove off as silently as he had come.

Justine's husband paced back and forth across the living room in his best attorney-for-the-prosecution style. "OK, babe," he boomed, orating toward an invisible jury, "you are off free and clear. Vidor Stark is not pressing charges. I counseled him that the press exposure he might receive from being put in the hospital by a woman half his size would be inconsistent with his manly macho image. The Cable Business Network is taking the seventy-five grand I offered them to replace their equipment. They won't prosecute either. Both the insurance companies covering Stark and the cable guys are happy that no one is filing a claim, so they're willing to forget everything. And the cops, as usual, are happy not to have to waste time in a couple of lengthy court cases. Ergo, you are a free woman."

Justine stared at the floor, looking less guilty than defiant.

"Now, my love," Harry continued, "we come to the tough part. The tough part is when you have to face the facts. Do you want to know what the facts are? Well, even if you don't I am going to tell you. The facts are these: First, you have let yourself get emotionally involved in this whole mess. PegaSys is merely a client, not your goddamned firstborn. Second, Thatcher and company are going to lose. The PegaSys ship is going down, and you are going with it. Third, merely by being associated with a disaster as visible as PegaSys is going to be a big black eye for your career, and maybe mine as well. Those are the facts, babe. Those are the facts."

Justine raised her head. "So what do you want me to do?"

"I want you to resign the account. I want you to put as many miles between Scott C. Thatcher and Justine Gold as you can. And, then, once you've done that, maybe I can help you find something useful to do. Maybe even profitable. There are plenty of better uses for your talents, Justine, than working for a bunch of guys who are going to be history in about a month's time."

Justine looked back at the floor, her lips drawn into a tight, thin frown.

12

THE MASKED AVENGER KNEW NO mercy. There was neither clemency in his soul nor forgiveness in his heart. His was the spirit of retribution, not reform. He did not absolve the wicked, he eliminated them. He was remorseless in his pursuit of wrongdoers; his mission was to punish, not to pardon. His justice was swift, brutal, and lethal. Night and darkness were his world, and the creatures of the night were his prey. Deep in their fetid lairs, the cringing minions of the underworld broke into greasy sweats at the mere mention of his name. The teeth in their stubbled, prognathous jaws chattered, their beady, feral eyes twitched, and they felt the scrape of cold, bony fingers along their misshapen spines. The Avenger's icy laugh brought terror to the bosoms of the iniquitous. Out there, in the swirling foggy gloom, the Masked Avenger lurked . . . stalked his quarry . . . and struck! Who knows what evil lurks in the hearts of men? Nee-ha-ha-ha-ha-ha! Roy Knight knows!

Roy Knight admired his handiwork and hummed a few bars of *Omphale's Wheel* (Camille Saint-Saëns, 1835-1921). Roy Knight smiled the vindictive, bloodcurdling smile that was the Avenger's hallmark. 6.5k bytes of very compact code. Very lean. Very elegant. A beautiful hack. World-class. 6.5k bytes. 10.83 seconds to download it into Wintergreen's machine. That was all it would take. If Wintergreen would just stay on the line, 10.83 seconds was all that was needed. Then it would be all over. Oh, Wintergreen might be fast enough to stop all his disk drives from autodestructing. He might even be fast enough to power down before every circuit in his computer was reduced to a puddle of molten silicon. But he would never, ever be fast enough—or smart enough—to interfere with the real mission of Knight's fiendish program. And what was that purpose? Ven-

205

geance! Justice! The gloating triumph of good over evil! The
Masked Avenger strikes back! The weed of crime bears bitter
fruit. Nee-ha-ha-ha-ha-ha! A permanent lock, a hardwired link,
from Knight's terminal to Wintergreen's. An open line down
which the Masked Avenger—

"Roy?"

Knight jumped. He had not heard Thatcher enter the room.
Thatcher's unnerving practice was to materialize unannounced
in his employees' offices. More often than not when he needed
to talk to someone, he went to visit that person rather than
summon the employee to his own office. Those who, like Knight,
had begun their careers in more formal organizations always
were taken aback by his surprise appearances.

"Hi, Scott. What's up?"

"I've been thinking about our mutual friend, the elusive Mr.
Wintergreen."

"Me, too. In fact, I have—"

"Good. Then you probably have reached the same conclusion as I have."

Not for nothing had Knight been a federal employee. He
didn't say anything. He simply nodded his head in an ambi-
guously neutral way. Thatcher continued, "Clearly, young Wintergreen is a man—or perhaps woman, we don't know, do
we—of enormous talent, misguided though that talent may be.
I think that talent could be better directed, don't you? It is a
shame to see someone so brilliant frittering away his or her skills
on mindless pranks and practical jokes. So, if you agree, and I
think you will, I think we should try to recruit the lad. Or lass,
as the case may be. Wintergreen is obviously a brilliant programmer, and we can always find a home for brilliance in
PegaSys, don't you think? In fact, it might not be a bad idea to
offer him a job here in security working with you."

The Masked Avenger wanted to cry.

Thatcher continued, "So, what I think I want you to do is to
contact him. You can do that, can't you? Just put out a message
on all the computer bulletin boards and hacker mail services.
Tell him to get in touch with you or me. He'll see one of them
and call in."

Knight shook his head and responded with glum hesitancy.
"Yeah, sure. But there is one thing. This one thing, I don't know
about it. It worries me. I haven't mentioned it, but it worries
me. I've been thinking about it for weeks."

"What's that, Roy?"

"Wintergreen may be a he. Or Wintergreen may be a she. OK. No problem. But suppose Wintergreen is an it?"

Thatcher arched an eyebrow. In his younger days, he had practiced eyebrow arching in front of a mirror. He has the gesture down pat.

"I mean, suppose Wintergreen is an AI?"

"Nonsense. You've been reading too much science fiction."

"No, really. Suppose he is one, an artificial intelligence. It could be done. Someone could write the code. Suppose you wrote the code, wrote an expert system for penetrating other people's computer security, and suppose you wrote it so that it modified itself, grew and mutated every time it ran into a new set of security logic. And then suppose the program escaped."

"Roy, really. The Software That Devoured Cleveland. I do, despite the decrepit antiquity of my years, retain some senile sense of the state of the art in software technology. And, for my money, the current claims about artificial intelligence have about as much credibility as Shirley MacLaine's claims about her previous incarnations. We are many, many years away from artificial intelligence programs that can behave as cleverly as Wintergreen."

"But suppose that there was a breakthrough. That some hacker out back in the garage actually has done it. I mean, breakthroughs happen. If it can happen someday, then it can happen now. You say that all the time. So, let's suppose—"

"Let's suppose this. Let's suppose that Wintergreen has an acceptable number of arms, legs, and heads and that those appendages are composed of standard, off-the-shelf organic materials. Let us proceed on that not wholly irrational assumption and attempt to contact him. Let us offer him or her a job, a salary, and an office. And then if, as an alternative to the size of his office, Wintergreen asks in how many megabytes of main memory we're going to domicile him in, we will know differently. Do I make myself clear, Roy?"

Knight knew Thatcher's mood. It was the sort of mood that brooked no dispute. He nodded and muttered, "Sure. I'll get right on it."

Thatcher said, "Good. I'll see you at the EMC meeting tomorrow, I trust. Let me know if you've heard from him then."

After Thatcher departed, the Masked Avenger sat silently in moody contemplation of the injustice of it all. A known hoodlum, a lawless denizen of the criminal classes, snatched from his grasp. Worse, the humiliation of having the miscreant working on his own staff. It was like telling Dirty Harry that the Boston Strangler was his new partner. It was like giving the Joker the keys to the Batmobile. It was . . . well, wait. Maybe . . .

On a parapet high above the sleeping city, the Caped Crusader waited and watched. His steely eyes peered out from behind his blue-black mask as he stared at the starry skies above Gotham City. Somewhere in the alleys below, the Penguin and his mob of thugs plotted another dastardly crime. The Batman was ready. The Batman would catch him. The Batman and his loyal companion, Robin the Boy Wonder.

13

LOUISE HAD BEEN STUNNED WHEN, some weeks earlier, Ash recommended that they "put their relationship on hold." It was totally unexpected, the proverbial bolt from the blue. It was a few weeks before AIW announced its raid, on a Monday in September, her first day back in the office after a ten-day vacation in Greece. She had been looking forward with damned near panting expectation to Ash welcoming her back in an appropriately amorous way. She was so eager for him that she actually left the office at 5:00 P.M. *(well, nearly 5:00)*. She had called him before leaving to announce that she was on her way home and would be waiting for him. Curiously, he replied that, instead he felt like taking a walk and would meet her at the 72nd Street entrance to Central Park. *Well*, she thought, *pleasure postponed is pleasure heightened. Besides, it will be good to talk, and maybe he has a heavy lunch to walk off. Then we'll get down to business.*

But instead, Ash took her as far as the Bethesda Fountain, and then walked her back. He barely looked at her. She didn't remember much of what he said, but the words "put ourselves on hold" were repeated several times. Likewise the words "time to take stock and think things through."

She didn't understand it. All she felt was a hollow, empty sensation. It was not a sense of rejection, nor even a sense of loss. Just a void in the pit of her stomach. She did not have much to say in response. She could think of nothing to say. It was not her style to complain, question, or cry. She was an adult and she was tough. Besides, she had been there before. She knew what rejection was all about.

The hiatus in their affair was short lived. Three weeks later, in early October, Thatcher had extended an invitation to Louise (and David Lefkowitz) and Mike (and Marilyn Lefkowitz) to spend a weekend at his estate in Connecticut. The embarrassment of a double—or quadruple, or whatever the mathematics were—date pairing off Louise, Mike, David, and Marilyn with the wrong partners was only exacerbated by the smiling, open-minded liberality with which Livy Thatcher assigned one bedroom each, with king-size beds no less, to the two couples. Louise had long since trained David to sleep on the floor, something he did with little grace but no complaints—albeit with a guilt-inducing wistful puppy-dog look about his eyes. As for Ash and Marilyn, who knew? Throughout Friday night Louise moped jealously about what she *authoritatively* knew to be Mike's satyrlike appetites, and on Saturday morning she suspiciously studied her best friend's face over breakfast, looking for signs of excessive contentment.

After breakfast, David went off to play tennis, a sport Scott abhorred, with Livy. Marilyn enthusiastically accompanied Thatcher to his sixteen-foot sailboat, and even agreed to clean such fish as the two might catch. The other houseguests went golfing, an activity hated by both Thatcher and Livy alike. Mike and Louise were left to themselves. They went for a walk.

Thatcher's property extended nearly a mile along the north shore of Long Island Sound. It was a rocky, quiet, private, and quite valuable mile. Thatcher once remarked that, were he to sell his estate to a land developer, he could buy Rhode Island with the proceeds and still have enough money left over to carpet it.

Ash had remained cordially warm to Louise after severing their physical relationship. Indeed, Louise thought that if anything he was a better companion after the breakup than before. It was as if the intensity of their sexual needs, and such emotions as accompanied them, had somehow blanketed the earlier friendship that had preceded—and perhaps led to—their becoming lovers. Louise was pleasantly surprised by the emergence, or rather reemergence, of the witty, fun-to-be-with, caring man she had invited into her bed one snowy night in Chicago. It seemed contradictory that Ash could share good times with her, or share good sex with her, but could not share both. She added this polarity in Ash's character to her long list of generic flaws in the male species.

Louise followed Mike as he picked his way among the rocks and bushes lining the rough shore. From time to time, they would find a high, warm rock on which to sit, and would rest, talking and looking out at the boats bobbing on the sound. From time to time she would think about Marilyn and about that oversized bed in the room that Ash shared with her *and the bath, don't forget about the big, tempting sunken bathtub—more like a Jacuzzi, really.* And she would try to think of some way to *subtly, ever so casually, not really interested, but oh, by the way, find out if, well, you and Marilyn . . . now that we . . . No, of course it doesn't bother me, I was only curious.* After a while the warm sun melted her questions, *nagging suspicions, really, and none of my business,* and she smiled and laughed and talked and suddenly, with no warning whatsoever, found herself being swept into Ash's arms.

And kissed.

Ash could kiss, *I mean really kiss.* He kissed with a single-minded, overwhelming, obsessive concentration. He kissed perfectly, with a firm, persuasive passion. He withheld nothing, but kissed with enthusiastic fullness. There was no hidden agenda to Ash's kiss; it was a straightforward, emotionally honest, and passionately sincere kiss. He put all of himself into it, giving and receiving all that could be offered or got. Ash's kiss was the concentrated essence of everything she could hope a kiss would be.

He held her up against him close and tight in a hug that brought heat to her skin. It had been too long. The time in Greece, the weeks of separation. The kiss was too, too good. Crushed to his chest in an altogether pleasing crush, her breasts surged. She felt her nipples tightening and, at the same time, an electric yearning urgently mounting down where Ash, hard already, pressed himself between her legs. One of his hands stroked and pushed at her buttocks. She thrust her hips forward, rubbing against him, and shook as her yearning grew.

Time was short. She knew that things would be out of her

control in minutes—in seconds. She wasn't ready for this. It was over, *damnit, over*. This was not what she had expected. She wasn't looking for it. She hadn't wanted it. *Damnit, over.*

She pulled back. Ash wouldn't let her pull back. She turned her head. Ash followed her, bringing her back with kisses. She turned farther, tilting her chin up. He went for her neck. That was worse. *No, better.*

"Mike." *Oh hell, woman, you are gasping.* "Mike, I thought this had end . . . ahhhh . . . stop that! Ended. You know, over. Done. Finished. Ended. How do you expect me to concentrate? We have to . . . stop that! I want to talk about . . ."

Mike slid his fingers into her hair, gripped, and turned her face squarely toward his. He said nothing. He just looked at her, looked into her eyes with an intensity she had never seen before. Just looked. Then drew her head forward and kissed her again. Longer this time, and deeper. Fiercer.

"We have to talk."

"OK. Louise, I love you. That's enough talk, so shut up."

"Mmmppffff!"

Ash bent her backward, lowering her to the ground. Absentmindedly, not really concentrating on the matter, she mentally sighed in relief that he had chosen a dry, grassy spot away from the pebbly shore. His hand was under her pullover. Her bra was unsnapped. Her pullover was bunched up around her neck. His shirt was open and his bare chest lay burning on hers. Her slacks were unbuttoned. He caressed her for a too short (*too long?*) moment. Her slacks and her panties slid down over her knees. His blue jeans were so swollen that his zipper was locked. He tugged it free. She was naked from the waist—*no, neck*—down. He was completely naked. He pulled her legs apart with neither gentleness nor violence. He knelt between her legs. He leaned forward. Her legs bent awkwardly, constrained by the slacks around her calves. Ash pulled them off, hurling them impatiently away. He straddled her, opening her legs. No foreplay, not really, because it was now. It had to be now.

He filled her and it was just right. She felt a belonging to the two of them, her with him within her, and he within, two needs that became the quelling of need. She was usually a quiet lover, but this time she cried out, over and over again.

They finished soon, but not too soon, and lay together, Mike still on top and inside her, each coated with the other's sweat and each relishing the sultry, smooth feel of the other's flesh. Mike pushed himself up slightly to lift his weight, still maintaining skin-to-skin contact, still softly in her. From time to time he brushed a light, affectionate kiss against her lips.

Time passed. Then Louise gave a start, realizing where they were and the condition they were in. She pushed at him gently. "Mike, we're in public view. Suppose someone comes along. People can see us from the boats on the sound. Scott's out there somewhere. Come on, roll off."

Ash wouldn't budge. He eased his weight back down on her to keep her from pulling away and kissed her again.

"Come on, Mike. I thought this relationship was over. Or on hold. Come on, before we are a public scandal. If anyone sees us, what will they think?"

Ash grinned and answered, "They will think envious, evil, lustful thoughts, that's what they'll think. Just like me. Besides, the nearest boat is a mile away and we're mostly behind the bushes anyway." He pressed another, harder kiss against her lips, shifting his weight a little to the left and cupping her breast with his right hand. He squeezed and stroked it, the tip of his index finger circling her nipple. Louise sighed and laid her head to the side. Mike began to kiss and nibble her neck just below the ear.

Louise affected a shy, little-girlish voice when she complained about something she really didn't want to complain about. She used it now, saying, "A public scandal. What will my mother think?"

He paused and lifted his head. "You mean about the photos in the *National Enquirer*?"

"Yeah, and the front-page headlines."

"Lust in the Boardroom."

"Naked Executives in Love Nest Romp."

"Yeah."

"Yeah."

Louise felt him harden within her. She had never had that happen before. Held inside her, he began to grow. He grew quickly and she found it vastly different than merely being entered. Better, too. Much better. Fleetingly, she decided that the night before Mike, or maybe Marilyn, it didn't matter which, had slept on the floor just like poor David. Stalwart a lover though Mike Ash was, even he was not energetic enough to come back this fast after a night of cavorting with another woman.

* * *

They spoke little as they walked back hand in hand to Thatcher's house. Ash once squeezed her hand very tightly and said, "You know, I do love you, Louise." Then he spoiled it by continuing, "Do you love me?" Louise silently looked away.

It wasn't until dinnertime that she realized that she had been without contraceptive protection.

The first time Mike and Louise had broken off their affair, it had been at Ash's initiation. The reconciliation, too, had been his doing. The second time, Louise thought, it would be her decision. And this time, the break would be final.

"I am," she announced to Marilyn, "calling it off with Mike."

Marilyn, sitting in one of the posture-improving Danish modern chairs in Louise's living room, blinked, shook her head, and in a not-at-all-kindly tone of voice replied, "What for? If the problem is that he isn't another one of your married men, we can fix that fast enough."

"That, Marilyn, is the shittiest thing anyone has ever said to me. Ever."

"Sorry, but for Christ's sake, Louise, the guy is the best-looking proposition I have ever seen. I mean from what you've told me about him, from what I've seen myself, he is just about wonderful. What's wrong? What's turned you off?"

Louise sighed. "Well, you know he's a good lover."

"Yes, I do."

"*Oh?* You do, do you?"

"What I mean is, from what you've said about . . ." Marilyn paused, looking archly at Louise. "Oh. Oh. I get it. Last month when we all went up to Chateau Thatcher. I was wondering when you'd get around to that. Well, for your information I slept in the bathtub, or Jacuzzi, or whatever that thing is."

" 'Meow,' said the cat," Louise replied. "Sorry. Anyway, that's all there is. I mean, being a good lover. There isn't anything else."

"Like for example?"

"Oh, long walks together. Dinner out. Talking about things. Sharing things. The stuff that makes up a relationship. I mean a real relationship."

"Setting aside the fact that the word *relationship* went out with the '70s, precisely how to you expect to go walking, dining, et cetera, while you spend most of your time hiding the fact that you two are even on a first-name basis. You're obsessed with keeping this affair of yours a secret from Thatcher. Christ, you two act like you have jealous spouses dogging your every step. Clandestine romance. Forbidden passion. How can you expect poor Mike to take you out for an evening on the town, if you are both paranoid that someone will spot you and turn you into that ogre, Thatcher?''

"He is not an ogre. He just has this thing about office romance."

"So what? If he doesn't like it, sue him for sex discrimination."

"Never. Besides, Marilyn, if you tick off the boss, no matter how right you think you are, you're going to suffer for it. I'm on my way to the top. Scott likes me—and I like him, by the way—and I am not going to cross him on anything he thinks is important. One of these days I may be in line for his job, and there is nothing, *nothing*, so important that I am going to screw up for it."

"OK. So that's a given. But still, as long as you two are furtively slinking around in the secret-assignation mode, you shouldn't really expect Mike to put flowers and chocolates on your desk every morning."

"And another thing, we don't have anything in common."

"Oh God! Oh, spare me! Come on, Louise! You have told me over and over and—"

"No, really. Oh, I thought we did. Back at the beginning. But it was all superficial. Actually, we are total opposites. We don't agree on anything. Look, just last week we took a risk and went to see *La Bohème* at the Metropolitan Opera with Jimmy Levine conducting. I loved it. I cried at the end . . .''

"You always do."

"Do you know what Mike said afterward? He said it wasn't an opera, it was Ringling Brothers, Barnum and Bohème. He said Levine was less a conductor than a motorman."

"Oh, for shame. Oh, horror, horror, horror, tongue nor heart cannot—"

"Don't be sarcastic. Another thing, he doesn't like Greek food. When we are out of town together, he refuses to go to Greek restaurants with me. I really came to like Greek cuisine when David and I—"

"Clearly grounds for divorce. Any judge in the country would award you a million-dollar settlement after hearing that."

"And he is so mean about David."

"Well, what do you expect? My dear ex-hubby is, if I am not mistaken, your lover."

"Was. Not 'is.' "

"Even when you and he went to Greece this September? On that long tour of the romantic Greek Isles? Leaving poor lonely Mike Ash back home all alone in New York?"

" 'Meow,' said the cat. It wasn't like that at all. You know Dave and I had been planning that trip for a year. We had our reservations before Mike and I . . . well, and anyway, David is my friend and he was really looking forward to the trip and I couldn't disappoint him and he didn't lay a hand on me. And, anyway, Mike never said a word about it."

"Ah, so you had separate cabins after all? I thought you told me—"

"No, but they were double bunks. He was on top."

"Just as I suspected. His favorite position."

"Marilyn! You are being a real bitch tonight. We didn't—"

"Not even once?"

"No."

"No?"

"I said, 'No!' "

"No, never? Or no, hardly ever?"

"No. Well. Well . . ."

"Well, what?"

"Once."

"Just once?"

"Twice, really."

"Do I hear three? Do I hear four? Do I hear . . ."

"Twice. He kept looking at me with those puppy-dog eyes, and . . . well, you know."

"Yeah, I guess I do."

"Besides, it's not like I was being unfaithful to Mike or anything."

"Ahh? Could you explain that for me? I seem to be a little slow tonight. I'm having a little trouble with the concept of your sleeping with Dave, and not—"

"It's not like Mike and I are married. He doesn't have any exclusive rights. And I don't either. Who is he to care who I sleep with? I don't care who he screws."

"Doubtless that explains your utter lack of interest in what went on when he and I were sharing a room up at Thatchers' place."

"That's different, and fuck you."

"Sure, it's different, honey. But don't you think, I mean for just one little minute, that maybe old Mike Ash is not quite as intellectually astute as you? Maybe he doesn't understand these subtleties with the same clarity as you. Don't you think that maybe Mike was a bit put off by your fling in the Aegean with the puppy-eyed Mr. Lefkowitz? After all, as I recollect, he was a mite chilly toward you when you returned."

"If he . . . if he was so . . . so paranoid to be that suspicious, that untrusting, then . . . then, why, that's just another reason to dump him!"

"Irrefutable logic, if I ever heard it. Look—"

"No! No, no, no. I will not have it! Ash has laid a two-month-long guilt trip on me about that time in Greece. Two months! I won't have it! I'm through with him!"

"Louise, you told me he never said a word about it."

"Exactly! Exactly! The son of a bitch! Now, I will not, I do not want to talk about this anymore. My mind is made up. It's over, Ash is history. I'm through with him. Finished. Done. Kaput. Got it? Finished!"

"Uh-huh, I got it. OK, then. Let's go out for a drink. Maybe we'll meet Mr. Right."

14

Nick Lee had finished his appetizer, had ordered a second vodka martini, and was eagerly awaiting the arrival of his veal Oscar. The pretheatre dining crowd was thinning and, consequently, service was quickening. Lee ate only one meal a day, and looked forward to it with gusto.

Shortly the waiter arrived, but he was not bearing veal Oscar. He was bearing a cordless telephone. "You have a call, Mr. Lee," he said.

Lee frowned. "I left explicit instructions that I was not to be disturbed." The waiter merely shrugged, and placed the phone next to Lee's butter plate. Lee picked it up and with little grace in his voice said, "This is Nick Lee speaking. How may I serve you, and it had better be important."

The speaker at the other end of the line had a heavy Japanese accent. "Ah, Mr. Lee. So sorry to disturb you, but Mr. Hidetake wishes to speak with you."

"Well, put him on then."

"Ah, no. He is shaving. He wishes to speak with you personally. He wishes that you join him for breakfast."

"What? Is he in America?"

"Ah, yes. We are at the Hotel Samurai Palace. Will you join—"

"What is he doing here? Why wasn't I told?"

"Ah, I cannot say myself. I am certain that Mr. Hidetake will explain these things to you at breakfast."

"Fine. At the Samurai, then. Shall we say 8:00?"

"Ah, excellent. This is just the time Mr. Hidetake asked for."

"Fine. Tell him that I'll meet him tomorrow morning in the breakfast room."

"Ah, no. You do not understand. He wishes you to join him for breakfast now. In a half hour."

"What?"

"When traveling, Mr. Hidetake keeps his schedule to Tokyo time. It is breakfast time now in Tokyo, and so it is breakfast time now for Mr. Hidetake. So then, you will be here in one half hour, yes? Yes. Good-bye."

Lee set the telephone down, narrowed his eyes, and began to worry.

"Mr. Lee," said Okinakao Hidetake, speaking in Japanese and taking Lee's hand, "it is good to see you again. I trust it was not inconvenient for you to indulge me in my little whim. I find international travel disrupts my mental rhythms unless I keep to Tokyo time. It is better, therefore, to disrupt the rhythms of my employees than my own, don't you agree? Not that you are an employee, but rather an honored associate. Please be seated."

"It is my honor to be your associate, and my honor to help you in any way I can," answered Lee in his reasonably fluent Japanese.

"I have taken the liberty of ordering for you so that we may talk and not be distracted by hovering waiters. I hope you will find a fruit cup and wheat toast appetizing.''

"Fine."

"Good. I am here in America for more reasons than merely this PegaSys affair. However, the PegaSys matter is part of the cause for my visit. I may speak candidly, I presume. Yes, I know I may. Then, Mr. Lee, I must tell you that there is a problem.''

Hidetake waited for Lee to respond. When Lee sat silently, Hidetake nodded appreciatively. Poker-faced silence was the right reaction. He continued, ''As you know, we once relied on the excellent services of Ferdinand and Imelda Marcos in such matters as the one at hand. Alas, events have deprived us of their cooperative and useful presence. Thereafter, I tried to use Taiwan, but unfortunately a country that derives an appreciable portion of its gross national product from the export of counterfeit Cabbage Patch Dolls is a most undesirable venue for serious financial transactions. Thus, instead, we have called upon our subsidiaries and certain of our allies in the Seychelles. It is in those islands that the laws are sufficiently flexible to permit your firm to underwrite certain financial instruments central to our goals. Unfortunately, Mr. Lee, unfortunately, the Seychelles are a most dogmatic Muslim culture. It is always so difficult to deal with Muslim law. Haven't you found that?''

Lee, being no fool, replied with an ambiguous ''Hai!''

''It is the prohibition against moneylenders that is so difficult to deal with. And, in these unhappy days of fundamentalist furor, one cannot flout such prohibitions easily. Another matter— the printers of those islands are, alas, of the Shiite sect. Not only were their sensibilities profoundly offended by having to typeset something written in English, the language of the Great Satan, you know, but to typeset something that dealt with equally Satanic usury—ah, me, well, there was a most disconcerting uproar.''

Hidetake watched Lee's face closely. *Yes, a tic, a faint tic in the left eyelid. How gratifying.*

''The result, Mr. Lee, the result is that we seem to have caused a rather widespread strike in those otherwise paradisiacal islands. And, we seem to have gotten the otherwise relaxed and cooperative government officials who oversee such matters as our endeavor in a bit of a snit. No one likes to see Shiites taking to the streets, Mr. Lee, and that is what might have happened had we not made certain arrangements.''

The word ''arrangements'' resulted in a rather stronger tic.

Hidetake took it as evidence that the time was ripe for increasing the pressure.

"Of course, Seppuku was deeply disgraced when it happened. The man responsible for managing, or rather failing to manage, this matter sends you this." Hidetake took a ribbon-banded scroll of rice paper from the inner pocket of his suit coat and handed it to Lee. Lee unrolled the scroll and found a *haiku* poem. Loosely translated it read, "To die in the hot white sun/ when snow covers the cherry trees at home/is sad beyond imagining."

Lee set the scroll down and looked questioningly at Hidetake.

"He made two copies," said Hidetake, "one for you and one to be returned to his wife with his head."

Lee's face blanched. *A most gratifying reaction,* Hidetake thought. *Perfection.*

"His head?" asked Lee, his voice rising. "His *head?*"

"Yes, of course. As you doubtless know, when a man does what is necessary to restore honor, he asks a friend to stand by him and remove his head. Otherwise, the agony of a slow death from the cuts in his intestines, Mr. Lee, the agony that might cause him to cry out and lose face. You Westerners call it 'hara-kiri,' do you not? One tries to write a memorable haiku before grasping the sword. The poem serves as a memorial for family and friends, and as an apology to those whom one has dishonored. In this way my deceased employee wished you to know that the disgrace has been removed from Seppuku Ltd."

Hidetake knew that his moment had come. Lee was off balance. There would never be a better time to strike than now. He drew two more pieces of paper from his coat and passed them to Lee, saying, "So then, honor is restored. But the Muslims must be placated. Here is an itemized list of the expenses we will incur. Arranging for the transshipment of such *large* items to Iran is most alarmingly costly, is it not? And with it is the invoice you must pay as your fair share of the burden. You will, of course, recognize that you no longer have any choice in the matter."

Nick Lee read the bill he had to pay, and blanched again.

15

It was almost 4:00 p.m. In the boardroom, the executives of PegaSys were beginning to gather for the company's November EMC meeting. The second Thursday of the month. At 4:00 p.m. Promptly.

Ash, arriving ten minutes early, strolled in bearing a bombshell in his hands and a smirk on his face. Grinning from ear to ear, he summoned a few of his cronies down to the end of the conference table. "Pete, Frank, Jack, come over here. I want you to see something." A few other PegaSys vice presidents drifted over to join the pack. Once a sufficient number were clustered around him, Ash unfurled the tightly rolled magazine he held in his hands, laying it flat on the mahogany table. "Here," he said, "look at this."

Around him there were a variety of appropriate noises: gasps of surprise, sharp intakes of breath, appreciative whistles, and dismayed comments such as "Uh-oh," "Disgusting," "Wait till Scott sees," and "Jesus, look at his tan." It was *People* magazine, and on the cover, beneath a bright-yellow banner that read "FROM MAGNATE TO MOGUL," was a picture of the prodigal son of PegaSys, Joe Jonas. Jonas was posed sitting on the hood of a Porsche 928. The Porsche was parked on a bluff overlooking the Pacific Ocean. There was a ("I'd give her a ten," someone remarked) blond sitting in the passenger seat.

More babbling from the background. "It looks like he's lost twenty pounds." "That car costs seventy grand." "I think his hair is growing back, growing back blond." "That is the most revolting thing I have ever seen. Open it up, I bet it gets even worse inside." "Yeah, quick, before Scott gets here."

Ash flipped the magazine open to the cover story. "FROM MAGNATE TO MOGUL—HOW CORPORATE EXEC JOE

JONAS BECAME HOLLYWOOD'S HOTTEST HONCHO.''
The photo on the opposite page featured Jonas in a Lake Erie-
sized hot tub holding a portable phone in one hand and a blond
in the other. It was a different blond. ''I don't think I can stand
this,'' someone muttered. On the next page there was another
picture, this featuring a tuxedo-wearing Jonas at a dinner table
with four of the equally tuxedoed kings of Hollywood. There
was an Oscar in front of Jonas. To his side, with her hands folded
on his shoulder and her chin resting on her hands, was yet another blond. ''What I find so profoundly offensive,'' said another voice, ''is that self-satisfied smile he wears in every one
of these pictures.'' ''Yeah,'' came the answer, ''and he's had
his teeth capped, too.'' Ash turned the page to reveal two more
photos, one of Jonas (flanked by a new blond assistant) at a
shooting location, talking to a covey of superstars, and the other
Jonas sitting behind a Macintosh II computer in his living
room—a room that looked as spacious as the Astrodome—
talking to two stunning, heretofore unphotographed young
women sitting languorously in front of his fireplace. ''Oh, for
shame, one of them's a brunette. I guess life in California isn't
perfect after all.'' ''No, that's not it. It's that he's used up the
supply of blonds and had to change flavors.''

Further comments from the chorus: ''California—the land of
fruits, flakes, and nuts.'' ''AIDS. They've all got AIDS out
there.'' ''See what happens when you leave the East Coast.
What a waste of time and talent.'' ''Skin cancer. All that time
in the sun causes skin cancer.'' ''He'll burn out and be dead
before he's fifty.'' ''He *is* fifty.'' ''Then it'll be any day now.''
''Smog. It's worse for your lungs than three packs a day.'' ''I
certainly would never want to live like that—I mean, perma-
nently. A couple of months, just to see what it's like . . .''
''Drugs. They all have thousand-dollar-a-day habits out there.''
''How fast do you think that car really goes?'' ''Forget the car.
How fast do those blonds really go?'' ''Earthquakes. The whole
state is going to fall into the San Andreas Fault.'' ''If we all can
rein in the shock to our delicate sensibilities that Mr. Jonas's
sybaritic depravity doubtless engenders in such people of taste
and breeding as we, then perhaps we can begin this meeting.''
Whoops. It was Thatcher, sneaking up behind the crowd.

In the ensuing embarrassed silence, everyone took his or her
place. Thatcher stepped to the head of the table and stood there
with his hands behind his back. After a suitably intimidating
pause, he began, ''Just that you might be aware of it, I have

always held, and continue to hold, Joe Jonas in the highest regard. I was disappointed when he left, and am not on speaking terms with him. Nonetheless, I can only view his accomplishments and the success of his new career with admiration. His lifestyle is one to which I do not aspire, but is his own business, not mine to criticize—nor, for that matter, a suitable topic for distracting the senior management of this corporation. I believe that we all have other issues to divert us.''

His hands still behind his back, Thatcher glared about the room. He paced to the left, turned sharply, and paced back to his original position. He was Captain Horatio Hornblower.

"This afternoon's agenda will be a departure from the usual. It will be brief, and I alone shall speak. Except, of course, for those of you who have questions. All right, then, let me begin. A month has passed since AIW announced its hostile intentions toward this company. I am profoundly disturbed at what has happened here since. I had hoped that we would be able to weather the shock of AIW's takeover bid with no disruptions to this firm's operations. My hopes have been dashed. In reviewing the flash reports on weekly results, I find the following disquieting factors. One, sales are down 4 percent. Two, factory rejects are up 8 percent. Three, employee turnover is up 5 percent. Four, employee absence is up 11 percent. Five, receivables are off by nearly 30 percent. And, finally, customer complaints are up 6 percent. These results are utterly unacceptable. Unacceptable. Do you take my meaning? Ladies and gentlemen, the health and prosperity of PegaSys are my—and should be your—paramount concern. The AIW affray clearly has hurt morale badly, and that loss of morale is weakening this corporation. It is, I suppose, natural for all of us, from those on the factory floor to those in the executive suite, to be upset by the attack of a predator who threatens both our careers and the enterprise to which we have devoted our lives. Upset though we may be, we cannot let this attack erode the quality of our work. If we do, we ourselves inadvertently becomes allies of the very people who would destroy this organization. I look to all of you to take the actions needed to reestablish the level of quality that is PegaSys's hallmark. I would not have us win the fight against AIW only to lose that which is best in our products, our service and our reputation.''

Thatcher paused and looked around the room. Every face wore a serious expression. He was pleased. Disturbed by the possibility of a successful takeover, his management team was drifting off course. He needed to bring them back.

Lying through his teeth, Thatcher continued, "I will not touch on this topic again. Are there any questions? No? Good. Next, let me update you on the tender offer. With considerable reluctance—you all know how I abhor such tactics—I have today secured board approval for a number of measures of the sort colloquially known as 'poison pills." These measures are intended to discourage raiders from acquiring us. Or, if they do not, to make the acquisition both expensive and distasteful. Gladys is down the hall at the Panasonic machine making Xerox copies of the board resolution now, so you should all be able to see them by the time this meeting is over. I want you to know that among the resolutions passed was a so-called golden para chute for all the officers of the firm. Except me. I am sufficiently wealthy that I do not need one; most of you, however, need to be assured of your personal financial security if we lose control of our company.

"Further, on this distasteful topic, I have not, and I will not, implement measures that threaten the long-term well-being of this corporation. In the face of vocal opposition from our investment bankers, lawyers, and other advisors, I and the board have rejected such strategies as selling off important subsidiaries, making imprudent acquisitions to burn off our cash reserves, or pursuing a leveraged buyout and taking on so much debt as would drain this company dry. I will defend PegaSys to the last extreme, but I will not use in its defense that which would destroy it. Question in the back? Yes, you Jack."

"Scott, there was an article in the *Times* about potential white knights or maybe greenmail."

"I saw it. The answer is no. We will not be greenmailed. Not ever. Greenmail is morally repugnant. Further, we will neither solicit nor accept offers from other corporations, from so-called white knights, to buy us in lieu of AIW. I believe, as I think you all do, that PegaSys's strength is inseparable from our independence. Our culture, our practices, our people, all of the elements that have made a success are sufficiently different from those of other companies that neither I nor the board can envision anyone buying us and still preserving what we treasure about this firm. We want to maintain the independence that has made us what we are, not auction ourselves off to the highest bidder and then let that bidder wreak rack and ruin on our customers, products, and employees. We have, by the by, received some ever-so-kind expressions of ever-so-well-meant interest from certain parts in Silicon Valley and elsewhere. With all due respect to the august senior management who initiated these doubtless sincere overtures, our response to them has been that the only difference between the disasters they would inflict on PegaSys and the havoc that Brian Shawby would produce is that with Shawby, we might at least get a chuckle or two out of the debacle. Yes, Phil, you have a question?''

"Scott, are we going to win?"

"Phil, I do not know. We will do our best. That is all I can promise."

"How does it look?"

"Both good and bad. Let me tell you why. First, the money side of the equation. AIW originally bid $85 per share for 80 percent of the company. Subsequently they've increased the offer twice. It now stands at $97 a share. That nets out to $16 billion and change. Big bucks. Our team has checked with every lender in the country, and no one, I repeat no one, would lend AIW a dime. If AIW were to borrow the money they need to buy us, the result would be $6.6 billion in equity and $17 billion in debt—a company that owed the banks two and a half times more money than it was worth. Even presuming a major asset sell-off, it would be a company whose combined earnings would cover less than 70 percent of the annual interest on that debt—forget about the principal. Now, one can always work a little accounting magic and conjure up some off-balance-sheet voodoo to make the numbers look better, but, ladies and gentlemen, the debt involved is so awesomely large that not even the wizardry of Merlin could prevail against it. No rational person could conclude otherwise than that the whole transaction is unaffordable for the likes of AIW. So, and here's my point, from a financial standpoint, the answer to your question 'How does it look,' is that it looks as pathetic as a pig trying to fly. It looks like it cannot and will not happen. Nonetheless, the shifty Mr. Shawby, and his shadowy advisors claim that the financing of the deal is a sure thing. They just won't say how or why. Not just yet. Of course, we are suing them to find out. Our lawyers say that the odds are we won't win, but we are suing them nonetheless.

"Let us now, however, hypothesize what happens if Shawby's gang does have the money. Let us stipulate, as the lawyers say, arguendo, that the laws of economics, physics, and, indeed, nature itself have been transgressed in some fiendishly preternatural manner, and that Shawby can get funding. Let us say that he has become the instrument of the devil, summoned up the powers of darkness, and sold his soul to the Prince of Evil. Although, according to all reports, Old Nick is a better bargainer than that! Let us say, by hook or by crook or by however, Shawby has got funding. Then, how does it look? The answer to that is, my dear Phillip, it looks lousy.

"The problem is who owns our stock—the problem is the institutional investors. About 63 percent of our shares are owned by the institutions, principally by pension funds and fund managers. These organizations self-righteously wrap themselves in the flag of 'fiduciary responsibility,' claiming that they are obliged to sell off whatever they own to any predator who offers them a fast buck in exchange. Coincidentally, a percentage of their fees stem from how fast a buck they can turn. Accordingly, they have not an iota of interest in long-term performance, and will tender our stock to Shawby at the drop of a hat. Were this country governed by officials who had a scintilla of business savvy or any genuine concern about the ultimate viability of American enterprise, someone would enact legislation that permitted the pension funds to buy and sell stock on only one day each year. Then we would see investment decisions based on the long-term prosperity of American enterprise and, a salubrious by-product, we would find large quantities of bright young MBAs seeking productive employment in those industrial sectors that contribute to, rather than detract from, our national economic well-being.

"But I digress. So, there is 63 percent of our stock that Shawby is almost certain to get; indeed, many of our funds have already locked in their sordid gains by selling our stock to the arbitrageurs. Shawby needs 80 percent under the terms of his offer, of which 63 percent will come from the funds. We need to keep the other 17 percent away from him. Let me restate that—we need to be sure that 21 percent of our outstanding shares will not be tendered. What can we bank on? Well, we can bank on the 7.5 percent that *I* own; of that you may be certain. I imagine that we can bank on the 4.7 percent that the people in this room and other employees of PegaSys own. And, we can bank on another 2.6 percent that certain friends of ours control. In sum, we can bank on just short of 15 percent, about two-thirds of what we need. Where will the other third come from? I do not know. If I did know, I would sleep better at night. We have, of course, taken a raft of advertisements in the newspapers arguing our case. We have written letters to all of our shareholders. We are now personally calling and visiting the institutional investors, for what little the effort may be worth. And, beginning next week, we will be trying to meet face to face with our other large shareholders, mainly wealthy individual investors. We need to persuade the owners of another 6 percent of our stock not to tender to Shawby. I hope and pray that we can. Does that answer your question, Phil?''

''Yes, but it raises another one. Does anyone have any guesses as to what Shawby is doing to raise the money?''

''Yup. But guesses are all that they are. Look, the traditional way to do a takeover is to line up short-term loans from a bunch of banks, then, after the deal is done, float some high-yield junk bonds to pay down the banks. Our best intelligence, as I said, is that no bank is touching the deal—and no one, not even Nick Lee's hoodlums at Lee, Bach and Wachutt, would underwrite junk bonds for such an impossible set of economics. Not even assuming that Shawby sold off our buildings, our lands, our patents, and everything else that wasn't nailed down to reduce the debt. Where does he get $16 billion? It is, after all, rather too large a sum to steal. We have three guesses. First, drug money. Don't laugh, apparently it has happened before. It is, when I think on it, a rather sorry commentary on the state of America that drug barons can make even more money helping takeover artists than they can peddling dope. Our second guess is some foreign government. That too, our investment bankers tell me, has happened before. Our third guess is that Shawby is fronting for some conspiratorial consortium of foreign companies. If either of the latter is the case, then we might normally expect to have no problem quashing Shawby. PegaSys manufactures what the laws call a 'strategic technology,' and there are a sizable number of statutes in place to keep strategic technologies from falling into the hands of foreigners. Unfortunately, the current administration, like its predecessor, has done little to enforce these laws; moreover, PegaSys has few friends in Washington. As a consequence, we can expect no help from the government. If it is the case that drug money is behind Shawby . . . well, who knows what happens? Any other questions? Yes, Frank.''

''Scott, this whole thing sounds like Shawby and Lee are pretty sleazy operators. Are there any dirty tricks going on?''

The expression on Thatcher's face soured. He had been hoping that particular question would not be asked. ''Yes, I am sorry to report that there have been. All in all, Shawby and Lee seem almost as interested in humiliating this company as they are in acquiring it. I fear that the business world these days has become a game of wolves. It seems that it is no longer sufficient to defeat your opponent, but rather that you cannot feel victorious unless you make him bleed as well. So, yes, there have been dirty tricks. Too many of them. You know we were burglarized three Sundays ago. Phones have been tapped, my own among them, and Mike and Louise, among others, have been approached with bribes—or something so close to a bribe that I cannot tell the difference. Further, there have been a fair number of attempts to besmirch the reputation of this company and my personal reputation in the media. Thankfully, none of these have succeeded. As yet. There have been some downright libelous letters sent to important shareholders, and a rather suspect mailing just today to the board of directors. Each of them received a horribly misleading white paper entitled 'The International Liabilities of American Directors in Takeover Litigation: How Foreign Courts Preserve Shareholders' Rights' from some British law firm called Quint and Claggart. I suspect that there have been other unsavory activities of which we are as yet unaware. Does someone else, yes, Jake, you have a question?''

"Is there anything that those of us here should be doing to help?''

"Yup. There sure is, Jake. Run your piece of this company like it should be run, and forget that Brian Shawby exists. If you do that, then if—no, when—we come out of this mess, we will be well.''

16

AFTER THE EMC MEETING ADjourned, Mike returned to his office with Louise. They had just sat down at his small conference table when, unannounced, Thatcher strolled in. Ash, who had considerable difficulty keeping his hand off Louise's thigh when they sat near one another, carefully put both hands on the tabletop. To make doubly sure that they did not wander off into unseemly temptation, he wove his fingers together tightly.

Thatcher perched his lankly frame on the credenza beneath Ash's window. The light from the window behind him turned his unruly white hair into a glowing halo. It also cast his face into shadow, hiding the expression in his eyes. Both Mike and Louise had seen him use the tactic before. He usually did it when he had something nice to say.

Thatcher folded his arms and turned his head, glancing out the window. Across the street a new office building was rising. It had already reached a height of forty stories; soon it would block the view out of Ash's window. An enormous orange construction crane sitting precariously on top of the new building was lifting the steel girders needed to add more floors to the tower. Thatcher looked at the name emblazoned on the crane— a name he had never heard of, a foreign name. It was Japanese or, perhaps, Finnish. "Sometimes I fear I am the only American manufacturer left in America," he mused.

Thatcher swiveled back to face Louise and Mike. He cleared his throat. "Ahem. Harumpf. Well. Well, we have been at this a month now, and I think the time has come for me to tell you how pleased I have been with what you two have done. It has been quite a long while since I have had the opportunity to work with either of you closely, and . . . well, I had a rather different perception of your talents before we started. You have done very well. I think between you . . . well, the two of you . . . in concert, you two are rather the single best executive in this firm."

Mike and Louise traded looks. Leave it to Thatcher to come up with a backhanded compliment.

"Don't take that amiss. Individually you are superb. But as a team, you are something special. You are putting out results that rival the best Joe Jonas ever did. And what Joe did was very fine indeed, bless him. So, I want to say that I am quite impressed. Yes, quite impressed. I want you both to know that after this is over, if we get through it alive and whole, I intend to put you in positions where we can capitalize on your talents. Mike, effective January first, you are promoted to the presidency of our software subsidiary. Louise, this is still confidential: Curt's doctor has diagnosed a heart problem, and he has asked for a medical retirement. You will fill his job as this company's chief financial officer. Also effective January first. Both of you will report directly to me. Both of you will draw down the compensation and the perquisites of senior vice presidents. Both of you will be moved to larger offices on a side of the building with a better view than that construction derrick across the street. Congratulations. Now, what do you think of that?''

"Uh," said Mike.

"Uh," said Louise.

"Jesus!"

"Shit!"

Thatcher frowned with perplexity.

"Run!"

"Get out of here!"

It was the most peculiar reaction to a promotion that Thatcher had ever seen.

Ash, white-faced with terror, flung himself out of his chair, grabbed Thatcher's shoulder, and wrenched him across the room. Louise hurled the door open and screamed, "Run, for God's sake, run!"

Thatcher, his ire rising at this altogether unseemly conduct, tried to tug back at Ash, but Ash merely yanked harder. Thatcher dug in his heels. Ash thrust his face to within inches of Thatcher's and bellowed, "Run, goddamn it, run! That fucking crane is falling!"

Crane? Oh. The crane.

Thatcher sprinted out of Ash's office. Ash dashed behind him. Outside, executives, secretaries, and clerks fled in every direction. Thatcher vaulted nimbly over a desk, clipping a table lamp with his ankle. The lamp crashed to the floor. Ash, dodging around the desk stepped on the lamp, crushing the broken ceramic into the carpet. Louise, athletic and fit, was far out in front. She beckoned them urgently onward, pointing to an emergency exit in the building's core. Ash swore under his breath at the eight cigarettes he had smoked so far that day. He heard a grinding sound behind. The crane was coming through the wall of his office. Where his office used to be. Thatcher yelled something Ash couldn't understand. It was gibberish. It sounded like a pagan war cry or an invocation to an unknown god. Louise slammed the emergency exit door open with her shoulder. There was a momentous roaring sound like a Boeing 747 landing. The crane was well into the building, and the building screamed. All fifty-three stories of PegaSys Center shuddered. Thatcher lost balance, ricocheted off of the emergency exit's door frame and floundered into the core stairwell. The building shook wildly. Ash stumbled and jolted face forward onto the floor, his momentum sliding him forward several feet. *Nine hundred dollars' worth of Hickey Freeman suit ruined.* Shards of flying glass tore at his back. *Nine hundred dollars' worth of Hickey Freeman suit ruined.* The ceiling came apart. Tiles and insulation blasted into a thick choking dust. Ash was coated white. *Nine hundred dollars' worth of Hickey Freeman suit ruined.* The crane thundered to a jolting stop, resting against the steel crossbeams of the floor above. It was suddenly very quiet. Louise reached forward, took Ash's wrists, and pulled him into the stairwell. Ash heard the fabric in his suit tear.

Ash stood up. Louise looked at him and said, "You know, that suit is ruined."

"Thank you for your concern, Louise," Mike replied, "and no, I am not hurt at all."

A chilly drizzle fell on Detective Ryerhurt's head. It was too light a drizzle to deserve an umbrella, but sufficiently thick to dampen his hair. He didn't have an umbrella anyway. The drizzle beaded the London Fog trench coat his wife had bought him four Christmases back. The trench coat embarrassed him. Every other cop in the precinct house made snide remarks about Sam Spade. The drizzle continued to fall. It was a little harder now. The firemen were all wearing hats. Their heads weren't getting wet. Maybe, he thought, he should get a snap-brim hat to go with the coat. Then the rest of the boys on the force would really have something to laugh about.

Thatcher opened an umbrella and moved close to Ryerhurt. Ryerhurt thought about moving away. He didn't want any favors from Thatcher. He didn't want any favors from anyone at PegaSys. PegaSys had been giving him too much business for him to feel good about accepting anything from PegaSys, least of all from its boss. Still, Thatcher's umbrella kept the rain off his head.

A fireman came over. He was wearing a rain slicker and a helmet. He had a steaming cup of coffee cradled in his hands. Ryerhurt wished that he had a cup of coffee, too. "Well," the fireman said, "that's that. We've been through the whole place. We've got everyone out now. You got a lot of lucky people in this building. No one killed. Not even a broken bone. Just some cuts and scrapes and bruises. A lot of lucky people. Guy in the cab on Madison Avenue wasn't so lucky. I-beam landed on him. Only fatality. Otherwise, a lot of lucky people today.''

"Thank God for that. Any structural damage to the building?'' asked Thatcher.

"Not as far as we can see. Engineers will have to go over it tomorrow, but I think mostly you just got a smashed-out wall, a floor or two of damaged electrical and air, and a lot of ruined furniture. If it was my call, I'd say everything except the fifty-first and fifty-second floors could be occupied again tomorrow. But it ain't my call, so you gotta keep your people off of everything above the forty-fifth.''

The fireman sipped at his coffee. Then he added, "This is the shits, you know. Every year or so one of them things falls over. You'd think the goddamned mayor or the city council or somebody would do something about it. People die. It's the construction industry, you know. They own this town.''

Shaking his head, he walked away. Ryerhurt and Thatcher stood silently beneath the umbrella. Minutes passed, and Ryerhurt's partner showed up. He had been interviewing the construction company's site manager and the crane operator. He looked at Thatcher's umbrella jealously.

Ryerhurt said to his partner, "What did they have to say?''

"About what you would expect. They were lifting a bunch of I-beams, the same as they have every day for the past two months. Then, bang, there is this grinding noise, and the operator feels the cab tipping over toward the street. He yanks on the brake and jumps. The crew boss was behind him and saw it all. A half dozen other guys say they saw the same thing. Metal fatigue, snapping bolts, who knows. A city construction inspector was there just yesterday and gave the whole thing a clean bill of health.''

"Yeah?''

"Yeah. I wonder what model Mercedes the construction inspectors are driving this year.''

"Yeah.''

"One thing though.''

"Yeah?''

"That crane. If you look up at it, you can make out a name on it.''

"Yeah?''

"Says 'Seppuku Ltd.' Does that ring any bells?''

"Yeah. Same name as was on the van those cleaning people used three, four weeks ago. The one the Yakuza boys with all

the heavy artillery used. Now that is a very interesting goddamned fact, isn't it?''

Thatcher pursed his lips and said quite slowly, ''Yup, Officer,
that is indeed a very interesting fact.''

''It was an accident, Mr. Lee, an accident,'' Hidetake said,
speaking rapid-fire Japanese into the hotel phone. ''How many
times must I tell you that?'' Hidetake listened for a moment
and, with mounting fury, snapped, ''You are not being logical.
What benefit could we gain? What possible profit would we
expect? What might we do other than shame ourselves and alert
our enemy to our intentions? We are not assassins! And if we
were, please give us credit for choosing a weapon more subtle
than a fifteen-story-tall, bright-orange crane with our company
name painted on it in six-foot-high letters! This was a blunder!
Happenstance! Coincidence! Do you understand? It was an accident, and you are an infantile fool to think otherwise! Now,
let me get back to work, and you get some sleep. There is much
that needs to be done, not the least of which is arranging transportation for the head of a certain employee of Seppuku's construction equipment subsidiary!''

17

THE PHONE WAS RINGING AS
Thatcher unlocked the door of his Sutton Place pied-à-terre. He
keyed in the security code that disarmed his burglar alarm and
entered the building.

He answered it. ''Thatcher here.''

A gravel-voiced, Brooklyn-accented man replied, ''Yeah, dis
Scott Thatcher?''

''Yup. To whom am I speaking?''

"Good. Real good. I been wantin' ta talk ta ya. Dis is Joey da Bridge."

"Pardon?"

"Joey da Bridge. Ya know, Joey Varrazano. Remember me?"

"Oh! Joey. Of course. For heaven's sake! It's been—what?—ten years or more since I heard from you. Joey, how are you?"

"Aw, I'm fine. Little fatter. Little balder. But just fine. How's by youse?"

"I have been better."

"Yeah. I can unnerstand. All dese scumbags tryin' to rape ya, huh? Shawby and his crowd? Dat's gotta suck."

"While I might not express the situation in quite those terms, you have captured the essence of my sentiments."

"Yeah, well, dat's what I called about. Ya know, I retired a few years back, left the union and spent some time off."

"Uh, I thought I read that . . ."

"Yeah, I took some time off down in Atlanta. Anyways, since I was, so ta speak, on sabbatical, dey made dis new guy prez of da union, see. And dis new guy tinks he is one hot shit. And ya know about all dat stock of youse guys we own—"

"Stock? Why, no, I wasn't aware that your union owned any PegaSys shares?"

"Oh, yeah. Way back when, aw hell, twenty-five years ago when I bought dat foist computer from youse guys, I figured, shit, dese guys know what de're doing. Dese guys are smart guys and smart guys make da money. So I started havin' da union pension fund salt it away. 'Course we don't put it all in one place, ya know. Ya don't want dat da Feds and da tax turkeys and da rest of dem joiks should find it, huh? Maybe dat's why you don't know we got it. It's all in a bunch a little hidey-holes. Squirreled away, like, for a rainy day. Here, lemme look at dis printout here, and see what we got. Sez we got 3,973,856 shares now. Approximately."

"Approximately," muttered Thatcher, rapidly calculating that the International Brotherhood of Craftsmen Union and Fraternal Society had somehow or another secretly accumulated a 1.9 percent ownership interest in PegaSys, a quantity of shares that would make a major dent in the amount needed to defeat Shawby's takeover bid.

Joey continued, "Anyways, like I was sayin', dis new guy is runnin' da union and I get back from Atlanta and he seems ta be doin' OK and what da fuck, I'm over sixty-five and I figure I might as well retire ta Palm Springs anyway where it is warm, which my old lady has been on my ass about for so long I'd rather not tell you anyways. So I'm packin' up and gettin' ready to go play golf with movie stars when dis shitty takeover t'ing comes along. So I asks da new guy what he's gonna do with da stock and he sez he's gonna sell it all to dis Shawby guy—''

"Joey, I would like to . . ."

"Don't interrupt. I don't like to be interrupted, huh?''

"Yup, sure, Joey.''

"Anyways, I say, now dat's a dumb idea. I say, dis Thatcher guy pays dividends every year and every year da price of the stock goes up and da pension is dere for da long haul so that da membership can retire in comfort and security in da sunset of dere years. Which is only proper. And dis new guy sez, fuck youse, I'm sellin' da stock. Which was not so smart. So den he comes down with dis disease and has ta retire.''

"Oh. Well, I am sorry to hear that. Nothing serious, I hope.''

"Naw. Fatal.''

"Oh.''

"Yeah. Fatal. Foist t'ing tomorrow morning. Anyways, so I'm back in da president's seat and I wanted ya should know that no way, nohow, does the union sell its PegaSys stock to dat bozo Shawby. We may be a whole bunch of t'ings, but disloyal to our friends we ain't.''

"Ah . . . well, my. Joey, I cannot tell you how much I appreciate this. We need the support of our shareholders, and your support will make a very important contribution to keeping us independent.''

"Aw, it ain't nothin'. It's just smart business. Like I sez, bet on da smart guys to make money. You're da smart guy, not Shawby. Another t'ing I think about, by da way, is dis. Maybe youse guys need some more help. Maybe it don't hurt so much if somebody torches dis guy Lee's office or snatches Shawby's kids. Or maybe Lee wakes up one mornin' and dere's Shawby's head at da foot of da bed, like in da movies. Ya know, somet'ing like dat.''

"I think not. Joey—''

"Yeah, yeah. I know. Straight arrow. Shit, I probably would of been disappointed if ya said yes. Well, youse go ahead and do what youse tink is da right t'ing ta do. Us guys is on your side all da way. And, hey, don't be a stranger. Give me a call sometime. OK, pal?''

"OK, sure, Joey. I'll do that.''

"Yeah, well, ciao, Paisan.''

"Ciao, Joey."

Thatcher hung up the phone and stared off into space. Joey's call was the first good news he had heard in weeks. Maybe the run of the cards was changing. Maybe Lady Luck had decided to move to his side of the table. Then, remembering that (like all good New England puritans) he believed in hard work, not good luck, he smiled, shook his head, and began taking off his coat.

The phone rang again.

"Thatcher here."

"Hi, Scott. This is Roy Knight."

"Roy, glad you called. Have you got things at the office under control?"

"Sure do. It will be business as usual tomorrow for everyone except the people on two floors, fifty-one and fifty-two. I have a couple of friends in the city government and managed to get an inspection team up on overtime. We're footing the bill for the overtime, but I figured you wouldn't have any problem with that."

"No, just as long as it is documented, and just as long as overtime is all that it is."

"And cab fare and four garbage pizzas and a six-pack."

"OK, but photocopy the receipts and send the whole shebang to the right people."

"Will do. Another thing, Scott, I have gotten hold of Wintergreen."

"Good! Congratulations. Who is he? Or she? Or it?"

"Don't know, except that he's a he. He says he'll give me his real name when we meet."

"Great. I'd like to talk to him, too. When will he be here?"

"Well, he lives in northern California."

"So what, we'll pay his plane fare."

"That's a problem, Scott, he doesn't like airplanes. He doesn't trust them."

"Don't blame him. What does he want to do, drive cross-country?"

"Doesn't have a car and doesn't have a license. And no girlfriend with a car to drive him."

"Aha! He sounds like a classic hacker! I look forward to meeting him. Well, look, it turns out that I have to be in California next week. In fact, Mike Ash and Louise Bowman and I all have to be there. I'll have Mike join you. Set up a meeting with this very talented young genius, and you and Mike try to woo him and win his loyalty to PegaSys. I want him on our team."

"Consider it done. Any particular day?"

"Wednesday."

"The day before Thanksgiving? What are you all doing out of town so close to the holiday?"

"Suffering fools, and not gladly. I'll fill you in tomorrow. Call me here. Since Mike and Louise's offices are now alfresco, we will all be working here in my apartment. OK?"

"Sure. 'Night, Scott."

"Good night, Roy. Oh, wait. One other thing. Tomorrow, noon at the latest, I want a full readout of an outfit called Seppuku Ltd. Tell the gang in the library to get cracking on it. And you tap your sources, too. I want the stops pulled out on this one. I want everything you can find out."

18

IT WAS FRIDAY EVENING. BRIAN Shawby groaned. He'd been groaning since noon. A salty tear oozed out of the corner of his left eye, dribbled down his cheek, and fell into the sink. He stared at the mirror, winced, and groaned again. He could not bear to look at himself. It was too horrible. He tried to turn away, but, irresistibly compelled by the same perverse urge that makes all mankind gape with shuddering repugnance at that which they most abhor, he found his eyes tugged back to the loathsome spectacle. He looked. He saw. He bellowed with anguish.

Jennifer rattled the bedroom door, asking if he was all right. Shawby tried to answer affirmatively, but all that emerged from his lips was a heartbroken shriek.

The doctor had been no help at all. The doctor had said there was nothing that could be done. The doctor had diagnosed his plight as a simple reaction to the drugs that Lee had given him before he went on television. "Look, Mr. Shawby," the doctor had said, with little sympathy in his voice. "The body reacts to medication in sometimes unpredictable ways. You ingested some pretty potent substances, and, I must note, substances that are illicit without a prescription. There are reasons why the law doesn't let people take certain medications without the supervision of a physician, and one of those reasons is that they can cause adverse aftereffects. As you now know. Besides, it's not the end of the world. Things much worse have happened to other people."

Shawby rested his head against the mirror and gulped a wrenching sob. If, he thought, a dog looked as bad as he did, the health authorities would have it put down. He pulled his head back. A stringy tuft of hair remained stuck to the mirror. His hair transplant was rejecting.

Andrei Bezukhov walked through Central Park, listening half-heartedly to the instructions for his mission in California. His controller issued orders one by one, slowly, stopping to confirm Bezukhov's understanding of each minuscule detail. He insisted that Bezukhov repeat each of his instructions back to him word for word. Bezukhov felt like a child in kindergarten.

Reaching the end of his litany, the controller said, "Outside of the airport, in the car rental lot, you will find a man waiting in the car next to yours. To him you will say, 'Is the weather here always like this?' Do you understand?"

"Yes, Comrade. Outside of the airport, in the car rental lot, I will find a man waiting in the car next to mine. To him I will say, 'Is the weather here always like this?' "

"He will reply, 'Most of the year. Where do you come from?' Do you understand?"

"Yes, Comrade, I understand. He will reply, 'Most of the year. Where do you come from?' "

"You will answer, 'From Poughkeepsie, where it is colder.' "

"I will answer, 'From Poughkeepsie, where it is colder.' "

"He will say, 'I was born there,' and offer to shake your hand. You will take his hand."

"He will say, 'I was born there,' and offer to shake my hand. I will take his hand."

"As you shake hands, he will slip you a package containing a gun, which you will hide beneath your topcoat."

"A gun," said Bezukhov, more enthusiastic than he had been. "A gun! What kind? A Browning 9 mm? Am I getting a Browning?"

"No, comrade, a Colt Airweight."

Bezukhov was chagrined. He wanted a Browning. He wanted a Browning badly. He had to have a Browning. It was the right kind of gun. It was the *only* gun. It was the pistol that all true revolutionaries used. Felix Dzerzhinsky had carried a Browning 9 mm. Che carried a Browning 9 mm. The Red Brigade, Al Fatah, Black November—everyone who was anyone carried a Browning 9 mm. Even the heroic KGB agents in the movies carried Brownings. They were a status symbol. As diamond stickpins are to plutocratic capitalist oppressors, Brownings are to revolutionaries. Bezukhov wanted a Browning. Anything else would be unmanly.

"Why can't I have a Browning?" Bezukhov sulked.

"Because the Party is giving you a Colt. Now, as you shake hands with the man in the rental car parking lot, he will slip you a package containing a gun, which you will hide beneath your topcoat. Do you understand?"

"A Browning is a much better gun."

"Do you understand," barked the controller impatiently.

Bezukhov sighed. "Yes, Comrade, I understand. As I shake hands, he will slip me . . . ."

19

ASH SPOTTED JOE JONAS GRIN-ning, or rather leering, at him; he braced himself for the worst. Jonas, all six feet five of him, loomed hairily above the crowd waiting outside the gate where TWA flight 849, JFK to LAX, had landed. Paradoxically, Jonas was elfin, yet enormous. He looked like an overgrown, hirsute pixie. Ash wasn't the only person in the Los Angeles airport to spot Jonas. Everyone saw him. They couldn't miss him. Tall, tanned, ruggedly handsome, his shirt open to the waist, three heavy gold bracelets on his wrist, and a half dozen gold chains on his hairy, muscular chest, Joe Jonas exuded burly, good-spirited machismo. He always had. Most of the people in the airport lounge knew who he was, especially the women. And even those women who didn't recognize him found themselves eyeing him sideways. Joe Jonas was catnip to the ladies.

Ash shoved through the crowd. Jonas thrust one of his enormous paws out, seizing Ash's hand in a bone-crushing grip. "Mike," he growled in a deep, affable voice, "great to see you! Jesus, you look . . . my, my, my, you look like shit! Christ almighty, your face is so white people out here will think you've spent ten years in the state pen. What's the problem? Rough flight? Or is it just the troglodyte lifestyle you live back East? We gotta get you out in the sun, my man! Tomorrow we go to the beach!"

"Hi, Joe," replied Ash, screwing up his courage. There was only one way to deal with Joe Jonas. Joe was king of the put-down artists; his preferred method for showing affection was insult. The more outrageous the insult, the more Joe liked you. Like Ash, Joe had been born and bred on the streets of New York. His repertoire of insults was, therefore, encyclopedic. There was only one way to handle Joe Jonas and that was to give as good as you got. "You look great," Ash continued, "What's happened, have you found the fountain of perpetual middle age?"

"Cute, Mike. That was cute. Who writes your material for you, Don Rickles? And if he does, who reads it to you?"

"No, seriously, you look fantastic. How much did the hair transplant cost and did they give you a package deal with the chin tuck?"

"It's fresh air, fresh food, and exercise. None of which have polluted your body chemistry in twenty years."

"Yeah, and a daily dose of minoxydil, I'll bet," said Ash as he extended his middle finger. Jonas cocked an eyebrow and said, "What's that? Age? IQ? Penis length? Number of white parents? Anyhow, come on, let's get out of here. We've got places to go and people to see and things to do."

"Uh, sure. I'm staying at the Westwood Marquis. If you can drop me off there—"

"Forget it! Remember, the blood of the Vikings sings in my

veins! The night is young! The moon is full! The wind is strong! Strong ale, beautiful females, rich plunder, and the red blood of mine enemies! Out the oars, and up the sails! Tonight we pillage Los Angeles! Besides, you're staying with me, pal. I wouldn't let my best buddy put up at some hotel.''

The women in the airport lounge kept their eyes pinned to Jonas until he was out of sight. Their fantasy lives were all a little richer for having seen him.

Mike Ash had not expected to spend the weekend in Los Angeles. He was planning on spending it with Louise. However, late Friday morning at Thatcher's Sutton Place home, a package of reports, clippings, and printouts had arrived. It was the material that Thatcher had requested on Seppuku. Thatcher closeted himself with it for an hour, then announced that he wanted Ash to call Joe Jonas. "I have reason to believe that he may know something about this organization," he said. "See if he will talk to you. You and he were always pretty close."

So Ash called Jonas's office in Los Angeles. Like everyone else at PegaSys, he hadn't spoken to Joe since his resignation. If Thatcher wasn't on speaking terms with Joe Jonas, then no one was on speaking terms with Joe Jonas. Ash's call cleared three reluctant secretaries, and then, to his surprise, Jonas came on the line. He was delighted to hear from Ash. He would be glad to talk about Seppuku. He wouldn't do it over the phone. It would have to be face to face. No, not next week. He was busy as hell, but, look, "I don't have any plans for the weekend, so get your ass on a plane and I'll meet you at the airport. Call back and let one of the secretaries know what flight you're on. And tell Miles Standish that I'll talk to John Alden any day." Jonas's booming laughter ended only when Ash hung up the phone.

"So?" asked Thatcher.

"He wants me to fly out tonight and spend the weekend with him.''

"Do it. Then fly up to Palos Locos on Sunday night to meet Louise and me. Then on Tuesday night, go over to San Francisco and meet Roy Knight. He is going out to link up with that Wintergreen chap I've been telling you about. Try to keep Roy under control. Try to keep Wintergreen under control. I want that young genius on the PegaSys payroll. I want him here in New York. Give him whatever it takes. Kidnap him if you must, but get him on our team."

"OK."

"You didn't have plans for the weekend, did you?"

Ash sneaked a peak at Louise. He thought she seemed oddly . . . oddly relieved. Ash told Thatcher that he had no plans, and began wondering what David Lefkowitz would be doing Saturday and Sunday. *And Friday night*, he thought. *Don't forget about Friday night.*

Ash looked at Jonas's car. It was a Porsche 952 Gruppe B. When they wrote about this particular machine they told you that Professor Porsche said it could do 195 miles per hour—but no one yet knew how fast it would *really* go. Parked, locked, and motionless in a dark corner of a Los Angeles International Airport's garage, it was a moving violation. Ash tried to remember how much it cost, but could think only of the U.S. annual defense budget. "God almighty," he said, "I didn't think this thing was street legal in this country."

Jonas answered, "It's not."

"Then how . . ."

"Let me tell you something about L.A., my friend. My first movie won eight Oscars, grossed $93 million domestic, and isn't even in foreign release yet. My second turned $11 million in its first weekend, and now, three weeks later, has racked up $53 of the same denomination. Out here they name streets after people like me. Freeways! Whole towns! Out here if people like me break the law, then they rewrite the law. And they keep rewriting it until I'm legal again! Let me tell you about the last guy to win as many Oscars as me. He drives out on one bright, sunny Easter morning wearing a raincoat and parks in front of this nunnery. The Convent of St. Wisteria the Six-Toed or something. He gets out of his car and takes off his raincoat and walks out into the middle of the street buck naked—except for an umbrella to keep the sun off because he's got delicate skin. Then for the next half hour he stands there wagging his weenie at the postulants! He did it on a bet to see if he could get away with it. And you know what? I'll tell you what. They didn't even give him a citation for jaywalking. Street legal? Street legal? Michael, my boy, if I'm street legal, this car is street legal! Welcome to Hollywood! Ain't it great?"

Mike walked around the Porsche, eyeing it the way he had eyed Louise the first time he saw her unclothed—and with similar emotions. "But, Joe," he said, "I thought you drove a 928.

There was a picture of you on the cover of *People* magazine, and—''

"Read the bumper sticker," Jonas answered. Mike did. It read, "My other car is a Porsche."

"That, Joe, is truly obnoxious. I mean *really obnoxious*! Hey! wait a minute, you've got New York plates on this thing."

"Yeah. I put 'em on about three months ago. They make all the difference in the world. Other guys on the road take one look at them and get out of my way. Ah, but it's a wonderful life. OK, chuck your bags in the back and get in."

Ash slid into the car, settling down into the low-slung leather passenger seat. He looked at the dashboard. It had roughly as many dials on it as the cockpit of a B-1B bomber. Jonas threw himself into the driver's seat and wrestled a key into the ignition switch. "Joe," asked Ash, "how fast does this thing really go?"

Jonas giggled like a mad ax murderer in an R-rated splatter movie. "Heh, heh, heh. You'll soon find out. Switch on! Ignition! Lift-off! Warp speed, Mr. Sulu! Aye, aye, Captain!'' Ash pawed at his seat belt, desperate to buckle up. It was the only sane thing to do.

Ash spoke only once during the ride. Actually, it was a scream. It was when he and Jonas left the ground at the top of the on ramp to the San Diego Freeway. Leaving the ground wasn't what made Mike scream. What made him scream was that, for at least a moment or two, they were on a collision course with a 747 incoming to Los Angeles International.

Later—he wasn't sure how much later because in his numb terror he ignored the passing of time—they skidded to a halt. "What's the matter," said Jonas, "was I going too fast for you, old buddy?" Mike opened his eyes and looked around. They were stopped for a red light at the corner of Wilshire Boulevard and Westwood. "Huh?" replied Mike, "what say? Oh, pardon me, you were taking it so slow and easy that I decided to catch a little nap."

"Ha! OK, pal, you asked for it. Later tonight, on the way up the coast to my place, I am going to really open this baby up. Hey! By the way, are you hungry? You want to get a bite to eat?"

"No thanks, I ate on the plane."

"Oh. You sure? I thought we might stop by The Palm. Eat something. They have my picture on the wall.''

"Did you say The Palm or the post office."

"Arggh! Hey, Ash, your sister swims after troop ships."

The light turned green, and Jonas sped away from the intersection. Ash's stomach stayed behind.

The streets in the Rodeo Drive area were as bright as those in New York, and as crowded. The crowd, however, was a different crowd. Very different. Younger, livelier, and, difficult though it might be to believe, harder-edged. Ash goggled as he tagged along the sidewalk with Jonas. It was brutal winter in New York, but in Los Angeles it was still T-shirt weather. *Tight T-shirts*, Ash mentally noted, *on the men and women alike. Well, not alike.*

Jonas put his hand on Mike's back and steered him through a dark doorway. Deafening music burst out of the opening door. Mike entered and squinted, trying to adjust his eyes to the flashing, flickering lights. Slowly he could make out the scene. The whole building shook to the thunder of rock music and the (*What*, he thought, *is the right word here? Orgiastic was too tame. Bacchanalian? Lupercalian? Babylonian? Corybantic?*) dancing of the crowd. Ash began to think about the way he was dressed—in formal business wear. He concluded that his costume was badly out of sync with the ambience.

A hostess walked over to them. Ash observed that her blouse was more opened than closed. Not that it made any difference, because it was three sizes too small and mostly transparent. Ash leaned toward Jonas's ear and whispered, "Excuse me, Dr. McCoy, but I don't believe we've been on this planet before."

"Right, Mr. Spock, and for pity's sake, don't tell the captain or he'll beam down and spoil it all. Meanwhile, set phasers to stun."

The hostess took one look at Jonas, recognized him, and broke into a blindingly white smile. The smile was for Joe Jonas, not for Mike. Him she eyed rather coolly. She chatted for a moment with Joe, then steered the pair over to what was surely the best table in the house. Above the din, Joe told Mike to sit down. But before they could take their seats, a quartet of cover-girl-like young women at a nearby table began to yell at them and wave them over. Clearly, the girls were friends of Joe Jonas. Close friends. All of them. Joe grabbed two chairs, and swung Ash over to meet his fan club.

"Oh, Joe. Where have you been keeping yourself?" "Come

on, big guy, sit down." "Over here by me, Joe." "No, here
next to me." "Who's your friend?"

This latter question was posed in a distinctly frosty tone,
followed by an every frostier silence. Ash stood waiting in the
ensuing hush, feeling increasingly uncomfortable about his all-
wool navy blue suit, all-wool navy blue vest, burgundy and
silver silk tie, white cotton shirt, and black nylon stretch socks.
The only part of his wardrobe that fit the local fashion were his
Bally loafers. Finally one of the four girls, a knockout with
huge, sparkling green eyes, broke the spell. She said, speaking
quite slowly and enunciating each word to withering effect, "Oh
don't be silly. That's no friend of Joe's. Look at the way he's
dressed. That, my dears, is the Xerox repairman." Everyone
except Mike thought this to be very funny.

Jonas replied with something that Mike couldn't hear, and
the girls broke into laughter again. Then he took Mike's arm
and led him into the men's room. There he made Mike remove
his jacket, vest and tie. He then stepped back a pace or two and
eyed Ash from top to bottom. "Open another two buttons on
that shirt. Go ahead. Hmm? There's still something wrong. Now,
what can—aha! I've got it!"

Shortly thereafter, Ash, shed of his undershirt, his white Cus-
tom Shop oxford open to his belly button, half of Jonas's gold
chains draped across his bare chest, and feeling an utter ass,
reemerged on the dance floor. The women at the table looked
at him more appreciatively as Joe Jonas introduced him. "Girls,
this is my long-lost brother, Mike. We don't talk about him
much in the family because of the scandal with the Vienna Boys'
Choir. But now that he's had the operation he's much better. Sit
down, Mike. Have a drink. Try not to slobber. Make friends
with my friends."

Ash replied, "Thanks, Joe. I am surprised that any of these
ladies are friends of yours. At your age, someone like my mother
would be more your speed."

"Mike, I would never touch a woman you've had."

There was another long, speechless moment at the table. Then
the gorgeous girl with the gorgeous green eyes spoke again.
"Gee, girls, aren't male bonding rituals fun?"

Joe Jonas's name was neither Joe nor was it Jonas. It was
Harald Olaf Johaneskanen. His mother was Norwegian and his
father was Finnish. He was the brawny offspring of four generations of equally brawny Bay Ridge seafarers. He was also a

man not be called "Harald" or "Hal" or "Olaf" or, least of all, "Olley." He was to be called "Joe Jonas." Called that by his friends (who were legion). Called that by his enemies (who were none). Called that by anyone and everyone who didn't wish to don a full body cast.

Later, at a different bar, but with the same women in tow, Ash asked, "So, Joe, tell me. How's . . . uh, how are things?"

Jonas looked narrowly at Mike, picking his words carefully. "What you mean is 'how's business?' Only because I'm a movie producer you don't want to use the word 'business,' do you? You simpletons back East don't think making movies or making television is a real business, do you? Well, let me tell you, Mike, it's realer than what a lot of you New York guys do."

"Ah, OK. So how's business, Joe?"

"Thanks for asking. Business is great. I've got three projects in development and they are all go. I've got a modern-day version of *Lysistrata* with Debra Winger, Bette Midler, and Theresa Russell that starts shooting for Touchstone next month. I've got *Duchess of Malfi*, only in a contemporary Mafia setting with Kim Basinger and maybe Robert Duvall. And, at Fox, Streep has signed for a feminist remake of *What Makes Sammy Run?* We're calling it *What Makes Samantha Run?*"

"Do you guys ever do anything original out here?"

"Yeah. What do you mean? Original? Yeah, sure, all the time. All the time."

"Joe, what is it that a producer does? I mean really does?"

"Really? You want to know really? OK, here's really. What a producer really does is two things. He ultimately has only two responsibilities. One, he makes sure that there is enough money for the project. Two, he makes sure that the cast and crew don't spend it all on drugs."

Ash was jet-lagged. Ash was drunk. Ash wanted to go to bed. Joe Jonas, on the other hand, seemed to be just warming up. His capacity for alcohol was supernatural. Mike rarely took more than three drinks in an evening. Jonas rarely took fewer than four in an hour. Ash felt like a fool on the dance floor. Jonas looked like poetry in motion. Ash was uncomfortable chatting with strange women. Jonas elevated it to an art form. As the clock ticked past midnight, Ash felt sluggish and tired. Jonas looked younger with each passing moment. *The man is a goddamned vampire*, Ash thought as he watched Jonas rollicking across the dance floor. *That's the only explanation. He only goes out at night, and drinks the blood of young virgins to renew his youth.*

Mike felt for the pack of cigarettes in his shirt pocket. He had already had his ten smokes for the day but, *what the hell*, there was a three-hour time difference between New York and Los Angeles that, *let me see, adds 20 percent to my waking hours, which means I can have another two. Besides, it's tomorrow in New York, so I can start again with a zero count.* He started tapping a Marlboro Light out of the pack. The girl with green eyes slapped his hand. The pack spun out into the crowd and disappeared, crushed beneath the grinding feet of frenzied dancers. "Ugh," she said, "what a nasty, filthy habit for such a nice-looking man."

Ash looked sadly after his demolished cigarettes. Less sadly, he looked into the girl's wonderfully sparkling emerald eyes. *Flecked with gold. They're actually flecked with gold. I always thought that gold flecking was something mystery writers made up.* "If it makes you happy to see me do without them," he said, "it makes me happy too." She smiled at him, and he suddenly felt young.

Joe Jonas cleared his throat. He arranged his face in a suitably sincere fashion, and in a neutral tone of voice asked Mike, "Tell me, how's the moustached misanthrope doing these days?"

"Scott? Scott's doing fine. No, Scott's doing lousy. I mean . . . he acts fine, but he is lousy. You know what I mean. The takeover is really getting to him. It's making him do everything he hates to do. He hates suing people, and he is having to sue a lot. He hates begging for favors from politicians, and he is having to grovel. He hates having to make decisions that are bad for the long term but expedient for the here and now. He hates having to be on the defense. And, I think he really hates not having you around, Joe. You were the one he always relied on. You and he were so close. . . ."

"Yeah. We were. We still are, even though we don't talk. I guess he told you about that, didn't he? Why we don't talk and why I quit?"

"No. He hasn't told me; he hasn't told anybody. No one knows why you left. Everyone knows that you won't talk to one another, but no one knows why you quit."

"Did you ever ask?"

"Hell, no. I figured it was none of my fucking business."

"So why not ask me?"

"Good idea. OK. Joe, why did you quit?"

"It's none of your fucking business."

Jonas stopped nibbling on the earlobe of one of the young ladies and turned to Ash. "Hey, I forgot to ask," he said, "how have you been?"

Mike replied in a calm, objective monotone, rather like the HAL 9000 computer in *2001: A Space Odyssey*. "I have been well, all things considered. Considering the fact that during the past month I have had lethal weapons aimed at me on three separate occasions. Setting aside the fact that the organization for which I have worked for nearly twenty-five years is about to be gutted by a man who is surely the most inept executive in America. Ignoring the fact that my friends, my colleagues, and the people whom I most respect in this world are facing unemployment. Disregarding the fact that two days ago, ten tons of steel girders and construction cranes threw a surprise party in my office. While my personal life is hopeless, while my nerves are a jangled mass of fused circuits, while my future prospects are grim, while my hairline shrinks as rapidly as my waist expands, while I struggle in the toils of midlife crisis, yes, Joe, I think that, all things considered, I can say that I am well."

"Good. Glad to hear it."

Many drinks later, in a different bar, Ash's world was fuzzy. It was painted in gentle pastel hues, and was soft around the edges. Ash rested his hand firmly on the table to keep it from floating away. Or perhaps, to keep himself from floating away. He felt his pocket. No cigarettes. Only business cards. Every waitress in every bar they'd been in had passed out business cards. He had the feeling that he had a lot to learn about California life.

He also had the feeling he was slurring his words. "Joe, I was surprised, Joe. I was really surprised when you said to come out. I figured, Joe, I figured that there was no way you were going to talk to me. I've been a shit, Joe, a real shit. I mean, I haven't spoken to you since you quit. I didn't even send you a card last Christmas. Did Scott send you a card, Joe? Did anyone from PegaSys send you a card, Joe? Christ, it's good to see you, Joe. It's great of you to offer to help us."

"Forget it. If you hadn't called when you did, I was going to break down and call his curmudgeonship myself. I let him know a month ago that I knew something about what was going on. I told Livy. Then I sat back and waited for the stiff-necked old bastard to call me. I should have known better. I should have known he'd never be the first to call. Hell, I would have gotten ahold of him this weekend to fill him in on what I know. But, by God, then he told you to call me! Leave it to that old stinker to break the ice without breaking the ice.''

"What do you know, Joe? What is going on that you know?''

"Tomorrow. I'll tell you tomorrow. We'll lie on the beach with a selected subset of these beautiful, seductive, sexy women, and I'll fill you in. Now's about the time to take your pick, by the way.''

"Pick? What do you mean, pick?''

"Upon the innocent flesh of which of the tender young maids who've accompanied us this evening do you wish to sate your sordid and lascivious desires? Take your pick, pal, take your pick.''

Ash tried to focus his eyes on the green-eyed girl. He couldn't quite make her out. She was . . . gone. "Where'd she go, Joe? Where did what's-her-name go?''

"Who?''

"You know. With the big green eyes.''

"Oh, her. Good pick. She went to the ladies' room with the other ones. They're working out the possibilities and figuring out who rides with whom if what happens. Her name is Pam, I think.''

"Oh. Nice girl. Smart. Sharp tongue—''

"Soft. Or so one hopes.''

"Oh . . . yeah. Anyway, pretty, too. But, gee, I don't know about . . . well, I'm not sure. I don't think I should really want to . . . well . . .''

"Michael, my friend. Mike, hold out your hand. Here. Got them? Those are the keys to my car. Now, when Pam gets back, you stand up, take her by the waist and lead her out to that car. Then you start it up and drive up the coast to my place. I'll write out directions, and—''

"Uh, I don't think I want to do that. I mean—''

"Goddamn, Mike! What do you mean, you don't want to do that? Look, pal, you gotta understand something! Let me tell you, it is your God-given right, your inalienable right as an American citizen to come to California, get yourself in a convertible car, and go rolling down the freeway with rock 'n' roll on the stereo and a hot blond in the seat beside you. Or, better still, with the blond driving! It's what America is all about! It's what George Washington fought for at Valley Forge! It's why Lincoln freed the slaves. It's what Roosevelt charged up the hill at San Juan for. The American dream, here it is, pal, on a silver platter! And you have second thoughts about it? What are you, some sort of commie fag pervert?''

"Joe, it's just that, well, she is a wonderful girl, but—"

"Christ, here we go again. For God knows how long after your divorce I tried to fix you up with women. I damn near decimated my inventory trying to find you a good date. All of whom you had problems with. Now, here's Pam. Bang! It's a hit! Top of the pops! She likes you, Mike. She likes you. You like her. Take the goddamned keys, Mike! I mean, you do like her, don't you?''

"Yeah. But, the thing is, well, let me put it this way, to say it directly, or better put, aw fuck it. I'm in love.''

"Don't be ridiculous.''

"No, really. I am really in love. Really.''

"As are we all, Mike.''

"I want to get married. I don't want to chase other women. I don't want anyone else. I don't want to wake up in the morning with anyone except Loui—oops.''

Jonas slammed his glass down on the table. "Who? Louise? What? Louise? No? Louise Bowman? The Iron Nun! The Ice Queen! Midnight Mary! You? You! You and Louise? No! You and Louise? I don't believe it. Do you know how many times I tried to get her even to go out for a drink? You! Aw, God, say it ain't so.''

Mike smiled a drunken smile. "Well, yes. I mean, no. I mean, yes, it is Louise.''

"God is punishing me. You and Louise. Christ! Wait a minute, is this love from afar, or have you and she actually . . . ?''

"For almost a year now. Since right after you quit.''

"I need a drink. This development is too much for me to deal with in a sober and upright condition. Oh, wait a minute. Here come the ladies. Hi, girls. Hope you all had a nice evening. Good night now. I'll call you all next week. Bye-bye. Shhhh! Don't say anything you'll be sorry for. Nitey-nite.''

Jonas waved the four deeply offended women off and the bartender over. He ordered a double of something that sounded lethal, and then turned to Mike. "Tell me about this,'' he said.

Mike, inebriated beyond any hope of discretion, did.

* * *

Mike had been speaking for more than an hour. He had paused only to boost his blood-alcohol level back well above prudent limits. With drunken dispassionateness, he chronicled events day by day, omitting not even the most minute circumstances. Joe Jonas had listened in unblinking fascination to Mike's clinically detailed narrative. Joe, like most men, had a weakness for gossip, and a ravenous curiosity about the amorous—both physical and psychological—behavior of women. In this regard, Ash's story was a feast. However, Mike was equally candid about his own emotional and mental comportment. Jonas found himself a bit embarrassed by those revelations.

At the point in his tale where he and Louise were concluding their open-air tryst on Long Island Sound, Mike stopped, patted his shirt pocket, and looked around vaguely. He pulled out his cigarette lighter and set it on the table. He stood up and felt his pants pockets. He patted his shirt pockets again, and sat down. "You wouldn't," he asked hopefully, "happen to know where I put my cigarettes, would you, Joe?"

"You don't have any cigarettes," said Joe, "and neither do I. I quit a long time ago. Your lady friend, Pam, disposed of your pack about five gin joints ago. Why don't you just suck your thumb or something?"

Ash looked sullen. Jonas continued, "Anyway, now is not the time to interrupt this epic. Tell me what happens next. There you and Louise are, bare-ass naked and rambling about in a state of what the lawyers call 'deshabille' on Old Ironjaw's estate. You are back in the sack with her, and you know full well that she has been off cavorting on the sandy shores of the Aegean with some other dude. By the way, they have a lot of nude beaches in that part of the world, I hear. So what comes next? Does little Miss Bluebeard appreciate that you might be just the slightest bit jealous? After all, you have been begging, wheedling, and cajoling her with vows of external devotion. In point of fact, Michael my boy, you have been exhibiting all the symptoms of a rare—of the rarest—disease of them all. Romantic love. There hasn't been a case of that in this country since 1960. So, is she reacting . . . Mike? Wakie, wakie, Mike. Lift up your head and face the day. Rise and shine, lad. Mike. Mike? Aw, hell."

Joe rose, pulled the comatose Ash to his feet, and tried to walk him to the exit. After dragging his limp friend a few yards, Jonas heaved a deep sigh, stooped, and hoisted Mike over his shoulders. No one in the bar even noticed.

20

ACTUALLY, IT WAS ALL A DREAM.
Actually, Ash never flew to California, never saw Joe, never met
the girl with the green eyes. Actually, Ash was still in New York.
Still in the PegaSys building. Trapped in the rubble on the fifty-
first floor. Pinned beneath ten tons of collapsed construction
crane. Ash knew it was all a dream, knew he was trapped by
the crane, because he could feel where it had landed on his head.
It was still on his head, all ten tons of it, pressing down.

They were coming now to dig him out. They had jackhammers. He could hear their ear-shattering clatter. Maybe the rescue crew would be merciful. Maybe they would have pity and
kill him where he lay. A jackhammer thundered nearby and one
of the rescue crew yelled, "Mike, come on, it's time to get up."
It worked for Jesus when he said it to Lazarus, thought Ash, *but
it won't work for me.*

"Come on! We've got to get down to the beach."
Lazarus come forth.
"I've got some coffee in the kitchen."
*Doubtless Jesus had waved a cup of Colombian premier in
front of the tomb. Some fine miracle that was.*

The shattering crash of jackhammers jarred him again. "Oh,
God," Ash groaned, "quit pounding on that door. I'm getting
up. I'm getting up."

"The shower is to your left. I'll see you in the kitchen."

Joe Jonas grinned wickedly, maneuvering a cup of coffee toward Mike's trembling hands. "Mike," he said cheerily, "you
look like you were in a stick fight and the other guy had the
stick." Mike said nothing. Mike was concentrating on grasping
the cup. He missed it again. It was his third try. "What's the

matter, cat got your tongue?'' Jonas asked. *No, not a cat. Not a cat on my tongue. Cat litter maybe, but definitely not a cat.* "Here, put your hands beneath your chin. Yeah, like that, keep them there firmly and I will slide this cup . . . there, got it? OK. Now, keeping your hands firmly against the chin, tilt your head back. Farther, farther. Aw, cripes, Mike, open your mouth.''

Ash felt something hot pour down his throat. Coffee. Life.

He drank again, emptying the cup. He stretched out his palsied hand, quaking less now, and accepted a refill. He downed it in one, two, three gulps. "Another,'' he croaked, and Joe obliged. Ash took a deep draught. His shoulders shivered; he shook his head and murmured, "Brrrrr! Ugh! Umpf! Look at my hands. No brain surgery for me today.''

"You know, Mike, you never were a good drinker. Hey, don't look at me that way.''

Mike continued to look at him that way.

"Here, let me get you something before you begin to feel it in your head.''

Ash shrieked, "Begin?'' Shrieking was a mistake. A bad mistake.

Joe stood at a countertop, dropping various ingredients into a blender. The juice from four freshly squeezed oranges. Half an orange rind. A dollop of brandy. Two cubes of sugar. Powdered malt. "Right here, we have Dr. Jonas's magic nostrum and alchemistic cure-all. Guaranteed to armor you against the dreadful aftereffects of a bout with demon rum. In your case, a losing bout.'' A pinch of salt. Something from the spice rack. Four raw eggs, shells and all. *Raw eggs.*

"Raw eggs. Raw eggs, Joe, forget it.'' Ash began to back away from Jonas. Jonas switched on the blender for a few seconds, then decanted its contents into an eight ounce glass. He whistled a little tune as he worked. *I know that tune: Offenbach, Hoffman, Dr. Miracle. Right before he poisons the heroine.* "Joe, there is no way that I am going to eat raw eggs. I am not Sylvester Stallone and this ain't *Rocky*. Joe, put down the glass. Just give me some more coffee.''

"Mike, do I drink? Yes? Do I drink a lot? Yes? Do I sometimes drink too much? Yes? Fine, then I am the expert in these matters, not you! In your condition, this can only help. Come on, man, how much worse can it get? I tell you what, if you don't feel better five minutes after drinking this, I will give you my watch. OK? Look, a fifteen-thousand-dollar solid gold Rolex. Here, put it on your wrist. It's all yours if in five minutes' time, you can honestly say you don't feel better.''

Ash adjusted the solid gold Rolex bracelet. He had never realized that Rolexes were so heavy. But it felt good on his arm.

"You're going to keep the watch, aren't you, you shithead?"

"You're goddamned right."

"But you feel better. I can tell you feel better. Upchucking like that always makes everyone feel better. It cleans out the system."

"I'm keeping the watch, Joe."

"Shithead."

"Hey, Joe, I thought you said we were going to go to the beach."

"Any time you're ready, Mike. It's right out the door to your left. Let's go."

And it was. Miles of it. Fine golden sand baking in a high hot sun, with only the slightest hint of a caressing, temperate breeze. Blue-green, white-crested waves rolled up and gently brushed the shore. A handful of sunbathers lay toasting a few hundred yards away. A child chased a retriever through the surf. Mike stepped out and felt the tension in his shoulders melt away. Most curious of all, he hadn't known that the tension was there. He had been carrying it so long that he did not notice it until it was absent.

21

As THEY LAY ON THE BEACH, THEY spoke. In light of Mike's late-night revelations about Louise, it was only fair that Joe go first. Looking up at the sky, he said, "Let me tell you about me and Scotty. You know, of course, that if you ever mention a word of this, I will break your knee-caps?"

Mike grunted.

"Did you ever wonder how he and I got along? Sure you did. Everyone did. Here is Scott C. Thatcher, Yankee patrician; straight A Harvard graduate; duty-honor-country Marine lieu-tenant with a medal from MacArthur in Korea; sober-sided, rock-ribbed stalwart of the Republican party; all-around straight arrow and full-time Boy Scout; faithful husband; dedicated fa-ther; committed church-goer; no-nonsense manager; and the hardest-working, smartest bastard in the Western world. In short, what we've got here is a straitlaced old prick. Right? The only things the son of a bitch has going for him are a good sense of humor, brains, and a sense of loyalty that would make Lassie look like Judas. Bottom line: he's the kind of guy God sends us from time to time so we'll all know what He *really* had in mind when He made Adam.

"And then there is Joe Jonas. Brooklyn born and bred. Scraped through CCNY with a 2.1 grade point average, taking as many crib courses as I could find. A draftee busted three times in two years to private no class. Hell on wheels. Cocks-man, street fighter, boozer, and full-time party animal. How in God's holy name can an ugly proposition like me get along with a guy like Thatcher?

"Well, first off, if you give me a job to do, I do it pretty good. I'm a fast learner. I can learn anybody's job. Anybody's. Then, too, I am a hell of a salesman. And people love to work for me; I can get them to get things done. I suppose that makes me a pretty good manager. Turned out that thirty-odd years ago I had a natural talent for systems engineering, too. I just understood it. No book learning, just an intuition of how computers work. It came easy to me. So somehow or another I landed a job at IBM, and, even more amazing, I kept it. Along the way, I get to know Scotty, who is a golden boy to say the least, and after a while I am reporting directly to him. He is on a fast track to the top, and I'm right behind him—carrying his bags. Oh, maybe my collar button is never buttoned, and my hair is too shaggy, and on Monday mornings my breath smells like the bottom of a rabbit hutch, but what the hell, I get the job done faster and better than anyone else. For a year or two, Scotty gives me The Lecture. 'Clean up your act, you dissipated scamp!' But after we've been together a few years, he just gives up and tolerates me. Anyway, by then I had figured out the difference between the things he merely disapproves of (that's a long list) and the things he absolutely won't put up with (that's a short list). And I never do the things on the short list—at least not where he can see me, or at least not more than once every couple of months.

"So we make a pretty good team, Scotty and I. We're going places together. Then one morning, ka-boom! Scotty strolls into my office—you know how he does that without ever warning you that he's on his way—and he says, 'Good morning, Joe, I just quit. Why don't you quit too and we'll go off and have some fun and maybe make some money?'

"This is Mr. IBM himself speaking. This a guy who not only knows all the words to 'Hail to Thee, IBM,' but sings them loud too. A lot of folks figured that he was Mr. Superstar, that he was going to replace Tom Watson, Jr., as chairman when Tom retired. Ka-boom. 'I quit.' Ka-boom. 'I want to start my own company.' Ka-boom. 'I want to make my own computer.' Ka-boom. Well, who could believe it? And, you know what, I didn't even think about it for a second. I just looked at him and said, 'Yeah, sure.' And then I stayed with the old bastard for twenty-five years. He was the number-one guy and I was the number-two guy. For twenty-five years. He'd get the vision, and I'd handle the implementation. He says, 'Hey, Joe! See that mountain over there? Well, I think it would be better in another spot.' And I say, 'OK, boss. No problem. Where do you want me to move it to?' And, guess what, every fucking mountain I moved really did look better in the place Thatcher wanted it. I never met a guy who was so goddamn right so goddamn many times. He would come up with things that I flat out thought were suicide. But he was right, and I was wrong. Once I'd done the job, he was right.

"And, yeah, sure, we would argue a lot. We would wrestle one another to the carpet twice a week. But you have to give him credit, I would *win* most of the arguments. That is what is so brilliant about the guy—you can persuade him that he is wrong. And, if he is, he admits it. Not easily and not graciously, but by God, he is smart enough to know when someone else in the room is right.

"For twenty-five years. Number one and number two. Me and Scotty. And here's the funny thing, here's how we got along so well. I was . . . I am . . . his best, maybe even his only, friend. The only one. See, when he started out he had lots of friends. But once he became a success, once PegaSys became a success, he didn't have any friends at all. He became too important, too powerful, too rich to have friends. All he could have were hangers-on and high-class moochers. No one just liked him for himself, or kind of just liked hanging out with him. When people looked at him, they didn't see a neat old dude named Scotty. They didn't see a good guy to sit down with and chew the fat. Instead, they saw the big-deal chairman of the big-deal PegaSys Corporation. They saw a man who could promote them, or increase their salaries. They saw a man who could give big bucks to their charities or to their political campaigns. They saw a man who could buy huge quantities of whatever they wanted to sell. They saw a man who was important, rich, admired by the press, powerful, or whatever. They saw somebody they wanted to persuade, not to befriend.

"Scotty is no fool. Least of all is he a fool. He figured the situation out fast. He figured out that there was no one he could talk to, no one he could let his hair down in front of, no one who didn't want something from him, no one he could trust. Except Livy, of course. And that witch doctor. And me. Scotty knew, and still does, that I just fundamentally don't give a shit about anything except having a good time. Hell, I never needed more money than I had. As it was, I socked away big bucks while I was at PegaSys, so I couldn't want more from him. All I wanted was interesting stuff to do, a weekend off every now and then, and two aspirin the morning after. Besides which, I just like the cranky old fart for himself. Not because he's rich and powerful and on the cover of *Fortune* magazine. But just because he is the sort of cantankerous old prick he is.

"That's how we got along so well. I did good work. I did the work he needed. And I was the guy he could be himself with. He didn't have to put on any acts with me. He never had to worry about my secret agendas, or my wanting something. It was just Scotty and Joe, and let's go out and have a brew and talk it over. Then we can come back to the office and get some work done. No role-playing, just Scotty and Joe. Number one and number two.

"That's also why I quit. I mean really quit, finally and for good. Late one evening the evil-minded old bastard crept up behind me in my office and said, and I quote, 'Well, Joe, I think the time has come for me to announce my retirement—and my selection of you to succeed me.' I mean it. That's what he said. Right out of the blue. He was serious, too. The son of a bitch was going to retire to some goddamned beach in Hawaii, and leave me holding the bag. Well, shit, I didn't even think about it for a second, I just stood up and said, 'Fuck you. I quit.'

"Then we argued. God knows we argued. For hours we argued. I told him that I was a number-two guy, a good number-two guy. Maybe even the best number-two guy. But that was all I was, and I knew it. I knew my limitations. I'd never be any good as number one. Well, Scotty won't even listen to what I'm saying. He yells and hollers and cajoles, and says that I am undervaluing myself, and that he knows me better than I know myself. I say that that's bullshit. I say that maybe I'm street smart, and maybe I can get the tough jobs done, but that there is no way I can fill his shoes. He is what a number-one guy should be, and I am what a number-two guy should be. Neither of us could swap jobs. What we are and what we do are simply too different. Thatcher doesn't buy it. We argue some more, but neither of us will give an inch. So then I start on how PegaSys can't get along without him. He won't buy that, either. He starts in on how old he is and that someday he will be gone. Spare me, I say. Christ, next you'll be breaking into the chorus of *Silver Threads Among the Gold*, or maybe, *Nearer My God to Thee*. That shuts him up. Then I tell him how I don't want to be in power. How I don't want to have to be role-playing all the time. How I don't want everyone I meet looking at me like a meal ticket. Boy, did that piss him off. It really pissed him off. It wasn't that he disagreed with that point, it was just that he wanted me to think that it wasn't all that bad, and to do otherwise was a dereliction of duty. Dereliction of duty gets him off onto the topic of loyalty, and you know how he feels about that.

"Now I know what you're thinking. You're thinking, hey, what is this happy horseshit? Old Joe is a movie producer. Old Joe is a numero-uno guy. Everybody in Hollywood wants a piece of him. He's got people fawning all over him. That's what you're thinking, aren't you? Well, you're wrong. Dead wrong. A producer isn't number one, he's number nothing. If a movie bombs out, all he's got on his conscience is the loss of a lousy twenty or thirty million bucks. Big deal, it's only money. Besides, a quarter of it got stolen and half got wasted before the negative was in the can. If things go wrong, it's the cast or the writer or the director who gets the blame, not the producer. Besides which, if the flick is a disaster, no one gets hurt, not really hurt, not forever hurt. No one loses their jobs. Their dreams don't die. Hell, even that guy who made *Heaven's Gate*, the biggest disaster in history, is back making lousy movies again. The other thing is this, sure people want things from me. Sure they look at me and see their ticket to the stars. But in the movies it's different. In the movies, everyone is right up-front about it. You know who is out to exploit you, because everyone is out to exploit you. It's refreshing, all that palpitating, unrepentant greed. A gal came up to me while I was making a pit stop last night. In the men's room, no less. She smiles, flashes some tit, and says, 'Hi, my name is Peggy and I give good head. I sure would like a speaking part in your next project.' It happens all the time. And it's a damned sight more honest than the way things happen back in Manhattan.

"Another thing, I confess that in lots of ways maybe Thatcher and I aren't so different after all. On the surface, we sure are. But beneath the veneer, we are just about the same kind of animal—smart, tough, and caring about the same things. Forget about my Viking berserker act; Scotty would have kicked my butt out the back door years ago if I was half as irresponsible as I like to pretend. But we are different, completely different, in two ways. One, I don't want power and authority, and he does. Two, he can take the stress, and I can't. Let me tell you, I could not handle it. I could not handle this takeover bid. Maybe I could do OK with the routine stuff, but there is no way I could cope with being where Scotty is today. He has tens of thousands of people whose jobs are on the line. He has his own dreams on the line. He has everything he has ever cared about on the line. It makes me sick to even think about being in his position. I couldn't deal with it. I'd crash and burn. That's why I always liked being the number-two guy.

"Anyway, we argued until after midnight. Finally, I just gave up. I just said flat out that there was no way I was going to take the job, and that I would quit if he insisted on it. I said that was that, and I didn't want to talk about it any more. I figured that would end the matter. But I was wrong. I never would have guessed what he pulls next. He leans back up against the wall, and he cocks his eyebrow up so high it's above his hairline. And his moustache is bristling. He folds his arms, and looks down his nose the way he does when he is really trying to show how mad he is. And he starts talking in that special voice he uses to intimidate people—using as many two-bit words as he can think of. And he starts lecturing me. For God's sake, all of a sudden, for the first time in twenty-five years, Scott C. Thatcher is role-playing with me. He is playing the chief executive of PegaSys giving a recalcitrant employee a stern lecture. Me! All of a sudden, he is not treating me like Joe Jonas, his best friend and steadfast number-two guy. Instead, he is treating me like one of them. One of *them*! One of the ones who want something from him.

"Well, hell. That tore it. I stood up and said, 'Scotty, no, excuse me, you're not Scotty. You're Mr. President. Mr. President, I will *not* be talked to in that manner. I will *not* take your goddamned job. I will *not* speak to you about the matter further. And, if you insist that I do, then I quit.' I guess he could tell from my voice that I was serious, because he stopped cold in his tracks. He didn't say anything for a long time. He just looked at me. Then he said, 'Joe, I am in the right and you are in the wrong. Once you come to accept this fact, we will speak again.' Then he walked out and slammed the door—and we haven't spoken since.

"So that's that. I played the New York game all my life. Then one day I found myself ahead of the house. So I left the table and cashed in my chips. You can't beat the house, Mike, don't even try. All you can do is maybe get a little lucky and get a little ahead. That's when you quit."

Later it was Mike's turn. He was lying on his stomach now, his head cradled on his arms. His eyes were closed and his face was a mask. Joe was sitting up, slapping suntan lotion over his ample, hairy frame.

"Joe, you realize that if you ever tell anyone about Louise and me, I will break your kneecaps."

"Yeah, sure. Mum's the word."

"OK. Here goes. There are a couple of problems."

"So I gathered."

"Problem number one is me. Deep down, in my heart of hearts, I worry that I'm not the right guy for her. She's . . . she's too good for me. Hell, up until last week at least, my career was at a dead end."

"What happened last week?"

"Didn't I tell you? I guess not. Scott's going to put me in charge of software. I get to be division president."

"Really! God, that's great! What a perfect fit! Shit, I wish I'd thought of that before I left. It's so blindingly obvious that you are the guy to run that can of worms that it takes someone as smart as Thatcher to figure it out. Congratulations."

"Thanks. Well, anyway, you know what they say—you know where you're going when you're forty years old because you are already there. Well, I was already there. A career staffer. No operating responsibility, just a nice-paying, dead-end job fixing things that needed to be fixed. Like Engineered Systems, which, as I recollect, you left behind in a rather untidy state.''

"Only as an intelligence test for my successors. Fixing that thing should have been a piece of cake.''

"Yeah? Well, like all simple things it took a while to puzzle out. Anyway, the thing is, I've gotten as far as I'm going to get. But Louise has not. She can go farther and faster than I ever could. She's five times smarter than I am and works ten times harder. So how can I weigh her down? Someone like me will just be a burden on her. That's part one of my problems. Part two is I don't know from women. I mean I really don't. I do not understand them.''

"Nor they you.''

"Oh? Well, perhaps so. But . . . well, the thing of it all is this, there is a darkness lying between Louise and me. I cannot see her through it—not clearly. And I don't think she can see me clearly either. I think she sees someone else. I think she wants someone else. Sometimes I even think she is trying to turn me into someone else. Someone who is not Mike Ash. Jesus, this is embarrassing, but right now I am Mikhail, Mikhail the gloomy Russian. She started calling me that a month or so ago. I asked her why and she said, 'I don't know. I guess it's that sometimes you just look like a Russian. You know, moody. Sort of morose. Sulky and introspective. Even when you're up and happy, you look like you'd rather be gloomy. You know, kind of like a Russian. Sad that you're happy. That's kind of Russian, too, I think. Besides, you look a little bit like Mikhail Baryshnikov. You've got that same sad smile. I think I'm going to start calling you Mikhail. Mikhail the gloomy Russian.' Earlier I was 'DJ,' short for Don Johnson, the star of her second-favorite television show, *Miami Vice*. Her favorite show is *Moonlighting*, but she doesn't think much of the male lead. Then for a while I was 'Indy' because something about me reminded her of Harrison Ford. God, but it's depressing, Joe. I always know who is in my arms when I'm making love to her, but I am never quite sure who is in hers.''

"Another thing is that she won't talk to me, not about the things that count. It would be good to talk seriously to Louise. Who else do I have? It would be good to share my fears, my worries, and my hopes with her. But she won't listen to me—listen in earnest. I tried once or twice to talk to her seriously, to tell her about my inner feelings, to sort out our relationship. She only changed the subject. We don't talk in bed. After we make love she retreats to the farthest corner of the bed and curls up for a nap. No hugging, no cuddling, no sleeping lightly on my shoulder, no talking. Once she is done, she is done and will not touch me—or want to be touched—until she is ready for sex again. For Louise, sex and affection are two different topics, and maybe her heart is in only one of them. Afterward, when we're done, she takes a nap. She awakens. She is self-conscious about her nakedness and tries to hide her discomfort by sprawling like a gawky teenager.

"She lolls about the bed, and I try and try again to force myself to look at her objectively and discover what lies beneath her skin. What makes her tick. How to reach across the distance between us in all things but sex and the office. There has to be a key to unlocking her. No one could be so passionate for so long, and yet remain so remote. But, instead of finding her secret, all I find is myself, becoming aroused again. Later, she will nap there on the corner of the bed for another twenty or thirty minutes, then get up, shower, and wave me off home to my apartment. She will give me a little peck of a kiss before leaving and tell me that she'll see me in the morning. Then I go home and sleep. Try to sleep. But I can't sleep anymore. When I'm away from her, my mind feels like an automobile engine, turning over. Turning over . . . in neutral, with some fool pushing the accelerator as hard as he can. Running at full speed, going nowhere. Is it that hard to love someone? It's not hard for me. Is it that hard to tell someone that you love him? Jesus, Joe, I do love her, but . . . oh hell, what's the use."

Joe Jonas rolled over on his side, resting on his elbow and looking at Mike. He squinted in the bright sun. "You do not," he said slowly, "make one whole hell of a lot of sense. But I think I understand what you're saying. Look, buddy, I've got a bit more experience with the fair sex than you. Let me see if I can come up with a couple of suggestions. Now tell me, what do you like most about her?"

"It's not 'like,' Joe, it's love. She's intelligent, fun to be with, witty when she wants to be, good looking, and sexy, too."

"Hmmm? Intelligence, companionship, wit, and sex? You've got your priorities backward there, friend Ash. Let me give you some seasoned advice, some words of elderly wisdom from one wiser in the ways of womankind than you. When I was, as Thatcher would say, a young pup and barely weaned, I, too, wanted women of character. I sought braininess, generosity of spirit, depth of intellect. Those were the qualities I wanted. Not just a bedmate, but a soul mate. I yearned for a woman, for women, with whom I could share the depths of my essential existential self. This was the early sixties and essential existential selves were blue-chip stocks in the market. Ahh, they came to me in abundance then, down in Greenwich Village where I lived. Their long, black hair parted razor sharp in the middle, tresses falling to their hips, coal-dark eyes smouldering with philosophic passion and bad poetry. Their minds chockablock with the wisdom of Alan Watts, Jean-Paul Sartre, and Jack Paar. Rail thin, with their legs crossed like a Buddha's, they'd sit on the carpetless floor of my pad—that's the word we used back then—debating life's great issues with me. Then, usually about two of a Saturday morning, with a sort of shy surliness, they'd shed their leotards and skirts and come make hollow-cheeked, bony love. It was less from lust than from politics, and such pleasures as they took in the act came from the thoughts they thought afterward. Or from a sense that by fucking me, they'd won whatever point we'd been arguing.

"Yeah, I remember those days. Woman as peer, as friend, as helpmate, as boon companion, as fellow intellectual voyager. Well, Mike, I'm still paying alimony to three such soul mates, and, quite frankly, the experience wasn't worth the expense. So chum, here's my advice, here's the wisdom of one both wiser and older than you. Where once I thought the most important thing in a woman was the mating of two true minds, now I realize that the most important thing is good tits. As a second choice, settle for long legs and a dirty mind. But, absent anything else, go for good tits. They'll get you through the good times and the bad times. Now that the autumn of my life is upon me, as my once-limber back stiffens and my once-stiff front limbers I recognize the one single overriding moral imperative of manhood and maleness. If you go for good tits, you can't go wrong.

"Now, we'd better get you back inside. That sun is hot, and Thatcher will have my ass if I get you sunburned. Come on, roust yourself up, and let's go get some lunch."

Inside the cool interior of Joe's house, Mike, with desultory interest, ate a ham and swiss sandwich. Joe offered him a bottle of imported Monniker beer, but Mike opted for iced tea instead.

Once lunch was ended, Mike retired to his room and went to sleep. He didn't awake until Sunday morning.

22

JOE JONAS BRANDISHED AN OVER-laden cherry cheese danish in one hand and a cup of coffee in the other. "The time has come," he said, "to tell you what I know about the yellow peril. What I think the devious sons of Nippon are up to. How they fit into Shawby's crazy little scheme to take over PegaSys. Or, more likely, how Shawby fits into their scheme. What I've got to do is go back a bit to the months just after I quit, so bear with me. When I left PegaSys, I decided I wanted to put as much space between me and New York City as I could. I didn't have a clue as to what I wanted to do with myself, except that I wanted out of New York and I wanted to be a long way away from Thatcher. I figured unless I put a continent between the two of us, the old fart wouldn't give up hounding me. So I came out here, and I bought this house, and I spent my time kind of just hanging out.

"OK. So, I don't have much to do. I go to the beach. I get together with some of the people I know. I look at a couple of venture deals up in Silicon Valley. But, basically, I am retired. Then at a party somewhere I meet this guy I haven't seen for a long time. He used to be with Allied Artists back when Manny Wolfe was running it. He asks me what I'm doing, and I tell him that I'm not doing much except making the odd investment. So he asks me to look at the script of a movie he is trying to get made. He says that everybody else he'd showed the script to had turned it down, but that he thought it had great prospects. Hell, I've never looked at a movie script in my entire life. What do I know? But, not having anything better to do with my time, I agree to read the thing.

"Well, I did read it. I loved it! It was great! I called this guy back and said that I figured it would make a wonderful movie—but, so what? I didn't know anything about making movies except that it takes money and connections. The guy who showed me the script had the connections, but no money. I had the money, but was not about to risk it on something I knew nothing about. We talked about it a bit, and finally I bought a small percent of the deal, just to keep it alive.

"We left it at that. But then the damnedest thing happened. One morning the phone rings. It's this Japanese guy. He says he understands that I am producing a movie and need some financing. He says his company would love to fund any project that I am involved in. He says that his company is Seppuku Limited.

"A week later, I *am* a producer and I've got the money to shoot the movie—a straight loan secured against the negative, at a point under prime. Which, as you know, we paid off with the first two weeks' box office. Anyway, the point isn't the movie. The point is that this little Jap guy keeps wanting to take me out to lunch. Every time we go out to lunch, somehow or another he steers the conversation around to PegaSys. He keeps asking me questions about the company, about the products, about the people, about Thatcher. The stuff he wants to know is nobody's business. It's sensitive stuff. But, what the hell, the guy is paying for the movie and paying for lunch, so I figure I'm obliged to tell him something. So I lie a lot. He seems happy with my answers, because he takes a whole bunch of notes. All the Japs take notes. It worries me when they do that.

"Well, we got the movie shot, and got it released, and I got rich and famous off the deal. Meanwhile, every couple of weeks this little Jap wants to take me out to lunch and ask me some more questions. Then, somewhere along the line, he asks if I could use money to make the next movie. I say sure, and this time we've got a deal that's three points under prime. Hell, who can resist that? Seppuku owns a big Japanese bank and a big brokerage house, and a couple of insurance companies too. I figure they have money to burn. So I am happy taking their money. If it means that I have to spend a couple of hours every week talking to this buck-toothed shrimp and telling him whatever lies he wants to hear, why then, I'm happy to do that too. Then about a month ago he asks me out to dinner. This is a first. I figure I'm coming up in the world. Maybe I'm going to get five points off prime for the next project. We meet for dinner, and I am ready to tell him all about my next movie. He's not interested in the movies anymore. Instead, he tells me that Seppuku loves me. He tells me that I am a paragon of virtue, a saint among men, and a warm and wonderful human being. He tells me that maybe I ought to go to work for Seppuku. He offers me a job. The job he offers me is president of PegaSys.

"Wait a minute, I say, PegaSys already has a president. Besides, Seppuku doesn't own PegaSys. PegaSys owns PegaSys. Now, he thinks that I hate PegaSys and that I hate Thatcher. That's on account of the lies I laid on him. He smiles and says Seppuku will own PegaSys—and soon. So I look like I am interested, and ask him how he plans to work this little miracle. Here's what he tells me. He tells me that Seppuku is going to help Shawby and AIW raise the money they need to acquire PegaSys, but that the financial instrument they are going to underwrite for Shawby will allow them to bushwhack AIW. AIW will buy PegaSys, but Seppuku will buy AIW. He says the whole scheme is very subtle. I ask him what kind of financial instrument they are using. He says he can't say, but all of it is being done off-balance-sheet and offshore. Nothing in the U.S., nothing subject to Securities and Exchange Commission review. Nothing that is subject to any American law. Then he asks me if I wouldn't mind giving him a photograph that they can put in the press release. I ask him, what press release is this? And he says it's the one they're going to send out after the takeover starts, announcing that I am going to return as president of PegaSys once AIW takes it over. That's when I left him, the little sushi-sucker.

"So here's what I think. I think that these guys are floating the damnedest financial instrument that ever was, and that they are doing it in every sleazy, second-rate financial market in the world. And, my friend, I bet that whatever else it is, this financial instrument is, as our august friend and compatriot, Czar Thatcher the Terrible, would say, the very instrument of the devil.''

Book Four:
The Last Word

"Mark how fleeting and paltry is the estate of man—yesterday in embryo, tomorrow in ashes. So for the hair's breadth of time assigned to you, live rationally, and part with life cheerfully . . . so very little is needed to make a happy life."

Meditations
Marcus Aurelius

Palos Locos, California.

Snuggled between the lovely Rio Frutas river and the scenic Sierra Lamina mountains, Palos Locos is the county seat of Nuez County, California. It is the home of the University of Eastern California—and of ninety thousand exceedingly affluent families. Palos Locos is yuppie heaven. It is the home of the most profitable BMW dealerships in the United States. It has more fern bars per capita than any other place on the globe. Likewise more Nautilus Centers, more Quiche 'n Crepes restaurants, more $17,000-per-year day-care centers, more human potential movement book readers, more pedigreed pet stores, more fresh cookie shops, more holistic medicine practitioners, more subscribers to *Architectural Digest*, more Jacuzzi installers, more wine emporiums, more Japanese gardeners, more German mechanics, and more Italian hairdressers. The typical family has a household income double the U.S. national average. The average value of a Palos Locos home is in excess of $350,000—in this town, any house costing less than $200,000 is considered a slum.

Palos Locos has no manufacturing base. There are no factories inside the city limits. Rather, the biggest industries in town are real estate and retailing. Nordstroms, Saks, Altman's, Bloomingdale's. The next largest industry is restaurants. All very upscale. If you want to go to a Kmart or a Burger King, you have to cross the town line. There are, of course, no poor people in Palos Locos. Members of the lower income brackets huddle together in a run-down ghetto called South Palos Locos, an unincorporated part of Nuez County abutting Palos Locos. South Palos Locos is 58 percent black; 26 percent Hispanic; 16 percent Oriental; and 100 percent poverty-stricken. The average family size is eight people. The average family income is $7,300. It has no school system, no sewer system, no police, and no fire department. Well water only. South Palos Locos has been trying to get annexed by Palos Locos for fifty years. Palos Locos will not take it. The city council says annexation is not in those poor people's best interest, because if they were annexed then all the property in South Palos Locos would have to be reassessed upward. Then no one living down there would be able to afford the taxes.

The Palos Locos Community Pension Fund, administered by the Palos Locos City Council, owned 1.5 percent of Pega-Sys's stock. Scott C. Thatcher wanted that stock voted against AIW's takeover bid. He wanted it very badly.

At 6:30 A.M. in the Palos Locos Holiday Inn, Scott Thatcher's phone rang. "Good morning, Mr. Thatcher, this is your wake-up call. The temperature is 76 degrees and the sky is clear. Have a nice day." "Thank you," Thatcher answered, "I will do my best." The operator sniffed as if upset by his response.

Thatcher's first act was to go for a brisk morning walk, a ritual he observed religiously whether at home or traveling. Then, having showered and shaved, he made his way to the motel's breakfast room. It was 7:45 A.M. Mike Ash and Louise Bowman were waiting for him.

Ash, reeling at the very concept of being awake at an hour earlier than 8:00 (despite the fact that it was nearly 11:00 New York time), was unhappily contemplating the watery miseries of California-style (which is to say, feeble) coffee. Louise, who had awakened at 5:00, jogged three miles, and swum twenty laps, was immersed in a stack of statistical reports, double-checking them with her antique Hewlett-Packard model 67 calculator.

Thatcher greeted them, sat down, ordered a fruit plate, and said, "OK. Let's get to work. The Palos Locos Community Pension Fund owns 1.5 percent of our stock. We need those shares voted for us. The city council wants me to testify before deciding how they'll vote. Tell me what I can expect this morning."

Louise answered brightly. "First, let me begin by telling you about Palos Locos. Background and demographics. You have to understand this place to understand the city council. This is a very wealthy community. It ranks close to Beverly Hills and

Silicon Valley in terms of per-capita household income. The voters are a very upscale, highly educated crowd."

Thatcher leaned back and smiled. "Good! If these are the people who elected the city council, then they are sure to have voted in the kind of good, solid Republicans who'll appreciate a cranky old Connecticut Yankee like me. Right?"

Louise replied, "Well . . . no, not really.

"The City Council of Palos Locos is pretty . . . how shall I say this . . . offbeat. The laws it has enacted have resulted in the city being dubbed 'The People's Republic of Palos Locos' by the nearest Republican-controlled newspaper. By the way, the nearest Republican-controlled newspaper is in Utah. The council is best known for advocating the designation of Halloween as a state holiday. The city government specializes in passing what they call 'quality of life' laws. For example, Palos Locos is the first city in America to declare its entire geography a 'nuclear free' zone—except for the building at 432 Winding Willow Way (which is the home of the NRA's local chapter head, and the denizens of Palos Locos hope that if the Russians ever drop a nuke it splashes down in his koi pond). Palos Locos has the unique distinction of being the only city in America to regulate the quality of cat litter."

Thatcher had lit up a cigar. His head was invisible, clouded in a wreath of thick, white smoke. From within the obscuring fog bank, his voice rumbled with displeasure, much as the burning bush's must have at Moses on his second trip up the Mount. "I think you are trying to set me up for something. I think you are trying to tell me that we are in a little trouble here. I think maybe you are telling me that getting the council to vote the PegaSys shares they control the way I want may not be a fait accompli. And, I think maybe you'd just better tell me a little bit about each and every member of the city council. Maybe you should do that right now, Louise."

Louise recognized Thatcher's tone of voice for what it was— a storm signal. Gale-force winds and high seas. Ships at sea should flee to safe harbors. Nervously, she began to rattle off the facts. "The City Council. Right. OK. First, Truscott Flood Forester IV: Age fifty-seven. He's the mayor. Chairman, Nuez County Republican Party. Trustee of the Felix Flood Forester Foundation. Hobbies: coupon clipping.

"Mrs. Harriet May Flood Forester III: Age eighty-two. Mother of Mayor Truscott Forester. Owner of the Palos Locos Center for Holistic Pet Care and Grooming. Trustee of the Felix

Flood Forester Foundation. Board of Trustees of The Palos Locos Pet Shelter. Hobbies: bird-watching.

"Darius Episcophagous: Chairman (whoops, that is 'Chair Person') of the City Council. Age forty-six. Defrocked Jesuit priest. Cofounder, California Gay Atheists League. Elected three times as official prom queen at the annual San Francisco Castro District Ball. Hobbies: unspeakable.

"Daphne X: Age thirty-six. Treasurer, Black Women Against Sexism. Former master sergeant in the Women's Army Corps. Author of *Armed Sisterhood—A Winning Strategy for Extirpating Sexist Exploitation*. Owner, Palos Locos's only licensed tattoo parlor and billiard hall. Hobbies: ninjutsu.

"Rama Krishna Shapiro, born Melvin Shapiro: Age forty-three. University of California, Berkeley, 1965–1973, no degree. Owner, Palos Locos Center for Wellness Therapy, Tibetan Massage, and New Age Head Shop. Claims to be the next reincarnation of Shirley MacLaine—albeit a premature one. Hobbies: pharmaceutical experimentation.

"Sister Mary Procrustes: Age indeterminate. Convent of St. Dominic of the Albigensians. Member, Governor's Advisory Council on Pornography. Chief movie evaluator for the Legion of Decency. Hobbies: autos-da-fé.

"Thaddeus Luther Black: Age fifty-eight. Ph.D. Christ College, Oxford. Medal of Honor, Korea, 1951. Nobel Laureate in Economics. First black member of the President's Council of Economic Advisors. Self-made multimillionaire. Fellow of the Hoover Institute for the Study of War, Revolution, and Peace at Stanford University. Commonly referred to as 'that uppity nigger' by Senator Helms. Elected to city council over his own protests. Has yet to attend a council meeting. Returns his paychecks unopened. Hobbies: unknown.

"Vladimir Illych Chernoeznamia: Age forty-two. Fellow of the Trotsky Institute for the Study of War, Peace, and Revolution. Founding member of the SDS. Professor and occupant of the Gus Hall Chair of American Constitutional Studies, University of Eastern California at Palos Locos. Hobbies: cane-cutting vacations in Cuba."

Thatcher sat silently, his head still cloaked by dense, pale cigar smoke. Mike and Louise waited nervously for him to speak. They waited long and patiently. Ash finally broke the hush, "So. Scott, as you can see, what we have here is just another typical collection of California politicians. Heh, heh, heh." Then he grinned sickly.

Silence. Thatcher was immobile. The cigar smoke slowly cleared. Louise could see his face. He was smiling at Ash's little joke. Faintly. Frostily. "I commend you, Louise, and you, Mike, on an excellent piece of political research. Of course, I do wish that you had researched the composition of the Palos Locos City Council *before* I decided to come out here and testify before them. If you had done as fine a research job before coming to Palos Locos as you have done after, I might not have bothered to take time out of my exceedingly crowded and unspeakably hectic schedule to fly out here. I might not have put myself in a position where I, my company, and my employees will be publicly humiliated testifying before an organization that makes Larry, Moe, and Curly look like the House of Lords. But, nonetheless I smile. I smile at what you have told me. More in sorrow than in anger. It is a pity that you have caused me to waste my time. It is a pity that this council controls 1.5 percent of our stock. Which, given the nature of that organization, will vote against us . . . will vote against any entrenched management. I guess we can just chalk it all up to experience. Live and learn. And, I am certain you have both learned an important lesson from this matter, a learning experience that will stand you in good stead during your future careers—careers that, I hasten to add, will not revolve around PegaSys Inc., because you are both fired."

2

LOUISE AND MIKE TACKLED HIM AS he headed out the door.

They yelled, begged, pleaded, wheedled, and cajoled. "No, Scott, you don't understand. Come on, chief, you gotta listen to us. It's not as bad as you think, really, Scott. Please, listen, we can win here. Really, we can. Please . . ."

Finally, Thatcher relented. He held up his hands and said, "OK. OK. Let it never be said of Scott C. Thatcher that he was unwilling to spare a few moments to listen to an ex-employee. Go ahead. What's your story?"

Mike said, "Well, Scott, what makes you feel we can't win this council's support?"

Thatcher glared at him, as if making a mental note to reduce his severance pay. "Young Michael," he growled, "if you gaze upon me with open and unbiased eyes, you will see standing before you the unrepentant personification of palpitating Yankee commercialism. White of skin, blue of eye, straight of limb, male of sex, long of nose, patrician of breeding, I am, succinctly stated, the true and absolute, flinty-hearted, starched-shirted, New England-bred, capital 'R' Republican antithesis of all that is chic in alternative ethnic, sexual, political, ethical, and religious fashions. I stand at the nethermost, polar extreme from frothy-mouthed communist revolutionaries, vapor-headed New Age psychics, and shrilly passionate advocates of intra-gender hanky-panky. Such people positively bridle at me. I am their opposite. I embody all that they abhor. Now this crowd on the city council, they are going to take one look at me, and it shall be as two cats in one bag. Fur will fly—and in abundance. They will all—all except, perhaps, Forester and this Thaddeus Black fellow—perceive in me the utter contrary of their quirky values. I, and I alone, am the very man against whom they marched in college, the great, the bestial bugaboo of progressive liberalism, the honky capitalist pig embodied, the incarnate oppressor of the poor, abuser of the weak, exploiter of women—"

"Scott—" interrupted Louise.

Thatcher pointed his finger at her. "And another thing . . . By the way, you're not fired, neither of you, that was just my way of expressing a little irritation over having my company's stock in the hands of these donkeys. And another thing, what grand sport such people find it to be to tweak the nose and twist the tail of a member of the Establishment. The envy of the outsider for the insider, the unspeakable joy of holding power over the powerful, the sweet revenge of seeing the strong sweat, and the wealthy—"

Mike said, "Slow up, Scott."

"Why? I am on a roll here. Let me further—"

"You're ranting."

"Good. I feel like ranting. It lifts the spirits, clears the system. Ranting is a laxative for the soul."

"Be that as it may, we just have time to make it to City Hall if we leave now. Presuming you don't just want to quit. Be a quitter and toss in the towel. Sneak out of town without a fight. You know Shawby is also testifying this morning, don't you?"

"What! Quit? Never! Shawby! Shawby, is it? So then . . . Why, by George, I will . . . I will . . . Hmpf. You are manipulating me, aren't you, Michael? That is what he is doing, isn't he, Louise?"

The limo pulled up in front of City Hall. Thatcher climbed out of the car and was promptly set upon by what appeared to be life-size Ken and Barbie dolls—the local television action news team. They descended on him like a biblical plague. The reporter brandishing the microphone had a teased bouffant hairdo that looked to be glued in place with a gallon of Aqua-Net, false eyelashes half an inch long, pancake makeup a quarter of an inch deep, baby-blue tinted contact lenses, padded shoulders, barely visible chin-tuck scars. The female member of the team was even more elaborately made up.

"Mr. Lee, Mr. Lee, we want to ask you a few questions about what your company is doing in—"

Thatcher growled that he was not Mr. Lee.

"Shit. Sorry about that. Cut! Stop the camera. I said 'cut!' OK. Take two. Ready. OK. Roll it. Take two. Mr. Shawby, we want to . . ."

"I am not Mr. Shawby either."

"Ahh . . . Mr., ahh, Mr. Ash?"

Thatcher shook his head.

"Aha! Mr. Thatcher! How nice to meet you. Oh, sorry for the confusion, sir. Excuse me for just a second, would you, Mr. Thatcher. Is that goddamn camera off? No? Well, turn it off, damnit, and rewind the tape. Now, you muttonhead! Right. Ready then. Mr. Thatcher. Yes, Mr. Thatcher. Sorry for the little, heh, heh, heh. Let me find my cue sheet, here. No wait, Mr. Thatcher. Don't go. Please, we want to ask you some questions about . . ."

As Thatcher stormed up the steps of City Hall, he could hear the reporter's voice intoning behind him, "And Scott C. Thatcher, number-one man from PegaSys, curtly refused to respond to your Action News Team's inquiries. I wonder if he's hiding anything, Sally." A female voice whinnied in response, "I don't know, Jeff, but one thing's for sure, this morning the eyes of all Palos Locos are on the action at City Hall. And from what we hear about the doings at PegaSys, everyone involved in that action has something to hide. Now back to Action News Team Six Central.''

In an understandably bleak mood, Thatcher and his party found their way to the crowded chambers of the Palos Locos City Council. They jolted to a stop at the door, thunderstruck at the decor and stared in awed amazement. Glistening metallic stalactites dripped menacingly from the ceiling. Luminescent plastic stalagmites thrust up from the floor. Bizarrely angled protuberances in lurid primary colors jutted in macabre directions from the walls. "This place," Ash whispered into Thatcher's ear, "looks like the inside of a Cuisinart." Thatcher whispered back, "And, like as not, we are about to be pureed."

The members of the city council had already arrived. They sat on a raised dais, suitable in style for the court of the Spanish Inquisition, although it is unlikely that any of that court's august members ever appeared on the bench of judgment, as did Mr. Shapiro, bedizened with a saffron robe and holding a prayer wheel. Or, as in the case of Ms. X, clad in construction boots, baggy denims, a grease-stained T-shirt (bearing the message "When God created Man, She was only joking") with a pack of Camels rolled up in the sleeve. Or, as in the present event, the chairperson, Darius Episcophagous, dressed in a violet sequined bombardier jacket, skintight lime-colored slacks, and mirror aviator glasses. Or was knitting in the style of Madame Defarge, which was what Sister Mary was doing.

The murmur of the standing-room-only crowd died down to silence as the last of the council members slipped into his seat. Seven seats were full. The eighth belonged to the eternally absent Thaddeus Luther Black, who prided himself on his refusal to appear in the same room as the rest of the council members of the city of Palos Locos.

The chairperson—he of the twinkling jacket and reflecting shades—gently tapped his gavel and the proceedings began. "Fellow community persons of Palos Locos, today's hearings deal with our community's post-full-time employment self-fulfillment fund, known for legal reasons as the community pension fund. Under community statute 74-118a, fifteen years ago we of Palos Locos established a special fund to handle the special caring needs of our fellow community people. Accordingly . . .''

During Episcophagous's fifteen-minute speech, Louise scribbled notes on a legal pad, and thrust them in front of Thatcher. "S. Listen to buzzwords. When u speak, use local lingo. Not 'citizens'—'community persons.' Not 'retirement'—'post-full-time employm't self-fulfilm't.' "

"And, so, in conclusion, the community persons of Palos Locos, and we whom you have elected to network decisions for you, are in the unasked-for and unwanted position of having to take sides in a conflict situation. So, with considerable reluctance, your community council must dialogue on the subject and interface a decision. We want, as do all of you, to tune into the mindsets of the people involved in this dispute, and find out where their heads are at. We want to vote for the company who has the kind of instructural community values that all our community persons can buy into, feel comfortable with, take ownership of, and sleep easy on. So we've asked Mr. Scott C. Thatcher, who runs PegaSys, and Mr. Brian Shawby, who runs American Interdyne Worldwide, to tell us what their realities are, and why we should support them. Mr. Thatcher, why don't you interface your gestalt with us first. Just step up to the lectern on your right; there is a microphone there. Oh yes, excuse me, there is one other thing I want everyone to know about. Here in Palos Locos we're not into majority rule. It's undemocratic. So what we council persons are going to do is decide on the percentage of shares we are going to vote for each side in this conflict situation."

As Thatcher rose, Louise leaned toward him and whispered, "For God's sake, stop gnashing your teeth. The microphone will pick it up. And for once in your life, try to be nice to a politician."

Thatcher adjusted the microphone, braced his hands against the rim of the lectern, and speaking slowly said, "Good morning. I am Scott Thatcher. I founded PegaSys. Together with my colleagues, two of whom have joined me this morning—Louise Bowman and Mike Ash, sitting up front there—together we have built what many people believe to be the finest corporation in the world. No one has questioned the quality of our products, of our services, or of any of the aspects of our business. Our shareholders have prospered accordingly. We do good work. We want to continue to do good work. That is why we want—and deserve—your support. Thank you, and I will be pleased to answer any questions."

Thatcher stood in the ensuing silence, looking calm, relaxed, and in command. After some moments, Episcophagous spoke up. "Ahh, that is all you have to say? I mean, your dialogue is finished?"

"Quite finished," replied Thatcher.

"Well, ahh . . . well, then, questions. Are there any questions from the council persons? Yes, Mr. Shapiro, do you want to go first?"

The saffron-robed Rama Krishna Shapiro, who appeared to have just awakened from either a meditative trance or a narcotic stupor, led the questioning. Shaking his prayer beads at Thatcher and speaking lengthily if not coherently, he theorized that PegaSys should discontinue its line of telecommunications products, relying instead on psychic vibrations to transmit data back and forth between computers. Thatcher appeared unable to think of anything to say in reply, so the questioning moved on to Sister Mary.

Sister Mary—knit one, purl one—spoke next. Her comments were terse, and dealt in the most part with the efficacy of chalk, blackboard, and yardstick (wielded with rapierlike swiftness anent the posterior portions of human anatomy) in drilling mathematics into the recalcitrant heads of third-graders. She contrasted these proven, time-tested tools to computer-assisted instruction techniques in terms of profound disdain. Again, Thatcher was left with little opportunity to speak.

Ms. X, in a voice of intimidating tone and timbre, rained rivers of withering scorn on Thatcher for bringing Louise to the hearings, referring to her as a "token woman," and, in accents of evermounting amplitude, hectored him about his personal membership in an all-male club. She concluded by roaring that PegaSys was the kind of company that exploits "women and other minorities." Thatcher, in beginning to review PegaSys's impressive record in hiring and promoting women and minorities worldwide, murmured that Census Bureau data said that women accounted for the majority of the population. Ms. X, bellowing with rage, cut him off. Her impassioned critique of federal statistics lasted more than thirty minutes.

Mrs. Forester looked up from the magazine she had been reading throughout the proceedings (*Cat Financier Monthly*) to ask what kind of pets Thatcher kept. "A well-informed pet owner is a good pet owner, Mr. Thatcher," she said. "And a good pet owner is a good person." Thatcher looked at her bleakly and replied that he was allergic to animals. With wistful hope, he hastily added that he had once owned a pet goldfish as a child. The dire expression on Mrs. Forester's face clearly indicated the long-defunct fish was to no avail. Scott C. Thatcher had been weighed on the great scales of life and been found wanting.

Vladimir Chernoeznamia's huge bushy beard muffled much of what he said, but the gist of his opening comments seemed to be a philosophical speculation as to whether or not a computer was a tool of production and hence subject to Marx's dictums thereon. He argued this topic with himself over the course of the next quarter of an hour, then, apparently concluding that he had lost the debate, embarked upon what promised to be a lengthy tirade on the fact that rather less than two-tenths of a percent of America's population owned more than 40 percent of America's wealth. Thatcher interrupted him to comment that if Chernoeznamia were to seize and liquidate all of the assets owned by all of the wealthiest two-tenths of a percent, he would have precisely enough money to buy every family in America a new Jeep. Chernoeznamia blustered like a wounded bull, and devoted the next half hour to a table-thumping lecture on socialist economics. He concluded his harangue by thundering that Marx had observed that capitalism sows the seeds of its own destruction. Thatcher replied briefly, endorsing this assertion.

Mayor Truscott Flood Forester's words were brief. He had but one question. "I'm long in your stock, Thatcher. Do you think it's going to get bid up any more or should I dump it now?" Thatcher blinked and said, "Personally, I'm holding," an answer that seemed to satisfy Forester not one whit.

The morning's hearings concluded with Darius Episcophagous announcing a two-hour lunch break.

"I have," snarled Louise as the trio stormed out of City Hall, "never heard so many non sequiturs in my entire life. No one asked any questions about the business. Nothing about the numbers. Nothing about the products. Nothing about the people. None of the stuff they yakked about has anything to do with the merits of the case—or their lack. This is worse than I expected!"

Mike, whose face was purple with rage, sneered, "The city council persons of the People's Republic of Palos Locos ought to be nailed up in crates, towed out to sea in a garbage scow, and sunk somewhere out beyond the twelve-mile limit."

Both waited for Thatcher to vent his wrath. But Thatcher was calm and collected. In a cool, relaxed tone of voice he simply said, "As I see it, Murphy's law has prevailed. Everything that could go wrong has gone wrong. I expect that you have heard the phrase 'worst-case scenario'? Well, now you know what it means. As of this morning, we have reached bottom. We have no further to fall. Accordingly, there is cause for optimism.''

He was wrong.

3

AFTER LUNCH THATCHER, MIKE, and Louise returned to their places in the council room to listen to the testimony of Brian Shawby, chairman and chief executive of AIW. Louise sat to Thatcher's left and Mike to his right.

Episcophagous repeated his meandering introduction as to the purpose of the hearings, then turned the floor over to Shawby. Shawby strolled to the front of the council chambers, looking unusually relaxed and confident. It was the first time Louise had seen him in person since they had met in Desuetude to discuss PegaSys's futile attempt to acquire AIW's video display division. Something about him had changed. His hair. He was wearing a rug.

Shawby opened his testimony by saying, "I have looked at Palos Locos closely. I have studied it well. I know it intimately. And I believe that the community persons of Palos Locos and the members of this city council are like me in certain regards, are like me in many regards. We are visionaries, you and I. We are not interested in what is. We are interested in what can be. We are not committed to studying the boring lessons of past history, but rather dedicated to the creation of new history. We do not want things to be the way things are. We want things to be the way things should be. That is our mission. That is our purpose. To that goal have I committed my company. And to that goal will I commit our new PegaSys subsidiary. You see, I have a dream . . ."

Continuing in a fervored oratorical style that blended in equally oleaginous parts the euphonious rhetorical habits of Jesse

Jackson and Jimmy Swaggart, he spoke of AIW's profound humanitarianism, devotion to its employees, consensus management style, egalitarianism, relaxed working environment, and community commitment. Periodically he dropped patronizingly saccharine quotes appropriate to his audience: the Maharishi for Shapiro, Torquemada for Sister Mary, Bella Abzug for Ms. X, Fidel Castro for Chernoeznamia, Ivan Boesky for Mr. Forester, Liberace for Episcophagous, and Garfield the cat for Mrs. Forester.

The audience applauded when he concluded his remarks.

Louise glanced sideways at Thatcher. He sat with his eyes partially closed and what appeared to be a faint smile on his lips. His face was wreathed in beatific serenity. Mike, on the other hand, seemed to be deeply concentrating on writing some thing on the yellow lined notepad in front of him. Louise arched her neck to get a closer look. It was his résumé.

Episcophagous invited the council to begin questioning Shawby. The first question came from the anarchistic Mr. Chernoeznamia. It was not polite. In a voice that dripped caustic disdain, he observed that among the myriad and far-flung businesses in which the AIW conglomerate participated were defense contracting and cable television—industries, he sneered, that were noted for their lengthy histories of sleazy misdoings, most notably bribery. He demanded to know if Mr. Shawby intended to bribe anyone in Palos Locos.

Shawby smiled boyishly and responded, "The stories you have heard are old, very old, and date back to the early days of the cable industry, before reputable companies such as mine got into the business. Specifically, I think you must be referring to the events in Pennsylvania some years ago, when one of cable television's founding fathers was sent to jail for allegedly disbursing shopping bags full of unmarked bills to local politicians. Tacky, tacky, tacky—at a minimum, proper business etiquette dictates the use of airline shoulder bags, not, for heaven's sake, shopping bags! No wonder the poor man went to jail. Now of course we at AIW are a much more sophisticated company. If we bribe anybody, we put the money in a nice matched set of Samsonite luggage!"

The city council and the audience broke into gales of laughter at this little joke. Louise did not laugh. Louise had a sinking sensation that Shawby was serious. She leaned over to Thatcher and whispered, "Scott, Shawby's—AIW's—principal cable operation is a satellite channel called 'Swedish Special Cinema.'

I have a list here of some of the programs they broadcast on that channel: *Bridget and Heidi's Vacation with the Boys; How to Pass Your Oral Exams; Hot Sauna Keepers; Kinky Nuns in Bondage;* and *Beyond the Valley of the Sex Starved Typing Pool.* What say we tell the council about them?''

Thatcher said nothing. He had an artless smile on his face. His eyelids were half-closed. He sat immobile, watching the proceedings.

With the wind safely taken out of Chernoeznamia's sails, the questioning moved on to Mrs. Forester. She perked up with a question about animal rights. Shawby in turn answered perkily, ''Mrs. Forester, let me first note that AIW, and specifically my company's Precious Pet division, is the creator of the designer cat litter industry. We are the ones who brought Kardin Kleanly Kat to market, and we are proud of it. Next let me give you my absolute assurance that once we own PegaSys, all of our computers will be constructed without the use of any animal material. At AIW we do not exploit helpless animals—unlike PegaSys's present management.''

''What?'' Louise leaped to her feet and screamed. ''What the hell do you think we build computers out of, catgut? That is the most ridiculous canard I have ever heard!'' Being products of the California school system, no council member understood the word 'canard,' and Episcophagous promptly gaveled her into silence.

Shawby went on to explain that he was an ardent supporter of animal rights, implying parenthetically that there might be some merit in determining whether parakeets should be given the vote. Mrs. Forester smiled her pleased approval of a man who, she clearly believed, personified all those virtues that Scott Thatcher lacked.

Louise again looked at Thatcher for a reaction. There was none. He had not moved, his eyelids still drooped half-closed, and a gentle look of angelic blissfulness showed from his face. In contrast, Mike had tilted his head back and was holding a handkerchief to his face to staunch a nosebleed.

Next Sister Mary asked her sharply pointed question about the use of computers in education.

Shawby replied by cheerily changing the subject. ''The issue, Sister, is less the medium than the message. What worries me is not so much how we teach, but what we teach. . . .''

To the wholehearted approbation of Sister Mary, Shawby sermonized eloquently, and at length, on the evils of salacious literature. He seasoned his preaching with frequent observations on the debasing and exploitive influence pornography has on women, addressing these latter sidebars to the fiercely smiling Ms. X.

When he concluded, the questioning turned to Mayor Truscott Forester, who throughout the afternoon had been scrutinizing Shawby with the kind of gimlet-eyed respect that one gifted liar reserves for another. Forester asked, "What should we do with the cash we get from selling our PegaSys stock to you? Should we buy AIW? Will AIW be a good value? Or do you know about something better?"

Shawby, who recognized precisely what Forester had in mind, answered, "I continue to believe that my company, AIW, is a superior investment opportunity. However, the nature of sizable acquisitions is such that it probably is a good near-term short. Which is what I personally am doing. But to respond directly to your question, I will have my good colleague and advisor Nick Lee give you a personal call with specific recommendations—"

"No illicit insider information, of course," interrupted Forester.

"Of course. I mean, of course not. Specific recommendations, I say, specific as to what might be a good, quick capital appreciation situation or two."

Louise looked at Thatcher to see what his reaction was to this blatant bartering of stock tips. There was none. Thatcher remained sitting in smiling silence, his eyelids at half-mast, and a look of childish happiness on his face. Mike, on the other hand, was sawing at the arteries in his left wrist with a rather blunt letter opener. Louise leaned over and offered him the use of the gift he had given her on her birthday, a Hoffritz woman's pocketknife.

Ms. X posed the next question. It stopped Shawby in his tracks, but only for a moment. She asked Shawby what his acquisition of PegaSys would to do for black people, especially those in Palos Locos. Louise smirked. There were no black people in Palos Locos. Shawby was trapped.

"Well, Ms. X, that question has troubled all of us at AIW. And we've come to the conclusion that the only fair, only just, only equitable, the only nonracist thing to do is to extend the benefits of AIW's corporate power to Palos Locos. And even more importantly to South Palos Locos. We feel bound by our commitment to equality and equal opportunity to do something to—I mean for, I say, for the underprivileged citizens of South

Palos Locos. No corporation which shares our high principles could do otherwise. Consequently, very early in our strategic agenda for PegaSys—once we acquire it next month—is a plan for the closing of current management's very expensive New York headquarters, and a relocation of its functions to South Palos Locos. And, of course, with the location of our PegaSys division headquarters in South Palos Locos will come jobs, jobs and income, income and new tax revenue, new tax revenue and . . ."

Louise felt her face become scarlet with rage. She turned to Thatcher, who still sat unmoving, just as he had for the past hour, with half-shut eyes and the expression of a sleepy, contented child on his face. In a hoarse whisper she demanded, "Holy Mother of God, Scott, do you hear this? We can't let this pass. Christ almighty, this clown is talking about 1,200 highly skilled people in New York! Scott, I have the numbers. Let me tell these folks the economic realities. Scott, I want to . . . Scott. Are you awake? Scott? *Scott!*"

The nurse awakened Thatcher. "Feeling any better now, sweetie?" she asked as she strapped a blood-pressure monitor to his arm.

"I just fell asleep," Thatcher said grumpily. "That's all."
"The hell you say," replied Ash. "You fainted."
"I did not. I was just taking a nap."
"Drivel."
"Don't you contradict me, Mike Ash. Or you either, Louise Bowman. It was jet lag or something. Now, you two just tell the local bone cutters to give me back my trousers and let me out of here. I was just taking a little nap, that's all."

Under light medication and bearing stern cautions about his age, Thatcher returned to the motel, where he promptly went to sleep.

4

WHEN TRAVELING IN THATCHER'S company, Louise and Mike kept their distance from each other. Fearful that even the least hint of a more than cordially professional relationship between them would fall beneath his sternly puritanical eye, they carefully chose rooms as distant from one another as possible, dined in different restaurants, and sat in separate sections of whatever airplane they traveled on. Occasionally they took separate flights.

On the other hand, they thought . . . on the other hand, Thatcher was, after all, asleep. Out like a light. Under medication. Slumbering like a baby. Could not possibly awake until the morning. Certain not to call upon either of them at 10:00 at night. Least of all to go rambling around the grounds of the Palos Locos Holiday Inn at that hour.

With nerves steeled by a sense of safety, a need driven by basic biochemistry, and a hunger born of a week of enforced abstinence, Ash had arched his eyebrows querulously at Louise. Louise nodded her head in reply and muttered, "At ten."

About four months earlier, Ash had discovered that Louise (infrequently, but from time to time), enjoyed fantasies. In a certain mood, her preference was for the kinkier kind. Tonight, he knew, the mood was upon her.

Mike, of course, was wholly incapable of constructing such fantasy episodes himself. When he had discovered that Louise occasionally liked lurid role-playing he hadn't known what to do. But Mad Mike, the creative genius, soon had a flash of inspiration. He started reading, avidly studying, and memorizing the most popular parts of Olivia Thatcher's pseudonymous bodice-rippers. They worked like a charm. The drama he planned, for example, would be plagiarized in its entirety (and updated to a contemporary setting) from a steamy Cecilia Mountbatten bestseller entitled *The Black Buccaneer's Bride*.

"The beautiful young career woman steps into the darkened motel room," Ash said. "She thinks she is alone. She does not know that a dangerous stranger is lurking in the shadows behind the door."

Louise came through the motel door.

"She sets her Crouch & Fitzgerald attaché case down in the foyer and reaches out for the light switch. Her fingers brush against the switchplate when, with terrifying quickness, a man's hand suddenly shoots out from the dark, rings her wrist with an iron grasp, and roughly jerks her forward."

Ash swept her up against his chest. "She was a tall woman, five feet nine inches. But he was taller. Her face was just below his, and she could see his eyes glint in the faint light." He spun her around sharply, twisting her arm behind her. Not hard enough to hurt, but firm enough to immobilize her. With his other hand he covered her mouth.

"He speaks in a deep, husky voice. His words come slowly, each one carefully pronounced for maximum impact. 'Don't speak. Don't cry out. Don't resist. You know what I want. If you try to stop me, you may get hurt. I'm not here to hurt you. Understand?' She nods her head."

Louise nodded her head. Ash took his hand away from her mouth and released her arm. Grasping her shoulders, he swung her around and pushed her against the wall.

He continued, "Holding her forcefully against the foyer wall, the stranger eyes her from top to bottom—slowly, coolly, with the look of a predator. He is tall, this brutal stranger, and handsome in a battered way. His hair is a dark blond, closely cropped and flecked with a premature peppering of grey. He is forty, perhaps. Perhaps older, but certainly no younger. He is muscular and broad-shouldered, and has the body of an athlete . . . the kind that plays rougher sports, like rugby or soccer. His nose is slightly crooked; it was broken once in a soccer game.

"He turns his pale, hazel eyes back to her face and stares at it curiously, as if seeing something there that he has never seen before. He wraps her luxuriantly thick, black hair around his hands and pulls her head back. He leans forward, his face close to hers, and whispers, 'Handsome. Woman, you are handsome. And beneath these clothes, I think, large-bosomed, too.' With these words, he grips her breast, squeezing and stroking it through the fine cotton of her blouse.''

And Ash did.

'' 'As I thought. Magnificent,' he says, almost reflectively. She stiffens as she feels his fingers probe and tear at her buttons. Middle button. Open. One up. Open. One more up. Collar button. Open. Two at the bottom, and her blouse parts. He strokes her bare midriff with the back of his hand. It feels cool against her skin, not feverish as she expected.

"His hands steal up, pause for a moment on her bra, and moves on to her shoulders. He takes the fabric of her blouse and balls it tightly in his hands, tugging it down off her arms. The blouse falls to the floor. She shivers at the cool touch of her pearl necklace against her bare skin. 'Now the bra,' he says, with mounting urgency in his voice. He slides the shoulder straps over her arms, gives it a sharp tug down, and lets it drop loosely around her hips. Now, except for a single strand of pearls, she is naked from the waist up. Her breasts, large and round, are exposed. She tries to step forward but he pushes her back, moving closer, his hands on her now, his mouth pressing her neck and seeking her lips.''

In Mike and Louise's little play there was no dialogue for the next minute or two.

"His hands glide over her, clutching, grasping, fondling her. His hands are smooth, soft, and his touch, while gentle, is tinged with roughness and demand. His mouth does not so much kiss her lips as it devours them, with a hunger that seems insatiable. There is a wildness in his caresses that she has not felt from other men, from the men whom she has invited to take her.''

Another minute or two when mouths must be occupied with things other than narration.

"Then she feels his hand slip lower, behind her, against her buttocks. She feels it clenching at the fabric of her skirt, working it up higher and higher. He presses her back against the wall again. Her naked skin flinches at the chill of the plaster. He stoops, grabbing the top of her hose and panties, and in one feline movement yanks them down to her ankles. He quickly stands and moves her forward, forcing her to step out of these underclothes. With one hand he continues to stroke her breast, with the other he probes beneath her skirt.

"She feels panic. This man is a stranger, an intruder, a violator of her privacy and a violator of her person. She struggles hopelessly in his arms.''

Louise's struggles, Ash confessed to himself, were pro forma at best. Her resistance lacked sincerity. Ash found it uninspiring. Nonetheless, he continued, "He pushes her back hard and holds his hand up as if to slap her. 'None of that,' he commands. 'You cannot fight me and hope to win.' She trembles violently at the threat, and tries to control the urge to flee.

"Again, his hand creeps between her legs. Uncontrollably, she feels herself becoming aroused, becoming damp. She despises herself for it. It is not that she is merely being used as a sex object. Other men have treated her as a sex object before. There is nothing new to that. When it happened in the past, it was insulting, but she could leave. But now, now she is being treated as something less than a sex object.

" 'You like this, don't you? Somewhere, somehow deep within you, you like it a lot.' "

Louise nodded a jerky yes. Louise never talked while she and Mike made love. And she never talked about sex later. The most Ash could ever get her to say about the physical side of their relationship was either a terse yes or an equally terse no. "Was that good for you?" "Yes." "Do you want to try it this way?" "No."

"Almost without her knowing it, almost as if it had a life of its own, her hand reaches down to his groin. It presses up against the place where his maleness strains against the fabric of his slacks. Her hand touches a hardness and rigidity that almost pulses.

"Again he places his hands on her shoulders. But now the pressure he exerts is downward. He forces her to the floor.

"He lowers himself down, stretching out, half covering her with his body. Pressing his lips on her, again with an angry hunger, he begins to kiss her. And, while kissing, removes his shirt. His slacks. His underclothes. Again his hands move across her body. Now they have a rhythm to their movements, a rhythm of urgent necessity. One hand strokes her breasts, the other rolls against her sex. Rhythmically. Rhythmically. And the rhythm of his hands is the same as the rhythm of her hips as they thrust against him.

"She is giving little cries as he takes his hand away, straddles her, parts her thighs, and enters. As he enters, her little cry becomes a larger one. As he moves within her, each cry becomes a little larger than the one before it. Soon there will be the largest cry of all."

* * *

Later, and in more traditional ways, Mike and Louise made love again. On the bed, not the floor. Twice. Louise did not utter a word until after they had both showered. The words she spoke dealt with the next day's business.

Ash lay beside Louise. He was waiting for his hair to dry, and would not spend the night with her. Not with Thatcher in the neighborhood. He lay beside Louise, but he lay alone. He had long ago given up trying to give Louise a post-lovemaking snuggle. She preferred to lie, curled fetally and unhugged, on her own side of the bed.

The problem, thought Ash, *the problem, now that I understand it, has three parts. Part one, I really want and need to talk seriously to this woman; it's long overdue; I love her, I want to marry her, and I want whatever this gap between us is bridged—no, closed. Part two, whenever I am alone with her, the hormones take over and all either of us can think about is having sex; so instead of talking, we make love; which is very nice but doesn't do anything else, and doesn't lend itself very much to long, meaningful conversations, if you know what I mean. Part three, after we're through, I am too blissed out and contentedly tired and brain-zapped to think straight, and the last thing I want to do is think about high-pressured personal issues. So instead I go off to sleep, and we never, never, never have a serious conversation. It's not my fault. I'm not dodging the issues. Besides, it's her fault too. If she really wanted us to talk through the issues, then she would say something. Wouldn't she? Well, somebody has to. OK. OK. Tonight's the night. I can't put it off anymore. I have got to know where this is going. No, I've got to let her know where I want it to go. No, I've got to make it go where . . . what time is it? Oh hell, it's nearly midnight, and we've got an early meeting with Thatcher. Maybe I can just tell her that we have to talk soon. Which we won't, because instead we'll be in bed. Maybe I can tell her let's get married first, and afterward we can talk about it. No, that won't work. Besides, what if she says no? Maybe I can just say that I love her. But all she does is grimace when I say that. Jesus, this is hard. How do I . . . what do I . . . I need to say . . . I need to say . . .*

Louise, for her part, was deep in thought too. *I hate this. We don't have anything in common except sex. And cats. Not endearment. Nothing close. I say hi, he says hi, we hop into bed, and bang, thank you very much, that's that. Where are all those affectionate words I used to hear? Where are any of the words I used to hear? Where are any words at all? Except hi and bang, thank you very much, you're pregnant. Probably. Probably not, just nerves. I mean, my period has been late before. This late? No. Yes. You're probably pregnant. Oh God, I hope not. What would he say if I told him? Probably some wiseass crack, "Welcome to the wonderful world of liberation, babe." Or maybe graciously offer to pay for the abortion. Or split the bill, more likely, the prick. Well, it's none of your goddamn business anyway, wiseass. Do I want an abortion? No. Yes. What's my choice? Besides, I'm not pregnant, it's just that I'm a little late. Yeah, more than a month. Arrrrggggh! I can't deal with this. Yes, I can. Be analytical, girl. How can you be analytical? Apart from having analyzed this relationship to death and knowing that it has to end. "Mike," I'll say, "Mike, it's all over. We're going absolutely nowhere, because there is absolutely nowhere to go. We aren't compatible. We're too different. It's not that we don't get along. It's that . . ." That what? Something, something, something, I'll say, "and we haven't got anything in common, except maybe the kid in my belly." I won't say that! Not ever. And he'll say, "OK. Good night." Son of a bitch. Why do I put up with him? The son of a bitch, doesn't he know my period's late? How could he not know? Doesn't he keep count? He probably does, but he's ignoring it. The prick. He knows. Do I love him? Come on, Louise, that's the real question, do you love him? No. Maybe. Yes. Maybe yes. I could, I suppose, and I suppose I do. Sort of. But, why bother, he'll just make me crazy and make me want to cry. He already does. And, do you really believe him when he makes noises about marriage? Marriage! Oh, no! Imagine what that would be like! Analyze that one, if you can! Besides, I know he isn't serious, and besides . . ."*

Ash sat up. Louise felt the mattress move. She didn't roll over to look at him. "Ahh, Louise," he said.

"Mmmm?"

"It's almost midnight and tomorrow is an early day. I'm, ahh, going back to my room now."

"OK, good night."

"We need . . . sometime, we really need to . . . ahh, you're half asleep. Anyway, well, ahh, I'll see you tomorrow."

"OK, good night."

"OK, good night."

Prick.

Ice queen.

5

THE NEXT MORNING THE PALOS Locos City Council, possibly encouraged by various unrecorded incentives offered by Messrs. Lee and Shawby, voted all its shares on behalf of AIW.

While Ash traveled across California to rendezvous at Stanford University with Roy Knight and the still-mysterious Wintergreen, Louise and Scott flew back to New York. Traveling with Thatcher was not an enjoyable experience, nor had it been since, a decade earlier, the airlines banned cigar smoking. Thatcher would sit, an unlit Macanuda clenched defiantly in his mouth, glowering at stewardesses and fellow passengers alike, complaining bitterly about whatever caught his fancy—the menu, the wine, the hors d'oeuvres, the movie, the seats, the cleanliness of the washrooms, the follies of airline deregulation, the price of first-class tickets, the substitution of "honey roasted" peanuts for the plain unvarnished real thing, and kindred issues. The only way to make flying with Thatcher bearable was to keep him diverted by talking about something other than air travel.

Louise, savvy in the secrets of managing Scott C. Thatcher's temper, had managed to occupy the hours between Palos Locos and the Colorado border with a postmortem on the city council's vote; all in all, it was a serious but not fatal setback, 3.1 million shares of PegaSys stock would be voted for Shawby, but PegaSys still might be able to keep the raiders from securing the full 80 percent they needed. From Colorado to the middle of Indiana she and Thatcher updated one another on the work being done by PegaSys's large (and steadily growing) defense team. By the time they reached the Pennsylvania border, Louise had exhausted other business topics, and Thatcher was looking about grumpily, seeking something or someone to vent his cigarless ire on.

In an effort to avoid hearing whatever tirade Thatcher was working up to, Louise decided to try the old nap ploy. She yawned and said, "Whew, Scott, I am really tired."

Thatcher looked at her and cocked an eyebrow. "Indeed," he replied before she could suggest that she wanted to close her eyes and sleep for the remainder of the flight. "I have been meaning to talk to you about that subject for some days."

"Huh?"

"You are tired—or at least you appear tired—all the time. You're getting dark circles under your eyes, and you look frazzled more often than not. It looks like you are putting on some weight too. I begin to worry that you are burning yourself out, Louise."

"Uh—well this AIW thing has been a tough time and—"

"It has been tough for us all. The pressure is crushing, and the physical demands of the hours we are keeping are brutal. People are wearing out. You are wearing out. When you wear out, you can't do your best. But your best is what we need, what we must have. Another thing. I think I know you pretty well, Louise. I have watched you work for many years now. I know who you are, how you react, and what you can do. I know what happens when you stretch yourself. That's why I think that, tired as you are, you are more tired than you should be. You will pardon me for saying this, but the stress of fighting off this takeover is not sufficient to account for your condition. There is something else gnawing at you, right?"

Louise sighed and nodded her head. She knew that it was Mike. Mike and a month's missed menses. The emotional tension of trying to decide whether or not to break up with him was showing. The possibility of being pregnant was more than she could deal with. It was interfering with her work. Mike was interfering with her work. Just as she knew he would. Just as any relationship would. Just as all her relationships had.

"Do you have someone to talk to about it?"

Louise shook her head. "No, not really."

"I will presume that it is personal, and I will presume that it is not the sort of thing an intelligent, attractive young woman wants a straitlaced old codger like me poking into. Neither of these two considerations will dissuade me from making a few wholly inappropriate comments. You know that, don't you?"

Louise smiled.

"Good. Here goes. Louise, I know your career is important to you, enormously important. Anyone's work is psychologically important, especially for smart, successful people like you. Good, hard, rewarding work can be, and I think is in your case, a source of enormous satisfaction and fulfillment. But it is not the only thing. Or at least it shouldn't be. Nor is it the most important thing. It cannot be your top priority, not if you want to be counted as a member of the human race. There is a good deal more to life than office life, and the greater rewards of existence are not to be found at Number One PegaSys Plaza. That goes for me as well as it goes for you. The best things in life are the personal things, not the professional things. Neither PegaSys nor even the potential takeover of PegaSys by that buffoon Shawby is more important than your personal, private life and your personal, private satisfactions. Louise, in absolute and utter candor, I will say that, if for one moment this Shawby situation endangered my family life and the things I do that make me a human rather than an automaton, I would hand the company to AIW on a silver platter. Or maybe a tin platter. I mean that."

"Baloney."

"No. Not baloney. Truth. Oh, it's more complex than the way I stated it, but the reality of the situation is, on a bottom-line basis, precisely this: some things are more important than other things, and the most important things are not named job, career, work, and promotion. I learned that lesson a long time ago. I learned it by watching other people sacrifice whatever they had to sacrifice to get whatever else it was that they wanted. When it was over, they had sacrificed everything they had, gotten something else, but wound up with nothing more than an empty feeling in their souls. And the pity of it all was that they couldn't understand why they had that empty feeling. Remember Goethe's Faust? Faust's bargain was that, in exchange for his soul, he could have anything he wanted. Anything. Not only that, he could keep his soul if he found one thing, just one thing, that was so wonderful that it made him 'say to the fleeting moment, *stop, thou art so fair.*' It was a pretty good bargain for the devil, because he knew nothing so wonderful existed. There is no one, single, grand thing so wonderful. There never has been. What makes life wonderful is not the single, grand things. What makes life wonderful is an abundance of little, good things. A warm day on a gentle beach, a cold day by the fireplace with a friend, a child's laugh, a good book, a—Yes. A good book. Have you read any good books recently, Louise?"

"Ahh. I've been a little busy and, well . . ."

"What's the last thing you read?"

"Ahh. Let me see. Well, there was Drucker's last book. It was really good and . . ."

Thatcher waved his hand in disdain. "I mean for pleasure. What was the last novel you read? Or poetry? Or even a short story?"

"The new Stephen King. When it first came out."

"Which was three or four months ago, if my aged and rapidly deteriorating memory serves. Well, what about movies?"

"Oh, nothing in the past few months."

"And the theater?"

"Nothing I really wanted to see so far this season."

"Refresh my memory. You did go on vacation earlier this year. But when was the last time before then that you took a few weeks off?"

"1985."

"And what magazines do you read?"

"Oh, lots."

"For example?"

"Datamation, Forbes, Business Week, Fortune, InfoSystems, U.S. News & World Report—"

"Your case is more desperate than I had imagined. Louise, do you have any social life at all?"

Louise sniffed irritably. "Of course I do."

"Friends?"

"Sure."

"People you go to dinner with?"

"Absolutely."

"Not counting Olivia and me, are there more than five of them?"

"That is a shitty and ugly question, and the answer is no."

"What about boyfriends? You will forgive me, I hope, for saying this—but then, after all, I am an irritating old man from an unliberated generation—I personally consider it to be a pretty sorry commentary on the state of American manhood that a woman as good-looking, personable, and downright smart as you has managed to go unmarried for so many years. So then, what about boyfriends?"

"Well, there's David."

"With all due respect to David, who is a charming and personable young man, he is not in your league, and it shows."

"I guess maybe I know that. Damnit, Scott, the thing is this. I work my tail off, and I just do not have the time for much of a social life. Besides, there may be lots of men out there, but not many of them are any good. I can't think of anyone I'd want to marry, and now that I think about it, why in God's name am I talking to you about these things?''

"Two reasons. One, I *am* your friend; and, two, it's pretty obvious that you need to talk to someone about them.''

Louise looked down in her lap, shrugged her shoulders, and softly murmured, ''Yeah, well, there is that.''

"And so?''

Louise inhaled deeply and, still looking down, said, ''Hell, Scott, I don't know. Sure, I want to get married. Sure, I want to have kids. But, to do that I want to find the right man, and finding him takes time. When I do it, I want to do it right. Only once. One man. One marriage. No problems. No fights. No incompatibilities. I don't want to add my number to the divorce statistics. The relationship I want has to be the best one, the perfect—''

"Perfect you don't get. They don't make perfect anymore. The stores no longer stock it. Perfect is out of inventory. You young people with your foolish yearning for the perfect this and the perfect that absolutely infuriate me. There is no such thing as perfect. The best you can find is good. Here you sit, you and everyone like you, smart as whips, tough as nails, skilled business people, brilliant managers, gifted negotiators. You can make any business situation work, you can fix any business problem there ever was. But for all your skills and talents, you can't make a simple personal relationship work. Your generation can't apply the genius you have in the office to the problems you find in your living rooms. It's too much trouble for you, or takes too much time. Instead, you keep moping around looking for some sort of perfection that does not exist. Perfect! Phooey! Name me one perfect, ideal, flawless relationship! Tell me who is the paragon and the model to whom we all should aspire. Whence must we look for the marriage of true minds and peerless compatibility?''

"You and Livy.''

"What! Me and Livy! The perfect relationship! My dear young woman, there has not been a week that has passed in our nearly forty years together that we have not argued, nor a month that we have not had a knock-down, drag-out fight. For Pete's sake, the melee began on our wedding day and hasn't ended since.''

"You're exaggerating.''

"No, I am not. I will have you know that Olivia and I argued so fiercely on the day we were married that we did not merely spend our wedding night in separate beds—we spent it in separate rooms. I hasten to add that we made up the next day, as we have ever since. But fight we do. Frequently and zestfully. The list of topics upon which we differ is vastly more lengthy than the list of those upon which we concur. And as for compatible interests, apart from a shared fondness for Italian food and a certain vulnerable affection for our children, our enthusiasms are quite, quite different. Oh yes, of course you see me squiring Livy to the ballet. I abhor ballet. Of course you see Livy dutifully manning the rudder when I go sailing. Livy loathes sailing. Of course you see us together doing this, that, or the other thing. Each moment of which the other finds stupefying, tedious, or childish.

"However, because we love one another and respect one another, we put up with each other's unedifying appetites for incomprehensibly tiresome things. As we put up with each other's frequently obnoxious behavior, unenlightened opinions, loutish poor taste, and distressing personal habits. We argue and I let her win—even though I know she's dead wrong. I love her and I compromise. She loves me and she compromises. We don't have compatibility. We don't have a perfect relationship. What we have is a good relationship based on mutual concession. What we have is the only kind of relationship that does work."

"And so you're saying—"

"Find someone you can deal with. Then make your deals. Make your deals."

"What about love?"

"It comes. It comes sooner rather than later, and it stays."

"I don't think I even know what the word really means."

Thatcher snorted, "Hmpf! What it means for me is probably different from what it means for you. What it means to men is different from what it means to women. But I'll tell you what the word 'love' means to me, if you want. First, it is an overwhelming sense of protectiveness; an irresistible compulsion to keep the loved one safe and cared for; to slay mammoths to feed her and keep saber-toothed tigers out of the cave. The second part is unabashed and unabated lust; a yearning far in excess of the kind of itch that the presence of a pretty girl just naturally brings along; yup, true love brings with it uncommon randiness. Third, for men, love triggers a shameless predilection for romance and romantic gestures; the grand ones and the small ones; 'tisn't much in fashion anymore, and the world and women are the poorer for it. Fourth, love and jealousy are pretty much synonymous for us male types; we find it pretty hard not to be possessive. That's about it for men. Love is protectiveness, high-octane lust, silly romance, and possessiveness. We're all still cavemen, we males, I suppose, but that's how we feel about love. All of us, I bet.''

Louise lifted her head and looked at him. Her eyes weren't moist, but they did sparkle a little. "Thanks, Scott," she said. "Thanks. I think you've said something to me that I needed to hear. I really appreciate it. Thanks.''

"You are more than welcome. Quite frankly, I welcome the opportunity to organize my thoughts and rehearse my comments on these topics. You are not the only person to whom I have to give this lecture. There is someone else around this company who needs a talking to, and who will get it whether he wants it or not.''

Whoops, thought Louise.

6

ANDREI BEZUKHOV GLANCED nervously to his left, and patted the gun beneath his parka. No one was looking at him. He glanced nervously to his right, and patted the gun beneath his parka. No one was looking at him. The young people ignored him. Tanned and golden in their cut-off blue jeans and tank tops, in light summery dresses or jogging shorts (the legs of Russian womanhood did not compare favorably with those on display before him), they drifted by him, walking with sassy impudent steps or cruising with indolent gracefulness on roller skates and bicycles. Andrei Bezukhov, walking slowly across the sun-drenched campus of Stanford University and wearing a fur-lined arctic parka, felt an utter fool.

The temperature was a balmy 78 degrees. Flowers bloomed.

The sky was cloudless. A gentle breeze ruffled the palm trees. It was paradise.

Bezukhov deemed the weather to be a fundamental violation of the laws of nature. It was, after all, late November. It was the time of year when the Moskva and Volga rivers froze solid, and when all good Muscovites braced themselves for marrow-freezing winds, head-high snow drifts, long glacial nights, and clanking heating systems that, when they worked, brought the room temperature up to 50 degrees—55 for those who bore the rank of major or above. It was cold, clammy, and miserable in Moscow. It was cold, clammy, and miserable in New York. Bezukhov had expected it to be cold, clammy, and miserable thirty miles south of San Francisco at Stanford University. That was why he had put on a parka. Over a heavy sweater. Over thermal underwear.

Andrei Bezukhov mopped the sweat off his forehead. He tugged at the neck of his thick woolen sweater. He fanned his face with a handkerchief. He looked around nervously and patted his gun. The gun was the problem. He couldn't take his parka off or everyone would see it, neatly tucked in a shoulder holster beneath his left arm.

Panting like an overheated cocker spaniel, Bezukhov made his way past the Stanford Graduate School of Business. Just ahead of him stood a tall, phallic construction, jutting high above the center of the Stanford campus—Hoover Tower, the rendez-vous site for Ash, Knight, and Bezukhov's target, Wintergreen. Wintergreen, the maniacally amok computer hacker. Wintergreen, who had downloaded the entire text of Barry Goldwater's recently published autobiography onto *Pravda*'s typesetting system. Who had reprogrammed the Politburo's mainframe to issue senior Party member food coupons to everyone on the janitorial staff. Who had summoned up unspeakably pornographic cartoons of Lenin and Stalin on the Eastern watch's radar screens. Who had left his calling card on every computer in the Union of Soviet Socialist Republics, who was now officially recognized as a formal enemy of the state, and who was to meet Mike Ash and Roy Knight—and nemesis, in the person of Andrei Bezukhov—at Stanford's Hoover Tower at 11:00 A.M. sharp.

There were, Bezukhov recollected as he reached the meeting site, only two notable Americans named Hoover. One was the late head of the FBI, a laughable oaf whose incompetent blunders were still recounted by KGB instructors who wanted to get a guffaw out of their students. The other was the president who had presided over the greatest depression in the history of capitalism, and whose incompetency after it had begun ensured an unrivaled economic debacle of global scale. Bezukhov was not sure after which of them the tower was named. It was a perplexing question. In Russia, people such as the two Hoovers would have been buried in unmarked graves, and their names expunged from the encyclopedias. But then, Bezukhov thought, Russian values were different from Californian values. Everybody's values were different from the Californians'.

Bezukhov knew that Stanford was the headquarters of a most peculiar body, the "think tank" known as the Hoover Institute, doubtless somehow or another associated with the Hoover Tower. The Hoover Institute was the organization that had most ardently preached the dotty dogma of supply-side economics, a theory holding that a government that makes less money than it spends, and then lowers taxes while increasing expenditures, will magically quash inflation, eliminate the national debt, erase its trade deficit, and produce boundless riches and prosperity for all. Bezukhov had authored several memos to his superiors urging that the Party anonymously contribute money to the Hoover Institute in order to encourage it to disseminate its theories more widely throughout other Western nations. These memos were sadly ignored.

Bezukhov glanced at his watch—10:52. Eight minutes to go. He glanced around to see if Wintergreen had arrived early. There was no one nearby holding the recognition signal that would mark him. Bezukhov moved over to the bubbling fountain in front of the Hoover Tower, and sat on its rim. He mopped more sweat off his brow. He patted his gun.

Mike Ash was leaning against a balustrade on the steps leading to Hoover Tower. He was dressed casually in grey slacks, a white oxford shirt, and a blue blazer. He had taken off his tie and left it in his rental car. Unable to find a parking place, he had abandoned the car in one of Stanford's myriad no-parking zones. As he stood relaxed in the sun, passing female students eyed him with interest, wondering what courses he taught and contemplating enrolling in them. One of them shamelessly walked up to him and said, "Excuse me, professor, you have a spot here on your jacket." As she brushed away at his spotless jacket, Ash, a little flustered, stuttered, "Oh, I'm not a teacher here." "Administration?" she asked hopefully. Ash shook his head. "Visitor." The disappointed girl walked away.

Ash watched her as she walked. She wore a loose, dark green T-shirt and matching corduroy slacks. The T-shirt wasn't tucked in and swayed fetchingly with her equally fetching stride. Her hair was long and blond, falling loosely over her shoulders. She moved with all the grace and possibilities of her age, *possibilities that seem so remote when you are in your forties. Likewise grace*, Ash thought to himself, as the girl continued to walk away in the sun.

Roy Knight was coming from the opposite direction. He looked like something that had escaped from the bowels of the computer science department, down deep where they keep the graduate students and don't let unaccompanied visitors go. His skin was etiolated. His wire-frame eyeglasses were bent askew. He wore unspeakably aged blue jeans, a lumberjack shirt, a square-cut black knit tie, and a lurid plaid jacket with sleeves that were several inches shorter than his arms. There were half a dozen ballpoint pens in his shirt pocket. He had no socks on, and his penny loafers had not been shined since the day they left the Florsheim store. He was the epitome of hacker chic. He waved at Ash, then craned his tall, gangling neck, looking for Wintergreen.

Ash watched him walk past the blond girl, the two not even noticing one another.

Knight reached Ash and said, " 'Morning, Mike. Seen our pal yet?''

Ash, his eyes still following the girl, answered, "No. What are we looking for again?''

"Blue jeans, Apple Computer T-shirt, holding the most recent issue of *Cerebus* comics. That'll be our boy.''

The blond girl was nearly out of sight.

Knight said, "Wait a second, I think that's . . .''

Almost gone now. Ash was pointing down toward the fountain.

Gone. Ash glanced in the direction Knight was pointing.

Knight said, "our . . .''

Wintergreen?

Knight said, "friend . . .''

A glint in the corner of Ash's eye.

Knight said, "Oh, no . . .''

A yellow acidic flash. A smell . . .

Knight said, "Jesus . . .''

Something red . . .

Knight said, "Look out!''

Something red where a student's chest . . .

Knight said, "a gun . . . —" and turned.

. . . had been. The smell of cordite . . .

. . . the smell of flowers . . .

. . . in the flowers . . . where Ash was rolling. *No, running now.* Running through the flower beds. Wintergreen was dead. Ash was running.

How did I get in the flowers? he thought. *Where was the bang? I didn't hear the bang! But it was a shot. I didn't hear the shot. Wintergreen is dead. I am running. Students are lying flat on the sidewalk. They have begun to shriek. Wintergreen is dead. I am running. Running.*

At the KGB academy, they teach you about fear You read studies on the subject, on its theory and its practice. You learn how to create it, how to use it, and how to react to it as best you can. Among other things, you are given a book by a largely forgotten American psychologist named William James. He tells the following anecdote. A man is walking in the woods. The man rounds a corner in the trail and comes upon a large, hungry bear. The man turns and runs. What has happened in this man's mind? James asks. Did his eyes register the bear's fearsome presence and promptly send a telegraph to the brain saying, "We're in big trouble, fellow. There is a hungry bear just in front of you. You had better decide what to do"? Did the brain receive this message and calculate, "Yes, it is a bear. Bears eat people. Let me consider what to do. I am in danger. If I am in danger, I must get away from it. I must escape quickly. This means I must run, and thus I should send an instruction to my legs to begin moving quickly"?

Or was it rather that as soon as his eyes spotted the bear, the man began to run? And once he was well under way, running in fear, then and only then did the brain tell him that he was running from a dangerous bear?

Was the sequence of mental and physical events *bear! danger! run!*—or was it *run! danger! bear!*?

James thought it was the latter. So did Bezukhov. He was a computer scientist. He was not an assassin. he had never seen a man shot to death before. It horrified him. He never, never, never wanted to see such a death again. He never wanted to see any death again. *Run! Danger! Death!*

* * *

Ash didn't know that he could run so fast. It felt good. The man with the gun was moving at a blistering pace, but Ash was overtaking him. The distance between them was eight yards and lessening with every second. The man with the gun had made a mistake. He had not dashed into Stanford's maze of cool, golden cloisters where he could have easily shaken a pursuer. Instead, he had run for the open spaces, out where it was simply a question of speed. If speed was the question, Ash had the answer. He closed the gap; six yards now. Ash wasn't even panting. It was easy. Five days without cigarettes and his wind was back. The man with the gun swerved toward Stanford's great oval, fifty grassy yards long or more, and bordered with bright flowers. He put on a burst of speed. It wasn't enough; Ash relentlessly closed on him. Someone ran alongside Ash, keeping pace with him. Ash guessed it was Knight, but kept his eye on his prey. Three yards now. The man with the gun leapt over the flower beds and skidded as his feet landed on the grass. Two male students casually flipping a Frisbee back and forth looked up, caught sight of the gun, and dived out of his path. Ash tensed, pumped his legs harder, and threw himself forward. He wrapped his arms around the man's thighs in a perfect tackle. The man running beside him piled on top a second later. Ash saw a gun tumble across the grass, far out of anyone's reach.

Vaguely he remembered the cautionary lecture he had been given by Detective Ryerhurt and his partner some weeks earlier. *Losing control. Howling at the moon. Drinking blood. Lashing out. Letting the mad dog inside of you slip its leash. Right*, he thought, *and it feels good!* He drove the palm of his hand into the base of his victim's skull. The man's face buried itself in the turf. There was an audible crunch as his nose broke. Ash cocked his arm back for another blow, but someone grabbed it, keeping him from striking again.

"That will do it," a voice said. "He is quite gone to sleep now, I think."

Ash stopped pummeling the man on the grass. He reached beneath the man's slack shoulders and rolled him over. The man on the grass was Japanese. He wore an elaborate silver-and-torquoise belt. Ash had seen him before. Ash felt his blood rising again.

The voice beside him said, "Excuse me, please." It was a peculiar voice. It had a faint, unidentifiable accent. Ash looked around and saw its owner, the man who had helped him chase and tackle the man with the gun. He was youngish looking and was plastered with sweat. He was wearing a parka. He said, "Excuse me, please, are you not Michael Ash? My name is Bezukhov, Andrei Bezukhov. I'm Russian."

Ash looked at him, cocking his head to one side. "Exchange student?"

"No. KGB agent."

Ash smiled, shrugged, and decked him with an uppercut to the jaw.

Later in the sheriff's office, where he sat numbly waiting for his statement to be typed, Ash began to shake.

It was evening. Ash lay in his room at Rickey's Hyatt a few miles from the Stanford campus. There was a tap at his door. He grunted, "It's open. Come in."

The door opened and Roy Knight entered. A young man, a bashful-looking teenager no older than seventeen, accompanied him. He was dressed even less tastefully than Knight. "Hey, Mike," Roy said cheerily, "guess what? This is Wintergreen. The other one, the poor bastard I was pointing at, was the wrong guy. By the way, they say he'll live. Anyway, Mike Ash, let me introduce you to Arnold Swift, aka Wintergreen. Arnie, this is Mike Ash. Come on, Mike, get up and let's go get a pizza. We got some talking to do with Arnie here."

Ash said nothing. He merely rose, walked into the bathroom, closed the doors, and vomited again.

7

Dᴇᴛᴇᴄᴛɪᴠᴇ ꜱᴇᴄᴏɴᴅ ᴄʟᴀꜱꜱ Rʏᴇʀ-hurt was sitting behind his scarred metal desk, a piece of furniture purchased by the city of New York at a military surplus sale in 1954 and last refinished during John Lindsay's first term as mayor. The precinct captain tossed a yellow telex in front of him. "A couple of your customers, I think," he said.

Ryerhurt read the message, winced, swore, wadded it up, then unwadded it and carried it over to his partner. "Here, read this."

His partner did. When he was done, he said, "Aw, shit."

"What we have here," Ryerhurt mused, looking up at the mottled once-white, now-grime-grey ceiling, "is the makings of a sinister international conspiracy."

"Yeah. Fu Manchu. Fiendish archcriminals. Sinister masterminds. A nefarious international conspiracy to keep me from going home for my Thanksgiving dinner," replied his partner unhappily. "A nefarious international conspiracy that sends telexes that talk about nasty Jap thugs running around with guns and shooting down innocent civilians."

"And then tell precinct captains to have their woefully overworked detectives clear any action they might contemplate with the weird boys in McLean. The cloak-and-dagger crowd. Some Russian has defected into the middle of this mess."

"The good news is that these unsocial behavioral manifestations seemed to have happened not merely in another precinct, but in a whole other state. Don't forget that. Like, out of our jurisdiction."

"But, unfortunately, this trigger-happy Jap bad guy is exactly the same trigger-happy Jap bad guy that we bagged the end of last month waving a piece of portable artillery around the otherwise decent, law-abiding and peaceful streets of our fair metropolis, and on whom we have a warrant out for jumping bail. But more to the point—"

"Yeah. Precisely to the point—"

"The son of a bitch that nailed the son of a bitch was a son of a bitch from the PegaSys company."

"Being precisely the same son of a bitch who punched out the son of a bitch's lights last time. Michael J., aka Mike, Ash. An otherwise quiet, unassuming guy; a sober, upstanding citizen; a prominent business executive even, who just happens to have this thing about punching out Japanese gunmen."

"Gunmen who just happen to have this thing about perpetrating felonies on and around the premises of PegaSys Inc. or, as it now appears, whenever they are in the immediate vicinity of PegaSys executives."

"So what's going on?"

"Beats the shit out of me."

"I think we maybe should just let this one sit. Tell you what, let that little Jewish broad, what's her name, Ms. Rambo, handle it. The Gold dame. With that tootsie around, all we need to do is wait till it's over and then send in the meat wagons. No? OK, what do you want to do?"

"Well, we got the outfit those cleaning people were working for, and we got the outfit that dropped a crane on PegaSys's head, and we got a telex that gives us this Jap bad guy's place of employment—and they're the same outfit. Seppuku. They're all Seppuku, and they're all Japs."

"And they're the guys that produced the TV show that the Gold broad ran amok on."

"Really? Do you suppose . . . Naw, that's too much. That's stretching."

"You're right. There can't be a connection there."

"So I say, what we should be doing is looking at this Seppuku outfit. Hard."

"And at PegaSys."

"Even harder."

"And Ash."

"Him, too. Soon as he gets back to New York, put a tail on him."

"Shit, there goes Thanksgiving."

8

THE KGB MAN WHO CALLED ON Quint and Claggart was, unlike Andrei Bezukhov, neither youthful nor handsome nor well educated. One look at him was sufficient to persuade Quint and Claggart that he did not speak on behalf of the more enlightened sectors of the Soviet government. Rather, he epitomized the more traditional—classic, one might say—values of the KGB.

"You get this gun," the KGB man said, reaching an enormous hairy paw beneath his far-too-tight overcoat and withdrawing a monumentally lethal armament. "This is a Dirty Harry gun, no? You ever see Dirty Harry gun before?"

Quint looked at the gun and felt quite ill. Claggart's eyes began to tear.

"You know Dirty Harry, yes? Is good movie. Is like real life is. Would make good Russian policeman, Dirty Harry. Even dresses like a Russian policeman, ha! Is my hero, is Dirty Harry. Ha!"

Quint received the full effect of the blast of fetid breath that propelled the KGB man's guttural laugh. He thought of long-dead nasty things found in sewers, and felt bile in his throat.

"Is Colt .44 magnum. Is not official Soviet pistol, but no matter, is good gun. Does not go bang. No, no. Bang is for sissy boys. Goes booooom! Ha! Boooooom! You like my gun, or are you sissy boys?"

"It is a lovely gun," squeaked Claggart.

"Indeed, quite the handsomest thing I have ever seen," croaked Quint.

"Good. Glad you like. I put here so you can admire it while we talk." The Russian, moving with bearish ponderousness, slowly set the blue-black revolver down on the table. He turned it so the barrel pointed at Claggart. Claggart winced. He shifted it so that it was aimed at Quint. Quint shuddered. He touched it lightly so that it angled between the two. "Now, while you admire my gun, we got some business, no?"

"Whatever you say," said Quint.

"Our pleasure," said Claggart.

"Is business with you, but deals with Japanese and with Yankees. Is business I don't understand, but my bosses say go do business with Mr. Quint and Mr. Claggart. So here I am. What my bosses say, is what I do. Ha! Understand? No good not to do what the bosses say. Could be trouble. Understand? Good! Is hearing, my bosses, that you are selling something maybe. Is what they call a convertible demand debenture. Is something called 'PegaSys' and 'AIW' and 'Seppuku' and 'Lee, Bach and Wachutt.' Means nothing to me. Means something to you, no?"

Quint and Claggart looked at one another. The Russian's sausagelike fingers stroked the gun's long, ugly barrel. Deciding that for once in their lives they confronted ample incentive to be honest, Quint and Claggart nodded affirmatively.

The KGB man's face broke into a broad smile. He bared his

mottled yellow teeth and roared, "Good! Good! Is delighted. You sell some, OK?" Claggart caught a whiff of his breath and reached for a handkerchief.

"Of course," said Quint. "Of course. We would be delighted. But . . . ahem . . . you see, there is a difficulty."

The Russian's head furrowed. "Deef-e-cul-tee?" he growled somberly. "You mean is problem."

"Precisely. Is problem. I mean, there is a problem. You see, we have . . . ahh, well, we have already sold off all of those instruments . . . those debentures that we had. Ours was a small allocation, and they are all gone. Yes, gone. Sadly all sold. And, ahh . . ."

The Russian lifted the gun. He cracked it opened and slowly counted the bullets in it. He lifted one out and held it up to the light. It shone with dull, lethal wickedness. He replaced it and closed the gun up. "Could be mistake," he said in a thoroughly unpleasant tone of voice, "or could be lie. Is hoping is not lie. Is hoping is not lie because is very big deef-e-cul-tee in buying bullets for .44 magnum Dirty Harry gun in London. Use up bullets you got, and you got to get more from another country. That's why is hoping is mistake. Is hoping that what bosses say is true and is hoping you make mistake. Let me tell you what bosses say. Bosses is saying that you was supposed to sell off all these debenture things, but that maybe you cheat a bit and keep a few back, waiting for the value to go up so you can sell at higher price, but is saying that you sold earlier at lower price. Is keeping the difference for yourselves. Or maybe you don't cheat because gentlemens don't cheat. Is maybe you don't count right because gentlemens don't count right. You sure you don't got none left?"

"Ahh," said Quint.

"Ahh," said Claggart.

"Now that I think of it," said Quint.

"Yes, now that we reflect," said Claggart.

"It could be that we miscounted," said Quint.

"There may be a few left," said Claggart.

"Is better be more than a few," said the KGB man, idly flipping the gun's safety off and on. "Is better be about 30,843 units, face value $100,000 per unit, pay to bearer, fourteen and three-quarters coupon, maturity December 25 this year, and is selling to me at big discount by whoever administers your estate unless we are doing business pretty soon now."

"As it happens," said Claggart.

"By a most curious coincidence," said Quint.

Claggart continued, "We just happen to have precisely, I say, precisely, the number of units that interest you. How fortunate for you."

The Russian, smiling again, nodded and said, "Is also how fortunate for you."

"If you care to write us a check," said Quint, "or perhaps you had a cash transfer in mind, we can even deliver the debentures to you right now."

The Russian shook his head. "No, is not wanting them now."

"Tomorrow perhaps?"

"Is not wanting them tomorrow."

"Ah, then, early next week, shall it be?"

"Is wanting them first thing in the morning on December 26."

"The morning after they mature," Quint said in a perplexed tone of voice, "after the deal goes through. Most unusual. Whatever for?"

"Is not wanting *unless* the deal goes through," answered the Russian, who was sighting the pistol at a tarnished brass lamp just behind Quint's left ear. "Is wanting after deal goes through, but dated before. But if is no deal, then is no sale. You is keeping them. Is not wanting them unless the deal goes through. Makes sense, no?"

"Not really," Claggart said, forgetting about the gun and adopting a tone suitable for lecturing a particularly dense child. "Of course you understand that the debentures will be worth more, a rather good deal more, than their face value on December 26—but only if the deal goes through. If the deal doesn't go through, they could easily be worth a good deal less. If you want us to wait until December 26 before selling to you, why, sir, then we will be assuming a very considerable economic risk. I'm not sure we are willing to deal under those terms."

"Is fair people, the Soviet government. Is not wanting you to go poor. Come December 26, is paying you 125 percent of face value in good Russian gold as of striking price Christmas Eve on London Metals Exchange, plus is giving you each lovely Russian sable coat with matching hat. Also is doing this through Lichtenstein banks with no tax records. And, guess what? Best of all, is not shooting you."

"Ahh," said Quint, turning white.

"Ahh," said Claggart, turning green.

"Ahh," said the KGB man, who was already a bright beet color and didn't turn anything except a bright, toothy smile.

9

"HOW LONG?" ASKED THATCHER, igniting his first cigar of the morning. His high-backed leather chair was tilted as far back as it would go. He was resting the heels of a glistening pair of Bally loafers on top of the equally glistening surface of his antique partner's desk. Gladys, whose list of secretarial prides and joys began with the shiny perfection of that desk's surface, sat to the side looking at his desecration with no forgiveness. She icily scribbled shorthand on a spiral-bound notepad, transcribing, as she had for the past five weeks, all of Thatcher's discussions relating to the takeover.

"A week at the most," Banks replied. "It's Seppuku that's bankrolling this deal. We know that now and we know it for sure. Joe Jonas was right, and we would have ferreted the little Nip bastards out—strike that, Gladys—the role of Seppuku out in a day or two ourselves. The question no longer is who, the question is what. We are sure that the pap AIW has fed the SEC is a pack of lies, but we can't prove it. What are they *really* doing to raise the bucks?"

Thatcher's stomach growled. He placed his hand across his belly and winced. "Excuse me. Too much turkey and too much mincemeat pie, I think. Don, I don't understand the issue. It would seem to me relatively easy to find out how the Shawby crowd are planning on getting—what are we talking about now, $18 billion with their latest offer?—getting their hands on eighteen billion bucks. This sum strikes me as being a little bit on the large size. Surely someone would notice it being raised."

"Not really, Scott, $18 billion just ain't all that much money these days, not in today's market. Besides, most of the money isn't in the banks and isn't in the treasuries. No one keeps a big iron vault with mega-zillions of loose change in it. No, most of the money is in the network. It's electronic money, and it's continually zipping around the globe. One minute it's in Eurobonds in Brussels and the next minute it's in a currency straddle in Singapore. In fact, Scott, I would go so far as to say that money isn't money anymore. At least not in the denominations we're talking about. Rather, it's information about money—digital, binary, electronic, stored, encoded, modulated, and demodulated information. Raw data. Money, real money, ain't green stuff with George Washington's picture on it; it's bits and bytes on the wires. It moves fast, it moves silently, and it moves secretly. Finding out who's got what, where he got it from, and where he's sending it to . . . well, it isn't that easy. Times have changed. Big currency transactions are bigger, but less visible. We'll need a week to smoke this one out.''

"A week it is."

Down the hall from Thatcher's office Louise dashed into the ladies' room. She locked herself in a stall and began to dab the tears forming at the corners of her eyes. She had just left Mike Ash's temporary office (his previous one still being under repair as a result of its invasion by the construction crane). She gulped a sob. Finally, she had the evidence she needed, positive proof that Mike did not love her. It was bad enough that he had not complained when she went to Greece with David, and instead had remained totally, stonily silent on the whole subject. Which meant he wasn't possessive about her. Strike one. It was even worse that he never, ever made mad, fanciful, romantic gestures. Strike two. But now . . . Damn, her mascara was running. But now . . .

"Mike." She had walked into his office and stood in front of his desk. "Mike, would you kill a monster for me?"

Mike, clutching the day's first cup of coffee in a death grip, and particularly irked by the fact that no one, absolutely no one, had noticed that he'd stopped smoking, glared up from the almost uninterpretable report on Seppuku's export operations he'd been attempting to decipher, and replied in a particularly surly tone of voice, "No. If you've got a problem, call the building management and have them send an exterminator."

Whereupon she had run for the ladies' room. No possessiveness. No romance. And now, no protectiveness either. Only sex. That's all it was, just sex. The evidence was clear. He didn't love her. Not only that, her stomach was upset. She lit a hated cigarette. More than merely queasy. *Morning sickness?*

* * *

Arnold Swift, aka Wintergreen, lifted the defunct ruins of a kingsize Famous Ray's pizza ("double everything except anchovies, we want triple anchovies") off Roy Knight's desk. He opened another can of Orange Crush. Knight passed him the bag of Oreos. Swift filled his hand to overflowing.

Roy, idly nibbling on some Lay's garlic-and-onion-flavored potato chips, ruminated. "Now what? I mean, it looks like we're in a closed loop on this takeover. Like, we're hung up and holding, Arnie."

"Bad karma, Roy. Like, if these are the Japs like Mr. Ash says—"

"Call him Mike. We're into first names at PegaSys."

"Yeah, sure. But it's like everyone here is a professor or administration or something, you know. I mean ties, Roy, you didn't tell me that they all wear ties."

"Yeah, I had trouble getting used to it too. But don't worry. It isn't important."

"Yeah, well anyhow, like I was saying, with these guys being Japs, you can't find out so much. There isn't that much in the public record. Heck, we've been through all the databases."

"Twice."

"And there's nothing there but gobbledygook. I mean, nothing that Mr. A—Mike or Louise or Scott can really use to figure out what's going on."

"Hmmm."

"They're real secretive, those Japs."

"Hmmm."

"They don't really tell anyone anything. Not really."

"Hmmm."

"There is probably no way you could figure out what they're really up to. Except . . ."

"Hmmm."

"Like, maybe the only way you could really find out what they are doing . . ."

"Hmmm."

"Yeah. Just what was on my mind."

The Masked Rider of the Plains and his faithful Indian companion looked at one another. Wordlessly, each knew what the other was thinking. Wordlessly, they both knew what they had to do. The evil cattle barons were plotting to burn the peaceful sheep ranchers out of their humble homes. Hired guns—black-hatted, moustached, cigar-chomping thugs from Tombstone—had been brought in to do the dirty work. Hot lead would fly. A range war was ready to burst into violent conflagration and race across the golden plains like . . . like, well, like a prairie fire. The sheriff was drunk and scared. The corrupt judge had been bribed by the cattlemen's association. The feisty young newspaper publisher had been beaten up when the Tombstone gang smashed his printing press. The sheepmen were all Quakers and wouldn't lift a finger to defend themselves. Innocent people, women, children, and young babes in arm would die. Unless . . . unless, the forces of justice, truth, and righteousness acted quickly. Desperate times call for desperate actions. The Masked Rider of the Plains sternly checked his pistols. All six chambers in both of his pearl-handled, silver-plated, gold-filigreed six-shooters were loaded. His faithful Indian companion opened the breech of his Winchester repeating rifle. It carried a full load. The two men clenched their jaws resolutely and nodded to one another. Then, with synchronized, fluid grace, they swung into the saddles of their noble stallions. The mighty horses reared. Justice was on the ride again. Heigh-ho, Silver, awaaaaaaaaay!

10

VIKTOR NADRAZNY, A FULL KGB colonel of long and honorable career, had made a little mistake. Minor, truly. The sort of trivial error that anyone could make. All he had done, the only thing really, was shuffle two 3 × 5 filing cards into the wrong order. A simple misstep, and not at all intentional. In and of itself, not anything worth becoming concerned about. Except, of course, for the consequences. Andrei Bezukhov, a rather timid low-level computer scientist whose card inadvertently was shuffled to the top, had been sent on an assignment intended for one of the KGB's more persuasive and less personable gorillas. And the gorilla, with his card misplaced on the bottom, had been sent on an assignment intended for Bezukhov. The gorilla had succeeded. Bezukhov had not. Bezukhov had defected. In public. Carrying a gun. In front of newspaper reporters. Who took pictures. Which found their way to Comrade Gorbachev's desk. Who circled them in red, and who wrote an exceedingly profane directive next to them. Who demanded an answer immediately. Right now. This very moment.

Accordingly, Viktor Nadrazny's bony rump now was being chewed upon. The chewer, to make a bad situation infinitely worse, was not his boss, nor even his boss's boss. Rather, it was Vladimir Aleksandrovich Kryuchkov, chairman of the Committee for State Security, born 1924 and appointed by Comrade Gorbachev during the 1988 purge. Viktor found him to be not the most sympathetic of men. Viktor found him to be precisely what you would expect the head of the KGB to be, glasnost and perestroika notwithstanding. Viktor wondered whether life above the Arctic Circle was as bad as he had heard it to be. Viktor knew he would not be wondering for long.

It was one o'clock on Saturday morning when Colonel Viktor Nadrazny received the orders that dispatched him several thousand thoroughly unpleasant miles north and east of Moscow. However, it was only five o'clock on Friday afternoon in New York.

"Another week," Thatcher barked. "Only three weeks to go until that tender offer closes! We don't have another week! Another week passes, and I'm history, and so is this company! This company is in the hands of a man—of men—who will strip it, fillet it, and leave its bare bones bleaching in the sun! Blast it, Don, how can we defend ourselves if we don't know the size, weaponry, and armor of the armies attacking us? Or the direction they're coming from? Or anything about them?"

"Scott, Scott, Jesus. Calm down. We are doing everything we can possibly do. It's just that these guys have covered their tracks unbelievably. We're doing our best, and—"

"Then that's enough. That's all I ask people to do. Their best. You can't ask for more than that. I pray to the Almighty that your best suffices."

"Scott, damnit, I know that speech. I've heard it before, and I know the rest of it. I know how it goes. Your own personal reading of the riot act. 'Most people are average, blah, blah, blah. That's what the shape of the bell curve is all about, blah,

blah, blah. So management's mission is to get average people to do their best, blah, blah, blah. The good Lord has not given the leaders of American enterprise much to work with, but blah, blah, blah.' "

"Oh, that speech. Don't get your back up. Cool off, I wasn't meaning to aim it at you. Heck, I know how good you and your guys are, it's just . . . well, I'd better not say it."

"Go ahead, I know what it is anyway. You were going to say, 'It's just that I hope you guys are good enough.' Damnit, Scott, don't I have enough pressure without my best client chucking brickbats—"

"Calm down. I wasn't going to say that at all."

"No. What were you going to say?"

"I was going to say, it's just that I hope your best is better than the other guys' best because they're going to be doing their best too."

Detective Ryerhurt stared in silent, overpowered awe at the sheer magnitude of the carnage. He'd been at Pleiku during the Tet offensive. It had been a kindergarten brawl in comparison. Property damage had been less.

His partner stepped out of the bedroom, his face pale from what he'd seen the medics having to do. Ryerhurt himself had seen the victim, and couldn't watch. Even under heavy anesthesia the poor man's screams had been too pathetic. The damage too heartbreaking. He'd had to step into the shambles of the living room and stop up his ears with his fingers.

"So?" Ryerhurt asked.

"So. He'll live. Maybe it won't be fun, but he'll live."

"What kind of an animal could do that to a man, anyway?"

"The female of the species, pal."

"What? Female? What the hell do you mean?"

"Didn't you catch the handle when the call came in? Didn't you spot the names on the mailbox in the lobby? This, good buddy, this apartment is the residence of our old customer, Justine Gold. Or what's left of it. And that thing back there in the bedroom is her husband. Or what's left of him."

"Jesus wept."

"Ditto the unfortunate husband."

"What is she, some sort of crazed fucking werewolf?"

"I'm beginning to think so. Did you see the color of the poor bastard's balls? Holy—"

"Don't remind me. It makes me want to throw up."

"We're going to need the SWAT squad to bring her down, I can tell you that. Christ, we'll need armored personnel carriers and elephant tranquilizers. Where do you think she is now, anyway?"

"Beats the shit out of me. Probably climbing up the side of the Empire State Building with Fay Wray in her paw."

11

THATCHER FINALLY GOT HOME AT 9:30. It was dark, and a chilly wet breeze blew in off Long Island Sound. A winter rainstorm was on the way. Thatcher pulled into his garage, parking his well-waxed and detailed twenty-two-year-old Mercedes 280 SL between Livy's Volvo station wagon and the battered Jeep Cherokee he used for errands.

Livy was waiting for him in the kitchen. She pecked his check, stepped back, looked at him, and shook her head. "My, my, my," she said, "it's been one of *those* days, has it?"

Thatcher nodded.

"And who were you today?"

"Father confessor from 8:30 to 9:00, Simon Legree in a meeting with poor Don Banks, Moses returned from the Mount in telephone interview with *Datamation* magazine, big brother to Louise Bowman again—I don't know what's bothering that girl—John Houseman playing the chief justice of the United States for the boys in the Storage Products Division, a druid wizard with the controller, Andrew Carnegie for the—aw, heck, Livy, I had to spin through my entire repertoire today, and create some new roles in the bargain."

"Poor Scott," Livy commiserated, as she assembled an overstuffed, cold turkey sandwich for him, "you have to be so many people. No one knows who you are. Why don't you just give it up and be yourself?"

"Can't do it. It won't work. It doesn't work that way. I've got all of these . . . these terribly smart, terribly different, terribly young people. I'm seventeen years older than the oldest of them except for Doug Wheeler. Setting aside the hoary antiquity of my own antediluvian carcass, the team at PegaSys are still in the tender springtimes of their youths. You need to be someone—you need to be *the* one to whom they can relate. If you want to handle them right, if you want to get them to give their best, then you have to be the person they need to give it to. Each one of them is so different, that's why you have to treat each one differently. You have to be a different guy with each of them. Besides, I don't mind doing it. It's my job. Never have minded doing what needs to be done. Who cares if none of them really knows who I am? Anyhow, if you know who I am, who gives a hoot about anyone else?"

"You're sweet."

"And you're good-looking." Thatcher took a bite of the sandwich and then looked up appraisingly. "You got any plans for the evening, beautiful?"

Livy looked back with an equally appraising glint in her eye. "I didn't, but I think I do now, you shameless—"

The front doorbell rang. It squealed off and on sporadically, as if someone were desperately pounding on it. "I'll get it," said Livy, leaving the kitchen. Thatcher set his sandwich down and stood up to follow her. "Sounds like trouble, maybe. I'll come too."

It had begun to rain heavily, and a strong, cold wind was blowing. Thatcher flung open the front door. Standing on his porch was an exceedingly wet and borderline hysterical Justine Gold.

"Justine!" said Livy.

"I've killed my husband," Justine shrieked.

Scott said, "Indeed. Is that so? Well then, you had better come on in."

"The no-good son of a bitch! He's dead and I'm glad!"

"It's raining, Justine. Come in. We'll talk about it."

"The bastard! He suffered! Oh, yes, he suffered! God knows, he died in pain!"

"The rain is blowing into the foyer, Justine. Come in here now. Now." Thatcher reached out and pulled Justine inside. Livy, straining against the mounting wind, pushed the door closed. Justine was wearing a pair of faded pink denims and a cardinal-red sweatshirt. Carmine dye ran off the sweatshirt and dripped lurid stains on Livy's carpet. "Screaming. Screaming for mercy! His black soul went screaming down to hell! I did it and I'm glad! Now I know how Lady Macbeth felt!"

"Livy, do we have a towel somewhere? And maybe a nice warm robe? There's a fire in the living room. Perhaps we should go sit next to it. Justine, can I get you a brandy?"

"I've killed my husband! The son of a bitch! Don't you hear me? And all you can talk about is—"

"OK. OK. I suppose we should talk about it. Tell me, Justine, just why did you kill your husband?"

"Because he was a lawyer and—"

"Say no more. I understand," Thatcher said calmly, "I'd do it myself."

Livy, returning with several thick pima-cotton towels, swatted him. "Scott, cut that out. You are not helping matters." She put her arm around Justine's shivering shoulders and began shepherding her toward the fireplace.

"Hey, wait a minute," Thatcher cried, his voice rising in irritation. "What do you mean, your husband was a lawyer? You never told me he was a lawyer. I had that man as a guest in my house. What do you mean by bringing a lawyer into my home?"

Livy, who was firmly drying Justine's dripping hair, said sternly, "Scott, stop it. Can't you see she's upset?"

"I've killed him. I'm on the lam. The law is after me. I'm a murderer. Oh, Jesus, what can I do?"

Thatcher handed her a brandy snifter. "First thing is, drink this. Second thing is, take a deep breath and calm down. Third thing is, tell us about it."

Justine gulped. "Yeah."

"Yup."

She sipped at her brandy and sighed.

"Feeling better?"

"Uh-huh."

"Want a bite to eat?"

"No, thanks."

"Gonna tell me and Livy what's going on?"

"I guess so."

"Well, go ahead. Get it off your chest."

"OK. Here it is. How I did it. Why I did it. I came home, see, I came home early. I had a meeting that was canceled, and I came home early. He was home, too. He didn't hear me come in. He was back in the bedroom, and . . . oh, God. This is so awful. Oh, God, I'm so embarrassed! Oh, God, I hate myself. The goddamned, no-good, rotten, four-flushing, shitty son of a bitch bastard!''

Livy took Justine's hand and stroked it to comfort her. ''Poor girl,'' she said sympathetically, ''it was another woman, wasn't it?''

''Oh, hell, no! If it had been another woman, I would have killed her, not him. Him, the fucker, him I would have only crippled!''

There being no obvious response to this statement, Scott and Livy waited patiently for Justine to continue. After taking another sip of brandy, she did. ''He was on the phone. I didn't even know he was there. I thought he was still at the office. I had some calls to make, so I picked up the extension in the living room. The mute button was stuck down or something, and he didn't know I was on the line. I overheard him. I heard every word he was saying. Oh. My. God.'' She started sobbing.

Thatcher knelt behind her and began kneading her shoulders. Livy poured another dollop of brandy into the snifter. After a few moments, Justine stopped crying and heaved an enormous, throaty sigh. ''The humiliation of it. The cocksucker. How could he do this to me? How could he do it you?''

''To me?'' said Thatcher, his voice becoming prickly. ''What do you mean, to me?''

''Sell you out. Sell me out. Sell us all out to Nick Lee.''

''What!'' The windowpanes rattled. It was not merely the violence of the rising storm that rattled them. The wind blustered, and so did Scott Thatcher. ''Nick Lee! Nick Lee? What precisely has your late, lamented spouse to do with Nicholas Lee? I mean precisely, young lady.''

''He's been working for him. He was talking to him on the telephone. My husband and Nick Lee. That's what I overheard. From what I heard him say, he's been working for him all along. From the day the takeover offer began. Every night I've gone home and told Harry—''

''Your husband?''

''My deceased husband, what happened during the day. And then the no-good, rotten-to-the-core, greasy, slimy son of a bitch passed it on to Lee. Everything. All of it. Strategies and tactics. Legal plans. Public relations. Lobbying. Shareholder relations. The money part of the game. What you said. What Don Banks said. What Mike said. What I said. What everyone said. Where we were going, and what we were doing. All of it. Everything.

The bastard couldn't have known more if he'd been in the room with us.''

Thatcher leaned backward, slid his legs out straight, and lay down on the floor. He folded his arms beneath his head and looked up at the ceiling. "My, my, my," he said. "Now this *is* an unpleasant surprise. Tell me one thing, Justine dear, just one thing. I want the truth now."

"OK."

"Did you really kill him? I mean, this is . . . what, your fifth or sixth husband? And you do have a reputation for, shall we say, inharmonious marriages and inimical divorces. He would not be the first of your spouses whom you've rendered unconscious. So, did you really kill him?"

"I think so. I think this time, I really did it."

"Good. I am delighted to hear it. Now let's go and get some sleep. We all can, I believe, rest with easy consciences, you most of all, Justine."

Later, lying in bed, Livy turned to him and asked, "Scotty, do you think she really did it?"

"Probably not. You know how she gets when she loses her temper. This is, by my count, the third time she's thought she dispatched a marriage partner to his eternal reward. And all of them lived. Happily ever after, too, given the sums she had to disburse to settle their claims. Justine can be violent, but she's not a killer. I'm sure the pathetic fool is just busted up a little."

"But what if she really went out of control this time? What if she actually did kill him?"

"Then she will be arrested, indicted, tried, and judged on the merits of the case by a jury of her peers. I will stand by her throughout the process. I will not help her avoid it. In any event, I'll make some calls tomorrow and find out what's going on. Once we know how serious this is, we'll decide what to do next."

"Justine," Thatcher said as he hung up the phone in the breakfast nook, "I have some news. Our attorneys have just returned from Beekman Memorial Hospital. They have finished negotiating matters with your husband. We have agreed not to initiate disbarment proceedings against him for surreptitiously collaborating with Nick Lee. In return, he has agreed not to prefer charges against you for putting him in a full body cast. This, to my mind, is good news. There is, unfortunately, some bad news. It is this: the doctors say that he will probably walk again.''

12

Nick Lee's office was deco-rated with primitive folk art. The walls were hung with Matabele masks from Zimbabwe, Maori greenstone war clubs from New Zealand, sheaves of arrows from a Jivaro tribe living at the headwaters of the Itacuai in Brazil, antique Yemenese scimitars, a matched pair of Tulomon shrunken heads, polymer-sealed Navajo sand paintings, Tibetan devil dolls, the topmost portion of a Chinook totem pole, Balinese finger cymbals, Tierra del Fuegoan beadwork, and, his most recent acquisition, one that had arrived unannounced and unexpected from one of his agents (who knew which one) just a week before, a most uncommon, intricately detailed, extraordinarily ferocious Hopi kachina doll.

Lee hated the stuff. He hated art in general, and art created by little brown people in particular. However, despite his antip-athy, folk art had the happy attribute of appreciating in value at a healthy pace. It was a good investment. Moreover, it was useful in making certain important impressions on visitors. One could, for example, look pointedly at the shrunken heads while making casual observations about the fate awaiting those who refused to pay greenmail at the rate of ten dollars per share over market.

At the moment, Lee was not thinking about his collection of primitive art. Nor was he thinking about PegaSys. PegaSys was a done deal. It was simply a matter of time—three weeks, to be precise—before it was bankable and banked. It was no longer worth thinking about. So instead, Nick Lee was thinking about Generals. He was thinking that no one had gone after any Gen-erals recently. He was thinking that maybe the time was ripe.

General Motors? No, too big. And besides, once you had it, you were stuck with it. No one would buy it back from you, least of all the Japanese. General Dynamics? Interesting concept. A business with its hands, or other appendages, deep in the knickers of the Department of Defense. A target worth thinking about. But then, the winds of politics can change direction abruptly, and who knew whether or not the next presidency would be as forgiving of dubious weapons systems as the current crowd—or, for that matter, Reagan's gang. Lee, thinking fondly of the halcyon days of the Reagan administration, suddenly remembered a favor given and long overdue for payment; he jotted himself a note to find out the favorite charity of a certain ex-member of the attorney general's office, and make an appropriately sizable contribution. General Electric, then? Still some good businesses there. Plenty of cash. However, too many friends in Washington. A hostile takeover there could turn into a particularly ugly affair. Still, there was all that cash. Lee put it down as a greenmail candidate. General Instrument? Aha! Tidy, bite-size, and—

The phone rang. He looked at it irritably. He was not in a mood for any distractions. However, the call was on his private line, an unlisted number, frequently changed and known to but the very privileged few. Likely the call was an important one. He lifted the phone off its cradle and purred, "Nick Lee. How may I serve you?"

"Oh, Mr. Lee. This is Jennifer."

Lee responded in a frosty tone. "Do I know you?"

"Jennifer. Jennifer Haze. Mr. Shawby's secretary."

Lee's voice warmed up, but only a few degrees. "Ah, yes. Miss Haze. How may I serve you?"

"Brian's shot himself in the foot."

"I'm not surprised. He does it all the time."

"Huh? No, Mr. Lee, I mean, like, uh, Brian's shot himself in the foot."

"I know, my dear. It's something we all have to learn to live with. He's a good man nonetheless. Tell me now, what is it that he has balled up?"

"Brian's shot himself in the foot, Mr. Lee."

"Quite so. Said the wrong thing to a newspaper reporter, did he? Or blundered a little management decision? Maybe trod on some politician's toes? Come, come, my dear Miss Haze, my time is precious. I'll see that it's taken care of, just tell me how he has shot himself in the foot."

"With my gun."

"Now, Miss Haze, that won't do. . . . With your gun? Whatever do you mean?"

"Brian's shot himself in the foot."

"If you say that one more time, I shall throttle you with my bare hands."

"But he did. You know that little .22 he gave me to carry around in my purse while we're in New York? Well, he was grabbing in my purse trying to take my credit cards away, and I was trying to get my purse back, and, well—"

"He shot himself in the foot."

"That's what I've been trying to tell you."

"You goddamned, brainless little bimbo, why didn't you say so!"

13

THIS WILL," THATCHER SAID slowly, speaking in his sanguine, unflappable drawl, "be an uncommonly brief meeting."

The assembled executives of PegaSys sat at their accustomed positions around the boardroom table. The monthly Executive Management Committee meeting was held on the second Thursday of the month. Promptly at 4:00 P.M.

"I have but one item on the agenda," Thatcher continued. "You know what it is: AIW. With considerable unhappiness, I must tell you that our situation is not promising. We may very well lose. Succinctly stated, there is an *eminence grise* behind AIW, Shawby, Lee, Bach and Wachutt, and their minions. It is a company called Seppuku. Seppuku probably is not known to you. It certainly was not known to me until quite recently. It is a gigantic, highly diversified, enormously powerful Japanese conglomerate. It is larger than we are and it is wealthier than we are. It apparently wants to acquire AIW once AIW acquires us. As best I can determine, it is bankrolling the AIW tender offer. How and to what extent, I cannot say.

"Accordingly, it is now appropriate for everyone in this room to begin considering their personal options in earnest—considering what they will do with their lives and their careers if this company of ours is destroyed. That is all I have to say. Thank you for your . . . thank you for many, many things. Our next EMC meeting will be held on January the fourteenth. That is, if it is held at all. This meeting is now adjourned. Good evening."

14

THATCHER GLOWERED AT THE newspaper. He glowered at Mike. He glowered at Louise. He glowered at Don. He glowered at Justine. He glowered at Gladys. He glowered at Denniston Howe, PegaSys's chief outside counsel. He glowered at Howe for a particularly long period of time. Snapping his finger against the *Wall Street Journal*, he said, "This is a lovely headline, Denniston. Just charming. 'Pega-Sys's Last Line of Defense Crumbles. High Court Rules Against Computer Company. AIW Takeover Seems Certain.' "

Howe, who was relaxed, confident, and not at all disturbed, responded, "We knew we'd lose the lawsuits all along. I told you that at the outset."

"The devil you did. You said, and I quote, 'The odds are against us.' Unquote."

"Yes, well. 99.9 to .1 against. That's what I meant."

"Oh, 99.9 to .1 against. You neglected to advise me of that little mathematical subtlety. Why then, pray tell, why, why, why, did we bother to sue AIW at all? Why did we accuse them of fraud, deceit, stock manipulation, conflict of interest, breach of faith, violations of the Racketeer Influenced and Corrupt Organizations Act, mail fraud, insider trading, misrepresentation of financial results, and all the rest? Why, Denny, did we bother if we knew the odds against us were one in a thousand?''

"Because of the one, not because of the thousand. Because, by some fluke, we might have won. Because they might have screwed up their defense, or the judge might have been senile, or we might just have gotten lucky. Besides, suing the other guy is the way the game is played. It's one of the rules of the sport. I try to buy you, you sue the pants off me. It's standard operating procedure.''

"Even though you know you don't have a chance?''

"Especially if you know you don't have a chance. It makes the opposition worry that you know something they don't.''

"And what did this little tactical gambit cost my company and my shareholders?''

"Oh, say $3 million in fees, plus court costs.''

"In other words, one year's average income for about one hundred and twenty American families.''

"Plus court costs.''

"On something you and your firm all knew wouldn't work.''

"It's the way the game is played, Scott.''

"Denny, please don't take this personally, but deep down in my heart of hearts, I truly despise lawyers. Truly. And the thing I despise most is that lawyers never quite seem able to understand why I despise them.''

"I resent that. That's unfair.''

"Merely honest. And now—''

The intercom on Thatcher's desk buzzed urgently. Gladys picked up the phone and whispered that Mr. Thatcher was not to be disturbed. She listened to the voice at the other end, debated with its owner for a few seconds, and then said, "Mr. T., this might be important. There is a young lady outside who insists that she see you. Her name is Haze and apparently she has some relation to Mr. Shawby.''

Louise muttered, "That's relationship, Gladys, not relation.''

Thatcher turned to Mike and asked, "That's the redhead, right?''

"Yeah. The one with the, ah, you know.''

"What do we do? Should we see her?''

"Yeah, sure. Why not? That sound you hear may be the clucking of chickens coming home to roost.''

"Denniston, what's your legal opinion? Do we violate either law or ethics—forget the ethics part, you're a lawyer—by talking to this woman?"

Howe answered archly, "Neither law nor ethics. Just be sure that I take a look first at any written material she might want to give you. We can't have her passing you stolen proprietary documents."

Thatcher arose and went to the door. He opened it, stepped into his waiting area, and introduced himself. "Ms. Haze. I'm Scott Thatcher. Delighted to see you again. We met before, earlier this year, when my colleagues and I called on Brian Shawby out in Desuetude. Won't you step into my office?"

Jennifer wore a pair of gold lamé slacks, matching shoes with three-and-a-half inch heels, a crushed-velvet purple pageboy jacket, quadruple strands of amethyst beads, two-inch gold hoop earrings and a three-quarter-length black mink coat on top of it all. She rose shakily and took Scott's offered hand. "Oh, Mr. Thatcher, thank you for seeing me so early in the morning." Thatcher peeked at his watch: 10:57 A.M. "I know I must look a mess, but after what's happened I just tossed on some clothes and . . ." She sobbed. A mascara-laden tear, approximately the color of Welch's grapejuice, rolled down her cheek.

Thatcher wrapped a protective, fatherly arm around her shoulder. "Now, now, it can't be all that bad. Please, come into my office and meet my friends."

He guided her into his office, took her coat, held a chair for her, poured her a cup of coffee, added the double dose of cream and three lumps of sugar she asked for, and then pulled another chair up next to hers. He sat down saying, "Now, Ms. Haze, let me introduce you to my friends. I want you to think of them as your friends too. This is Don Banks, and this is Denny Howe. Over here is my secretary, Gladys. And Mike Ash and Louise Bowman. You might remember them from when we visited Brian out in Missouri. And, please, call me Scott. 'Mr. Thatcher' is too formal, don't you think? And I hope I can call you Jennifer. Can I do that?"

"Oh, yes. For sure, Mr. Thatch—I mean, Scott. Everyone calls me Jennifer. Everyone except that awful Mr. Lee. I hate him."

"Well, I'm not terribly fond of Nick Lee myself, Jennifer. Is that coffee all right? Are you sure? Good. Now to what do we owe the uncommonly pleasant surprise of your company, Jennifer?"

"I'm mad, and I want to talk to you."

"Why are you mad, Jennifer?"

"Because, because, that, that Mr. Lee, he called me a bimbo!"

"No," Scott exclaimed in an aghast tone of voice. Everyone else in the room made "tsk-tsk" sounds.

"And so did Brian. And then Brian had him take away my credit cards!"

"Unspeakable."

"Just because of the tiara."

"How triflingly petty."

"I really needed that tiara. You know, for when you go to fancy dress parties. It really is an awesome tiara. Anyway, and then, and then Brian told him to only give me fifty dollars a day in spending money while he's in the hospital."

"Beg pardon? Brian Shawby is in the hospital?"

"Uh-huh. Monday night, he shot himself in the foot."

"Not surprising. He usually does."

"With my gun. And another thing, when I went to visit him today, I overheard the doctors talking, and they said he has crabs."

"I am speechless."

"Which he didn't get from me, I can tell you!"

"No one would ever imply."

"So I decided to come see you. I want to say something. Maybe Mr. Lee is right. Maybe Brian is, too. Maybe I am only just a bimbo. But if I am, well, let me tell you something, bimbos are people. Bimbos have nothing to be ashamed of. There are a lot worse things you can be. A lot. Besides, bimbos have hearts. Bimbos have souls. Bimbos have needs, the same as anyone else. Bimbos have goals. Bimbos have self-images. Bimbos want self-fulfillment, just like you or Brian or anybody else you can name. Bimbos want self-actualization, as they say on PBS. Us poor, pathetic, downtrodden bimbos want to satisfy our own fundamental human yearnings, and find our rightful places in the greater order of society."

Ye gods, thought Louise, *a new minority movement! Bimbo liberation!*

"And, how do bim—how do you do that, Jennifer?" Thatcher asked.

"Shopping."

"Of course."

"And there's another thing I want to say."

"Yes."

Jennifer lifted her head and thrust her chin out. Her eyes took on the appearance of burnished steel, and her voice deepened with emotion. She took an index finger, gesticulating like a turn-of-the-century politician haranguing a crowd by torchlight. "I'm bored. I'm just bored stiff. I'm bored to tears. I mean, like, I've been going with Brian for two years now, and all I do is hang out in that dumb office, reading dumb books, watching dumb people go by, and waiting for dumb Brian to get horny. Which isn't worth waiting for, even if I do say so myself. And maybe once in awhile we go somewhere and do something, but it's always someplace he wants to go, and something he wants to do, and usually somewhere where there aren't any good stores anyway. Places where he's got factories! Give me a break. And then what happens? We got to go to New York for a month, and what do we do? We don't do anything, that's what we do. And Brian makes me stay in my room all day, and takes away my credit cards, and won't give me any money to go shopping. I am fed up! Believe that I'm fed up! I'm through with Brian Shawby, Mr. Thatcher, I'm through. He can't dance, and he doesn't like rock'n'roll, and he's no fun at parties, and he can't take a joke, and he is dull, dull, dull. Brian Shawby is a wet blanket on my soul."

"Well put. You have my most sincere sympathies. But tell me, Jennifer, why have you come here? Why are you telling me these things?"

"I want a job with you, Mr. Thatcher. I want to work for PegaSys."

"Ah, well, hmm. I'm not sure that's wise, Jennifer. Brian is trying to take over PegaSys, and the odds seem to favor his success. If you came to work for us, well, in a couple of weeks he might own the company. Then you'd just be back working for him."

"Oh no, I wouldn't."

"Oh?"

"Because he is not going to take over PegaSys. That ugly little Japanese guy is. Him and Nick Lee. They're double-crossing Brian, only Brian isn't smart enough to have figured it out yet."

"I can't believe you gave her a job," Mike said.

"She will make a fine Xerox operator, Mike. As long as she stays down on the seventh floor with the copying equipment, she will do very well. She will do the very best she can, and you can't ask more than that.''

Banks looked up from the crumpled wads of paper in his lap, Jennifer's gift to the PegaSys team. He shook his head in amazement and proffered a handwritten page to Scott. "This," he said, "appears to be the nut of the thing."

Thatcher took the page from his hands and squinted at it. "Don, are you sure we are on firm ground looking at the stuff?"

"Absolutely. None of this belongs to anyone except Ms. Haze. Not one page of it is internal to AIW, Lee, Bach and Wachutt, or, for that matter, Seppuku. All it is is notes she made on her own behalf, and not in any capacity as an AIW employee. It belongs to her, not them. We're clean. If they sue us, and they will if they find out, we'll win—99.9 to .1 says we'll win."

Thatcher groaned.

Louise asked, "What does it say, Scott?"

"Hmm. Well, I gather she was parked outside Nick Lee's office waiting for Shawby when a call came in from Hidetake, the chief exec of Seppuku. This is dated a couple of weeks ago, by the way. It seems that Lee had a couple of his henchmen in the office with him, so he put the call on the squawk box with the volume turned on high. That's how she heard it. Hidetake was speaking through a translator. First off, Lee and Hidetake exchanged some pleasantries. Then Hidetake rattled off a bunch of numbers and names. The names are of people he called 'our paper boys.' Jennifer didn't take down any of the numbers, but she got some of the names. I'll try to make them out. Somebody had better take note of them so we can run a check on who they are. By the way, where are Messrs. Knight and Swift? They are supposed to be part of this team, and responsible for getting us information fast. They're the ones who should be chasing down these names."

Mike answered, "They're camped out in the computer room. Incommunicado. In a state of mystical trance, doing something arcane on the computer. I tried to get them to take a break and come down, but all they did was grunt that they were on to something hot and tell me to go away. You know how obsessive Roy gets when he's on a computer terminal?"

"Yup."

"Well, Arnie's just as bad."

"Good. I am delighted to hear it. OK. Here, take these names down. Dear, dear, but poor Jennifer does have problems with spelling. First name. Quint and Claggart. Second name, Glendower Associates. Third name, Sobel, Rosenburg and Company. These are all corporations, I think. Arnold & Cassius. Ali-ibn-Abi Tariq. Double-check the spelling on that. Mugawawe Exports. Nihon-Faberstein-Junker. Compaigne Javert. Kai Lee Fong. Panama-Colombian International Investments. Then she wrote, bless her heart, 'and a whole bunch of other funny-sounding foreign stuff.' What have we got, eight or nine names? Well, it's a start. Gladys, get this list up to Knight and tell him that no matter what he's doing, I want a rundown on who these people are, what they do, and what his best guess is on their role in this affair."

"How about the rest of Jennifer's notes, Scott?"

"Yup. Next Lee says that he is unhappy at having to pledge what he's pledged. Hidetake replies that he has nothing to worry about. Then Hidetake asks whether Shawby's still in the dark, and Lee says, quote 'The phrase fat, dumb, and happy takes on new meaning with our boy Brian.' Hidetake asks about Mark Cass—that's Shawby's son-in-law—and Lee says he would barter his soul to replace Brian as chairman and chief exec of AIW. Then there's some discussion of new AIW board members—aha! I see what's going on. In return for the financing they've given him, Shawby has given Lee and Hidetake seats on his board of directors. Shawby believes he still has a majority, but Lee and Hidetake have suborned some of the people Shawby thinks are on his side. As soon as AIW acquires PegaSys, they plan to oust Shawby and replace him with Mark Cass. Young Mark has sold his father-in-law out."

"Cute," sneered Don Banks. "They're a real bunch of sweetie pies all right. Unfortunately, knowing the Borgia-like family relations at AIW does us not one whit of good."

"And," added Thatcher, "we still don't know how Hidetake and Seppuku are financing the deal."

The great detective scrutinized the list of names Mrs. Hudson had delivered to his apartment at 221B Baker Street. It inventoried a most intriguing catalog of desperados; doubtless high lieutenants in Moriarty's legion of devilishly cunning criminal fiends. Sliding his long violinist's fingers through his thick brown hair, he turned an aquiline profile and eagle-like eyes toward Watson and said . . .

"The game is afoot."

"Huh?" replied Arnie, who was scanning freshly printed out columns of hexadecimal data.

"I mean, like, uh," continued Roy Knight, "I think this is the piece of the puzzle we've been missing. You know, under the authorized agent file."

"You think so?"

"You betcha. Let's log back in, use these names to turn a key or two, and see if anything unlocks."

Watson, you may wish to bring your service revolver on this affair. We face the veritable Napoleon of crime, and dark deeds may be done this night. For myself, I would be obliged if you would hand me my sword cane.

After the meeting in Thatcher's office adjourned, Mike and Louise walked together to their respective offices. As they stopped outside Louise's office Mike said, "You look haggard, Louise. You're burning yourself out."

She answered, "I know. As soon as this is over, one way or another, I'm going to take some vacation. I figured on going down to Antigua or something."

"Sounds like a fine idea to me."

"I thought I'd go with David."

"Fine," said Mike, jerking his head back slightly. "Just fine. You do that. I've been expecting something like that." He spun on his heel and walked away quickly.

What was it that Joe Jonas said about him and Thatcher breaking up? Ash thought. *He wanted to put a continent between him and Scott. Yeah, a continent between them. A continent between you and your problem. That's the right answer.*

15

On Monday morning, December 13, Thatcher expected Don Banks's readout on how AIW planned to finance its raid. He also expected his core team, Ash, Bowman, Knight, Swift, Howe, and Gold, to be present at the meeting. He was disappointed in both regards.

"Gladys, where the devil are Louise and Mike? Where's Justine? Where are Roy and Arnie? Has life in this organization become so casual that we cannot start a meeting punctually? Are we changing our corporate name to 'PegaSys-Lite'?"

Gladys answered, "I've called Mr. Knight's computer room three times and there's no answer, Mr. T. And no one seems to have seen Ms. Bowman or Mr. Ash since Friday morning. But Ms. Gold did call in and say that she was tied up and to start without her. Mr. Howe is here, but I think he's in the washroom."

Thatcher growled. "Nuts," he said, "I'll start without him. And finish, too. What's the bottom line, Don?"

Banks cleared his throat and opened his briefcase. He fumbled at some papers, cleared his throat again, and closed the case. "I don't know how to say this, Scott," he muttered.

Thatcher bent forward, his eyebrows raised with mounting ire, and said, "You've struck out, haven't you?"

"Completely. Dry as a bone. Nothing. A goose egg. All of our efforts to identify how the transaction will be financed have been fruitless. We have found nothing. Whatever they are doing is so well hidden that not even God could find it. And if God can't, well then, neither can Morgan, Teech & Kidd. We're continuing to work on it, but, Scott, I have no confidence that we will succeed."

"And so," Thatcher said with finality and profound resignation, "it's over."

"Scott. Oh, hell. Scott, we've known each other for more than twenty years. Christ, I can't lie to you. I think, at this point, the answer is . . . the prudent thing to do is . . . to plan that it is over. To make your personal plans on the basis that two weeks from now, AIW will own PegaSys."

"I have always prided myself on being realistic, Don." Thatcher shrugged, heaved a sigh, and turned to his secretary. "Gladys, do me a favor. Get the maintenance people to bring some cardboard boxes up to my office tonight. Tomorrow, I think I want to do some packing."

Gladys made a note on her pad, broke into sniffles, and excused herself from the room.

Banks looked down at his shoes and, in a very soft tone of voice, said, "There are several points I need to counsel you on relating to leaving PegaSys, and pertaining to the specific mechanics of the transfer of power. But before I do, there is one last chance you might take, one final—"

"For Pete's sake, Don, don't drag it out. Speak up, man. I don't care how remote the odds are, I'll do whatever I have to, presuming it's legal. Out with it, man."

"Hidetake's in town. He's been camped out at that new hotel, the Samurai Palace, for the past week. You might go and confront him."

"What would that accomplish?"

"There's no telling."

Thatcher narrowed his eyes and smiled fiercely. "Nothing ventured, nothing gained, huh? OK, I'll go beard him in his lair." He punched the button on his intercom and bellowed, "Gladys! Have a car and driver outside the front lobby in five minutes! Cancel all my meetings for the rest of the day! And, in respect for the courtesy that one senior executive owes another, call the Samurai Palace Hotel. Ask for Mr. Hidetake. Tell him I'm coming over in a half hour to cut his heart out."

Gladys's voice came back. "Do you mean an informal one-on-one meeting to frankly review the issues, Mr. T?"

"Yup. I suppose so."

16

OKINAKAO HIDETAKE OCCUPIED
the hotel's presidential suite: two bedrooms, two baths, a kitch-
enette, formal dining area, a living room, and a conference
room. The half-hour warning that Thatcher had given him was
more than ample for him to prepare himself, and to set the stage
to his liking.

Thatcher stood in Hidetake's living room, waiting while his
arrival was announced. He looked around idly and noted a stack
of magazines resting on an end table. He stepped over and rifled
through them. They were Japanese comic books. Hidetake, like
most Japanese businessmen, was an avid comic-book fan. He
had them air-expressed to America so that he would not miss a
single thrilling episode of his favorite characters' adventures.
Hidetake enjoyed most the saga of Riki-Oh, a muscular Japanese
Rambo; in the pages of *Business Jump*, he waged never-ending
war against the global military-economic cabal formed by a sinister partnership between the Nazi-refugee organization Odessa
and the international Zionist conspiracy. Second only to Riki-
Oh, Hidetake enjoyed RapeMan, who was commissioned by
humiliated husbands and rejected lovers to wreak brutally violent and defiling sexual vengeance against their women.

Thatcher flipped open a story about Lover Boy, another of
Hidetake's favorite characters. In graphic detail, the cartoons
illustrated a fresh-faced teenage girl, bound and naked, as she
was flogged. A few panels later, her abuser lit a candle and
slowly dripped searing-hot wax on her breasts. Then she was
shown being sodomized. Thatcher threw down the magazine in
disgust.

Moments later, he was led into the conference room. It was
bare of all furnishings except for rice-mat floor coverings, a

three-foot-high, twelve-foot-long lacquered conference table, and two thinly stuffed pillows, one at the head of the table, and one at the foot. Hidetake sat cross-legged at the head of the table, his elbows arched out and his hands resting on his knees. He was clad in a dark burgundy kimono, patterned with white interlinked squares. Resting on the table in front of him were his antique family swords, drawn from their scabbards by about a quarter length.

Hidetake stared impassively forward as the translator led Thatcher into the room. He showed no sign of acknowledging Thatcher's entry or presence.

The translator, a petite young Japanese woman wearing large, black-rimmed glasses, said something deferential in Japanese. Hidetake replied with a series of harsh, guttural syllables. The translator turned to Thatcher and said, "Hidetake-san welcomes you. He wished to know if I am an acceptable translator, or if you wish to bring your own."

Thatcher grinned. "Thank you very much," he said. "However, I will not be requiring any translation services, nor will Mr. Hidetake. He graduated *cum laude* from Cornell with a master's degree in engineering, a feat which, I believe, requires at least a nodding acquaintance with the English language. I expect that we will be able to understand one another rather well."

The translator blushed. Hidetake broke into a deep, rumbling laugh, and said, "You have done your homework, Thatcher-san. I congratulate you, and apologize for this simple ploy. Trust, however, that I too have done my homework. As for you, young lady, you are no longer needed. Leave us."

As the abashed translator scurried out, Hidetake waved at the cushion and said, "Please, sit down. Can I get you some tea or coffee? Or perhaps you'd like some soda pop. Coke? Diet Pepsi? Orange Crush—or is that Mr. Knight's preferred beverage?"

"Nothing, thanks." Thatcher sat down, mimicking Hidetake's posture, and grinned again. "So," he said.

"So."

"You have a certain interest in my company."

"A certain interest, yes."

"A silent partner, so to speak."

"Silent partner. Yes, that is an apt phrase."

"A silent partner, then, but a partner of fools. I've studied your company during the past few days. I've studied you. You are no fool, Mr. Hidetake. How is it that you've allied yourself with the likes of Brian Shawby? He *is* an utter idiot, you know.''

Hidetake barked another laugh, ''But of course he is! He is hopeless. So, too, is Mr. Nicholas Lee, despite his fearsome reputation. They both are fools. But then most men are fools, are they not? There are more fools in the world than there are wise men. Tell me, Thatcher-san, do you not find it difficult being a rational man in a world of fools?''

''Fools don't last long at PegaSys.''

''Nor at Seppuku. Indeed, the longevity of incompetents at my company may be even less than it is at yours. But that is not my meaning. We, you and I and the few like us, must deal not only with our tiny empires, but also with the greater world outside. Suppliers, competitors, customers, politicians, the public. How tiresome they can be. What fools the larger part of them are. If I may speak colloquially, what turkeys. Yes, turkeys waiting to be plucked. There is no challenge in dealing with them. They are so inept, so blind, so innocent, that there is no sport to stalking them. Your eloquent American phrase 'fat, dumb, and happy' (which Mr. Lee uses so frequently) is particularly felicitous. If one's customers are fools, selling to them is no challenge. If one's competitors are cretins, defeating them is no thrill. If one's suppliers are imbeciles, bargaining them down gives no satisfaction. For a superior man to prove himself better than fools is not so gratifying, I think. This is my meaning.''

''Do you mean to say that the reason you allied yourself with Shawby and the reason you are trying to take over my company is for the challenge and pleasure of defeating someone who is not a fool?''

Hidetake laughed again, long and hard. ''How ingenious of you! How insightful. Why, no, I had not meant to say that at all. Honestly, the thought had never crossed my mind. But I do believe, yes, I do believe, now that you mention it, somehow unconsciously such a motive doubtless exists. You are a psychologist, Thatcher-san, to have read in my mind what I myself did not know was there. But, I must assure you, this consideration was at best secondary. The source from which my ambitions for your company spring really are quite different.''

''Do you care to tell me what they are?''

''Of course. At this late hour, I see no reason not to. Especially since you have been so clever as to discover my participation in the takeover of your company, and also because you have been so alert as to tell me something about myself that I did not know. I shall be totally candid. You will forgive me in this candor, but we are mature men, are we not? First, I will give you the least important reason. That reason is that I hate and despise you as the son of a man whom I hate and despise. Your father caused the Japanese people much loss of face. His testimony at the so-called war crimes trials in Tokyo held my nation up to worldwide scorn. His explicitly detailed clinical descriptions of what he called 'barbarous torture' of cowardly prisoners of war were most uncalled for. That he spoke as a prominent physician made his defamations that more potent. More to the point, when General MacArthur ordered him back to America, he insisted on repeating these slurs during his testimony in front of your Congress. Then he allied himself with the self-styled 'hang Hirohito' group of slanderers who crusaded against all that I and my nation hold holy. He set himself up as a morally superior judge of our honorable adherence to values and codes of ethics established not merely centuries but millennia before your upstart country was born. He splattered offal on my people, on my flag, and on my God, the Emperor. And on me, Thatcher-san. And on me, an imperial officer of the Kempeitai. Your father sought to have all my corps punished for what he called war crimes and what we of the Kempeitai called duty. As I hated him, so do I hate his son."

"The war is over, Mr. Hidetake. Long, long over."

"But the disgrace of defeat is not yet eradicated. We have only begun, Thatcher-san, only begun to restore our besmirched honor."

"I date from an era when America was triumphant in war, magnanimous in peace, honorable in alliance, envied in its wealth, and the exemplar for all in the freedom of its citizens. Accordingly, I sometimes find it difficult to adapt to contemporary realities. My recollection of those years is that my nation treated yours with magnanimity. Accordingly, I find it difficult to understand your bitterness."

"Then let that pass. My bitterness does not matter. I wave it by. It is, as I said, the least important of my reasons for helping AIW acquire you. At best, it is a grain of sugar added to already sweetened tea. We need not speak of it. Let me instead speak of national goals. In my country, unlike yours, we make no distinction among national goals, corporate goals, and, indeed, personal goals. Japan's policy and the policy of Japanese business are the same. Policy is what we do; it is what you debate. Consider this: more than a decade ago we set as a national policy achieving leadership in the financial world. Your nation held this position, and our policy demanded we surpass you. Look at the results. Today only one of the world's twenty-five largest banks—the eighth—is American. Seventeen are Japanese. The entire economy of this planet is held in thrall to decisions made in Japan, and every corporation in the world operates at the discretion of Tokyo. We hold the purse strings, and we call the tune—but softly. For the moment, we call the tune softly. If Japan decides to take a certain action, then Japanese businessmen do not whine and complain about next quarter's profits of shareholder value or tax consequences. On the contrary, Japanese businessmen march in disciplined ranks toward the national goal. Toward implementation of national policy."

"What does this have to do with your meddling in my company's affairs? With your helping Shawby and his crowd?"

"Quite a good deal, I fear. Computers and software are a national priority. Regrettably, they are something at which we have not had much success. We have spent enormous sums to develop a mainframe computer that could compete with IBM in the 3080/3090 class. Alas, we had to take certain shortcuts in developing the operating system software for it, and, as a result, have been most disgracefully accused of industrial espionage by your Federal Bureau of Investigation and by IBM. And software, Thatcher-san, computer software. America holds a 54 percent share of the world market, and Japan only 9 percent. This situation is a dishonor; it is *hinomaru*, an affront to the Japanese flag. We have done all in our power to overtake your nation. We subsidize 160 billion yen's worth of software research every year. Under the Information Technology Promotion Act, the Japan Development Bank extends loans to computer companies at the lowest imaginable interest rates. We created JECC with government funds to lease computers to Japanese corporations on lavishly favorable terms—only Japanese computers, of course. We have erected every imaginable barrier to the success of your systems. It has not worked. And why is that? Why is it we have failed? It is because you refuse us the help that is our due. Your computer companies refuse to license the most critical of their technologies to my country. You hold back that which is most valuable and most proprietary. You, Thatcher-san, you yourself have held back PegaSys's trade secrets—secrets that my nation must have to achieve its destiny. To date, you have merely postponed the inevitable. Now the day of reckoning has come. Your last president, whom we most mournfully miss, opened up your nation's doors. Opened them to our imports, and opened them to our acquisitions. They will never close again. No American businessman will ever again be able to slam a door in Japan's face and deny us that which we need. Now, it is simply a case that if you have something we desire, and we can't build it, and you won't trade it, then, by my Emperor and by my ancestors, we shall buy it! We shall buy it whether you wish to sell it or not."

"Fair enough," Thatcher said through tightly clenched teeth. "No doubt there are a few other reasons."

"Of course there are. Of course. Your company is a superb one. Your profit margins are three times higher than Seppuku's, and Seppuku's profits are double those of the average Japanese company. We shall ensure that some of your profits pass from AIW's coffers to ours. Further, our deal with AIW is a good one. I spoke of fools earlier, didn't I? Well, there is one joy in negotiating with fools, and that is that you can always profit. Our arrangements are lucrative and, quite frankly, risk free. Of course, you would like to know specifically what they are, wouldn't you? You can't have found out how—"

"You mean about Quint and Claggart and all that crowd," Thatcher interjected, taking a shot in the dark.

Hidetake stopped cold. He scowled and stared suspiciously at Thatcher. Not a muscle in Thatcher's poker face moved.

Finally Hidetake spoke again, "Hear my reasoning. If you know everything about the financing, then there is no reason for me to speak, for you already know what I would say. If you know something, then I should not speak, for risk that you might learn more. If you know nothing, then again silence is called for. I believe this logic is flawless, don't you, Thatcher-san?"

Thatcher smiled as evilly as he knew how. "Absolutely flaw-less. Precisely the same chain of logic leads me to conclude that I should not tell you what I do, in point of fact, know."

Hidetake grimaced. "Touché. You are a worthy opponent. It does me credit to have you as an enemy, and it will be my honor to defeat you."

"In that regard, I should like to add two more American colloquialisms to your already excellent vocabulary, Mr. Hide-take. The first is: don't count your chickens until they are hatched. And the second is, it ain't over till it's over."

"Sadly, you have not expanded my vocabulary. Both these axioms are known to me. I will take note of your use of them.

However, we have become diverted from our discussion of the principal issue, and I was enjoying speaking of it with you."

"Then please continue."

"Reasons. Reasons for helping AIW take you over. Accept, if you will, that it is an economically desirable situation. My next reason is that my own company, Seppuku, has a desire to achieve strategic leadership in computers. Quite simply, by acquiring your company—or rather, by helping the truly lamentable Mr. Shawby acquire you—we shall achieve that leadership. It is worth billions to us. Billions of dollars, Thatcher-san, not billions of yen. As a final reason for Seppuku's role in this affair, I will confess to one of my own personal weaknesses. That weakness is ego, Thatcher-san, ego. You must understand egoism, I think. You cannot have become the person you are without a large ego. You cannot build and manage a great endeavor unless you are a considerable egoist. All leaders, great and small, are egoists. You, me, all the others. So, with some modest embarrassment, I confess that my ego motivates me. Overturning a mighty corporation will gratify me. Teaching a humiliating lesson to America will please me. I am a small man, Thatcher-san, from a small country. The thought of tumbling a giant appeals to me. I am David, and you are Goliath. When you fall in the dust before me, I shall feel proud. You understand this, I hope. It is a picayune emotion and probably not worthy of me, but nonetheless, destroying your company shall make me feel good."

"I believe," Thatcher said quite slowly, "that I understand you completely."

"Good! Excellent! But now, I have spent much of my valuable time talking to you, and you have spent very little talking to me. I should like to hear you speak. Tell me—tell me, since I have opened my heart and given you my true reasons for my actions, tell me your true reasons for opposing this takeover."

Thatcher puffed out his cheeks and blew between his lips. "Hmpf. That's not an easy question. Nor is it one that I feel obliged to answer, Mr. Hidetake. I will say this, however. I will leave this room today with rather more reasons for fighting the acquisition than I had when I entered."

"I am sorry to hear that. Will you not even tell me one?"

Thatcher stood up and brushed the seat of his pants. "Yup, sure. One reason is that I don't think of my customers, or my competitors, or my suppliers as being fools, and I would mortally hate to see my company in the hands of someone who did.

They deserve better. That is all I have to say to you, Mr. Hidetake. Good day.''

Thatcher stepped to the door and opened it. He started to walk out, but then halted. He turned to face Hidetake, who was still sitting at the distant end of the room. ''Oh yes, one other thing, Mr. Hidetake.''

''Yes?''

''You have studied me, I believe.''

''Oh yes, of course. My agents have compiled quite a thick dossier on you.''

''Then you know that one of my personal idiosyncrasies is that I don't use strong language. I never swear.''

''Yes, indeed, this is a fact that I have noted.''

''Good. Well, I have one more thing to say to you then, Mr. Hidetake.''

''Yes?''

''Fuck you.'' So saying, Thatcher turned and left.

Book Five:
Christmas Gifts

"Whether she be good or bad, one gives one's best once, to one only. That given, there remains no second worth giving or taking."

Puck of Pook's Hill
Rudyard Kipling

1

VERY EARLY ON TUESDAY MORNing, Thatcher arrived in his office to find Louise, Mike, Roy Knight, and Arnie Swift waiting for him. They were not a pretty sight— less so, smell. They exuded the sour odor of exhaustion, of long hours worked in a poorly ventilated room, of fast foods eaten too hurriedly and washed down with too much coffee, and of tension stretched to the breaking point. None of the men had shaved (albeit, Arnie was a year or two away from needing to), and Louise's normally impeccable clothing, hair, and makeup were in such disarray as to render her almost unrecognizable. It was certain that all four were wearing the same clothes and linen as on the preceding Friday. It was likely, in the cases of Knight and Swift, that their clothing had been worn even longer.

Thatcher recognized the feral gleam in their eyes, and it made him cautious. Their eyes sparkled like those of nocturnal carnivores, ravening brutes who hunt in packs and who had just caught the scent of prey on the wind. Their eyes were the eyes of things that smelled blood, and were hungry.

Thatcher hung up his coat, then skirted around them to his desk. Taking his seat, he said, "Looks like you've got something for me. Anyone want to tell me what it is?"

Louise rose from where she was sprawled on his sofa. Half her blouse dangled untucked out of her skirt. She had discarded her panty hose some days earlier, and stubble had started to become visible on her legs. Her eyes were yellow, shot with red. Her voice was harsh. "Yeah. Yeah. I want you to know that we got it. Not all of it, but some of it. More than anyone else has got. We got it. Us. Us four. No one else. Not Mr. Denniston Howe. Not Mr. Donald Banks. Not Morgan, Teech & Kidd. Not the finest minds in investment banking. Not the whiz kids.

No. Us. We did it. Me, Arnie, Roy, and Mike. We got it right here. We've got some real data on how AIW and Lee, Bach and Wachutt and Seppuku are financing the deal. Not all of it, but more than anyone else has been able to find out.''

She pointed an ink-stained, broken-nailed finger at a stack of printouts. ''And let me tell you one other thing. Never, never in a million years would Banks have found this out. Never in a million years would anyone have figured it out. No one in the world. Except us. We did it, and no one else could. No one else ever could. What we've got here is a start. It doesn't tell us everything, but it tells us more than we knew before.''

''Do you want some coffee, Louise? Should I send for breakfast?'' Thatcher asked solicitously.

''Not for me,'' she answered, ''I'm running on adrenaline.'' The others shook their heads, except for Arnie, who asked for a box of Dunkin' Donuts—''You know, a mixed assortment, with all the icing and sprinklings on top. Oh yeah, and maybe a jar of peanut butter to go along with it. The crunchy kind if they have it.''

Thatcher made a call to the security desk in the lobby, and dispatched a guard to fetch Swift his donuts and peanut butter. Then he rested his chin on the palm of his right hand and said to Louise, ''Before you tell me what you've got, you'd better tell me how you got it.''

Louise turned to Arnie, telling him to answer Thatcher's question. ''Gee, Mr. Thatcher, I mean, Scott, it was neat. I mean, it was radical stuff. We started, aw gee, sometime last week, I think, with AIW. Now that wasn't neat. I mean, my kid sister could have done that. They got a simple password system, and the passwords never change. I mean, you just zip in there and type something like 'computer' and, bang, you just log on to their mainframe. They got no priority levels and no protection. I mean, once you log on, you can get anything you want, applications, databases, dictionaries, source code even. It's all wide open. It's just the tackiest security system I've ever seen. Well, so Roy and I bust in, and, I got to tell you quelle kludge. These guys at AIW are wall-to-wall big blue. I mean like, they've got nothing but 3090s. But their applications are true gar-bàge. I mean, we are talking stuff that was written thirty years ago and hasn't been updated since. We're talking 3090s running in the Autocoder emulation mode. And their databases are all flat file stuff. I mean, we aren't talking hierarchical here, not structured, much less semantic like we use. These bozos got maybe $30 million worth of shiny new IBM iron, and they are running software that, like, belongs in some museum somewhere. True munge. Anyhow, it's absolutely no sweat to do a dump of everything they've got. So Roy and I download the whole enchilada—core, online-storage, and all—and start looking through it, trying to find something we can use to help you fight this takeover stuff. Well, there isn't anything that we can see. I mean, it's just all dull, dumb stuff. Mostly it's payroll, personnel, and financial applications and databases. So we look at it, and even though we aren't finance guys, it pretty much looks like there is nothing worth talking about on any of AIW's computers.

"So once we get through cleaning everything AIW's got in its systems, we decide to go for big casino. We decide to take a run at Seppuku. Actually, I made a pass at 'em before, while I was in California, before you hired me. They spotted me, I guess, and shut me down. Maybe that's why they sent that guy to ice me. So, anyway, Roy and I, we hit 'em. Roy knows what he's doing, and, wow, radical! Let me tell you, those Japanese guys take security serious. I mean, like, real serious. All the really neat stuff. One-way trap-door algorithms just get you to ground floor. Stuff that's way beyond RSA to do anything serious. And they've got some of the most truly bizzaro booby traps I've ever seen. One of them, if you're not careful, uploads a really nasty virus to any computer that penetrates their protection schemes. And another thing, these guys at Seppuku are using Kanji boxes, front-end, back-end, and everywhere in between. You know how if you break into just about any computer system in the world, your command structures are all English language. Not these boys. These guys are using some really exotic 32-bit words, so that everything is in encrypted Kanji. It was a bear figuring out what was going on. We finally had to hotwire a link through the NSA codebuster at Fort Meade to the mainframe at the Defense Language Training Institute at Monterey, and get us some real-time translating and decrypting going on. Nice system they've got in Monterey. I wanna get back and look at it more some day.

"So, anyhow, here we are hardwired into Seppuku's mainframe, and hardwired into Monterey, and we're issuing commands in English, and routing them through Fort Meade and Monterey, and the output is coming back Kanji to Monterey, and then back through Fort Meade, and on to us in English. I mean we are boogying with this stuff. And what we're getting is the right stuff, I gotta tell you. We're not sure what it means, but we know it ain't gar-bàge. So we're looking at this stuff, and we're trying to figure it out, and we decide to get Louise and Mike to come take a look at it. So Louise walks in and says holy whatever and Mike looks at it and says—"

Thatcher slapped both of his palms down on his desk with a resounding crack. His jaw was clenched and he ground his teeth audibly. "Enough!" he barked. "That is just enough! Do you four mean to tell me that you have spent the past weekend breaking into other corporations' computers? AIW's and Seppuku's? Do you mean to tell me that you have been engaged in computer piracy?"

Mike replied, "Well, yeah, Scott. I know you don't approve, but this is so important that—"

Thatcher shot back, "So important that you decided to break the law?"

Louise interjected, "Scott, look, no one got hurt, and no one will ever find out. Besides, breaking some stupid law is not the issue when—"

"It is the issue," Thatcher said menacingly, "it is precisely the issue. There is no other. Law and ethical behavior are the only issue. They are fundamental to the policies and precepts with which I manage this corporation. They are what PegaSys is all about."

Mike stood up and waved his hand in a pacifying gesture. "Look, Scott," he said in a calm and apologetic voice, "I know this kind of thing ticks you off. I knew it the moment last Friday night when I saw what Roy and Arnie did. Isn't that right, guys?"

He looked at his three companions for support. All three nodded their heads.

Thatcher glared at them. "Even though you knew that what you were doing was wrong—even though you knew you were breaking the law, violating corporate policy, and engaging in the kind of outright criminal burglary that I personally find abhorrent—you decided to go ahead."

"Yes," Louise said, "it was too damned important."

"Nothing is that important. Hear me out. Do not dare to interrupt me. Nothing is more important than behaving honorably, ethically, and legally. Nothing. I should hope that in all your years of working for me, you would have learned that one lesson if no other."

"Yeah," Mike said ruefully, "we learned it. But we also know that if this company isn't in business anymore, the lesson isn't worth all that much."

"Then you've learned nothing."

Louise shook her head irritably and snapped, "Enough, already! Maybe we did the wrong thing, but it's done and over with. What we did isn't the point. The point is what we know. We know how the Shawby gang has structured this deal. We know where the bodies are buried. We've got the names, we've got the times, we've got the places, and we've got the dollar denominations. And, with what we've got, we may—given the grace of God and a little luck—we may just be able to stop this acquisition. We may just be able to figure out how to win, Scott, and that, not ethics, is what we should be talking about. So let's get down to facts, OK?"

Thatcher leaned back in his chair, folded his arms, and replied, "Let's not. I do not want to hear one word about whatever it is you have uncovered."

Louise strode to the front of his desk. She put her palms on its gleaming surface and leaned forward. "Cut it out, boss. Time is short. We can't afford to play games. We've got the goods on Shawby, Lee, Seppuku, and the whole crowd. So you just sit there while we fill you in."

Thatcher shook his head. "Nope. No way, Louise. You four have violated the law. While what you have done is bad enough, for me to listen to it would be worse. I will not have you dragging me into what is utterly and unarguably a criminal conspiracy. I will not have you entangling this corporation in violations of the law. I will not listen to you."

Louise thrust her forefinger at him and in a furious tone of voice shouted, "To hell with that, Scott C. Thatcher! To hell with that! You are going to sit there, and I am going to tell you what's going on, and you are going to goddamn well listen! Right goddamn now!"

Thatcher's moustache bristled with rage. "Louise, if you say one further word—if any of you say one further word—if you attempt to disclose one iota of the information you've pilfered from other people's computer systems, I will fire you on the spot. I cannot hear, I cannot use, I will not tolerate any of it."

"Oh, don't be silly, Scott."

"I mean it. My mind is made up. I am serious. I will not have the law violated further. If you utter one word, you are fired. And fired for real."

Mike Ash had edged around to the right-hand side of Thatcher's desk. "It starts with a sale-leaseback deal."

Thatcher glanced at him and then looked down at his desk.

He spoke slowly, and almost in a whisper. "Mike, your employment with PegaSys is terminated as of this moment. Please go to your office, collect your personal belongings, and be out of this building in an hour. Roy, as head of security, I want you to make sure that Mike's card key and ID badge are handed in before he leaves."

Roy Knight, still sitting on Thatcher's couch, stared up morosely. Thatcher's face was stone. Mike, on the other hand, wore a peculiarly smug grin. Mike nodded at Roy and then twitched his head at the window behind Thatcher's desk. He pointed surreptitiously at the drapes. Roy frowned, thought for a moment, and then understood his meaning. He said to Thatcher, "Sure, I'll do that. But first you should know that the sale-leaseback involved all of AIW's assets."

Thatcher's head jerked up. "You, too, Roy? Is that the way it is? Well, then, Roy, your employment is terminated too. The same things I said to Mike apply to you. You have an hour to clean up and leave."

Louise frowned, not quite catching Ash's ploy. She watched him reach out to the drapes. She saw his smile—the loopy leer of Mad Mike, PegaSys's boy genius, the one who always came up with an off-the-wall solution to insoluble problems. Mad Mike. Unpredictable, erratic, sometimes flaky, but always original. *Mad Mike has an idea.* She suddenly understood it. *He may be a bastard, but, goddamn, he's a brilliant bastard,* she thought. *I love you, you rotten goddamn brilliant bastard.* A faint, cunning smile began to form on her lips as she said, "Then all of the assets were securitized by Seppuku."

Thatcher did not look at her. In a deeply saddened tone of voice he said, "I am not surprised. You and Mike have always been something of a team. One hour, Louise, then please leave the building."

Arnie, who didn't quite comprehend why Mike Ash was fumbling with Thatcher's curtains, spoke up, "Gee whiz, well, I don't know what to say. I guess you'd better fire me too, Mr. Thatcher. Because they did, what's the phrase, they did a private placement with what they'd securitized."

"You're fired, Arnie. Go back to California where it's warm and there aren't people like me who have to fire people they . . . care for. Now, all of you please leave my office, I want to— What the dickens!"

Thatcher yelled and tried to twist in his chair. He couldn't. Ash had yanked the cords off the drapes and lassoed him. Ash swiftly wound the nylon ropes around Thatcher and bound him fast. Thatcher was immobilized, trussed to his chair.

Louise rested her pert rump on the edge of Thatcher's desk and leaned close to his rage-purpled face. "You know, Scotty," she said with a sunny smile, "you are a wonderful person. I love you and treasure you and really wouldn't ever want to work for anyone else. But you know, sometimes you can be an absolute pain in the ass. Now you just sit there, and swallow your holier-than-thou pompous pride, and listen to us. Don't worry about breaking the law. You can't break the law, because you are no longer operating under your own power. You're a prisoner, and can't help hearing what we're going to say. And another thing, PegaSys isn't breaking the law either. It can't. You fired us. Since we're no longer PegaSys employees, anything we do has no relationship to PegaSys. Now then, pay close attention. The boys and I want to tell you a little story."

2

THATCHER'S INTERCOM BUZZED. Ash leaned across Thatcher's desk and pushed its "on" button.

"Yes," he said.

Gladys voice came back. "Is Mr. T. in there with you? He has a call from Mr. Banks."

Thatcher replied, "Tell him I'm all tied up."

Louise giggled.

"This is not," Thatcher said sternly, "a laughing matter, young lady. I have been sitting here, kidnapped, for an hour and a half. Besides, my anatomy itches."

Gladys came back on the intercom. "Mr. Banks says he's coming up right now. He'll be here in twenty minutes."

Mike replied, "Thanks, Gladys. When he gets here, just tell him to come right in."

"Oh, Mr. Ash, there are some donuts out here. And . . . it looks like . . . peanut butter."

"Someone will be out to get it, Gladys. And one other thing, when Don Banks gets here we want you to stay put. There is no need for you to come in and take a transcript of this meeting. Just send Banks straight in. By himself." Ash switched off the intercom.

Roy, who was slumped in an exhausted heap in an armchair, looked up hollow-eyed and said, "Anybody got a suggestion how to handle Banks when he gets here? He'll be even more disinclined than Scott to listen to what we have to say."

Thatcher snickered. "Well, well, well. It is a predicament. It is perplexing. It is a puzzlement. Yet, there is a solution, and I am disappointed that you four felons haven't thought of it. After all, the litany of your crimes is sufficiently lengthy that multiple life sentences seem inevitable. Computer burglary. Assault and battery. Kidnapping. Several others, too. Ask yourselves, what's one more piece of villainy when, tried and convicted, you step before the judge? What's one more blemish on your already blackened souls when you face Saint Peter? How do you handle Don Banks, you ask. The answer is obvious. You'll just have to tie him up, too." Thatcher grinned his trademark wolfish grin.

An hour later Thatcher said, "I think you can take the gag out now."

Arnie stepped behind Banks, undid the knotted handkerchief, and removed it from the investment banker's mouth. He carefully refolded the cloth and tucked it into the breast pocket of Banks's coat. He stepped back a pace from the chair to which Banks was bound and critically examined the results of his efforts. He reached back to Banks and nudged the tip of the handkerchief a little to the left.

"Cut that out," Banks said.

"I'm just trying to get it right," Arnie replied defensively.

"Just leave it alone, huh?"

Arnie sulked back to his spot on the sofa.

Don Banks looked around the room. Roy Knight was sprawled in one armchair. Louise sat in another, her legs tucked up beneath her. Arnie had folded himself into the lotus position on the sofa. Ash was standing with his rump resting on the back of one of Thatcher's guest chairs. Thatcher himself was tied firmly to the high-backed green leather chair behind his partner's desk. Despite the fact that he was bound hand and foot, Thatcher looked resolutely in control of the proceedings.

"We are all," Banks said morosely, "going to go to jail."

Thatcher shook his head. "Nope. These four hoodlums, maybe, but not me and you. We're victims, not criminals."

"I have at times asked the gods to inject a little larceny into your heart. I now regret my prayers."

"We had no choice but to hear what we heard. The right metaphor, Don, is Odysseus, bound to the mast as his ship sailed past the siren's rock."

"Yeah, well, maybe so. What I want to know is this: What are we going to do now?"

Thatcher thought for a moment, then answered, "I suppose that the right thing to do is to call the FBI and have these four arrested. Then, probably, we should call Nick Lee, Shawby, and Hidetake and tell them what's happened."

"Yeah, that's probably the right thing to do."

"On the other hand . . ."

"On the other hand . . ."

"We could sit here and debate whether or not this is one of those rare situations where the rule of law is at fundamental odds with the precepts of ethics. Where the legal statutes say one thing but right reason says another. I could quote from Thoreau's *On Civil Disobedience*, or Martin Luther King's speeches, or even, I suppose, Marcus Aurelius. We could do that, Don, don't you think? There are, after all, some grounds for contending that in the case at hand the right thing and the legal thing are different."

"I suppose so," Banks grudgingly acknowledged.

"Of course, I don't *know* that they are different. All I'm saying is that the question is open. They could be different."

"They could be."

"Then we should take the time necessary to talk it out. Unfortunately . . ."

"Unfortunately . . ."

"We don't have the time right now. The meter is running. Time is short. And, besides, we don't have all the evidence. Therefore, I propose that we defer reaching a decision on the legality and morality of these matters until we have sufficient time for reflection. And until we have assembled all of the evidence and duly considered it. Do you agree?"

"If these people will untie me so I can go pee, I'll agree to anything."

"OK. Louise, Mike, Roy, Arnie, you are all rehired and back on the payroll. It should go without saying that your salaries will be docked for the past three hours or so during which you were not employed by PegaSys. Further, you are on probation, and I will make a final determination as to your employment status on December 26, after AIW's tender offer expires. That is, if I am here to make any determinations whatsoever. Now, both Don and I would appreciate it if you would be so courteous as to release us. We will take a ten-minute break, and reconvene here to sort out our options."

Banks looked up from the mass of printouts that he had been reviewing for the past several hours. He wiped a hand across his brow and shook his head. He looked up and said, "This deal that Shawby and Lee are working is like an M. C. Escher drawing—architectures that warp dimensions beyond recognition, but are still perfectly logical. You look at it and you know that there is something wrong, that what you are seeing is somehow or another devilishly awry. It can't exist, but it does. It's right there in front of you. And the more you look at it, the crazier it makes you."

Thatcher said, "I think we've got all the data we need, but we don't understand what it means. Let's review the bidding. Let's try to make it simple. Can anyone here get this story down to its simplest level? I want to hear the simplest possible summary. Twenty-five words or less. What are the basic basics? Mike?"

Mike stroked the thick stubble on his cheeks and shook his head. "I don't understand it, and I don't think it can be simplified."

"Let me try," said Louise. "Forget everything AIW has told the SEC. What Shawby has really done is a sale and leaseback of all of his assets to Seppuku. All of them. Lock, stock, and barrel. Lee has done the same with Lee, Bach and Wachutt. And both of them have pledged all of their personal assets as well. Literally, to finance this deal both men are renting the very clothes on their backs from Hidetake. Seppuku has taken all of the assets and securitized them. Including, God help us, the goodwill. Hidetake is operating under the laws of some island in the middle of the Indian Ocean; his bank has a subsidiary there, and he can do whatever he wants. Then Hidetake has taken the securities and sold them through a bunch of sleazeball agents on a private placement basis. The paper he's pushing is registered only in the Seychelles, and he's not selling anything in the United States. He's a Japanese company doing business outside the U.S., and claiming immunity from the Securities and Exchange Commission, which would, I hasten to add, land on him like a ton of bricks if he even thought about peddling his trash in this country. The buyers of his paper are mostly very rich guys and some of the smaller, flakier national governments. Cripes, he's even got the Albanians in the deal for $50 million. Everyone in this thing—Shawby, Lee, and Hidetake—has raised a lot of cash. But the problem I've got is that the cash isn't enough. Look, Shawby's hocked, say, $2.5 billion worth of assets. Lee's hocked everything his company has for, round numbers, $5 billion in cash. The dubious debentures Seppuku floated have pulled in another $6 billion in what is effectively unsecured debt, selling at seven-point discount under face value. All this cash has wound up on AIW's account at the Seppuku Bank in Tokyo. Needless to say, it is not drawing interest. You have to credit Hidetake for that. So Shawby's got $13.5 billion in folding money. That still leaves them about four and a half billion bucks short of their last offer for our stock. They don't have enough. What I want to know is where the hell are they planning to get the remaining four and a half billion from?''

"I bet I know," Mike answered. All eyes turned to him. "That $4.5 billion is exactly one-quarter of the AIW offer. It's 25 percent of what they say they are going to pay. So that means AIW will sell off 25 percent of PegaSys to cover the tab. What does PegaSys own that comes in one bite and is precisely 25 percent of our net worth? Come on, people, hasn't anyone looked at our annual report recently?'' Ash picked up a copy from Thatcher's coffee table and brandished it. "It's right here in the back. Under international assets. Our Japanese subsidiary tallies to exactly, let me repeat, exactly 25 percent of our assets. Hence, it is worth 25 percent of the takeover price. Hence, the minute the takeover goes through, brother Shawby will sell PegaSys-Japan to brother Hidetake. Hence, brother Hidetake will pay $4.5 billion. Hence, they will be able to fund the total $18 billion tab. Hence we are fucked. That is how the deal will go down.''

"And the result will be," said Thatcher, "a PegaSys that is three-quarters the size it is today and so burdened with debt that it will sink like a stone.''

"Not exactly," Banks answered. "Seppuku gets all your Japanese operations at what I must objectively term a fair price.

But whether or not it sinks like a stone is another question. Look at what happens on December 25, when the transaction closes. Shawby pays $18 billion to buy you precisely at midnight. Then the debentures that AIW is using to finance the deal expire precisely one hour after the deal is consummated. How can Shawby hope to pay off those debentures? The answer is, he can't. So what happens? I bet that Seppuku will extend Shawby and Lee a loan to retire those debentures. They, in turn, will issue him junk paper. Callable against equity, I bet, at some market-price formula. Then Hidetake will wait for a few months. When the time is ripe, he'll pull the pin on those bonds, call 'em for equity, and take over the whole package. By the time he exercises the call, the value of PegaSys will be one hell of a lot less than it is today because it will be stuck with a ton of debt, and unable to meet its interest commitments. And, Shawby's son-in-law will be doing everything in his power to drive the worth of the company down. When it gets low enough, Hidetake will strike. He will get all of PegaSys on the cheap. I'm sure that after it's all over, he can pay Nick Lee a nice off-the-books premium and still will have wound up buying PegaSys for less than he would have in an aboveboard transaction. What he is doing is, if you'll forgive me for saying this, brilliant.''

"Maybe, but it's too complex," Thatcher said. "Why not just do the simple, straightforward thing? Why didn't he just underwrite some junk bonds for Shawby on the day the takeover began?''

"I can answer that," Don Banks said. "The Japanese hate risk. They'd do anything to avoid it. Hidetake was afraid that Shawby would screw up the thing, or that some problem would emerge. Maybe over PegaSys's strategic technologies. So he put together a no-risk deal. If it came unglued, he'd own AIW and Nick Lee's company. If it went through, he'd own you. Either way he's ahead of the game.''

"OK, clear the decks," said Thatcher. "I want to hear some options. Now that we think we know what they're doing, I want to hear how we can torpedo them. Let's get to work.''

3

By two o'clock in the morning Thatcher had given up. He and his team had reviewed four times over every piece of data that Roy and Arnie had pirated from AIW's and Seppuku's computers. The data told him, four times over, that there was absolutely nothing they could do.

Every piece of information they analyzed confirmed Ash and Banks's hypotheses about the ultimate structure of the takeover. AIW, Lee, Bach and Wachutt, and Seppuku had created an unstoppable money-raising juggernaut. Slipping between loopholes in international law and sliding through cracks in the structure of international finance, the trio had assembled the wherewithal to pay $18 billion at 12:01 A.M. Christmas Day for control of PegaSys. At 12:02 A.M., one-quarter of the company would be transferred to Seppuku. At 1:01 A.M. the same day, the high-coupon, discounted debentures with which the acquisition was financed would expire. One minute before they expired, Seppuku would loan AIW the money it needed to pay down the debentures. It would receive high-interest junk bonds with some very peculiar redemption and conversion terms. Very little mathematical savvy was needed to conclude that within a matter of months Seppuku would exercise its options under the bonds and take over both AIW and PegaSys.

It was foolproof. Nothing could halt the acquisition. Thatcher tossed in the towel. "We're done for. We can't win. It's over. Call it a night. Everyone go home. No need to come back tomorrow. Take some vacation."

Mike, who was crouched over an untidy pile of printouts on the floor, turned and said, "Wait a minute, Scott, there's something here. I know it. We're missing something. I know it."

"Mike," Thatcher said in a disconsolate voice, "there is

nothing here. Truly. We've seen it all. I have been around long enough to know the odor of defeat, and I smell it now. Shawby's won. We've lost. Let's not fool ourselves any further. They can't be beaten. They never could. Go home. Get some sleep."

Ash ignored him and began searching through the paper at his feet. He picked up one document, eyed it, and threw it down. Then another, and another. There was, he knew, something that had eluded everyone. Something that whispered at him. Something that called out to him in a faint, distant, and as yet inaudible voice. He could not hear what it said, but he knew that it spoke to him. It was a piece of the puzzle. It was the key piece. If he could only find it and set it in the right place, the whole puzzle would fall into place. It was one tiny element of data lost in mounds and mounds of paper. It was a number, or a sentence, or a name, or a place, or a company, or a phrase, or a word, or . . .

Thatcher shrugged, ran a hand over his face, and said to Louise, "You talk to him, Louise. Tell him it's useless."

"Mike, Scott's right. You've been through this stuff. I've been through this stuff. We've all been through this stuff. We know what it says. It says that AIW is bulletproof. We can't stop them. There's no way. There is no magic wand we can wave to win. We're stuck. We've been beaten. You're beaten. Let's quit, Mike, and we'll all go home."

Ash didn't even look at her. He rifled through the paper obsessively. Something with a soft, furry paw stroked at his perceptual doors. It gently stroked the outer limits of his consciousness. It was like hearing a cat purr across a large, darkened room. He knew it was there, but he didn't quite know where there was. It was maddening. It was like being a high school student taking a fill-in-the-blank test. He knew the answer to the question. He knew that he knew the answer to the question. He just couldn't remember the one word, the right word, that belonged in the blank spot in the test booklet. The word was in his mind, but it wouldn't pop out. That one word was the difference between passing or failing his final exam.

Louise stood up and began noisily packing her briefcase. "Ash," she snarled, "you meathead. We've crapped out. The party's over. Quit fooling around. You're acting like some mad scientist in a bad movie. Give up. It's goddamn over, Ash!"

Ash ignored her. He stared at another sheet of paper. Louise began heading toward the door.

"Wait a second, Louise," Thatcher said. He looked at Mike.

"Wait a second. Just wait. Look at him. I've seen him like this before. Maybe he's got something. Mike? Mike? Do you see something we've missed?"

Ash rubbed his finger across his upper lip. He bit his thumb. He looked at the sheet of paper.

Thatcher knelt by Ash's side. "Mike, if it's there, you can find it. I know you, Mike. You can find it if it's there. Show me, Mike, show me. We can help."

Mike irritably waved him away. He began tracing out the document line by line, word by word."

Louise said, "This is hopeless. It's a waste of time."

"No!" Thatcher answered. "No. He's seeing something, I can tell. He's onto something none of us noticed. Mike, if you love this company, if you value its people, if you care for any of us . . ."

Ash looked at the paper and rubbed his cheek. It was infuriating. It was on the tip of his tongue. He just couldn't . . . quite . . . put his hand on it. *Mad Mike*, he thought, *the creative dervish. The idea man. The idea-a-minute man. Where's the idea now? I know it's here. It's here somewhere. I can feel it. Perhaps I can think of a synonym. Or perhaps I can think of its category. If I could just remember its category, I could jog it loose from memory. It's a number, or a sentence, or a name, or a place, or a company, or a phrase, or a word, or—What else? A number, or . . . like a number. Like a number? A phone number? No. An address? Uh-uh. An account number? Nope. A date. No. Not a date. Not a date, but close. Like a number. Like a date. Like a time. A time? A time. It was a time. Goddamn! It was a time!*

Ash stood up beaming. He threw out his chest and cried like a circus barker, "Ta-DA-DA-DA! A trumpet fanfare, if you please. Ladies and gentlemen, boys and girls, children of all ages. Step right up. Hurry, hurry, hurry. The big show is about to begin!"

He strutted in a circle around Thatcher's office, flourishing a single page of Knight and Swift's illicit printouts. "Observe, my friends, if you will, this tiny scrap of paper. Examine it closely. What mysteries might it contain? What secrets might it unveil? Yes, sir, you sir, with the grizzled moustache and silvered hair. Cast your eye on this single sheet. Tell me, what do you see?"

Ash held the page in front of Thatcher's face. Thatcher, knowing that Ash's erratic creativity might just have paid off, humored him. He said, "I see black characters on white paper. I see the text of the debenture issued, or rather under-written, by Seppuku Limited. Nothing more.''

"And so you do, fine sir, and so you do. But you see only the superficial reality on this sheet of paper, and do not see the underlying and greater truth that lies beneath it. Had you but eyes to see, why then, fine sir, you would see—salvation! You, young and beauteous lady. Step closer, and read to me the words writ upon this page.''

Louise, who had lost her sense of humor several hours, if not days, earlier, said in a voice one step removed from a snarl, "I don't see why. God knows I've read the goddamned thing a dozen times today.''

"Just once more, fair damsel, for me. Read it aloud.''

"OK,'' Louise said with resignation, "just once more. Quote, 'American Interdyne Worldwide, Inc. $100,000. Subordinated debenture. $6 billion issue. 12.5 percent coupon. Due December 25 at 1:01 A.M. This debenture is—' ''

"Stop!'' Mike yelled. "That's enough! You have read the magic formula. You have chanted the secret words. Genies, de-mons, sprites, angels, fairies, and elves shall now appear and work feats of wonderment. Don't you see them? Here they arise as per your conjuring!''

"I don't get it,'' Louise said.

"Nor I,'' added Thatcher.

"My, my, my,'' Mike sighed, "tired, aren't we? Haven't spotted it yet, have we? It's right here. 'Due December 25 at 1:01 A.M.' ''

"We all know that,'' Louise said. "We've been over it a dozen times. 'Due December 25 at 1:01 A.M.' Shawby has to pay back the money he's borrowed to buy us an hour after he's bought us. What goddamn good does it do us to go over that point again? We've beaten it to death.''

Mike flashed an enormous toothy grin around the room. "And precisely why, dear Louise, precisely why do you think he has to pay back that money an hour after he's bought PegaSys?''

"Goddamn it, Mike, I'm tired of this game. I want to go home. We've lost this company and it's no time to play 'riddle me this.' ''

"Why, Louise, why? Tell me why you think he has to pay an hour after the deal goes down.''

"OK, goddamn it! Because it goddamn says so!''

"Oh no, it doesn't'' Ash shouted, breaking into laughter. "Oh, no it doesn't!''

"Ash," Louise sneered, "you're spacier than my kid brother and he's in astronaut training. What are you gibbering about?"

Mike's laughter tapered off. He surveyed his audience. Roy and Arnie merely looked perplexed. Louise looked furious. Thatcher appeared hopeful, but quite confused. But Don Banks—Banks's eye had a faint, but swiftly growing, gleam in it. Mike rushed on to his punch line in order to keep Banks from sharing his triumph. "The way I read this, he has to pay the money thirteen hours before he acquires us. I repeat, *before*!"

Four people said, "Huh?" Banks said, "Right. Son of a bitch! He's right!" Then he doubled over laughing. Ash joined him. Both reeled backwards in hilarity, slapping one another on the back. They collapsed together on the sofa. Their guffaws deepened, and they wrapped their arms around one another, roaring at the most supreme of supreme jests.

Thatcher, who had stood to watch Mike's cavorting, triumphant antics, sat down. "Pardon me," he said, "but I am merely a poor innocent old man, and I am lost in these confounded thickets of knavery. We seem to have some sort of an in-joke here to which I am not privy. Will one of you two be so kind as to enlighten me?"

Mike couldn't stop laughing. Banks giggled to a halt and took control of himself. Wiping a tear from his eye, he said, "This is a classic. This will go down in the history books. Oh, Jesus, Scott, it's wonderful. The language on the debenture—don't you see—it says that it is due on December 25 at 1:01 in the morning. But it doesn't say where. Don't you see? It doesn't say where. It doesn't say what time zone."

"So?" asked Thatcher.

"Whoopee!" Louise shrieked before Banks could answer. "Hallelujah! Hosanna! Praise the Lord! They left off the time zone! Oh, my God! They left off the time zone! That means you can call that debenture at 1:01 A.M. Hong Kong time. Or Singapore time, or Tokyo time, or anywhere else on the other side of the international date line. Don't you see, Scott? When it's ten in the morning in New York, it's midnight tomorrow in Tokyo. There's a fourteen-hour difference! They're going to start executing their tender offer for PegaSys at one minute after midnight on Christmas, December 25, New York time—Their debentures are due one minute after one Tokyo time. And one minute after one Tokyo time is one minute after eleven in the morning in New York—*the day before*! December 24! You can call that debenture in for payment fourteen hours before they can take us over. You can make them pay up all the money they have fourteen hours before their tender offer expires. You can buy them before they buy us!''

''Why'd they do it?'' asked Banks.

Thatcher cried, ''Who cares? What matters is that they are delivered into my hands!'' Then he gave a war whoop of the sort that had not passed his lips since he was nine years old.

4

AFTER THE EUPHORIA DIED DOWN, Thatcher ordered everyone off to a nearby hotel for five hours' worth of sleep. Before he left his office, he called (and awoke) both Denniston Howe and Justine Gold, and ordered them to be in his office promptly at 8:00 A.M.

At eight Thatcher's team convened. Its first order of business was to calculate the financial implications of their new defense strategy. This task was completed swiftly, although Don Banks and Louise, who both prided themselves on uncommon mathematical wizardry, briefly debated the finer points of the sums involved. In the end they agreed that about $13.6 billion would be needed to purchase all of the debentures Seppuku had floated on AIW's behalf. In redeeming the debentures, PegaSys would receive back slightly less than $13.5 billion—the sum total of the AIW/Lee, Bach war chest, plus all of the personal assets of Messrs. Shawby and Lee. It was, at best, a less than break-even deal, but in Thatcher's estimation, a bargain nonetheless. He counted himself lucky that the AIW/Lee, Bach debentures were so heavily discounted. After all, their face value was $14.5 billion.

Banks, when asked if he could arrange a short-term loan of $13.6 billion, merely smirked with unquestioned superiority and muttered something about being bored by the lack of challenge afforded by such a trivial sum. The money would be available by lunchtime. He also smugly asserted that Morgan, Teech & Kidd would guarantee that when the debentures were offered up for repayment in Tokyo, every American bank and brokerage house in that city would stay opened and fully staffed after midnight, local time. They would take the steps needed to see that full payment through the Seppuku Global Marine Trust bank was promptly and expeditiously concluded. By 11:15 on the morning of Christmas Eve, New York time, PegaSys would own every penny of cash in AIW's bank account, and more to the point, would be owed the additional seven points in principal that represented the discount at which AIW had been required to sell its debentures. In short, AIW and Lee, Bach and Wachutt would have no cash and would owe PegaSys just short of a billion dollars. They would both be bankrupt.

On the subject of bankruptcy, Denniston Howe, who was neither privy to the sordid details underlying how Thatcher's team had secured their data on the AIW financing nor desirous of becoming so, assumed responsibility for the legal aspects of the transaction—and its immediate aftermath. For once in his life, Thatcher was pleased to have the highest-powered legal firm in New York on his side. Howe made a few quick phone calls, lining up one sympathetic judge and several sympathetic law officers. The services of both would be needed.

Justine borrowed Gladys's word processor. She began hammering out draft press releases. She also prepared a note for hand-delivery to the Board of Governors of the New York Stock Exchange explaining why a halt in the trading of PegaSys and AIW stock was called for. All the material she wrote was dated December 24.

As for the actual mechanics of purchasing more than $13 billion worth of debentures, Banks and Howe agreed that it would be preferable if some third party, acting as an agent for PegaSys and concealing PegaSys's identity, executed the purchases. Members of Banks's or Howe's firms, much less PegaSys employees, could be recognized and AIW, Lee, Bach, and Wachutt, or Seppuku might be tipped off to what was afoot. It was not desirable for the enemy to know what was going on, or for them to have an opportunity to try to stop it.

Thatcher pondered their advice for a moment or two, then said that he knew of a perfect third party, an international organization with representatives in every country. They were men who could easily acquire the debentures on PegaSys's behalf.

Indeed, he observed with an artless smile, the organization was noted for its uncommonly effective negotiating techniques, and, therefore, might be able to obtain a price for the debentures lower than the amount estimated by Don and Louise. He then asked everyone to leave the room. When they had gone, he picked up his phone and dialed a number in New Jersey.

The phone rang three times before it was answered. A hoarse, gruff voice grunted, "Yeah. Dis is da Varrazano residence. Whatcha want?"

By lunchtime, all the details were ironed out. Everyone knew his or her marching orders. Don Banks confirmed that the money PegaSys needed was now available and sat ready awaiting Thatcher's beck and call. The team adjourned, and everyone hurried off to do what needed to be done. Everyone, that is, except Mike Ash. He lingered until the last of the team left Thatcher's office. Then he shut the door behind them and sat by Thatcher's desk.

He looked silently at Thatcher for a few seconds before saying, "This is tough. Scott, what I'm going to say is tough. I don't want you to feel that it has anything to do with you, or anything to do with PegaSys. I've been happy here for twenty years. But, hell, Scott, in the past two months everything's gone sour. Crazy people have pointed guns at me three—no, four— times. Ten-ton cranes have collapsed into my office. People have tried to bribe me. Nutball KGB agents have defected into my arms. Policemen follow me. You've fired me twice. And another thing, I don't feel particularly good. My stomach is upset, and I don't sleep at night. I think maybe this is all Mother Nature's way of telling me that something is wrong. I'm not happy. And, well, anyhow, the thing is this—when I was out in California, Joe Jonas talked to me. I don't want you to think that he tried to talk me into leaving PegaSys. He'd never do that. But he's happy, Scott. He's happy, and it's real nice out where he is. He's got a good life. It's better than mine, that's for sure. It doesn't have loony-tunes waving guns, and it doesn't have four consecutive days without sleep, and it doesn't have Nick Lee or Brian Shawby. I'm not happy, Scott. I guess what I'm saying is that I want to quit. I want to move to California and be like Joe. I want to be an ex-New Yorker."

Thatcher snorted. "Phooey. There is no such thing. Do you take my meaning?"

"Maybe. But, anyway, I want to give it a try. I want out.

Once this thing with AIW is over, I'm going to resign and move west."

"Umpf," Thatcher grunted, "if that's what you want to do, then that's what you should do. Do it with my blessing."

"Thanks, Scott. I think I'd better get back to work now."

"No, not quite yet. First, I want to make sure that resigning is what you really want. I want to make sure that I fully understand that litany of problems you just rattled off."

"Sure. OK. But my mind's pretty much made up."

"I know it is. Now, let's see. Where to begin? You spoke about people with guns, and long hours, and lots of pressure. But (curiously enough, in my estimation) you didn't talk about the one thing I thought you'd talk about."

"What was that?"

"Your love life, or absence thereof. Let's talk about that for a moment, hmm? It seems to me like a very logical place to begin."

Thatcher was a handler. Handling people was what he was best at. When he was done, Mike Ash didn't even know he'd been handled.

5

OVER THE COURSE OF THE NEXT eleven days, quietly and stealthily, AIW's debentures were bought and sold. The buyers' sometimes draconian, but always simply stated, terms were remarkably persuasive. They rarely had to ask twice. They offered a fair and equitable price, but did so with a tone and demeanor that suggested grave disappointment if refused. They were not the sort of men that anyone would want to disappoint.

Curiously, given their otherwise timid mien, Quint and Claggart were the sole and singular holdouts. Despite Thatcher's admonitions to Joey the Bridge about avoiding threats of violence, much less the real thing, several personal calls of steadily increasing sternness were made on the pair. However, not even wholly unsubtle hints about the amount of time it takes to recover from broken kneecaps could budge the two from their adamant refusal to sell.

Quint sat in the sparsely furnished library of his club, sipping a brandy and ginger ale. In the armchair next to him Claggart rested, reading a fascinating magazine about unusual rubber implements. Behind them a coal fire sparked and crackled, and the faint, tart, not entirely displeasing, odor of coal smoke wafted into the room. It was nearly Christmas, and the club was quiet. Most of the members were visiting their otherwise estranged families.

Claggart heard the noise first. The sound of voices raised in heated argument. Then a distant shriek of agony. "Whatever do you think that is?" he asked, turning to Quint.

"Lovers' quarrel, I'll warrant. Or one of the junior members cornered down in the steam room again."

"Seems to have died down now. Bloody nuisance. Like my peace and quiet, I do."

The door at the end of the reading room crashed open with a shattering impact. A tiny figure, clad from head to toe in electric red, whirled in. The figure stood for a moment glaring around the room, then spotted Quint and Claggart and began to approach them. Neither liked the way the figure moved. It slinked like a stalking leopard.

"My God," exclaimed Quint, "it's a beastly, bloody woman!"

Claggart arose, towering to his full, albeit unimpressive height. He puffed out his chest and wrathfully cried out, "Indeed! A woman! See here, young woman, this is a men's club. No frilly lacy girlish things allowed! Men only. No females. Now you just bustle on out of here. Speakee English? Do you understand me, madam? You and your sex are neither wanted nor welcome in this establishment."

Justine Gold placed a red-gloved hand against Claggart's chest and shoved. His heavy haunches toppled him off balance and back into his chair.

"You Quint?" she demanded.

"No, madam, I am not. The gentleman next to me is Mr.

Quint. I am Mr. Claggart. And neither of us wishes to see you, hear you, or speak to you, whoever you may be.''

''Tough shit.''

''Oh. Oh, dear,'' Claggart said.

Quint said, ''How, my dear young lady, just how, if I may ask, did you manage to gain entrance to this club? The doorman has strict instructions to admit no one of the feeble sex.''

''The doorman, huh? Yeah, well, don't worry about him. There's no need to call an ambulance. Just tell him to put an ice pack up against it for fifteen minutes or so and the pain will go away. Or at least begin to subside.''

''Oh,'' said Quint.

''My, my,'' said Claggart.

''What happened to the poor man?'' asked Quint.

Justine smiled with enormous, albeit unpleasant, satisfaction. ''The same thing that's going to happen to you, only more so, unless you two fuckers sell me those AIW debentures you own. Right fucking now.'' She waved a Knirps folding umbrella in Quint's sallow face, wielding it like a war axe.

Quint's face turned a bright red shade, nearly matching Justine's boots. He stood up, bristling with ire. Standing up was a mistake. Justine swung the umbrella like a police truncheon. It traversed a short, swift arc that ended between his legs. Quint shrieked and sat down.

''Just put an ice pack up against it for fifteen minutes or so,'' she said. ''The pain will go away. It will be swollen for a while, and you'll have trouble peeing, but it won't hurt so much.''

Claggart drew his legs up beneath him and pushed himself back into his chair. ''Uncalled for,'' he said, ''quite, quite uncalled for. You must be reasonable, young woman.''

''I am being reasonable,'' Justine replied. ''I am the very personification of reason, decorum, and good fucking behavior. Hear how reasonable I am. Right now, this very minute, you go and get me those debentures. In return, I will pay you precisely the price you paid for them plus accrued interest. Otherwise, I might not be so reasonable for much longer.''

''I cannot do that. I will not do that. You can't intimidate me. They are not for sale at any price.''

Justine drew a red glove off her left hand. Then she tugged its companion off her right hand. She arched her fingers so that her long, red gleaming, unspeakably sharp nails twinkled in the firelight. Claggart watched them as the rabbit watches the snake.

Examining her nails, she said, ''Have you ever thought about blind men? Those poor tragic people with white canes and trained dogs—the ones you see selling pencils out of a tin cup in Charing Cross Station. 'Pencils. Pencils. Buy a pencil and help a poor blind man, guv'nor.' Have you ever thought about those unfortunate men, Quint? Have you ever pitied them? Have you ever dropped a few pence in their cups and said to yourself, 'There but for the grace of God go I?' ''

"I'm Claggart, and if you look in that briefcase on the floor, you will find precisely what you want. We've been expecting a rather Russian gentleman to call for the debentures and have been carrying them wherever we go.''

Justine picked up the briefcase. It was a deep maroon, Moroccan affair, bound with a complex network of straps and buckles. She opened it, removed the debentures, and said, "Nice bag. How much did you pay for it?''

"Seventy-five quid.''

"Tell you what, call it ninety and I'll add it to the check.''

"Whatever you wish, madam, just so long as you conclude this transaction and depart as hastily as you arrived.''

Justine scribbled out a check (in red ink), waved it twice in the air, and dropped it in Claggart's lap. He winced.

"Just get an icepack and your pal will be all right,'' were her last words as she left the room.

Some time later Quint, clutching an ice bag to his groin, ruminated aloud on the shape of the globe and the latitudinal and longitudinal positions of the land masses thereon. He concluded that, as near as he could envision it, the most distant point, the utter antipodes, from Moscow was somewhere in the South Pacific. The farther one was from Moscow, he reasoned, the farther one was from a certain large, homicidally inclined KGB agent.

Claggart warranted that this was not necessarily a bad thing, what with scads of scantily clad, sun-browned native boys splashing in the waves, the clear, warm waters causing their loincloths to cling against their muscular little buttocks, the golden beaches lined with deep foliage that would hide from sight certain lurid acts, and the cool, airy grass huts being wonderful places for trysts. Then too, there were the prospects of visiting sailors, especially the American kind in their tight, ever so fetching, white bell-bottom trousers . . .

As Claggart ambled about the room weaving these idyllic fantasies, Quint thought about Russia. He thought about Russian literature. He thought about tales of troikas dashing across the snow. He thought about troikas being chased by packs of hungry wolves. He remembered that, in the last dire extreme, the passengers of such troikas were reputed to toss one of their fellows overboard. "Wolf meat" was the phrase they used. The theory was that the wolves would be diverted from their pursuit if one of the travelers was tossed to them. Thinking such thoughts, he reached a cautious hand into his trouser pocket and began fingering his penknife. He did not notice that Claggart, also deep in thought, had stopped in front of the fireplace and was weighing the heft of a cast-iron poker in his hand.

6

THE DAY BEFORE CHRISTMAS EVE, Roy Knight and Arnie Swift tapped into the New York Stock Exchange ticker tape. They looked at one another and chortled as they watched the tape fly by on their screen. They could see that PegaSys and AIW stock prices were moving in the right directions. The marketplace instinctively knew that Shawby was going to lose, even if Shawby himself did not.

There was, they decided, absolutely no reason to tell Thatcher about any of this. Least of all to tell him how they had—just as a safety measure—hacked into the extraordinarily sophisticated computer systems used by the world financial community. All of them.

Better that Thatcher never knew. Better that he never even suspected. And better that he never learned of the last-ditch defense that Roy and Arnie had concocted against the possibility of AIW actually trying to close its tender offer. Thatcher probably would have been more than upset at the ideas they had. Ideas that, now, would never be implemented.

Roy sighed, reached over to his console, and typed "< FILE

APOCALYPSE. FILE PURGE.'' Somewhere in every computer room in every bank, brokerage house, and stock exchange in the world, a disk drive whirled, a head descended, current flowed, and a few hundred lines of computer code were erased. The world financial market never knew how close a call it had.

7

At 11:15 a.m. on Christmas Eve, Thatcher stood looking out of his office window over the Manhattan skyline. Cold, dark, snow-laden clouds were blowing in from the west and north. Near the horizon the sky was a sickly yellow cream, tinged with blue. Higher up, the blue blended into slate grey, and the clouds were lined around the edges with darker, shadowy tones. The weather was grim and foreboding now, but later would produce that loveliest of circumstances, a white Christmas in New York.

Don Banks stood in the center of the office with a cellular mobile telephone glued to his ear. He listened intently to the party speaking to him. He grinned and gave Thatcher a thumbs-up signal. Thatcher stepped back to his desk, lifted the phone, and dialed the seven-digit number for Nick Lee's private line. Lee answered on the second ring.

"Nick Lee speaking. How may I serve you?"

"Nick, this is Scott Thatcher."

"Yes, Scott. What a pleasant surprise. I had not expected to hear from you at all."

"Nope, I suppose not. Well, I guess today's the day. It's all over, isn't it?"

"Just so, Scott. It is all over and you will eat crow."

"Ehh. Umpf. Our little wager—I'd almost forgotten that. Well, look, the reason I'm calling is that I thought we ought to get together and end this thing on a gentlemanly note. You, me, Brian, and our teams.''

"Excellent. Well done. I would like that. Brian and I will come over right away.''

"No. No, I don't want to meet here. When this thing started I said that Brian Shawby would never enter our offices while I was still chairman, and I meant it. Instead we'll come to see you, if that's acceptable. What say we come down right now? I think we can be there in, oh, say forty or forty-five minutes.''

"So be it. Brian is here with me now. We will be awaiting your arrival.''

They met in Lee's office. Thatcher, Ash, Bowman, and Banks represented PegaSys. Lee and Shawby stood for the American Interdyne Worldwide side. Thatcher noticed that Shawby could hobble only with the assistance of a cane.

Nick Lee graciously showed Thatcher's team his collection of primitive art, commenting knowledgeably on the origins, styles, and ethnic meanings of the pieces. Then the six sat at the small conference table at the west end of Lee's office. Lee moved to sit at the head of the table, but Thatcher got there first. Lee bowed gracefully, smiled, deferred to Thatcher, and sat beside him.

"Well," said Thatcher, "Nick, Brian, and all of you. Let's make this a short meeting if we can. I have some papers here. Let me open my briefcase. Let's see. Ahh, yes. Here it is. First we have a photocopy of this note, this debenture. One hundred grand denomination, secured against all the assets of AIW, all the assets of Lee, Bach and Wachutt, and all of the personal assets, possessions, properties, and belongings of Messrs. Lee and Shawby. My, my, my. You boys really bet the store floating this paper, didn't you?''

Lee jerked back and hissed, "So you know. So what? I care not. Little good will it do you now at this late hour.''

"Actually," Thatcher said blandly, "it does us no good at all. Not at this late hour, as you say. However, earlier today when we exercised it, and all the others you folks issued, it did us a great deal of good. Because, Nick, in exercising it, we acquired all of AIW's assets, all of your company's assets, and all of—now, how does this little gem read—all of your and Brian's personal assets, possessions, properties, and belongings.''

"Drivel. Nonsense. Poppycock. Hogwash. The notes cannot be called till tomorrow.''

"Which we did, at midnight promptly."

"Tomorrow, you ass, they're not due today."

"More precisely at 1:01 A.M., December 25."

"And today is December 24."

Thatcher smiled thinly. It was not a real smile. He said, "In New York, but not in Tokyo. It's the other side of the international dateline. In Tokyo, Nick, it is almost two o'clock on Christmas morning. Merry Christmas, Nick. Merry Christmas, Brian. On this Christmas morn, Santa has brought me a very nice present. Santa has given me my company back. And he's given me both of yours as well. We called those notes in Tokyo. We cashed them in. Nick, Brian, you two lads owe me $14.5 billion. You were only able to pay me $13.5 billion. Boys, in lieu thereof, I own your ass . . . ets. All of them."

Lee ripped the photocopied debenture out of Thatcher's fingers and bounded up out of his chair. His eyes flamed as he read it; his eyes sparked as he tore it to shreds. He threw his head back and shrieked an eerie, piercing scream. Clenching his fists, he glared around the room snarling, "Of all the half-witted blunders! How could you find out—this is . . . this is . . . what cretin is . . . who . . . I'll rip out their—"

"Temper, temper, Nick," counseled Thatcher.

Lee turned on him, purple with rage. "This is a mere technicality, damn you. It doesn't matter. Your stock has been tendered. You're in our grasp. You are ours. We have you! No goddamned duck-farting legal minutia is going to keep me from buying you!"

"With what?" Thatcher was cool and relaxed. "You haven't any money. You haven't any assets upon which to borrow any money. We've got it all. You've got nothing. I remind you that you secured your paper with everything you had. Your pockets are empty. If your pockets are empty, then how can you buy us? Dear Lord, Nick, my reading of that debenture and the law behind it is that right now you boys can't even afford to buy a cheese danish at the Chock-Full-O'-Nuts."

"Fuck that! I'll . . . I'll see you in hell, Thatcher! No! Better! I'll see you in court!"

Thatcher smiled elfishly. "Ah, yes. Indeed you shall. In a few minutes, as it turns out. This other piece of paper from my briefcase appears to be a summons. It demands your near-term presence in the Federal District Court for Southern Manhattan. It alleges unkind things about your and Brian's solvency, as well as the felonious nature of attempting to pay for billions of dollars of stock when you don't have two nickels to rub together. Doubtless there will be a few other lawsuits when all of those people who've tendered up PegaSys stock to you learn that you can't buy it. Oh yes, now that I think of it, I have another summons here as well. This one deals with the bankruptcy laws. It seems to say that my company is putting you two boys' companies into liquidation. And this third summons, well, it says much the same thing—only it doesn't deal with corporate bankruptcy, it deals with personal bankruptcy.

"Oh yes! How could I forget? There is another legal matter with which you boys must contend. I believe certain law enforcement officers will want to discuss it with you personally. And at length. Misrepresenting the way in which you planned to finance your tender offer was very, very naughty. The law frowns on it. Seems that you have violated . . . how many statutes was that, Louise?"

"One hundred and sixteen. Adds up to eight hundred and three separate charges."

"Dear me, Nick and Brian, you *are* in the soup, aren't you? Ahh well, they say federal minimum security facilities are not at all uncomfortably furnished. Besides, you'll have plenty of company, because, if memory serves, many of Nick's best friends are already guests there.

"The various hearings on these matters start in twenty minutes, so you'd better get a move on if you are going to be on time. But, one thing, you are going to have to walk over to the courthouse. Don't expect to be squired in that tarted-up Rolls Royce limousine of yours, Nick, because, if you look out the window, you will see a couple of federal marshals seizing it. They should be towing it away right now."

Lee dashed over to the window, looked down forty-one stories to the street, and howled in anguish at what he saw. He rounded on Thatcher and roared, "Oh Thatcher, you shall pay. You will rue this day. The vengeance I will wreak on you will stand as a lesson to every man, woman, and child in this country. I will bleed you dry and dangle your desiccated carcass up over my doorway. Your children shall weep and your wife shall mourn and men shall shiver at your name. I shall—"

Thatcher stood up and sharply cut him off. "You shall shut up, that's what you shall do. I have had quite enough of you. I have had enough of your silly Mephistophelian posturing. Of your speaking in bad pentameter and misquoting Marlowe and Goethe. Quite enough. I have had quite enough of you and your minions' efforts to destroy my company, suborn my employees, subvert my management, and peddle off my most valuable assets to the Japanese. I have had quite enough of your smearing me in the media. I have had quite enough disruption of the orderly operations of my enterprise. I have had quite enough. Quite enough. For two full months, Nicholas Lee, I have had to swallow my pride while you and your hapless crony here, poor dumb Brian, have embarrassed me and all who work for me. I have suffered, and now I am going to suffer no more. Rather, my good man, you are going to suffer. Your suffering does not begin in bankruptcy court, Nick Lee. It begins here and now. I own, officially, legally, and outright by the terms of your debenture, all of your assets. As the owner thereof, let my first official act, be to kick you two out of here. Right now. I want you off *my* premises!''

Thatcher strode to the door and flung it open. Detective Ryerhurt and his partner stood there. Both, having been briefed by Mike Ash as to both the grand design and subtle details of the preceding two months' events, were smiling from ear to ear and eagerly awaiting the roles they would play in the drama at hand.

Thatcher raised his voice a few decibels as he spoke to the two policemen. "Officers, these two gentlemen, Mr. Brian Shawby and Mr. Nicholas Lee, are trespassing on property legally belonging to me. I wish you to escort them from the premises as expeditiously as possible. I expect a Japanese gentleman to be calling for these two shortly. He will want their heads. Quite literally, I'm afraid. It is a bad habit of his. So please get these people out of here before Mr. Hidetake arrives and causes an unsightly mess on *my* carpets and *my* wallpaper.''

Thatcher's smile broadened. He slowly walked around the conference table, pausing to pat Shawby, who was quite distraught, on the shoulder.

Shawby, his eyes moist with tears, looked at Lee. "Why, Nick? How did this happen?''

Lee rounded on him. "You cretin! Don't you know how much money a day's worth of interest on the money we're borrowing is? Six billion dollars, that's how much, bozo! I figured that by letting the bonds expire Tokyo time rather than New York time, there would be an extra $6 million in interest!''

"But you never told me,'' Shawby whined. "You never told Hidetake either. I bet . . . I bet you were going to keep it all for yourself. Weren't you? Weren't you, Nick?''

Lee snarled, "Brian, the thought may or may not have crossed my mind. Whether it did or it didn't is irrelevant. What's relevant is this: if you ever articulate that scurrilous accusation again, I will sue your useless ass from here to doomsday!''

Meanwhile, Thatcher had stopped by Lee's credenza and picked up the newly arrived kachina doll on it. "This," he said, "belongs to a friend of mine. He sent it here only temporarily. I'll take it with me when I leave." Then he stepped to Lee's side. Lee was slumped back in his chair like a rag doll. Thatcher said, "But, officers, before you remove these gentlemen from here, I want you to let Mr. Lee eat his lunch." With a look of angelic innocence on his face, Thatcher reached into his briefcase and drew out a small package wrapped in white paper and bound with twine. He undid the twine and unwrapped the paper. He set the contents on a paper plate, in front of Lee. It was a dead crow, *"Bon appétit,"* he said.

8

THE SOOTY GREY MIXTURE OF RAIN and sleet that had begun to fall during the early afternoon finally metamorphosed into thick, white snow. By seven o'clock the snow had begun to stick to the streets and sidewalks, sending late commuters, already dizzy from office parties and holiday drinks, skidding and slipping as they dashed to Grand Central Station. By eleven o'clock three inches had fallen, and with that fall a hush of reverence fell, the reverent silence that a heavy snow brings to New York City. The streets were empty of traffic. Sirens no longer shrieked. People spoke in soft tones, and the thick blanket of new-fallen snow soaked up such sounds as they made. By morning Manhattan would be a magic isle, cloaked all in white, and silent but for the happy squeals of children who, at last, were able to play in the street. On Christmas morning, cynical city dwellers would glance out of their frost-glazed apartment windows at the sparkling landscape and feel a bright sense of wonder and cleanliness. Not even the mayor, unable to persuade the street cleaners to get to work, would be wholly unhappy.

On Sutton Place as the hour approached midnight, Scott Thatcher, his back turned to a roaring fire, raised his glass. "A toast," he said, "a toast to Christmas, a Christmas even more worth celebrating than most."

Don Banks cried, "And to villainy vanquished!"

Livy added, "And good triumphant!"

Roy Knight chimed in, "And to the good guys, who are us."

Scott, Livy, Don, Roy, Arnie, Justine, Louise, and her date for the evening, Dave Lefkowitz, clinked each other's glasses.

"I believe," Thatcher announced, "in honor of the occasion, I shall go to the piano and play a Christmas carol or two. Livy, do me a favor and call the tardy Mr. Ash. Tell him that he and his lady friend should be here now, as opposed to being off doing whatever it is that they are doing." Thatcher sat down at the piano, popped his fingers, and began to tap out a quite credible version of "God Rest Ye Merry, Gentlemen."

His guests, hesitant at first, slowly gathered round and began to sing. Louise, pushed by champagne punch far beyond her normally temperate limits, slouched her back against the piano. Her long, black hair tumbled loose across her shoulders. With her elbows propping her up from behind, she fell into a sultry posture not seen in America since Bacall made her last movie with Bogart.

The doorbell rang. Justine went to answer it, and a moment later returned to the living room with Joe Jonas in tow. Joe wore a camel overcoat; its pockets bulged with wrapped Christmas presents. Joe roared out, "Ho, ho, ho. Season's greetings from Santa."

Thatcher, his fingers still dancing across the keyboard, turned, glowered, and said, "I'm still not talking to you."

"You just did!" Jonas shouted, "And Merry Christmas, you nasty old man!"

Livy returned to the room and threw her arms around Jonas, kissing him solidly on the lips. "I've got a Christmas present for you, Livy," he boomed. "It's a box of smuggled Upmanns, the finest cigar in Cuba. Judicious administration of them will keep your cantankerous spouse fawning at your feet for a month."

Thatcher turned again. "You always were the rottenest person

I ever knew. It's the only thing about you that I like. Merry Christmas, Joe, and welcome home."

"Yes, Joe," added Livy, "welcome home."

The doorbell rang again. Livy opened the door to find Mike Ash, his hair frosted with snow and his topcoat unbuttoned, waiting on the doorstep.

"Where's Marilyn?" Livy asked as she unconsciously dusted flakes of snow off his shoulders.

"Home, I guess," he replied in an oddly cracked voice. Mike stepped into the house and thumped the snow off of his shoes. With his overcoat still on, he walked into the living room. Thatcher, still at the keyboard, turned to look at him and said, "Hi, Mike. Merry Christmas. Only minutes now to midnight. Welcome. Take your coat off and join the party."

"Nope. Thanks, but I'm only going to be here for a second."

Ash looked furtively to his left and right as he approached the piano. Thatcher watched him, as usual having a pretty good idea what was going on. Ash took a deep breath, then, speaking rapidly, as if anxious to get something off his chest, he said, "OK. Here it is. I have done some thinking and I have made some decisions. This situation I'm in has gone on long enough. I've had it. I'm fed up. I can't take it anymore. So . . . So . . . Louise and I are getting married. Come on, you, you're coming with me." He seized Louise's wrist, and started pulling her toward the door.

Louise stumbled forward a step or two before the implications of what was occurring fully penetrated her uncommonly inebriated consciousness. Then she yelled, "What the hell? You son of a bitch! What are you up to? Marriage! To you! There is no goddamned way—"

Thatcher's rising voice droned her out. He boomed, "Good! Excellent! It's about time. I endorse the idea. I am thoroughly sick and tired of all the clandestine antics you two have been going through to keep this little romance secret. Sneaking about. Looking over your shoulders. Pretending you barely know one another. Silly waste of time. Childish nonsense. I'm glad to see it's over."

Ash stopped in his tracks. *People know things here,* he thought, *that I didn't know they knew.* Louise very nearly slumped to the floor. Her voice broke as she whispered, "Oh no. You know about—"

Livy spoke up, "Of course we do, children. Everyone knows. Everyone always has. You two are so obviously in love."

"Me? In love?" Louise shrieked. "With him? Never!"

Ash tugged her arm firmly. "Louise," he said, "shut up. It's over. I'm marrying you. You're marrying me. You don't have any say in the matter, so just shut up."

"No say! What the hell do you mean, no say?"

Mike began dragging her to the door. Louise struggled backward unsuccessfully. She bumped against a small end table. It fell over with a clatter. Louise shouted, "Caveman!"

Joe Jonas cheered, "Go for it, Ash!"

Ash said sternly, "Quiet, woman. You try my patience. I am a violent man when aroused. Never knew that, did you? And as for you, Scott Thatcher, you knew about this thing all along, did you? Well, screw you."

"And a Merry Christmas to you too, Mike," Thatcher replied gleefully, "and a very happy New Year!"

"From me, too," Livy added, "and all of us. Oh, Mike, one other thing. Since you're going to be her husband, and such a caveman too, maybe you can get her to stop her closet smoking."

Louise screamed, "Arrrrrrrrrgh! Aren't there any goddamned secrets left in this goddamned world?"

"Speaking as a mother myself, I know it's no good for children, and certainly not at all the safe thing for someone who's pregnant."

Huh? What? thought Ash.

"Arrrrrrrrrgh!" To this Louise added, as Mike opened the door and began to pull her outside, "Damnit, Ash. Wait, goddamnit, until I get my coat. Ash, you goddamn animal! What about my coat!"

"Fuck it. You'll need a new one anyway if you're pregnant." Then he wrapped his arms around her, locked her tightly to him, and pressed his lips against her soon unresisting mouth. They stood together, sharing one long, long kiss, with the silent snow drifting down on them, illuminated by the warm yellow light pouring out of Thatcher's open door, until the clock ticked past midnight and it was Christmas morning.

ABOUT THE AUTHOR

Joseph Garber is a well-known business analyst, futurist and consultant. He grew up in New Hampshire, spent most of his career in New York, and now makes his home in northern California.